Dancing
Lessons

Dancing Lessons

a novel by Olive Senior

Canada Council
for the Arts

Conseil des Arts
du Canada

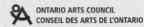

ONTARIO ARTS COUNCIL
CONSEIL DES ARTS DE L'ONTARIO

Canadian   Patrimoine
Heritage   canadien

Canadä

The publisher gratefully acknowledges the support of the Canada Council
for the Arts and the Ontario Arts Council for its publishing program.
We acknowledge the financial support of the Government of Canada
through the Canada Book Fund (CBF) for our publishing activities,
and the Government of Ontario through the Ontario Media Development
Corporation, an agency of the Ontario Ministry of Culture, and the
Ontario Book Publishing Tax Credit Program.

LIBRARY AND ARCHIVES CANADA CATALOGUING IN PUBLICATION

Senior, Olive
Dancing lessons / Olive Senior.

ISBN 978-1-77086-047-6

1. Title.

PS8587.E552D36 2011   C813'.54   C2011-904032-8

Cover art and design: Angel Guerra/Archetype
Interior text design: Tannice Goddard, Soul Oasis Networking
Printer: Marquis Imprimeur Inc.

Printed and bound in Canada.

RECYCLED
Paper made from
recycled material
FSC® C103567

This book is printed on 100% post-consumer waste recycled paper.

Cormorant Books Inc.
215 Spadina Avenue, Studio 230, Toronto, Ontario, Canada M5T 2C7
www.cormorantbooks.com

The ladies, in particular, ought to dance with a sort of amiable circumspection and a becoming grace, which, indeed, add to their charms, and heighten their attractions. Gentlemen ought always to be attentive to their partners, and they should all of them move in unison in every step and attitude.

— CHARLES DURANG,
The Ball-Room Bijou, and Art of Dancing ...
with Rules for Polite Behaviour, 18–

To Earl Senior and Fay Harrison,
who were there from the start.

Dancing
Lessons

I

HOW WAS I TO know he had a bad heart? All I wanted was to dance one more time in my life. I heard the music playing in his room that was right across from mine and something came over me, a joyous feeling that I had had in my life only once before, so I went over and asked him to dance. What's so wrong with that? It's true he had just moved in and we hadn't been properly introduced. But I didn't "drag him around and assault him and cause him to freak out and have an attack," as Matron told Celia in this overly dramatic mimsey-mamsey way of hers, all hands and eyebrows and jangling earrings and shoulders working.

She believed it, of course. Not that she said anything, in that lawyer-ish way of hers. Nothing showing on her face. I sat there like a schoolgirl in Matron's most uncomfortable chair trying to look comfortable. My arms and legs crossed. I didn't say a word. I never do. One thing I've learnt in life is to hold my tongue. Which is why She knows nothing. Though O how I cringe every time that scene pops up before my eyes, the most embarrassing moment of my life, a moment — I might add — totally and absolutely out of character. I truly, truly do not know what made me do it, me, the shyest person on earth. But how will they know that, since I have no intention of confessing?

It was madness! But once that raucous music bounced through his open door across the hallway and snaked into mine, my shoulders started to twist, my hips started to shake, my feet started to beat a staccato across the polished mahogany floor.

"Come, come," I remember saying to him, arms outstretched as I belted out the words that came back to me after all those years:

> *If you wanna go crazy and act the clown*
> *Be the laughing stock all over town*
> *That's YOUR RED WAGON ...*

I certainly didn't drag him around, as Matron claims, though I did try on one of my spins to clasp his hands in mine. But I could see he was an unwilling partner and I continued to dance and sing by myself:

> *That's YOUR RED WAGON*
> *So just keep dragging YOUR RED WAGON along ...*

until *braps!* The music swooped to a sudden stop and I found myself standing in this strange man's room, with him looking as frightened as a little brown mouse and me hot and red as a pomegranate. He gaped at me, his mouth opening and closing, but what he said I do not know, for I fled to my room and slammed the door. O my Lord!

Maybe I did frighten him, for he's built on the compact side and I'm a bit taller, but Matron doesn't have to make me out to be such a clodhopping giant. To be honest, I am a teeny bit bigger than I was before I came here, for I've been eating and eating ever since. Am I going to turn down good food prepared and served by someone else at exactly the same time every day? I spend my day waiting for my meals. I don't understand all these people here complaining and picking at what they are served, but I ignore them and wipe my plate clean. Let them skin up their noses all they want, especially those three who share a table with me.

We sit at these little round tables with lovely china and real linen napkins that remind me of the only thing that was nice about my childhood. It's like heaven to me. But of course I don't let them know that, those three Pancake Sisters From Hell. Names of Ruby, Babe, and Birdie, if you can believe it. They are not really sisters, but have been friends all their lives. Killed off their husbands I'm sure so they could end up here together at Ellesmere Lodge gossiping and betting on the races and drinking martinis and playing bridge. They are as alike as gungo peas in a pod. They look like dried gungo peas too, their skin yellow and speckled with brown splotches all over and their hair pulled off their foreheads and puffed up and dyed this wishy-washy brownish blond like their skin so that their heads look round like pancakes flat on the plate before the maple syrup.

It's funny, I had never had pancakes before, but it was the very first breakfast that was served to me here at Ellesmere Lodge. I gazed down at my plate that morning and was so struck by the resemblance I nearly died laughing inside. I could tell they noticed the little smile on my face, for they couldn't take their eyes off me. I'm good at taking in everything, even when I have my head down. But I just kept on eating and ignoring them. Who are they fooling anyway, thinking they're so elegant and aristocratic, always on about Daddy and School and Sister-This and Sister-That as if they are still seven years old, not ten times that (at least!), but let's not bother with them. It's She I am concerned about. She is now so thin she is almost at vanishing point, and if she vanished, what would I do? I poke that thought down every time it comes to the surface for I don't even know where the others are anymore, Junior and Lise. I know Shirley is in a cemetery in Brooklyn I'll never see. Never a word from the others. The odd Christmas or birthday card. A hundred-dollar bill enclosed. She is the only one who cares. Well, not cares really, I don't think she cares, but she shames easily and so she wouldn't want anyone to know I'm living on the street, would she?

2

NOT LIVING ON THE street exactly, but I would have been perfectly happy staying down there in the country with the old wooden house collapsing around me, battered and torn apart by the hurricane. It's what I'm used to, isn't it? Hardship. Hardship and lies. A pummelling from life every way I turn. O, I'm nicely set up here, everyone would say, Ellesmere Lodge, ha! The Best Retirement Home in the city, in the whole of Jamaica, in the British West Indies, the World! Though from the way Matron treats some of us, well, one of us exactly, you'd think we were in boarding school. It's certainly the most expensive, the one where all the rich people park their parents. And that's the trouble, isn't it? They're not used to someone like me. From the time I came, I could hear them sniggering behind my back, eyeing my work-hardened hands, my large awkward feet, my brown calico skin coarse as a grater. Inviting me to their stupid teas just to watch my hands tremble as I handle the delicate china cup. Though She tried, I have to give her that, she tried her best to get me fixed up for this place. Threw out all my old clothes and bought me lots of new ones. Everything new: suitcase, underwear, toothbrush, the lot. Not allowed to bring a single thing from my old life. Okay, a lot of it was rain-soaked, but it was she who made me throw it all out. Nothing old to be brought here. Except myself. And that's the trouble, for it's really myself she doesn't want.

She took me to the hairdresser for a smart cut, and this woman, herself sharp as glass plastered with makeup, is going snip-snip and feeding her all the shards of gossip and all the time under her hands I feel her contempt as if she would snip-snip my head off too for someone as unfashionable as me daring to come into her place. I'm not beautiful, don't think I don't know it, which is why She also took me to this place to have them give me facials and rub my skin with all kinds of oily gobs and do my nails and put lipstick and eyebrow pencil on. Ha, me, who has never used more than Pond's Vanishing Cream, well, Jergens maybe, and a little dab of face powder.

Now you see all this expensive stuff She keeps buying me, perfumes and such that I don't touch littering my dressing table, but it comes in useful when I want to curry favour with one of the girls who works here. Or even Winston, the miserable gardener, who will take the fancy box of soap or the perfume for his daughter, he says, though everyone knows it's for some young girl he is chasing. But what do I care, if he doesn't tell about my picking the Bombay mangoes off Matron's very own tree. She only claims it's hers because it is by her little cottage, which is on the Ellesmere Lodge grounds. I think she talks to those mangoes at night they grow so fat and beautiful and inviting! For what else does she have to do once she has finished terrorizing us (well, one of us). Winston tells her anyway, the old goat, to save his skin, but by that time I've ripened them in brown paper inside the shoebox at the top of my clothes cupboard and they are well and truly eaten. Vanished evidence. It does pay to say nothing. Even when caught in a stickup.

I nearly died laughing inside at the scene played out later right by the mango tree. Me and Matron. The mango caught my eye and she caught me! I admit I was lurking, but what right had she to be going into her cottage at that hour of the day when she is supposed to be at work? There I was, gazing up at the shiny ripe mango right at the top of the tree. A red-gold sun that waved at me as I went for my morning walk. It pulled my feet in that direction. I picked up the crook-stick that was conveniently lying there on the ground and was positioning it properly in relation to the mango when a banshee wail sliced the morning and a fury in acid colours barged into my angle of vision.

"Mrs. Sam-phire!"

The stick could have been a snake, I dropped it so fast. My

heart fell clear to my foot-bottom but I kept my head; I stood up straight and looked innocently around as if searching for a lost sheep. To buy myself time. This couldn't be me, caught in the act.

"Mrs. Samphire ... ask you ..." I was forced to focus on Matron, who was now waving her arms around and screwing up her face. "... leave my mangoes alone." Orange-coloured sandals (bronze metallic toenails!) came to a halt inches away from my own feet, which had suddenly attracted my scrutiny. I hoped I looked contrite. Matron paused then, as if she expected me to say something, but I didn't. Such a long pause took the wind out of the sleeves of her caftan and she finished rather lamely, dropping her hands to her side. "And stop. Asking Winston. Think I don't know. What's going on." Long pause until she managed to fill her sails again and wave her finger at me, but I could tell she was trapped between annoyance and the consciousness that when all was said and done, I was still a Resident. With a capital R, for that's how the rest of them acted. She ended rather sulkily: "My private space. No right. Out of bounds. Must I put up a sign?"

I shook my head then; this was easy: No.

"Ne-ver," she said, heaving her not very extensive chest and holding her head high in a facsimile of indignation. "Ne-ver has another Re-sident intruded in this manner."

No, I wanted to say, the other Residents never get up off their bony asses.

I'm not sure Matron has the stomach for fighting, really; she gazed at me some more, huffed and puffed, then turned on her heels and took off like a rainbow streak.

As soon as her back was turned, I took up the stick and touched the mango, which fell right into my outstretched hand. I secured it in my pocket and I continued on my walk, practically killing myself with suppressed laughter as I ran my hand over the smooth skin of the fruit and anticipated the forthcoming feast. Ha, I thought, this one will be blamed on Winston for sure. She won't believe I could be so bold. And serve him right, too, for having the cheek to accept bribes and not keep his mouth shut.

Still, a little worm of anxiety is eating at me, for I know I shouldn't be taking chances with Matron, my situation here is still shaky. I will vow to get into no more trouble and do as She commands.

Once a week, when the manicurist and the hairdresser come here to Ellesmere Lodge (not the facety one, this one is much more humble or else she wouldn't be bothering to come and shampoo a bunch of old people, would she), She pays for me to have "treatments," they call it. Just like the others. Torments, I say, but I go, just as I go to the doctor who is the other person who gives "treatments," unwillingly, for I know what She is trying to do. The hairdresser — Morveen, if you please — is like a little overdressed schoolgirl in her tiny skirt, chunky-heel sandals, and skinny top, with blond highlights in her hair and at least six earrings in each ear. As she eases me down in the chair to shampoo my hair while this other little one — Kyisha — is getting ready to mess around with my toes, she, this Morveen, says, "Relax, Mrs. Samphire, you are much too tense, Miss. Relax and enjoy yourself."

3

YES, I AM ALWAYS tempted to say, once over fifty years ago I relaxed and enjoyed myself and look what I brought down on my head. Well, that was before yesterday happened. I frown and become even more tense when I think of this because I'm mad at Her, always at her, for I know she is doing all of this not for me, but for her own self, so she won't be so ashamed of me. Shame, that is all that has ever ruled her life, which is why she is like this dry stick now, all bones and hair. She always had lovely hair, the only nice thing about her, well, nice teeth too and lovely skin, pale as dry bamboo leaves and a manner as brittle as dry bamboo sticks. They love her in here, they love her there, everywhere, for everyone knows her, she is a celebrity, now she even has her own talk show on television. Our Doctor, the guru. Only she isn't that kind of doctor, the one that can provide us with "treatments," but the know-it-all kind, spending years studying, now doing something up at the university, always off to conferences and things. I don't know how her husband and children put up with it, but then I hardly know them. You'd think she would have taken me home to live with them in that big house, rooms and rooms and swimming pool, but O no, not good enough for them. Her children as distant as she is, on the rare occasions I've been privileged to see them. Unnatural, all of them. Not that I care. Just to spite her, I no longer ask after them. Up to now I don't even know what she's been studying. She's on every committee and board around. Which is why they treat her like a goddess whenever she comes to visit and why they put up with me. Don't think I don't know. You'd expect me to know more about her, wouldn't you? But it's always been like that. The one at a distance. With Shirley and Lise and Junior, now, we had some laughs together, didn't we? Let our hair down. Things we shared. I mean, they were human and though they have turned around and done some things that ... well, let's not go into that now, but at least they didn't act as if they were so way above the rest of us. But She always did, didn't she? It was a mistake to let her go and live with those people, that Reverend Doctor Something and his wife, I can see that now, but at the time it seemed such a god-sent opportunity for at least one of them to get a good education and there was never any doubt it would be her. No warmth at all. Never. Her head always buried in a book. At the time I thought it was such a good thing that one of them at least liked reading, for I liked reading and my own life would have been different I know if somebody had bothered to educate me properly.

It is true I was going to St. Catherine's Academy at the time. They did plan to send me to nursing school. I can still hear it, Aunt Zena's cackle: "Ha-ha, you made your own bed, girl, you must lie on it," as they washed their hands of me. Well, he did have his own bed, I'll say that now, and a lovely horse when I met him, for this was just after the war and there was no gasoline, and he put a roof over my head and food in our bellies, I'll grant him that. So despite everything, I could still hold my head high every time I passed their house, for they refused to have me back in. And when they passed mine on their way to church, sanctimonious old wretches, I peeped through the curtains to watch how they cast their eyes slantwise at all my flowers blooming. Flowers that annoyed them no end, I'm sure, since I planted the loudest and commonest ones I could find: zinnias and marigolds, Joseph Coat and sunflowers. No pale roses and itty-bitty violets for me. They could keep their heads higher than mine because they lived in a much bigger house, on the hill, the biggest around, and they had straighter noses. Come to think of it, She is so like them, with her powdery skin and straight nose. It is that side of the family she takes after, the ones that are so full of you know what. Except she has her father's crinkly nayga hair. And his white people's eyes. Don't worry, I don't swear, or use bad language, never have, I've always been careful of my speech, was forced to be as a child when I lived with them. Some things are just too drilled into me to lose, though I sometimes think some nasty words to myself. Maybe one day I'll shout them out loud. If they bother me enough I will. If they try to send me away from this place I'll grab hold of the veranda posts and hang on for dear life and shout and shout till the petals fall off their bloody roses and shame them all. And She will be standing there, shame tinting her dry bamboo skin. But then I think perhaps I won't, for suppose she really gave up and abandoned me then. Whatever would I do?

4

ABANDON. ABAN-DON. A WORD with a nice swing to it. Like a hammock. Well, no. More like something slung out. Thrown up. Thrown away. Dumped. Forlorn, forsaken. Or some-body.

Hea-vy. A-ban-don. Did She think I abandoned her when we allowed her to go and live with those people? I hardly ever saw her after that, it's true, but was that my fault? Her father certainly went visiting, got quite chummy if you please, though what the Prince of Darkness had in common with those self-righteous paleface people is beyond me. But he was the one with the car. Did he ever once offer to take me?

Apart from rushing me to the doctor with a sick child, did he ever once take me anywhere? I knew he never wanted to be seen with me, once he and the children turned me into a witch. I saw it in the way he looked at me, or rather, the way he let his eyes slide off me with the smoothness of a green lizard. And whose fault was it? Did he once give me money to straighten my hair? Get a new dress? Buy a box of face powder? Lipstick? Rouge for my cheeks? For that's what he liked. That girl Esmie Roche with her penny hair straightened and wrapped up in a pound worth of bows. Think I didn't know? Think I didn't know of Mrs. Carter's daughter, the mealy-mouthed schoolteacher with the skinny legs and the lisp? Think I didn't know of that girl who worked in the office at the estate? He liked them young and dark-skinned, ripe and bursting like starapples. Pretty faces and hair upswept. Young and easy to break in. Easy to break. Until he met his match with that one there, that hard-back woman who finally lured him away — and broke him. That story was music to my heart. But of course he bounced back. He always did. That's the Samphire men for you. But why am I wasting my time thinking about him?

5

I can't truthfully say my mother abandoned me. But she upped and died when I was only a few days old, so what would you call that? My father's mother, Miss Celia, and his sister, Aunt Zena, took me in and I grew up in the same house with my father, only I never knew he was my father until I was about eight or nine years old. I never knew I was related to them. Truly. Nobody told me anything. First he was away at the War and then he was there and wasn't there, if you know what I mean. He wasn't like the other men who went to the fields or out to a job. He just wandered around the place not doing very much and sometimes he got boisterous. He disappeared for long periods of time, returning without a word, at least not a word to me. They said it was the War that did it, shell-shocked him, though I didn't know what that meant since at the time we didn't even have electricity. I knew about the War because several of the men around had gone over to England to fight in it and were known as the Old Soldiers, and very proud of it they were too, wearing their old uniforms and hats and medals on Poppy Day. But he did things sometimes that made his mother and sister afraid of him, and even when I was too young to know what was going on, I could sense their relief when he was not around. I was afraid of him too, the only man in the house, but only because in those days I was afraid of everyone and everything. I could never do anything right. When Aunt Zena wanted to be nasty, which was every day, she would say to Miss Celia, "Well, what do you expect? The child of a slug and a madman."

It took me a long time to figure out that it was me she was talking about, and after I realized it I would cry and cry inside myself for I didn't want to be the daughter of a slug. I didn't understand why Aunt Zena would insult me so, calling my mother the lowest, most hateful thing there is on God's earth. Once I told this to my husband and he nearly fell out of the bed laughing. He leaned over, gave me a hug and kissed me on the forehead, and wow wasn't that a nice surprise and couldn't I have done with more of that, and he said, laughing still, "'Slut,' 'slut,' you little idiot. Not slug." I didn't know what slut meant and he wouldn't tell me, he just kept on laughing, his eyes dancing for me the way they never did at any other time, and it certainly made me feel better. For it is only in other people's gaze that we see ourselves, isn't it?

Already those were the days when I couldn't look into his eyes without feeling pain and humiliation, for I knew now they made four so easily with others, so reluctantly with mine. I didn't know how to make my wishes known, how to please him, how to hold his gaze. And when I did manage to do so, it was like falling into water that was not the river or the sea but a pool with endless depth, like the blue hole at the riverhead where dangerous water spirits lurked. He only gazed at me now with anger or exasperation, or to issue commands. I'd look, and look away, drowning.

6

I only ever danced this one other time in my life and it turned into the saddest thing that ever happened. It was like this. Once I knew my father was my father, and I can't remember how I knew, I would watch him closely, not that there was anything between us, he never paid any special attention to me. It was always "Girl this" and "Girl that" if he needed anything, I don't think he ever called me by name. But I loved him just the same for he was the only thing that belonged to me or the only person I could say I belonged to, for I never knew my mother's family and Miss Celia and Aunt Zena acted as if they would rather I didn't belong to them. Maybe I was a slug, or some sort of obstacle cast into their world that they were forced to walk around, to their great inconvenience. Maybe it was this thing of my mother being a slug that made them watch me so closely, for I never had space to breathe. If I wasn't at school I was put to work in the house and on Sundays I was straight laced and jacketed and marched off to church with them. Tied up tight as a knot the whole time and never a kind word, a tender smile, from them or anyone else, for all took their cue from the Richards family. I was the one who had brought disgrace on them, though how, I didn't know.

One time I thought it was because of my hair, which Aunt Zena would not even touch; when I was little it was Dulcie's job to comb it. Dulcie, the maid who had been with them forever, long before I was born, so I think she too hated me from the way she pushed my head and pulled that hair. It took me a long time to realize that my hair was more like Dulcie's than Aunt Zena's, so then I thought that was the disgrace. For me. For them. And I didn't have their nose either. Nice and straight. I only realized that much later, as if my body parts were becoming visible to me piece by piece, a jigsaw puzzle fitting into place, revealing a strange hatchling.

To this day I remember looking at myself in the mirror, staring hard as if seeing myself for the very first time, and suddenly having my nose jump out at me, a large and fleshy nose that took up most of my face. Not at all the shape and beauty of theirs. Once I noticed it, I became preoccupied with this nose. It was all I could see when I looked in the mirror. I began to steal glimpses of my reflection everywhere, even in the distorted lenses of the dinner cutlery, the shiny pots in the kitchen. It was all I thought people saw when they looked at me. Nose Girl. Then I must have gotten over that for I became obsessed with other parts of my body. I ran my critical eye over my features, piece by piece, and nothing I saw pleased me; I was not like them at all, those others in the house I occupied. My face was too large, my forehead too broad, my cheekbones too high, my lips too thick, my eyes too muddy, my skin too dark, my hair too coarse. I looked like nobody. I couldn't see below my neck in the bedroom mirror so I would steal into Aunt Zena's room when she was out to stare at multiple reflections of myself in her three-way mirror, gasping anew each time at the big head, the long, coltish limbs, the knobby elbows and knees. I was so shocked to see myself, my ugly self revealed, that I felt true heartbreak, for I had no idea where I, this strange person in the mirror, had come from.

For a long time, I was haunted by my own ugliness, yet I

took a perverse pride in it too, for it gave me a reason why no one could love me. To this day I have no idea if as a child I was really ugly or beautiful, for I had no one to tell me. And I have nothing to look at. No one ever bothered to take a picture.

Here's something funny when I think about it now, funny to anyone who believes in signs. The wedding as non-event. The photographer who was hired to take our wedding picture messed up and the pictures didn't come out. We were supposed to dress up in our wedding clothes again and go to his studio. For years the poor man kept trying to make an appointment with us, for he was mortified, but it just never happened. Well, within a few months of the wedding it would have been impossible for me to get into that dress anyway, for my first child — She — was on the way.

I don't know if such pictures matter, because I am forever haunted by all these other pictures in my head, so clear to me even now I could print and paste them into an album, though they are not all pictures I would keep if I had a choice. Except for the one of my father laughing and singing, the one time he danced with me.

7

THIS HAPPENED DURING A period when my father was at home for a good long while. Since he never went to church, I got it into my head that I would stay home that Sunday, pretending to be sick, even though I knew it would mean castor oil and no Sunday dinner, when Aunt Zena came home. But even if nothing happened with my father, it would give me a chance to read the book I had borrowed from the school library and hidden under the bed. They went off and left me, to an empty house, for Dulcie too went to church, eleven o'clock service. All the respectable did. Except for my father.

I was lurking in the doorway of my room, looking down the hallway to where his was, wondering what to do, when from his room came the most marvellous sounds. I knew it was from the gramophone he had brought from his latest time away. I hadn't heard him play anything on it, though he must have done so when I was at school, for at the dinner table Miss Celia called what he played the devil's work and asked why he couldn't have brought home some hymns. But now the minute her back was turned this noise started up and what he was playing certainly sounded like the devil. It was the strangest cacophonous music I had ever heard, though I had never heard anything more than hymns and school songs. It was raucous and loud, with a driving rhythm like horses galloping overlaid by discordant gawps and boops and bleeps. It shocked me so much, I felt tilted into another world. Without thinking I walked down the hallway to his room and peeped in.

He was standing by the window overlooking the veranda, facing into the room where the windup gramophone stood, conducting this music with one hand and moving his head and shoulders to the beat, with a smile on his face that I had never seen before. It was some time before he noticed me, and I had time to study him and to wonder anew at what a handsome man my father was. He was tall and well built, his limbs gangly and loose, with the triangular face and straight nose of his mother, for her parents had come over from England, Miss Celia was always proudly saying. Which is probably why she hated me. My mother's family had come from out of the canefields, I once heard her say. But where her husband came from, I don't know. All I ever saw of him was a picture in a large oval frame of a fierce-looking man with bushy hair and a moustache and skin that was very much darker than the young Miss Celia, who sat primly in a wicker-work chair with her legs crossed at the ankles while he stood behind her beside a small wicker table with a vase of artificial-looking flowers.

But while Miss Celia and Aunt Zena's skin was white and mottled with freckles, my father's was logwood honey. And while their hair was brown and dead straight, both the same, his was rich dark brown with lots of kinky waves and red highlights. He wore it longish, swept back from his broad forehead. The more I looked and admired, the more conscious I became that I was nothing at all like him, except for the long legs. This day he was wearing what I thought of as his uniform when he was at home, his cream linen pants with cuffs, his red suspenders, and a pale blue chambray shirt with the sleeves rolled up to his elbows that brought out the blue in his hazel eyes and reminded me that mine were dirty brown.

When he saw me, he didn't look surprised, he smiled but didn't stop moving to the music. A curl of his hair that had been plastered down with pomade came loose and flopped about in time to his movements. I couldn't believe anyone who looked so young and carefree could be my dad.

"Hey, Girl," he said when the record stopped. "Know what music this is?"

"No, sir." I shook my head, suddenly feeling my body shrink with shyness.

"Well, this is the greatest music in the world. Jazz. American music. This is ragtime. The devil ripping it up." And he threw back his head and laughed, showing his beautiful teeth. He picked up the record sleeve and started to read from it. "Harry James and His Orchestra 'One O'Clock Jump' composed by Count Basie; Louis Jordan 'Choo Choo Ch'Boogie'…"

After that, it was talk, talk, so much talk in a non-stop stream. He'd put on a new record and smile and move his body until the record stopped and then he'd start talking again, getting almost as fast and frenzied as the music, his eyes bright, his face and body mobile, the lock of hair dancing to its own syncopation. At first I was simply entranced, so happy to be there, alone with him, feeding on his energy, as if he were an incandescent spark. But this went on for so long, this talk about things I knew nothing about, it drained me until my chest tightened so much I could hardly breathe. I wanted desperately to go back to my room, but having put myself into the picture, I didn't know how to pull away. I didn't want to go without getting what I'd come for. I so desperately wanted him to talk about me, us, my mother, him, that I exerted all my mental faculties. Please, please, I remember saying silently to him, please, please talk to me.

I don't know what I actually conveyed, but as if he sensed my mood, he took a record from a different album when the music stopped and said as he wound up the gramophone,

"Listen to this!" As soon as the needle touched the record, I was lost in the most joyous, raucous sounds I had ever heard. This one had a beat I could understand and a woman's voice like a razor blade. My father sang along with the chorus:

That's YOUR RED WAGON
just keep dragging YOUR RED WAGON along.

I had no idea what the words meant, but the beat, the mood, transported me out of that room in that country house to another world and my head was still spinning when the record finished.

"Like it?"

I nodded, and he played the record again.

"Come, Girl, sing with me," he said. At first I felt small and my throat dry as I tried to follow the words.

If you're gonna play horses and blow your dough
Don't you run to me if they don't show
That's YOUR RED WAGON …

He kept putting on the same record, and repeating the words, and soon I could belt them out as good as him and we were singing along at the tops of our voices:

… just keep dragging YOUR RED WAGON along.

So when he said, "Let's dance" and took hold of my hands, "Like this," I didn't feel awkward and clumsy as he showed me what to do. I felt careless and free. How easy I found it to follow him. He nodded in approval as I caught the beat and soon we were dancing to that music as if there were devils after us, inside his room and into the hallway, where we galloped up and down, into the dining and living room and back down again. Each time the record stopped he would go and put it on again and we would resume our dance through the house, singing at the tops of our voices, stomping for emphasis, getting wilder and wilder:

> *So you fell for somebody who pinned your ears*
> *Baby don't be bringing me your tears*
> *That's YOUR RED WAGON —*

Badoom! The loudness of the mahogany front door crashing against the wall as it swung open with force stopped us in our tracks, at the far end of the hallway. We froze together, my father and me, hands clasped, each with a foot in the air ready for another round, the words dying on our lips:

> *So just keep dragging ...*

Miss Celia stood in the doorway, Aunt Zena behind her, and the maid Dulcie: I remember still the quivering of their churchgoing hats like the tips of windswept palm trees. They were deadly silent, the entire world had hushed, but for the scratchy music that played on: we were caught red-handed with the evidence hot as the devil. I could feel my father's hand tighten, grow cold. Suddenly his body slumped, like a child's. Aunt Zena brushed past Miss Celia into the hallway. That terrible tightness in my chest came back for I knew exactly what she was going to do. My father knew it too. He didn't move. The words "No. Don't." broke away from him. But it wasn't from the smiling man of a moment ago. It came out high-pitched and anguished, like a child's. His hand still held mine, but it was as if he had suddenly become the child and he was holding on to me, not the other way round. I could feel his hand, then his whole body shaking. I felt as if I wanted to faint. My head started to grow big, for I knew something terrible was about to happen.

As Aunt Zena scuttled into my father's room he moved, down the hallway, in quick strides, but she slammed the room door just ahead of him and turned the key in the lock. I closed my eyes tightly then so everything came to me as sound: my father pounding on the door and bawling out, then howling, then sobbing as he beat against the wood. Miss Celia yelling at him, "Fabian, stop it! Stop it at once! I won't put up with it one more time. You hear me! Stop it!" Dulcie calling in the feeble voice she always put on for Miss Celia, "Come Mass Fabian … listen to your mother." And then, from inside the room, the sound of the needle ripping across the record, a sudden silence followed by the breakage of records smashing on the big rock outside the side window and, not long after, the sound of an almighty crash, and splintering, the tinkle of metal on stone. I knew the gramophone had gone too.

At that sound, my father went quiet, but I could hear him throwing his entire body at the door which finally burst open and hit the wall just as the front door had. I could hear the sound of objects thrown and Aunt Zena in his room sliding around the polished mahogany floor in her Sunday heels and screaming, "Murder! Mama, do something." And finally the heels beating a staccato as she fled from the room back to where her mother and Dulcie still stood in the front door for

I hadn't heard them move. Then the front door slamming and the sound of their Sunday heels clattering across the wooden veranda and down the steps, fleeing. Fleeing from what, I didn't know, for I was still frozen in the hallway, pressed against the wall, my eyes squeezed tight. When I opened them there was nothing to see but the empty hallway, the closed front door, my father's room door, which was slammed shut by Aunt Zena in her flight. From behind this closed door came the sound of whimpering, of words babbled and broken off. From the front yard came the noise of women shouting, of male voices, and above it all, Miss Celia calling across the fence to our neighbour whose son had a buggy, "Miss Mirrie, please ask Jacob to go to the station as fast as he can and ask them to bring the Black Maria. Mister Fabian gone off again."

I couldn't stand it then. I stumbled into my room, which was right there at that end of the hallway, closed the door, threw myself on my bed, and willed myself to sleep. Sleep is what I did then when I didn't know what to do.

8

That's one of the things they have against me here, isn't it, that I'm such a good sleeper. Not that I boast about it, but it must gall them to hear me snoring away all night when their own sleeplessness is all they ever talk about. I mean, how much conversation can you get out of that topic? My table-mates, each taking her turn to narrate her tale of nocturnal woe. Though they always seem bright enough in the daytime to me.

Too bright, perhaps.

It usually starts with an ostentatious yawn from one of them as she slowly unfolds a snowy white napkin and places it on her lap. This morning it's Birdie, sweet and ditzy, short and pigeon-chested, with her tits hauled up to her neck, the most likeable one of the lot because she seems the least threatening; everything she does is slow. She looks just as outrageous as the others, though, coming in to breakfast at 8:00 a.m. wearing a delicate, frilly, white organdy blouse over white linen pants, high heels, a huge string of pearls, and purple lipstick. Hair upswept and stiff and held severely in place by a whole can of spray. Face powdered and made up. It's not because she is going anywhere, that's how they dress all the time.

"Wazzamatta gurl, you didn't get your beauty rest last night?" This from Ruby, the skinny one who dresses like a macaw and speaks the way I imagine a macaw would speak. Raspy. Her throat lining etched from the cigarette she always has burning. Like now. At the table. I'm glad I sit farthest away from her, but even so, every few minutes I wave my hands about to indicate my disapproval. Not that it matters to this woman, she is a law unto herself down to her bright blue eyeshadow and the spot of rouge covering each cheek-bone, the only part of her face that isn't creased. I guess the eyeshadow is meant to pick up the colour of the amazing sapphire ring she wears on her right hand, the one she never takes off while the others keep changing, for she seems to have an endless cache of jewellery. Ruby's sapphire is as large and splendiferous as Princess Diana's engagement ring, and as she waves her cigarette hand about, I can hardly take my eyes off it, though of course I don't give the slightest hint of my interest.

"Ruby, it's not a joke you know. I never closed my eyes all night."

"Oh, that wasn't you snoring down the place at midnight then?" This is Babe, who looks over at me and winks.

I don't wink back because I believe Babe is the one who laughs hardest at me behind my back. I look down at my porridge and scoop up the first spoonful. I like to behave as if they're not there, though I sometimes follow their foolish chatter. Babe is the one who wears a succession of outrageous glasses that make her look like that singer there, the one who sang at Diana's funeral. That song. Or better still, Dame Edna, the comic I've taken to watching on TV. Though I don't think a comic effect is what Babe is after even if she does have the jowls for it. Babe is one of those women who has spent her life basking in the admiration of men. Don't ask me how or why, but that's the impression she likes to give. And, though there are so few ambulatory or with good enough eyesight around, she still spends her time coyly preening, the hands with the fake fingernails frequently touching the hair, the mascaraed eyelashes fluttering, the silk blouses always tucked in with belts to show off the waist, the pants or skirts tight enough to show what was once a bottom. The sandals. The painted toenails.

They spend the whole time chattering about how they spent their sleepless nights as if this is a completely new topic each time and they don't see each other every minute of every day. I tend to tune back in when they get around to advising on the best cure, Ruby, the vulgar one, usually ending with "A good ---- always did it. When my Jorge was around." Then her eyes sort of retreat into her head as she goes into a sulk. Any mention of the long-dead Jorge always brings that on. I pretend not to hear (and I can't bring myself to write the word) but I know my ears turn bright red, which is why Ruby says things like that. She is not known to observe propriety, though don't ask if she doesn't play the Grand Dame if anyone should dare to take what she considers liberties with her. Obviously nobody bothered to wash out Ruby's mouth with soap when she was little. She talks dirty all the time, about the great sexual life she had with this Jorge, who was, I think, husband number three. Nowadays I think she just knocks back the Valium or whatever sleeping pills her doctor prescribes.

Babe, surprisingly, makes no mention of sex or pills, favouring a nightcap of brown alcohol. "It has to be brown, dearies — rum, brandy, or whiskey." With honey and warm milk, the latter taken up to her room each night in a Thermos. How much does she consume, I wonder, but am afraid to ask. I suppress the thought that Babe is really a sick woman, or has been close to death's door, with at least four major operations to her credit.

Birdie in her muddled way is given to trying everything — pills, alcoholic nightcaps, mint tea, St. John's wort, and listening to tapes of birds twittering in the Amazon rainforest through headphones, after she is exhausted watching TV — though the bird sounds sometimes give her nightmares of huge black raptors swooping down to carry her off, which makes her wake up in fright. Just as she is dozing off. Birdie has a querulous way of speaking, like Archie Bunker's wife in *All in the Family* that I'm seeing for the first time in reruns on TV. But this very hesitancy makes her kind of endearing, a tremulous dove in an aviary with a parrot and a hawk.

I don't bother to tell these people that if they weren't so bone idle they would sleep better, born rich with nothing to do all their lives the lot of them. Where I come from, nobody complained about not being able to sleep, everyone was up at dawn working hard all day so we could hardly wait to fall into bed when night came. There was nothing better to do anyway, no television and such in those days. I'm proud of the fact that I sleep soundly at night and sometimes in the days as well, which I know annoys Matron no end since she is one of those always complaining about not sleeping. One would think there was a plague on Ellesmere Lodge. But her not sleeping is no surprise considering she has nothing to do but mind my business, phoning Her every two minutes. And she always comes flying up here as soon as Matron calls her, you can be sure. You'd think she had nothing better to do, either.

So here it is, the morning after I am supposed to have killed the said gentleman, his ghost was enjoying a hearty breakfast in the dining room . I watched his every move two tables away: orange juice, fish fritters and callallo, fried plantain, two slices of toast, orange marmalade, and two cups of coffee with milk, three sugars each cup. And here we are in Matron's office with her in full flight, her bony arms flapping about in her favourite sunflower-bedecked caftan, the bright orange lipstick already smeared, the eyebrows, pencilled in of course, all the way up to the bangs on her forehead, and the earrings, cascades of seashells, jangling. She claims that dressing informally takes away any hint of the institutional, though her attitude — to me at least — is pure Holloway.

"Im-agine," she is saying now to Her, in this fake manner she has of speaking, as if she has somehow mixed up in her head the speech of two entirely different people. Which is not surprising, since she loves to tell of the wonderful years she spent in "Henglan," as a nurse she says, and that grand person in her head is clashing with some little country girl not quite jettisoned.

"Im-agine. Ken you believe? After she almost keels that poor gentleman. Meester Bridges. And they are trying to ree-vive him. In his room" — which she makes sound like "woom" — "Mrs. Samphire 'as the gall. To go to sleep. And snore loudly."

Everything she says ends on a high note, but "sleep" hits the highest note of all, almost a screech, so we know what's really bothering her, don't we? "In the woom," she continues. "Right across from his. Middle of the h'afternoon." There we go again. "Snoring. While he is almost dying." Lying! That's how she speaks, I swear. Fake accent. Short sharp bursts. Punctuated by eyebrows and earrings.

The two of them are behaving as if I am not in the room, though I have been summoned to appear before this Magistrate's Court, and I'm sitting in Matron's most uncomfortable chair trying not to laugh as Matron's eyebrows crawl like centipedes up to her hairline. Of course She says nothing, or nothing more than is absolutely necessary. Always been like that, even as a child, with that round face pale as the moon and just as forthcoming. A face that never reveals what the owner is thinking is probably what makes for a good television host. For her job is to provoke her guests — "probing questioning," I think the papers call it — so they'll get all excited, and shout and yell and wave their hands about, while she maintains her cool and speaks in such soft, reasonable tones that the audience is left in no doubt as to who is the upholder of Truth and Justice. Well, maybe some of them hate her for it. Just for being so totally cool in a country where yelling and screaming is the norm. Is she normal? But she does manage to get people to blurt out things they wouldn't normally say — which is exactly the technique she tries to use on me, except, here she has met her match. For I am the great revealer of nothing myself. I say even less. With me it comes naturally.

I don't mean to be bitchy about my own daughter no less, but there she sits each week, Little Miss Perfect, wearing some beautifully crafted outfit, in this wicker chair on this fake veranda with white painted railings and fake palms, a bowl of unmentionably vulgar flowers on top of the glass-topped coffee table which is artistically positioned between her and her guest seated in an identical wicker armchair. The only equality on this show. The chairs are white. The background wall is painted an astonishing shade of blue to mimic some impossible sea or sky, I suppose. It is the perfect foil for her crinkly yellow hair and bamboo skin and the garments in the soft tones she favours; not always so fortunate for those guests whose dark skins or darker suits sometimes fade away into the blue. All the better to chop you to bits, my dear — which she does with razor-sharp precision and immaculately charming voice, perfectly modulated. This show is a new one, called *Quest* if you please, tailor-made for her. Though, I have to say she's good, and she's served a long apprenticeship as a panellist and expert on many other shows, so she is already a household name. She does have a reputation otherwise of lending her name and her time to causes — the Battered Women's Shelter, the Street Children's Fund. She sits on all sorts of cultural foundations and boards. She's certainly not an idler. She's a sociologist. That's what she teaches up at the university.

I've been watching her new show only since I've been here at Ellesmere Lodge. My old television set at home conked out long ago, like so many other things. Not that there was anything worth watching. Here we have a large TV in the lounge, smaller ones in our rooms, and a satellite dish out back, so for the first time I am able to see her in action. Oprah she isn't — though they both have high foreheads, wide-set eyes, and the same sort of gruelling sincerity. But this is a two-bit local station in a two-bit place, even the lighting goes a bit wonky at times. There are no experts to call, no gifts to be given away, and no audience to be seen, though the audience is heard all right, and that's the best part of the show. After she's put her guests through the wringer, in this civilized kind of way, she turns them over to the wolves. While her guest might try to squirm out of answering, it is her job to pin him, for it's mostly men, to the board till he begs for mercy, or gets angry, or charmingly lies, or sulks. There she is, interviewing week after week a parade of idiots who come before her — parsons and politicians, businessmen and contractors, academics and trade unionists, all big fishes in a very small pond. These are all public figures out there, spending public funds or messing about with the public's trust or not messing with the public's garbage collection. They come in smiling, ready to undo the little lady, but at the end of it all they are undone. She does her homework and she knows just when to drive in the barb. The public love her, for the quest is on their behalf, of course, the little people; she of the shining armour is out there fighting their fights without once having to wave her skinny arms about. Don't we love people with the gift of the gab, and doesn't she have it where it counts? On television. She hardly ever opens her mouth to me.

I am proud of her. I beam with maternal pride when others praise her. But she does get my goat when she tries to use her charming technique on me and my business. The Listening Ear. The Voice of Reason. The Quest: Are you okay, Mother? Or, better still, implied, as in: Why can't you settle down and be a good girl and save me all this grief? As she's doing now in Matron's office while Matron continues her silly dance with her hands and eyebrows. As if I'm used to answering to anyone.

9

I MUST HAVE STOPPED listening to them, for I found myself pulled back to that other day long ago when I woke up in my bedroom, the house all quiet. I realized most of the day had gone, for the room was darkening already and the sky reddened with a vanishing sunset. I got up to open the door and discovered it was locked. Aunt Zena. She had done it before, locked me in as punishment, though I couldn't remember what for. Once for three whole days. It's only now when I think of it that I wonder if it was those times when my father was off his head that she locked me in. For once I was confronted with the truth of his behaviour, I began to recall other times, fragments of memory throughout my childhood of voices raised, furniture crashing, screams and shouts, an air of tenseness and exhaustion in the morning. I'm wondering now if she locked me in to keep me safe, to keep me from witnessing. But I don't want to believe that, for it would show that she had a caring side and I know she didn't.

This time I didn't even bother to rattle the door, for I knew no one would come, no one would come until they decided to let me out. So I stood still and listened again, and I heard sounds, men's voices mostly, but they were not the usual loud country voices. They were muted, flattened the way voices are when someone has died. I moved to my window when I realized that the voices were coming from that side of the house where there were the clotheslines, the chicken coops, and the mango tree.

10

MANGO. THAT'S THE FIRST food he ever fed me, stopping his horse at the Clovelly Cascades and lifting me down, then holding the horse's bridle in one hand and my hand in the other as he led me off the bridle path down to the river. It later became a well-known beauty spot, pictured on calendars and postcards, but at the time it was just part of the wild country we were passing through, with the dirt road zigzagging through the craggy limestone rocks with the occasional windblown, stunted tree, the dusty roadside bush and furze. The sound of the roaring river as we approached, the wild landscape somehow matched my own sense of wildness, of being, finally, in flight. I held tightly to his hand. It was the first time anyone had ever held me since I danced with my father and the feeling was almost too much to bear. I could hardly breathe. I couldn't speak even if I wanted to.

He stepped carefully down the path, and it was only much later that I would wonder how many girls he had led there. But this day I had no such thoughts in my head, for I knew I was the one, the chosen one, the chosen one, as the falls roared out to the pounding of my heart. Cold spray sprinkled us as we walked past the falling water, but I welcomed it, for the day was already too hot. Farther down where the river broadened out and it was quieter, he set the horse free to graze and he hoisted me up onto a flat broad rock. I opened my eyes to a different landscape, green and lush like the Garden of Eden, shaded by the broad-leafed anchovy trees that lined this bank, their trunks hidden by the profusion of wild pines and orchids that covered them, the long roots of wiss tangled up with the philodendron stems that hung almost to the ground like a green curtain. In the damp soil at our feet wild coco leaves held up their heart-shaped faces to the cool spray, and even the small smooth rocks in the river were covered with moss on the shady side.

He hoisted himself up beside me on the rock, an island in this green world, and I ached in trepidation. This was the moment I had hungered for, and my heart got ready to burst. But instead of putting his arms around me as I expected, crushing me to his body, he turned aside. Taking off his canvas knapsack, he unlatched the metal buckles, opened the flap, and put his hand inside. I watched, mesmerized by the golden hairs on the back of his brown hand, his long thin fingers, excited by his nearness, his acrid, smoky smell, dying to see what he was bringing forth. Two mangoes was not what I expected, but that is what he took from the bag. He handed one to me with a quirky little smile on his face and my disappointment vanished when I saw what it was. A Bombay! The finest of mangoes. I greedily took hold of it as he polished the other on his shirt sleeve, and I forgot everything, where we were, what I had done, as we tore into those mangoes like children, peeling off the skin with our teeth, biting into the fruit and letting the juice run down our chins, sucking the seeds until they were white, then rushing to the river to wash our hands, splash water on our faces, the discarded mango skins glistening like flowers on the black sand.

When we returned to the rock and he lay down with his head in my lap, I never knew such joy or such terror, the terror muted by the awe of knowing he had brought me Bombays, the finest of mangoes, more spoken of than seen in our part of the country. There were mango trees everywhere, it is true, but not these, these never grew where we lived, as if they required a more rarefied form of cultivation, a richer soil. They were rare, treasures, and I had never eaten one before.

Now I recall that as I gazed at him lying there with his face to the sky, his eyes closed, hearing behind me the chomping and snorting of the horse, the scent of mangoes perfuming the air, I felt the first little worm of anxiety, as if the mangoes were somehow tainted. I wondered where he had gotten them. Whether he knew beforehand today would be the day and had brought them specially to tempt me, their subliminal scent luring me to him, as the snake tempted Eve in the garden. Or whether, like Persephone, having bitten into the fruit offered by the Dark Lord, I was now condemned never to return. But there was no question of my returning, it was as if that morning my feet had set off down a path of their own and I could only follow where it led me. It had led me out of the district and away from everything I knew, beyond the cultivated plots and the increasingly isolated houses, into this wilderness, where even the birds sounded strange and aloof and lonely, leading to what ending I did not know.

It turned out he didn't know either, he had gotten no further than seduction. Once he got me, like Miss Celia and Aunt Zena, he had no idea what to do with me. He never called me by my name. He called me "Girl" like everyone else, though with him it became "Girlie" and then "G," which is what everyone came to call me. I was a girl, a child, for I was not yet sixteen. Maybe it was that childish self that revealed itself to him with my delight in the mango, how easy it was to satisfy me. Or maybe what it revealed was a hunger that was deeper than he had realized, a hunger he, the Man-of-the-World, already knew he could never satiate. For he suddenly sat up, put his arms through the handles of his pack, and, jumping up, extended his hand. "Come," he said, pulling me to my feet, and for the first time since I had set out on this runaway adventure, I was afraid, for he showed me the closed face of a stranger.

He kept hold of my hand, but tightly, as I stumbled behind him back up the rocky path to the dirt track, for my feet felt less sure now and he seemed to be moving much faster. I never knew till the horse moved off whether we were going to go back the way we had come or carry on. Up to then, since I left home that morning, I had not spoken a word, my tongue as tied up in my head as it always was.

He lifted me onto the horse and we carried on in the direction we were headed. He lifted me down again when we reached our destination. He never touched me again until we were married, although all I ever wanted was his touch. I was wearing my navy blue pinafore over a white shirred blouse and my shoes and socks in which I had left home that morning when he took me home to his mother.

11

MY FATHER CALLED ME by my real name, once, and that was the time I lost him. The time I climbed out of my bedroom window after everyone had left and night had fallen. Under the orders of Miss Celia and Aunt Zena, they had tied him to the mango tree, his mates from the war, Mass Eustace and Mr. Beard. By the time I awoke, he had become quiet. Soon after I started to watch from behind the gauze curtain, the crowd in the yard had wandered off in ones and twos until finally no one was left. I could hear Miss Celia and Aunt Zena. Other voices at the front of the house. Pans clattering in the kitchen. Life back to normal. I climbed out of the window. Some light of day still lingered; in the western sky a pale moon was rising. I could see my father clearly. I saw nothing left of the man who had danced with me. His hands were tied together in front and a rope was looped around his waist and wound loosely around the tree trunk then tied, so he couldn't move far. But he didn't look as if he wanted to go anywhere: his body was slumped and his head was down, almost touching his chest, and all life seemed to have gone out of him. He seemed more like a half-empty sack than a man. When I came close and saw that, I couldn't help it, I threw myself at him, trying to hug him, burying my head in his chest, uttering loud sobbing cries that drained me till I fell on my knees at his feet. "Papa," I cried. "Papa."

I had never called him that before, never called him anything but "Sir." But the cry was torn from me, along with the sobbing that I could not control, for I knew I was the one who had brought him to this. None of it would have happened if I hadn't stayed home that Sunday. I vowed that if only He Up There would turn the clock back to that morning, to the way it was before I left my room and went to his, before we danced, I would never ever again even think about him being my father. I would be good, for all times, forever and ever, amen.

I quietened down a bit, waiting on God, and I felt my father's hand in my hair, stroking me, until I gradually grew calmer. "Don't cry," he repeated, and the words came out strangely, as if his tongue was swollen or he had rocks in his mouth. "Please don't cry." And then he called me by my name. My sobs ceased instantly. Everything seemed lighter. For once in my life, I had this feeling of belonging, as if I had a right to be in the world. He knew my name! He called me! I felt so drained, I couldn't move for a long time, I just stayed there, on my knees, my hands still wrapped tightly around his legs, my tears soaking through his clothes.

I don't know how long I stayed like that, but when I heard voices approaching I got up quickly and dried my eyes. It was Mass Eustace and Mr. Beard, returned with chairs and blankets, food and the water canteen from the war that Mr. Beard held to my father's mouth for him to drink. I could tell they planned to spend the night. They followed orders, for fear of the Richards women, but they would not desert their old comrade. I could see there was no place for me. I was too happy anyway to care, too wrapped up in the solace he had given me. I didn't look at my father as I got up off the ground or as I hoisted myself back through my bedroom window with the long legs I knew I had inherited from him. I felt I had all the time in the world to get to know him. My father. That from now on he would always be there for me.

So just keep dragging YOUR RED WAGON along...

I couldn't help singing and jerking my body to the beat as I headed for my bed, like sticking my tongue out at those two women and the rest of the world.

The next day they put him in a straitjacket and they took him away in the Black Maria.

12

"MRS. SAMPHIRE WEALLY SHOULD try harder. To feet in."

I return to this buzzing in my ear which is Matron still complaining. She's never referred to me as Her mother, as if she can't believe in that possibility. But what makes me want to laugh is this business of "fitting in," for that is something I have never managed to do. Because there's never been a place for me to fit in to.

Perhaps by "fitting in" she is referring to my refusal to go to church on Sunday with all the old hypocrites, led by Mrs. Humphrey the Minister's Wife, or rather, the minister's widow. Though I don't think she realizes the Reverend Mister is late and she is no longer required to enforce the moral code of their county parish. Anglican, of course. The rest, Catholic. Nothing less elevated than that in our lovely Home except for Mr. Levy, who is Jewish and goes to the synagogue on Saturday.

Of course going to church gives the ladies a chance to dress up and show off. They all come out of their rooms at the same time, doors shut with a collective bang and keys turned, rouge and lipstick askew and perfumes sending out challenging signals left and right as they gather in the forecourt, leather handbags laden with prayer books, mints and tissue swinging martially, as if they are ready to have a go at each other, eyes narrowed and glasses glinting, weighing up the competition to see who is wearing more rouge. Who has a new outfit. The Over Seventies Handbag Heavyweight Bash of the World!

All except for Miss Loony Tune, actually Miss Louella Dune, professional spinster. And singer. Who carries only a change purse. Beaded. By herself. To match her eyes? Probably. And her covered hymn book. Beaded, etc. And who now tends to sniff at makeup but only because she says her skin became overly sensitive after years of stage makeup. And Mr. Radcliff, whom I mentally call Heathcliff for reasons that are obvious to me. He is the only male among the churchgoers, being principal, retired, of a progressive co-ed school and self-appointed attendant to Miss Loony because, I think, her trim figure and scrubbed face remind him of schoolgirls.

Off they go, piloted by Matron who is herself a vivid sight, in her Sunday uniform of tailored pantsuit in extreme purple, canary yellow, or pure white, with floating scarf and earrings. All handed into Matron's estate wagon, courtesy of Ellesmere Lodge. Except for those whose relatives and friends come to collect them, in a loud hallo-ing swarm, for these people all seem to know each other and I think recommend the Home amongst themselves when an old relative needs to be parked. So you can see how well I fit in! Among the chauffeured are the three Pancake Sisters — Catholic — who are driven back and forth to these events by one who looks like Old Family Retainer — I swear they speak like that — in a car that could only have belonged to Daddy.

Of course they all come back exhausted and eat a hearty lunch and have a no-sleep snooze and then spend the rest of the afternoon in the lounge or on the veranda tearing other churchgoers and one heathen resident, usually absent but cleverly listening, to shreds.

Every Sunday morning it's the same tune, or even beginning from Saturday: Matron asking me if I'm joining them for church this week. Why she bothers, I don't know, but it clearly worries her, and my refusal is obviously a great addition to her dossier of my not "fitting in." Though she finds it a problem with me and no one else, because others don't go to church — none of the men except for Heathcliff, who just likes to be with the ladies. I don't bother to tell her that I was raised by people who were the world's greatest churchgoers, and more mean and spiteful people I have never encountered in my life. Ditto for some of the people here, but I am calling no names. All will be revealed on Judgment Day, as every good churchgoer knows.

13

IT'S FUNNY HOW I'VE had this journal for so long and I never felt like writing a single thing in it before and now I'm having so much fun with it. The morning after the fiasco with the gentleman and my being dragged onto Matron's carpet — a threadbare raffia mat, actually — when I returned to my room I had to admit to myself my gut-wrenching, acute embarrassment over my own behaviour, which I still cannot account for. Jesus wept! I acted the clown all right. But it was so out of character it made me wonder if it might not be something they are putting in the food here and if I shouldn't make a note of it, just in case. Without thinking any further I headed for the bureau drawer and took out the book and a pen and started writing in it, just like that, as if it were the friend I needed. I'm beginning to think my days here are numbered anyway — not that I have a friend here. I have never had a friend. Not a real one. Perhaps that is what I thought he was going to be: Friend. And not just friend but lover, father, mother, brother, sister, all those missing from my life suddenly rolled up into one person. Well! He wasn't even a good husband. But let's not go into that now.

It was She who gave me the notebook. Without a word, as usual, gift-wrapped with other Christmas presents — she has never been stingy with me, I can say that. But it's stayed in the drawer ever since, along with all the pens and pencils and markers and crayons she has of late taken to giving me. Enough to open a shop. None of them used up to now. Every time I open the drawer and see the pens and pencils, I get a little twinge and I wonder, does she know? Why does she keep giving them to me? Well, I'm sure she doesn't know since only Matron would tell her, and the whole world would have heard about it by now if Matron knew. Maybe I should stop pilfering pencils, though it's hard to break the habit of a lifetime. But people are getting cranky, especially that Miss Pitt-Grainger when for the second time in as many months she couldn't find her crossword puzzle pencil, which she was absolutely certain she had left on the small table beside Her Chair in the lounge, along with Her Newspaper, neatly folded into a square, open at the half-finished crossword. The Cryptic Puzzle, she is always very careful to point out, not the Quick and Easy, as she calls the other one. She says this in a voice that implies moral as well as intellectual deficiency and casts daggers at the

Pancake Sisters, who argue loudly over the clues in the Easy every morning and whose necks you can see she would wring if they had dared to attend her school. For Miss Pitt-Grainger has spent her life as a teacher in the colonies, culminating in the headship of The Best Girls' Boarding School on the Island, as she is fond of saying.

When Miss Pitt-Grainger gets up steam, it's like a whale blowing or, since I have never witnessed that, how I think an alligator would sound if it spoke with an accent like hers, sawing the words up the length of its mouth and spitting them back at you. Her teeth are like that too, saw-edged. Unlike Matron, who tends to fade out words as she speaks, like a sputtering candle, Miss Pitt-Grainger is given to emphasizing them, sometimes with a hand gesture to signify pounding of the furniture, even if she's standing in the middle of the room, as she is now. I was just passing through the lounge and stopped when I heard the commotion.

Miss Pitt-Grainger is standing there waving her arms around, an unfortunate gesture as it makes the ample flesh on her arms jiggle, as does most of her when she speaks, for that is the most emphatic thing about her. Miss Pitt-Grainger is built like a tree trunk that has lost its firmness and is slowly being squashed, for fat seems to have gathered in strange places on her body so that when she walks or talks, different parts of her move, varying according to the mood she's in. This time it's mainly the upper arms and the jowls to match. Poor Annie the unofficial housekeeper is standing there saying nothing, but no doubt feeling the icicles darting from Miss Pitt-Grainger's blue eyes. Her straight snow-white hair bobs up and down as she speaks, looking as usual as if she had hacked at it herself. Her face has never known makeup, leaving her plain but regular features looking strangely vulnerable behind the thick glasses. Don't let that fool you.

Miss Pitt-Grainger (or the Pitt-Bull, as I have come to think of her) is the opposite of the Pancake Sisters, for everything about her proclaims the Death of Style. She wears simple short-sleeve cotton dresses in what used to be called a sprigged print, of the type not seen for many a year, so I can't help wondering where she gets them, probably from the same place she gets her shoes. The type of clunky sandals you'd only see in English magazines of small print and cream paper and dark muddy photos with advertisements in even smaller type with woodcut illustrations for goods which can be purchased only by post from furtive mail order houses located in places with names like Slough and delivered in plain brown wrapper. Big chunky sandals with small wedge heels and tiny decorative perforations in the leather and thick soles that will never wear out. Built for people like Miss Pitt-Grainger, for she has them in three colours — brown, black, and white. She reserves the white for daily wear. Why, I don't know, unless she uses it to do penance, for believe me, white means white. Miss Pitt-Grainger is the only person I know who still uses that horrible white liquid to clean her shoes, the kind all of us as children had to use on our crepe shoes. She does it every day.

Who am I to criticize another's style, you might well ask, but at least I just throw on any old thing that will fit me, I don't bother to make the effort, while Miss Pitt-Grainger's clothes are always neatly pressed and shoes shined or whitened faithfully, clean cotton handkerchief at the ready and handbag always by her side, even in the lounge.

Poor Annie! Miss Pitt-Grainger's jowls are acting in concert and the right hand is beating an imaginary drumstick in the air.

"There!" she is saying, pointing at the small table where the neatly folded square of newspaper rests, the crossword uppermost. "That's where I left it. For just one minute. To get ice" — icicles thrown at Annie — "since no one bothered to bring me any." O yes, we know what for at 11:00 in the morning. We know what's in the handbag. We know who took her pencil, don't we? I had passed there a few minutes earlier and don't even know how it happened, I leaned over to take a peek at how far she had gotten and next thing I know, as I walked away, I felt the pencil in my pocket.

I feel a little stir of remorse at seeing Miss Pitt-Grainger's rage, directed at Annie, the nicest of the staff here, but I value my life too much to confess. "Oh dear," I say, and Miss Pitt-Grainger's head snaps towards me. "Er, maybeyoutookit-withyou?"

She gives me an alligator snort and I'm surprised she even heard what I said. But she explodes. "Mrs. Samphire! My short-term memory is excellent, as everyone knows. I left my pencil right here. And you know it!"

Uh-oh. This is serious business, and I start to back out of the room. My eyes meet Annie's and she rolls hers at me, which makes me feel better and I try not to smile. For Miss Pitt-Grainger can abide no frivolity and particularly loathes Heathcliff, the only other English person here and who is given to salacious little witticisms with all the ladies, even me. Of course I won't bother to tell her how many times I have gone into the empty lounge and picked up her crossword and filled in a clue or two. Or occasionally changed what she had, to something quite nonsensical, just to annoy her. Serves her right for using a pencil with an eraser. And for abandoning her things to go and get ice for her mid-morning gin and tonic. She hasn't caught on to my messing with her stuff yet, or maybe she just thinks it's her age, despite what she claims, but the pencil thing is another matter. Pens too. I admit I swipe them when I see them. Can't help it. Have been known to ease them out of handbags and pockets. A nice little cache since I've been here, but so cleverly hidden that I'm sure no one can find them. Or have they? If they have, surely Matron would know? Plus the girls who clean, Cherry and Maisie, and who are the chief talebearers to Matron, know that I have a drawer full of all these new pens and pencils, still in their packaging. I sometimes open the drawer right there in front of them and hand them brand new pens and pencils as gifts for their children, so why would I want to take other people's?

I leave Miss Pitt-Grainger with her rant and another "Imsureitwillturnup," which only makes her glare at me anew.

"It had better," she says. "Or I'll have to think that I'm staying in a place where people *steal* things. Something that never happened before —"

Before what? I'm too scared to hear the rest of it so I make a fast getaway and head for my room to download the loot, which is burning up my pocket. Why O why O why, I ask myself. Miss Pitt-Grainger's anger has shaken me because she's made the taking of a half-used pencil into such a major thing.

I can't help worrying since I'm already in everyone's black book. My daughter is ashamed of me. The residents hate me. Matron wants to turn me out. My house is destroyed. I have no one to turn to. So, after sitting on my bed and thinking for a while, I've decided that I'd better turn myself into a model citizen. From now on. Seriously.

I will take a vow and, see, I am writing it down in my journal, a real vow, signed and sealed — there, my fingerprint even, in black marker — TO USE ONLY MY OWN PENS AND PENCILS FROM NOW ON.

To show that I am serious, I am going to make a point of taking the new ones out of their packaging. There! I have lined them up in the drawer. More than one layer. But the worry is still there, and I'm thinking it would be prudent for me to start returning some of my borrowed loot until the current charges against me blow over, just in case. Not to their owners, of course not, as if I could remember, but to nooks and crannies throughout the house, which is old and has many, down the sides of sofas and under cushions, in dark unswept corners, so they'll look nice and cobwebby as if they have lain there for ages, even out in the canna lily beds, inside Matron's car, her office even, all places where, over time, they will be found. No evidence left to convict me. Unless Matron has bought a fingerprinting kit, which I wouldn't put past her. A good plan, I think. And I am proud of myself, for I have never been good at planning.

14

YOU'D THINK I HAD everything all planned out the day I left home, wouldn't you? But it was a Friday afternoon like any other. For as long as I could remember, on Friday afternoons Aunt Zena sent me down to Mr. Lue's grocery with a list of the next week's requirements and payment for the previous week, since on Fridays there was no school after lunch. I wasn't expected to carry anything home — I was, despite it all, being brought up as a young lady. So Mr. Lue would put everything together and the yard boy, Danny, would go on Saturday morning to collect it, carrying everything in a basket on his head. I loved these errands and looked forward to Friday afternoon with a passion, for it was the only time I was ever let out, so to speak. Not that the leash wasn't tight, for I was warned not to speak to anyone on the way, and Aunt Zena actually timed me: I was expected to take one hour, no more or less. There was no time for dawdling, even if I wanted to. But with the three-pence she gave me for myself, I was always able to buy Paradise Plums and gumdrops, wrapped icy mints and sticks of black licorice, and sample each on my leisurely walk home. I always made sure I had enough left in my pockets, heavily rationed, to tide me over the week. For years, nothing happened on these walks, I said hello to people whose houses I passed, all of whom I knew, and they said hello to me. There was never any traffic on our country road, except for the red Royal Mail bus morning and evening, which I took to and from school, the parson's buggy on Sunday, and the truck that delivered Mr. Lue's provisions once a week. Not counting the market dray that left laden on a Wednesday night and returned on Saturday, or the farmers and market women on their donkeys.

And of late, him, Charles Leacroft Samphire, sitting loosely astride his horse in the shade of the big almond tree where the road widened, just around the bend before Mr. Lue's grocery and the church, looking bronze and handsome like all the Samphires, his feet in leather boots, his pants tight-fitting blue drill, his shirt white linen rolled up at the sleeves, no collar or tie but a bandana knotted around his throat, his leather hat pushed back on his head. That's the way he always dressed, from the first time I saw him out of the corner of my eye. I managed to take him all in before dashing those very eyes to the ground, for looks could kill, I knew that. Dressed and looking like no one else I had ever seen, but in body, in that loose-limbed casual way he had, reminding me of my father.

Of course the minute I saw him I stepped to the other side of the road. My face grew hot under my straw hat, then my entire body, as if fire ants were attacking me. I made the mistake of glancing at him and he raised his hat and smiled, but I didn't smile back, for I would have been smiling at the devil, or so Aunt Zena would have said. Oh, I knew who he was all right, everyone knew Charley Samphire, or Sam, as they called him, especially fathers with grown daughters who kept their shotguns to hand. Or so Aunt Zena said. Sam was in fact my father's relative, of a large clan that lived some miles away, but while the women of the family were regarded as decent, Sam and his brothers were not allowed to cross the threshold of our house. For what reason, I never knew, except that they were bad and wicked. Sam and his brothers were many years older than me; they were in the category of adult, so I never paid the stories much mind. Or Sam either, for that matter, on the few occasions I had glimpsed him in the past. Mostly at a distance, once at the wicked end of the common where Harvest Festival sales or Emancipation Day picnics were held, where the young men gathered to smoke and drink out of cream soda bottles filled with white rum, and ogle the shameless girls who promenaded arm in arm in twos and threes up and down past them. But that was a long time ago, before I had shot up almost to my father's height and sprouted breasts and hair under my arms and other places too embarrassing to mention and Miss Celia had silently handed me one day *What Every Girl Should Know*.

Well, did that book help? Of course not. I remained as green as a sweet-cup shell and as thick. I had no girls my age to share secrets with. I was never allowed to dawdle after school or keep friends and I never made any. "You sleep with dogs, you rise with fleas," Aunt Zena would intone, as she timed my coming and going. I only realized later, of friends Aunt Zena could not speak for she had none.

15

WHEN I WAS LITTLE, my only friends were books and pencil and paper. I was quick as a child and learnt to read at an early age. At first they were proud of me and encouraged my reading and writing. I can remember Miss Celia giving me spelling exercises every day and checking them off on my slate. All ticks, usually. She taught me to add, too. All before I went to school. Unlike the other children around, I had to speak proper English. I had no difficulty in school answering questions or responding when spoken to, but I would never volunteer speech, not even to other children. After my father left home, that time for good, I found it harder and harder to speak. I would try, but the words seemed to crawl under my tongue and bury themselves there, refusing to come out. My vocal cords tightened to the point of pain. Yet there was so much I wanted to say! Once I got old enough to discover I could put my thoughts on paper, I started to do so. I had only fragments of paper to write on. Soon I discovered that I could not leave these fragments carelessly, for someone would find them and I would be cross-examined. "What do you mean by 'lonely, lonely, lonely,' child? Do you think you are a poet or something? And who is 'The Wickedest Person in the Whole World'? Yourself?" So I learnt not to leave words hanging around, and I started to hide my bits of paper. I no longer scribbled words in my exercise book, for they checked those from time to time with dire results. And since paper was hard to come by, not like today, I resorted to tearing blank pages out of books, saving brown wrapping paper, peeling off the insides of labels, opening old matchbooks, saving paper from packaging, anything that came to hand. I became a real paper rat. I scraped up pencils too, wherever I could, for I couldn't stop scribbling, I was writing more and more, longer pieces. It wasn't for the sake of writing so much as for the refuge these scribbled words provided, so I hid them securely, as tightly as a snail's shell, my soul hidden inside. Until the day Aunt Zena discovered the cache. She read them all aloud to Miss Celia while I stood there, my face flaming, and then she tore them to bits, piece by piece, and threw them at my feet. I vowed after that not to commit anything to paper again. Not to keep anything in my heart. Not to show anything on my face. Not to say more than I needed to. Not that I stopped writing. But from that day on, other than my schoolwork, it was all written inside my head, waiting.

16

SINCE I'VE BEEN HERE at Ellesmere Lodge, I've offered more than once to help Matron in the office. I have no doubt I could be useful there but it's really because I want to learn how to use the computer. That idea came to me when I realized that writing in a journal wasn't a safe thing to do and I remembered Mr. Levy explaining about his laptop to Heathcliff and telling him about passwords. I thought of asking Her to buy me a computer; I have never asked her for anything before, but I imagine it is too much money and she's already spending so much on me. Suppose I can't learn how to use it? But Mr. Levy is much older than me and there he is, typing away — he says he is writing his memoirs. Well, so am I, come to think of it. So now I have this itch. I really need to check out this computer thing, but I am too much in awe of Mr. Levy, who is a patrician old gentleman with snowy white hair and a lovely manner, to ask him anything. So it was to Matron again, making my offer, willing her to say yes and invite me in, but she smiled sweetly and said again in that smarmy way of hers, "Oh that is so nice of you. Mrs. Samphire. Thenk you. Very much. I will bear it in mind." And that's been the end of that. I didn't expect anything, of course. Because I'm silent, and I don't have the kind of background the rest of them have, she too thinks I'm stupid. Or maybe it was just the way I mumbled it so it came out in a rush, all nonsense sounding.

I don't think it's because she's afraid I'll go through her files and ferret out her little secrets. Not at all. I'm sure she doesn't think me capable of that. I have already done that, of course, the few times she's left me alone in there, for I'm quick like that. Always have been. I like to know about the enemy. Which is how I found the picture when I was searching through Aunt Zena's bureau one day when they were both entertaining visitors on the veranda. A picture of a man and Aunt Zena, wearing a wedding dress! Without a doubt, it was her, looking much younger and happier, a long, clinging white lace dress and a veil which in the photograph was so long it was draped on the ground all the way around the two of them almost in a full circle and her arm linked tightly into his. I didn't have a chance to have a good look at him that day as I didn't want to press my luck, but I later confirmed my first impression of a portly man with a broad, flat face and straight black hair, and skin darker than hers, like an Indian's, the one on the cigar box that Miss Celia kept her sewing things in, not the other kind, and not unhandsome.

That was a shock to me for she seemed such a solitary one,

as tightly wound up and dangerous as barbed wire. I couldn't imagine anyone getting close to her and wondered when this wedding was and what had happened to the husband. Maybe she cut him to pieces. I had no idea then she had ever been away from home, for although Miss Celia was her mother, she was very much the ruler of the kingdom. Of course I couldn't ask and no one ever told me anything. As soon as I appeared the adults shut up or changed the subject if they were talking about anything the least bit interesting. So of course they turned me into a spy, creeping around and listening. But about Aunt Zena's husband and married life, not a word did I ever hear. Until one day after I had gone to live with Ma D, Charlie Samphire's mother, I had the brilliant idea of asking her, for she knew them.

"Ah, Zena," she said, in response to my question as to whether Zena had ever married. Ma D smiled a twisted little smile and paused in the middle of what she was doing, which was cutting out a piece of cloth, the scissors already slicing the material. It was beautiful silk material, salmon coloured, she was cutting to make a blouse for me. I stood across the table from her with my mouth open, torn between wanting to hear the story and keeping one eye on the scissors and praying her hand wouldn't slip and ruin the material. But of course Ma D was a pro on both counts. Not that she told me very much then, I think she still regarded me as a child and not yet ready to be let into adult secrets. But at least she wasn't as rude about it as the others.

"Married," she laughed. "Oh yes, she rather made a habit of it."

"What!" I'm sure my voice rose in disbelief.

"Well, it depends on what you call marriage." I leaned forward eagerly, but all Ma D added in a very dry voice was, "She's been churched once." And, though I waited to hear more, the fact that she had resumed cutting where she left off made me understand that no more would be forthcoming, at least for now. I didn't press her for more, I was too shy to do so anyway, but what she had said left my head spinning, as I tried to figure out what it meant. Was there so much more to Aunt Zena than the little countrywoman I had grown with and never learned to love? The foremost mystery in my mind had always been that of my mother. Now I filed away Zena's story as the second. What wouldn't I give to know things?

17

OF COURSE NOW I think about it, I treated my own children the same way, for I never told them anything at all. Not a word did I say to them about their sister going to live with someone else. "Soon come back" was all I ever said. Not a word did I say about my black eyes and split lip and noises in the night. Not a word when their father left. Didn't I of all people know the awfully destructive power of silence? Yet I silenced my own children with a look, forced their own words back inside them with a hand raised to strike. For I hit them, O yes, and don't tell me anything now about child abuse and cruelty. What did people like us know? Though I can't say I myself was physically beaten as a child, that didn't stop the anger from pooling inside me, ready to burst on my children. Not all bruises show.

I couldn't take it out on him, could I? Women just didn't do that. In his presence I was always too frightened to speak or make a move and once the moment of high anxiety passed, the pressure dropped and I could not build the anger up to boiling point again.

I suppose I felt I had to protect them, shield them from the worst of it, as if I could stop his straying. Every time he found a new girl he would go and get drunk and come home and take it out on me. It took me a long time to figure out the pattern. My first thoughts were always for the children and as soon as I heard him coming down the road, singing drunkenly, some-times alone, sometimes with others, I would rush to shut the door to their room. When it first began, after Junior's birth, we had only two bedrooms, and the children were all piled up together on the bed in theirs.

It didn't happen that often I suppose. After my initial shock and outrage, I learned to deal with it. For he never beat me when he was sober, nor did he ever touch the children. He was sometimes too drunk to stand up straight, most of the punches missed, and we usually ended up going round and round with him holding on to me for support while trying to hit me, banging into things, knocking over furniture, like we were in this crazy drunken dance, and I would finally waltz him off to bed. He never raised his voice to me at those times, it was all silently done, just him grunting as he aimed a punch or a kick. At first I cried out for him to stop, but that woke up the children. To this day I can still see Her stricken moonface at the bedroom door, so I bore it in silence.

The next day he would wake up and behave as if nothing had happened, and I did the same, hiding the bruises on my body, preparing explanations for my black eye, my swollen lip in case anyone asked. But no one did. I hardly went anywhere outside the house and field anyway. When I did, people averted their eyes from me as they laughed with him. He was the one everyone knew and loved, for many miles around — after he got the car, for hundreds of miles no doubt. I hardly saw him: our roving ambassador. And there came a time when I was thankful that he roved.

Well, he did take care of us, I'll give him that, as far as he was able, though it got to be less and less as he needed more and more for his drink and his women. He put a roof over our heads and food on the table, when he could, and sometimes money for clothes and the children's schoolbooks. When Lise, the last child, was eight or nine he left home as usual one day, and he never came back. Sent me nothing but a note asking me to deliver his clothes to the messenger, and I'm proud to say I didn't rip them to shreds as I wanted to. I behaved in a civilized way. I packed them neatly in his bags and I handed them over, even offered the man something to eat while he waited. And I just carried on. For I was the one who had kept the little farm going all along, the four acres of family land he was given when we married, and I was only glad he didn't want to bring the other woman there and throw us off it, for by now I believed him capable of that. No love of farming in him, I could see that from the start, so it was fortunate that I took to it, with help only with the hard work, the digging and hoeing and weeding. A boy to cut the bananas when they were ready and climb the coconut trees or dig the yams.

He did try at first to help in a half-hearted way, but after the third child — Charles Junior — was born, and we were still so desperately poor, he got the job as a bookkeeper down at the sugar estate, keeping track of the men's work and paying them, maintaining the records. He was good at that sort of thing. Suddenly having a regular income coming in made a big difference. He was able to extend the house, he bought the car, and for a while we were much better off than we had ever been. For the first time since we got married I could see a path opening before us.

Sam had a good head on his shoulders and some education. He and his brothers had all been sent to a fine boys' school — the same one that took Charles Junior — though how long they lasted there I have no idea. I can't say he was at heart a wicked man, but he was a weak, vacillating one, hollow at the core, and I think that made him cruel. I think all of them had been injured too much by their father to really make a go of anything. But he did stick to this work, probably because it was so undemanding, and it gave him an excuse to be away from home.

When he failed to come home that last time I knew where he went, don't think I didn't have my channel to everything that was happening. Millie who came to help out when I had the first child for some reason remained true to me all her life, and as she ironed or cleaned the floor, she kept me informed. She came from a family of hard-working women with their tentacles spread wide — one sister worked at the post office, two others worked for the best families in the district, and her mother was a higgler who went to the city market every week. Of course I had no way of knowing how much of what occurred in my own household made the rounds. But somehow, if I came close to trusting anyone it would be Millie, for she has known me better and longer than anyone else, and when I came to Ellesmere Lodge it was in her care that I left my house and land. Perhaps I trust Millie because she was the only person who seemed to prefer me to my husband. I could see it in the way she acted whenever he was around, and she was ever so sympathetic to me, always, though I wasn't sure how much of it was simply out of opposition to her twin sister, Kay. Don't ask me why, but those two girls had to disagree on everything, they were like night and day, and since Kay was a big fan of Sam's, I think Millie was duty bound to despise him and champion me. So she kept track of his business, and could announce with glee one day that his new woman had thrown him out.

It wasn't even Millie's day to work for me. By then I could only afford to employ her for two days. But she dropped by anyway, so urgent did she consider the news. When Millie went to work she went barefoot and dressed in a blue cambric shift with her hair in little plaits covered by a cap, and she assumed a manner to match. On her days off, when she had a tendency to wander around the district, Millie was a sight, for even in the middle of the week she could be seen dressed up in red boots that laced in front and a tight hobble skirt that showed off her bottom and a frilly blouse that showed off her breasts. Hair upswept, smelling sweet with the coconut oil she applied to her skin so it shone and the khus khus perfume she dabbed behind her ears, she walked with careful, rolling steps that showed off her finer points. In later years of course it would be hot pants, Jheri curls, and Afro-glow, and later still a track suit, trainers, and a blond wig, for Millie kept up-to-date.

Millie was a sambo girl, rather plump with squashed features, so she wasn't really pretty, but she had something that was sweet to men for they were attracted to her like honeybees. Unlike the other girls around who couldn't wait to get a man, and usually got a baby instead, Millie said she wasn't ready to settle down and flirted and laughed with them all, showing the gap between her front teeth that was supposed to be the sign of a loose woman. But I don't think she was; though she had a reputation as a "walk-bout," Millie didn't care. Unlike her younger sister Vie, who had to stay home to mind the three children she already had at age twenty, Millie was "free, single, and disengaged," as she liked to describe herself to any who dared to criticize her.

"Why me should stay coop up a yard like cunno-munno and me nuh have man or pikni to mind?" was her standard question, hands on hips. She was proud of her independence and, indeed, was the only one of those girls who would eventually settle for nothing less than marriage. Since she and her other sisters all worked out of the house, they left poor Vie not just to mind pikni but do the cooking and the chores for the rest of them. So Millie on her days off was free to walk. And talk. She walked to the shop, she walked to the post office, she walked miles to visit her friends and relatives when her mind took her, in the process harnessing all news and gossip and trailing behind her the ugly chat-chat that followed women who did not stay at their yard and — even worse — had no children of their own. Yet, because Millie had such a pleasant, smiling face, with dimples, and a temper to match, everyone liked her, even the women, so the remarks passed behind her back were nowhere as stinging as they would have been were she less well liked, or less well connected in the marketplace of gossip.

That afternoon, on her way home from her walkabout, she stopped off to visit me.

I was actually seated on the back steps beating chaklata in the mortar when she came around the side of the house. "Miss G," she greeted me, and I could see from the dampness of her clothes and the sweat running down her face that she was coming from far. She stopped by the tank to take up the little tin cup that stood there, dipped up water from the bucket, and drank in deep gulps before she came and seated herself on the bench under the breadfruit tree that faced the steps. Before saying another word, she pulled her cotton hankie from her sleeve to wipe her face and stooped and picked up a dried breadfruit leaf from the ground to fan herself. I continued with my work, scooping up the last of the beaten chocolate and cinnamon from the mortar and shaping it before putting it aside on the tin sheet to dry with the rest of what I had already pounded and formed into balls. Then I started to take up more of the parched beans from the Dutch pot and drop them into the mortar. But I didn't raise the mortar stick, for though I had a million things to do before the children came home from school, I was eager to hear the latest news and welcomed the break.

I settled back, for I expected this session to be the usual leisurely affair, but Millie hadn't even finished wiping her face before she burst out laughing. "Then Miss G, you nuh hear? One autoclaps at Cross Path Friday night!"

I must have looked blank, for the name meant nothing to me. Then I remembered it was where Sam had gone to live when he left me, a little township down on the plains, near to the estate where he worked. At the mention of Sam I felt a tightness around my heart, but I looked at Millie and said nothing.

"She throw him out, for it was her house you know? Lock, stock, and barrel. All him tings she tumble out inna yard. Is so him come home and find them."

Her eyes were filled with laughter as she looked at me, but I was busy trying to envision the scene, one that I had wanted to enact myself but lacked the courage to do.

"Him get out of him car and him see the whole house lock up. Him don't say a word, him try the front door with him key. Well, hear this now!" Millie was virtually crowing. "She nuh get the lock change?"

She was laughing now till tears came to her eyes and she had to wipe them with her kerchief. I didn't feel like laughing, I don't know why. Millie didn't notice, she was used to my silent ways.

"Well, him start to batter the door and bawl out for her. For him walk right round the house but every door and window lock. So him come back round to the front door and start to kick it in.

"By this time, crowd gather you know. Nayga standing

there on the street a watch the play. So she must be inside waiting till she have a big audience, for before the door yield, she throw open a window at the side and start off one big bawling. 'Murder! Police! Wai-O him gwine kill me. Unno run for the constable for me. Do!'"

Well, Millie said, nobody moved since everybody knew this was part of the sport. But Sam, who I know was always embarrassed by scenes, spoilt their entertainment. For he stopped kicking at the door, looked out at his audience and smiled broadly, shrugged his shoulders, picked up his things, threw them into the car, and drove off to cheers and waves.

At the time I heard this story I'm ashamed to say I never crowed as I should have done; the only thing I took away was that he was free of that woman, free to come back to me. Already I was mentally planning how I would greet him, how I would not utter a word of reproach, how I would cook his favourite dishes, press his shirts the way he liked, cater to him in every way so he would never again leave me. How pathetic can one get? For the next minute my ears tuned into Millie again in time to hear that the quarrel was over another woman he was seeing. Now his car was parked over at her yard. I was so ashamed of my feelings I felt soiled, for I had truly thought when he left that I was done with him. But Sam was the kind who infiltrated, like birdshot pellets that could stay in your body forever, a foreign agent colonizing you. Causing you just enough pain to bring on a perpetually nagging awareness; too near to the heart to cauterize from consciousness.

What on earth did Sam have that made us women ready to be such willing slaves? I don't know, for after that initial contact I never did personally experience much outpouring of his charm. But I saw it work on other people. The way he had of making you feel as if you were the most important person in the world to him, for just that moment he had you in view. For just as long as it took him to extract what he wanted.

In the middle of Millie's recital and my own emotional merry-go-round, a dreadful thought came to me. Millie! Why hadn't she fallen to his charms the same as everyone? Weren't they two firesticks who had known each other much longer than he knew me? Why hadn't sparks flown between them? Hadn't they been thrown into close proximity over and over again in our house? Why wouldn't he exercise his master's prerogative as they all seemed to do?

Was Millie wilful and independent enough to resist him? Why hadn't he taken her as he seemed to have done many of the girls around? Or was it perhaps that he hadn't? Is that why Millie was so scornful of him? Her attitude wasn't natural, was it? I could feel the panic rising inside me until I trembled and I shook my head to force the thoughts down, for I knew I was treading on dangerous ground. Not Millie. I didn't want to lose her, too. She was the only one I had to put steel into my resolve whenever I needed it. I forced myself back to that place where I trusted her. Trusted her, at the very least, not to be a hypocrite. Like so many others I could name.

Millie came and went with news of Sam from time to time, but eventually he moved away and I lost track of him. By this time his mother — my dear Ma D — was dead and I had no contact with the rest of the family. I struggled on alone with the children, once more mired in work and making ends meet.

Was I bitter? Did I resent Sam? You bet. Especially after I found out that behind my back, all this time he was in touch with the children, bent on seducing them away from me.

When She got married he showed up at the wedding. More, he had a leading role. It was such a blow to me, on what should have been a happy occasion, to see him looking a bit battered but still cocky and full of life, dressed in a fine silk suit, his hair white but freshly cut, as if he had just stepped out of a fancy barbershop. I thought it was just like her, wasn't it, to take away from me every drop of joy there was that day, bringing him back on the scene like that. I thought he had totally vanished from my life as my father had done. I thought that was how it was with me and men.

18

WELL, MY SON WANDERED off too, didn't he? Even before he was old enough to consider himself a man. Charles Junior. After that I made sure he became his father's responsibility. To tell the truth now, I wasn't too bothered by his going — I was actually relieved, for the boy by then, at sixteen, was more than I could manage. How a good boy could suddenly turn so bad, I don't know. Up to his third year in boarding school, Junior was the sweetest; he was easygoing, polite, willing to do what you asked, did well at school. Much easier to raise than the girls, I would say.

I don't know if his father going off like that had anything to do with it. Junior was about thirteen at the time. I never

said a word to those children about Sam. Even after I sent off
his clothes I didn't tell them he wasn't coming back. I didn't
want to talk about it, seeing everything I had invested in life
bouncing and scattering like dried pimento grains falling from
a badly sewn crocus bag. I suppose the children noticed his
clothes were no longer in our room, his shaving stuff had
disappeared from the bathroom, come Monday his clothes were
not among the washing on the line. But they said nothing, not
even Miss Big-mouth Shirley. It was as if the man of the house
had fallen into space, leaving this silence behind that wasn't
a silence really, more like a painful ringing in the ear. I didn't
realize how his absence dragged us all down. How mistaken
I was to think I was the only one who suffered because I was
the one who had been shamed. Say what you will, the children
loved their father. When he was around, he was good with
them. He was affectionate and playful and indulgent the way
I never was. But there, he left, and the only one in the house
who mentioned his name was the little one, Lise. About a week
after he left she came right out and asked, "Where's Papa?"
Nobody answered.

He and I did exchange letters about the children's schooling.
Junior had done well in his first few years and I didn't want
to have to take him out of school, so I swallowed my pride
and asked his father to continue paying the fees. He did too,
though it was still a struggle finding money for everything else
he needed as a boarder. But I truly wanted my children to have
the best, and as I saw it, only education would give it to them
since I had no legacy.

If only Junior had kept at his lessons, who knows what he

might have turned out to be. He was bright, make no mistake. Even in that school with boys coming from these rich homes, he did well, never coming less than third in his class. He got prizes too, for good conduct, athletics, maths, and others I can't remember. I was so proud of him, though I'm not sure how I showed it. I think now I was more concerned with the fact that he hadn't come first. Well, I thought that was the way to urge him on to do better. What did I know?

Then sometime around third or fourth form something happened that turned him into this monster. That's the only way to describe it, the change that suddenly came over that boy. Like he spun around and turned himself wrong side out.

My first thought was to blame it on the friends he was making, but these were boys from good homes, not the types you would expect to lead him astray. It's only when I look back that I realize the bad egg was that Pinto boy, nice, good-looking, his mother was a businesswoman and his father a lawyer who had turned into this big-time politician. The other best friend was Michael, the son of a doctor. Good homes, all of them. And where did Pinto end up? In a federal prison in the U.S. as a drug trafficker. And the other one? That Michael? Shot to death in his own home, gangland style, his blood draining into the pool, his wife and daughter watching. Junior is lucky to be alive, I suppose, though I'm not sure how long his connection with them lasted. For that's where the rot started, the summer he begged off coming home because Pinto had invited him to their beach house. How proud I was that my son was making such important connections. How happy I was that I was finally getting him away from the poor barefoot boys of the district he used to hang out with.

You know what it's like raising a boy child who listens to nothing you have to say? It's a father's job to raise a boy child, but by the time Junior was a teenager, his father was no longer around. And there I was, stuck with him, another Samphire man. Tall, good-looking, charming when he wanted to be. After that summer, his mood, his personality, his behaviour, everything changed and I no longer knew who he was. As soon as he got back to school I started getting letters from the principal. I wrote to his father then and asked him to deal with it. I guess he did do something, but it was too late. When the school expelled him, it was his father who took him home. I didn't want to see him. He did come to get his things and then I didn't see him again for several years, until we patched things up at his sister's wedding.

Maybe I shouldn't have given up on Junior, if that's what I did. It's not that easy. Knowing just what combination of flavours goes into creating people. He certainly got his stubbornness from me. His silence too, for once he turned into a teenager I never knew what was in his mind. That was the crazy part, not knowing how he felt about anything. I've spent years thinking about what Junior turned into. Well, I don't really know what that is, do I? I don't know anything about my children once they left home, Junior or Shirley or Lise. Except for Her, the one that escaped, the one who was raised by other people. So what is that saying about me then?

19

WHILE I'M ON THE subject, it is clear that that Charlie Samphire was setting up for me, like a mongoose waylaying a chick. He looked a bit like a mongoose too, for his family all had sort of narrow pointed faces with straight noses and that coppery skin and coarse crinkly hair of almost the same colour as their skin and water-marked eyes, sort of bluey green as I saw the first time I looked into them. That was to be some time yet. He played this teasing game with me. The first Friday I saw him I hurried past, but I could feel his eyes all over me and my clothes were damp with perspiration by the time I reached Mr. Lue's. I stayed in the shop longer than I normally did, catching my breath, cooling off, taking my time choosing my sweets from the big jars on the counter, because I was terrified to pass him a second time. But my terror of Aunt Zena won out and I was relieved when I neared the tree to see he was no longer there.

The next week, part of me was hoping that he would be there, the other half in terror that he wouldn't. But he wasn't this time, or the next. But the third week after that, there he was, and my feet almost knocked together in fright as I walked past him. Again the lifting of the hat, the smile. The fire raging in my body. It went on like this for quite a long time. Some months, anyway. He would be there, he would not be there, and after a time, though nothing was said, I realized that his being there was not accidental, he was there because of me.

I was certain of this when he was there two weeks in a row,

the first time that had happened. By this time I could think of nothing, dream of nothing but him. Of him kissing me, taking me in his arms, dancing with me. *What Every Girl Should Know* was of no help in taking me beyond that point, but I knew it was a plunge into something dark and dangerous, my aching body was telling me so.

After seeing him two weeks in a row, I left home the third week with my head in a turmoil, praying, Please God, let him be there. Let him be there. That's all I could think of as I hurried down the road. I knew I would just carry on straight past the square and throw myself into the river if he wasn't. I came to the tree and saw that he was not there. Tears came instantly into my eyes and were streaming down my face.

The road was usually empty of people at that hour, but I didn't care if anyone saw me, I only cared that he wasn't there. When I was almost at the shop, about to step onto the piazza, I turned my head to the right and through my tears I saw a dark shape under another tree beyond the shop, at the cross-roads where the school, the post office, and the church were located. As I stared, the shape coalesced in my sodden eyes and I saw that it was him, Charlie Samphire, sitting there on his horse, a smile on his face, for me. It was as if he was challenging me then, daring me to take that step. I had to be the one to do it. I didn't hesitate. I held up my skirt and ran towards him. He held out his arms and I flew into them. He hoisted me up. And I flew away from my old life. Just like that.

20

I'LL ALWAYS WONDER WHAT Charlie Samphire ever saw in me. Why he did what he did. I always think of it that way, as if I had no say in the matter. He did marry me, after all. He didn't touch me until after the wedding. What if he had done the expected, taken me and got me pregnant and abandoned me? The nightmare in those days of every decent girl. Whatever would have happened to me then? Yet every time I reflect that he treated me with decency, I run headlong into the other consideration that he only married me because his mother blackmailed him into doing it.

I have this secret thought that will never find an answer. I think Sam's mother, Ma D, and my father had something going at one time, which is why she cared so much for me. To her, I was always "Fabian's girl." Why can't I, even to this day, believe she simply liked me for myself?

21

I DON'T THINK ANYONE ever liked me for myself. Whatever that means. Liked me unconditionally, without barriers and hesitations. Maybe I'm not likeable. Maybe I need to grow some tentacles that will reach out and pull people in. Like that Ruby. She just doesn't care, does she? A hundred if she's a day, yet she does exactly as she pleases and says anything at any time to anyone. It is so embarrassing. She gets away with it, too. You can see that Ruby is a favourite with everyone. Well not with me, for I pay her no mind, not even when I know she is throwing words at me. It kills her, doesn't it, that I won't say anything. Not even when she teases.

"Hey, Mrs. Samphire. When are you going to give us dancing lessons?"

This is at the dinner table. I want to reach over and strangle her, for I'm sure the whole dining room, the entire world, hears. I feel my face grow hot. I know I should get up and leave, walk out and keep on walking, back to my own yard. But they are clearing away the soup dishes and I'm dying of hunger. I'm smelling the roast chicken with stuffing and I'm rooted to the spot. My plate is put in front of me and I keep my head down and tuck in, glad of something to do, knowing that Ruby is there looking at me with that little smile on her face. She moves her eyes to exchange looks with the other two. But I am saved by Birdie, who never seems to know what is going on and so can be relied on to change the subject by introducing something irrelevant and confusing. Something that she's seen on television, for Birdie is a great consumer of talk shows.

"Did you see this girl on Montel who was adopted and found her real mother and ended up killing her?"

"What, what?" Babe crows in a slightly irritable tone. She can be counted on to miss half of what is being said because she is too proud to admit she is deaf and a hearing aid would clash with her gaudy diamond earrings. This table talk follows the usual pattern: Birdie in full flight, talking nonsense, Babe clucking "What, what?" throughout, and Ruby adding the multicultural chorus that punctuates Birdie's recital as if she is paying attention to it all: "Mama mía!" "You don't

say!" "Caramba!" "Santa Caterina!" "Rahtid!" "Rasta-far-I!"
"Je-sús!" All of which amuses me so much by the end of the
meal I've usually forgotten to be annoyed.

I don't always listen because not much of what they say
makes sense. Sometimes I like to let my eyes rove around the
rest of the room, without being too obvious, studying the
body language at the other tables, and at one particular table
in recent times. But right now my ears are practically waving
"over here." I want to hear all about the adopted girl who
kills her real mother. I really do. But to my intense annoyance,
Birdie nimbly switches in mid-sentence to something else. I'm
dying, just dying to ask her to tell me more about the story of
the girl, but I can't get the words out of my mouth and I sit
there stewing in frustration, willing her to find her way back
to it. But she doesn't, and I spend the rest of the night trying
to work it out for myself, creating my own scenario.

I know it is nonsensical, for my daughter is a good girl
who takes care of me, doesn't she? What relationship she had
with her adopted mother I don't know, for I met her only a
few times and she is dead now, so I'll never find out. Him too,
the Reverend Doctor Whatever. Him of the booming voice
and the crewcut and the argyle socks and the black string tie.
Things I'll hate for the rest of my life. Well, we never meant
to hand her over to them, did we? It just happened, the way
you can set off down the road one morning intending to carry
on with your regular life and find yourself on a different path,
not knowing how you got there.

That's how it was, wasn't it? They came and borrowed her
for a few weeks, then for the long holidays, then it was for

a school year, and then forever. I did see her from time to time. She came home, though less and less as she grew older. She wrote to me. Letters that are engraved on my heart. *Dear Mama*, she started out, for that is what my children called me. Then it got to be *Dear Mother*, and then *Dear Mummy*, and finally, *Hello Mum*. What did it all mean? I spent more time wondering about the salutations than I did the body of the letters, for these were always short and to the point, only her spelling and handwriting changing over the years. The letters didn't say anything really, not what I wanted to hear. *I hope you are well*, she always said. *I am fine*. After that it was a recital of things learnt, goals attained, places visited. *I am learning to play the piano. I got 99 per cent for my English. Lots of love. XXX*. Did she really mean that, the love bit? Or was it cancelled out by the Xs that she started to put in after a year away? Those Xs seemed so artificial to me, as if they were part of a sophisticated lifestyle I knew nothing about, and I came to hate them, especially when in some letters they blossomed into a whole line. A reproach to me, that's how I read it, like crossing your fingers to ward off the evil eye.

Even more perplexing was her name. First she signed as *Junie*, which is what we called her at home, then it was *June*, her proper name, and by the time she entered high school *June* disappeared and *Celia* appeared in her place. It was her middle name, but I was confused. Where had my Junie gone? After that, I could call her that name only in secret, for when she came home she insisted that her name was Celia and refused to answer to anything else.

Signs, all signs that I was losing her. I kept those little letters and read them over and over and they broke my heart every time. For they never said what I wanted to hear: *I love you more than anyone in the world. I miss you. Please come and take me home.*

I should know about letters, for I wrote them to my own mother. Hundreds I am sure. In my mind. A letter a day in my childhood, pouring out all my longing. I had no mental image of her, so I created one, a beautiful white-skinned Madonna with a mass of wiry black hair who hovered over me as I wrote, slightly to the left of my shoulder, her cinnamon breath warm on my neck. She always answered my letters, poured out her love and words of consolation even as I was sending my words to her. The funny thing is, she spoke in languages I had never heard, none I could decipher. But it didn't matter. From some deep well of connection we understood each other perfectly. There were no cross XXXs between us.

22

WHO PUT THOSE CROSSES between my children and me? Was I the Bad Mother? Maybe I was, but my plea is I didn't know how to be a mother, good or bad. There was no one to teach me. I had babies, tried my best. Washing the nappies. Keeping them clean and fed. Rolling along. How do all these other mothers manage, the ones who produce these children who live good and productive lives and in turn fuss over their mothers and love them dearly? What did they do that I failed at? Where are all these fine children who should come by and love their mothers and fathers at Ellesmere Lodge? How come I never see them? Most of the children seem to be living abroad, and the ones who do drop by are like mine, hurried and frantic, juggling their old parents along with everything else in their busy lives.

23

I DID GO, ONCE, to bring her back home. She was my child after all. We hadn't signed any papers. It was when he first started to sleep out. The first time he stayed out all night, I sat up, sick with worry, imagining an accident, all the terrible things that could have happened. He came home at daybreak. He washed and changed his clothes and left again for work. Not a word to me. He came home that night, but stayed out a few nights later. Soon it became a regular thing. Sometimes the children and I wouldn't see him for an entire weekend. I didn't ask him where he'd been, the smell was all over him. I wanted to smash him then, beat him to a pulp, but the impulse was all in my mind. I remained quiet as a mouse, asked no question, showed nothing on my face. Spoke only if spoken to, did as I was asked. Perhaps that is what infuriated him after all, my compliance. Who wants to sleep with a doormat? What would have happened if I had stood up for myself from the start? But that was something I had never learnt to do, not until he left me there with the children, all on my own. I wanted to hurt him, get back at him in some way for this final insult. His rejection of me was plain for all the world to see. His current sweetheart lived only a few miles away. Everyone in the district knew her. They all laughed at me, I could feel it. I don't know if this is what made me get it into my head one day to go and bring her back, take her from those people once and for all. To replace what had been taken from me.

As I did with everything else, I made no plans. I woke up in the middle of the night with the idea coming to me, fully blown, and by daybreak I was walking down to the crossroads to catch the bus. He hadn't come home yet, but this time I didn't care. He was the last thing on my mind. I got up, washed, and put on my one good dress, a blue and white polka-dot cotton shirtwaist with a sweetheart neckline and three-quarter sleeves. I put my change purse and a letter I had with the people's address and a clean handkerchief into my purse and jammed my hat on my head, a little cream leghorn with a narrow rim and a wide band, like a schoolgirl's as I recall now. I was being borne up on such a wave of the rightness of my mission that I was out the door before I remembered the other children. I hesitated for a moment, unsure what to do. Then I went back in the house and woke up the youngster Ken who had been living with us on and off from when Celia was a baby. I told him that I had to go somewhere urgently and would be gone all day and to tell the Mister when he came he needed money to buy food for them. School was out, so I didn't have to worry about getting the children ready. By the time I reached the road, though, I was feeling a twinge of conscience and I turned back and asked Ken to give them breakfast and to ask Millie to keep an eye on them. Ken was a good boy and I knew I could rely on him, but he himself was young and not entirely bright. He'd been abandoned by his mother and his grandmother was too poor to care for him, so he adopted us. First he would come for meals, then I was sewing him clothes, then he more or less moved in with us before we even noticed. Ken was a bit of a wanderer, though, and came and went between his grandmother's place and ours. At this time he was probably fourteen, and when he was around, a real help with the children and the yard.

Looking back, I am appalled at the self I was then, the one who could walk out the door and leave the children. Lise was just a toddler. But I truly wasn't thinking of anything else but the duty — as I saw it — that I had to perform, one that couldn't wait. The one action that would put everything in my life to rights.

I had no idea how long a journey it would be. I had not eaten and had brought no food. At one or two stops on the way, vendors came to the window and I remember I bought a roast corn from one, which made me so thirsty that I bought a cream soda at the next stop. But soon I was nauseated from the drink, the food, the heat, the fumes from our bus and everything else on the road, the bone-shaking ride. I took off my hat and fanned my face until I suddenly remembered that in my haste I hadn't combed my hair. I looked around quickly, shamed in case anyone had noticed, and jammed the hat back on. I concentrated on breathing deeply to settle the turmoil in my stomach.

After what was beginning to seem to me like a whole day's driving, I was dying of thirst, but I dared not use up any more of the money I had with me. It was a weekday and the bus was not overcrowded. At least there were seats for everyone. The other passengers chattered as they passed the time, but I spoke to no one. I had only been to the city a few times before, and then I had travelled with people who knew their way around. On my own this time, I got more and more frightened as we got onto the main highway and the traffic steadily increased. Our driver seemed to get manic with his driving, and the heat inside the bus, even with the windows down, was almost unbearable. I wanted to faint, to pull on the bell and ask the driver to stop and let me off so I could catch a bus to take me back home. But I checked the impulse each time for I would conjure up her face, moonlike, upturned and beseeching me. By now I had convinced myself that she knew of my coming, was packed and standing with her little suitcase at the door waiting for me, ready to leap into my arms.

The bus let us off in the busiest part of the city, near the main market. The appalling stench, heat, noise, dirt, and confusion overwhelmed me. I hardly knew what I was doing as I stumbled towards the nearest taxi. I told the driver the address and he took off with a jerk. Only after we were stuck in traffic a few streets on did I come to my senses and begin to wonder if I had done the right thing and even if the battered old car I was in was in fact a taxi. For there was just an empty hole where the meter should have been and the driver looked suspiciously like a Rasta, his hair bundled up inside a knitted tam in red, green, and gold stripes. When I realized this, my heart fell down to my shoes, for at that time Rastas were scary people. This was in the early sixties. They were madmen, everyone said, who had their heads turned by smoking ganja and then went berserk and chopped up people with their cutlasses. We didn't have any down where we lived, not then, but I saw them sometimes in the town and walked in dread of ever being accosted. People were gleeful whenever the police caught one of these "Beardmen" and shaved off his locks and beard, for it was as if they were literally flying into the face of everything considered decent, with their frightening shouts of "Babylon!" and "Fire!" and "Natty Dread!" The market women, like Millie's mother, were always bringing new Rasta jokes from town, for at the time they were figures of fun as well as fear with their strange ways of speaking and behaving. Millie was always telling stories about them to me. There's only one Rasta joke I remember now: This fine lady was walking down a side street when she suddenly came face to face with a dreadlocks Rasta with long natty hair and beard. "Jesus Christ!" she exclaimed. In her fright dropping all her packages. At which the Dread put his fingers to his lips and admonished her: "Go in peace and tell no one that you have seen the I."

That Rasta driver certainly drove as if he was filled with some spirit, with one hand either on the horn or flung straight out of the window in a salute to other taxi drivers or people on the sidewalks who called out to him, for he seemed to know everyone downtown. "Lion!" they shouted. "Zion!" he shouted back. His radio was thumping out what passed for music, my headache was pounding in time to the drumming, and he was singing along — "When I reach Mount Zion / I gonna ...." — beating out a rhythm with his fingers on the steering wheel. He leaned his body into every curve, which he took at top speed, as I clutched the seat with both hands to keep from bouncing.

I wanted to ask him please to drive slowly, to turn down the radio, to stop singing, but I couldn't bring myself to do so. After a while I found myself paying more attention to the passing scene than to the driver. We had left all the noise and confusion and crowded streets behind and were climbing up into the hills. Here the streets had nice sidewalks, all the houses were substantial and set far apart and had gates and thick hedges and beautiful lawns and fresh air. I would have enjoyed feasting my eyes on this scene had I not started to worry whether the driver could be trusted, if he was taking me to the right place, if he had put me down as the country-woman I was the moment he saw me and was planning to take me somewhere to murder me for the few coins in my purse. Which then brought me to another worry, were all the twists and turns he made necessary? Was he prolonging the journey to increase his charge? For it suddenly occurred to me that I hadn't asked him what the charge would be. I had heard enough of people taken in by the cheating city slickers. I was almost sick with worry by the time he turned down a street of even grander houses than those we had passed and shifted down to a crawl as he started to look for the address.

"What was the number again, Dawta?" he asked.

I was so flustered I couldn't remember and had to fish in my purse for the letter that had the address on it. He didn't have to drive much farther before he rolled up in front of number 30. Before I got out, my heart sank as I looked up at the black wrought-iron gates that were firmly closed, and the freshly painted white two-storey house set some distance behind an ocean of flower beds and lawn.

The driver turned around to look at me fully then and he must have sensed something in my expression. "This is the place the Dawta want?" he asked in what seemed a kindly voice and he actually smiled, showing several gold teeth. I was surprised to see he was middle-aged, older than I thought from his driving, for I hadn't looked at him properly when I got in.

I nodded. I paid him what he asked; it was almost half of what I had left. I was shocked at the amount, but still had no idea of whether he had cheated me or not. The street was empty as I got out of the taxi and watched it move off slowly, looking shabby and out of place. I went to the gate and gazed up at the house. I picked up a stone to knock on the metal mail-box attached to the gate to attract the attention of someone inside, for that is what we country folk did. But even though I raised my hand with the stone in it, I couldn't for the life of me bring it down. It was as if I was suddenly seeing myself in slow motion. My unkempt hair pulled back and knotted at the back with escaping strands like steel wool. My plain cotton dress with my breasts straining against the fabric for it had gotten too small for me. I could see the large sweat stains spreading from under my arms and feel the dampness and rank smell. My feet were stockingless in my one pair of good shoes that weren't that good anymore as I had bought nothing new for myself since I married. Surely these people inside would take me for a madwoman. Would they recognize me? I was only in my early twenties then, but I knew that my plain and care-worn self was that of someone much older. How could Junie claim me? It struck me for the first time that day: what if she didn't want to? What if she refused to come with me? What if she simply said no and closed her face? During the miserable journey to get there, I had not once thought about that. In the world I occupied, as it was then, children had very little say about what they did or didn't want. Their job was to obey adults. But in my heart of hearts I knew that obedient and polite though she might have been, her own wishes would matter terribly to me. She had to want to come.

I felt so overwhelmed by everything my entire being began melting away, becoming insubstantial and faint. I knew I couldn't go through with it. I dropped the stone and held on to the gate, my head bowed, trying to gain control of myself. It took a while, but I finally pulled myself up from that abyss and turned back to the street, with no consciousness of where I was, with no plan in mind. It took me a while to focus. When I did so, I was surprised to see the taxi parked on the grass verge on the other side of the street. It was a dead end, and I suppose the driver had merely gone to turn around. I cringed with shame at the thought that he must have been watching me. How long I don't know. I had lost track of time. I walked towards him, still with a sense of remoteness, still outside of myself. As he reached behind and opened the back door I got in automatically.

"De I-an-I not dere then?" he asked as I got in and shut the door.

"No", I said.

"Where the Dawta want to go to now?" He had turned around and was looking at me.

I stared at him, my mind still a blank.

"I-man a forward a bus station, seen?"

I nodded, glad to have the decision made for me. As the car moved off, I found myself sobbing, loud dry sobs. I stuffed my handkerchief into my mouth to stop, and eventually the sobs ceased. I sat, ashamed, for I could see the driver glancing at me in his rear-view mirror from time to time. I noticed that he had turned down the radio and this time he did not sing along. He seemed to drive at a more sober pace too, as if to accompany my mood.

It wasn't until we were back in the crowded section of town near the bus station that I came to my senses and realized that I would barely have enough to pay for this taxi ride, and once I did so, I certainly wouldn't have enough to pay for a bus ticket to take me back home.

I had no idea what I would do, and what is more I didn't care, I didn't care what happened to me. When we got to the station, the driver turned around and watched as I drew the notes from my purse and fumbled with the coins to make up the amount to what he had· charged me before. I held out the money to him. He didn't take it. Instead, he gave me a searching look and I thought he was going to ask for more.

"De Dawta going far?" he asked. I told him.

"Clear to there?" He made it sound as if I came from the end of the world. I nodded.

He thought for a bit and shook his head. He said, "Is all right, Dawta. I-man was coming back down here anyway." It took me a while to understand he wasn't charging me. I stared at him in disbelief. "Jah-jah seh, Not one of my Idren shall go hungry and beg for bread. The I can see you have a heavy burden to bear. Go in peace. Selassie-I."

I was so confused I'm not sure I thanked him properly as I got out of the car and shut the door. For just then another passenger came up. The driver turned and smiled at me and nodded. I held up my hand in farewell and stood there long after he had driven off, buffeted by the flow of people, struck by the first act of kindness anyone had shown me in a very long time. Then I got hold of myself and pushed through the crowd to find my bus. Before I got on I bought a coconut from the vendor and drank the water, but though he cut the nut in two and offered me the jelly, it couldn't pass my throat. I was lucky to get a window seat again, and as the bus pulled out I put my head against the woodwork and, despite the rattling and the shaking, I closed my eyes and slept all the way home.

This is the part that really shames me, even now. Throughout that long, awful day I never gave a single thought to my other children. But even before I opened our gate I could hear the uproar from the house. I had no idea what time it was as I didn't have a watch, but I knew it was late. The house was in darkness. I called out as I walked through the door and was met by instant silence, and then shrieks of "Mama come" and the children exploding around me, all arms and legs. Ken came out carrying the baby, who was bawling her head off, but she too stopped as soon as I reached out to take her.

"Ken, what's happening?" I demanded. I knew my guilt and anxiety made me sharp with him.

"Nothing, Miss. Is so they been carrying on all day. From you leave."

"They're not hungry?"

"No, Miss. Miss Millie come over and we feed them. They not hungry, Miss."

"Mass Sam came?"

"Yes, Miss. But him gone again, Miss."

He must have felt the hardness of my gaze, for he added, "Him just change him clothes and gone from morning, Miss." He paused, and then finished lamely, "And him don't come back yet, Miss."

"He didn't ask for me?"

"No, Miss. I tell him you soon come, Miss."

I looked at Ken, suspicious that he was laughing at me, but somehow I didn't think he was. I was suddenly too tired to question him further.

I was flooded with guilt. I had never before left the children for so long and I hadn't prepared them for my absence. I silently cursed myself, wondering why I couldn't be thankful for what I had, instead of setting off on foolish quests. I inhaled the baby's sour smell and hugged her to me so tightly she started to scream.

I was suddenly overwhelmed by it all, by my hunger, my tiredness, my frustration, the smell of urine and damp, the eerie shadows cast over that dark little house by the one oil lamp that was lit. I felt as if I had seen a possibility of light but then had been dragged back down into a kind of darkness, and for once, and I swear it was only that one time, I was glad that someone had escaped it.

With the baby still in my arms I sank onto my bed. The two other little ones crept into the bed too and curled up tightly against me, their hot, sweaty little bodies stuck like glue. I eased my shoes off and stretched out with my back against the headboard, unable to stop my tears falling, thankful they were too young to understand.

24

I WAS MISTAKEN AS usual, wasn't I? Many years later when Shirley was grown up and angry with me about something, she brought it up, the whole business of my going off. This was just before she left for New York, and her behaviour was getting as erratic as Junior's had been. Shirley had gone from placid to flying off the handle for no reason, saying anything that came into her head, no matter how hurtful. This from the child who had been the most loving and thoughtful of all of them.

"She's the only one you cared about," she flung at me. "'Celia this' and 'Celia that.' That is all we ever heard. Nobody else mattered to you. Not even Pops."

"But —"

"Mama, don't say a word! You know it's true. You could never accept the fact that you gave Celia away."

"Wha—?"

"No, let me finish. Celia was like a little ghost haunting you, haunting me, all of us. She left a hole in my heart too, you know. My sisi! How could she have left me? But after a while I got used to it, pleased that it was just the three of us now, Junior and Lise and me. Celia was some big girl who came to visit and was fun when she was there, but I no longer ached to have her back when she left. And it would have been all right if you had left it alone. But no, you couldn't help holding her up as a shining star to us. Every day of our lives. It was 'Celia this' and 'Celia that' —"

Shirley was crying now. Tears were running down her face, but she made no attempt to wipe them. I was torn between stopping her outrageous accusations and comforting her.

"Celia could do no wrong while the rest of us could do nothing to please you. You have no idea how sick of Celia I was."

"But you loved Celia. You idolized her!"

"Well, I did when we were little. Then I couldn't stand her. I hated her. I wanted her to die. Then you'd care about me."

Shirley stopped talking and opened and closed her mouth abruptly, shocked at what she'd said. But it also stopped her crying. She took the handkerchief I handed her and wiped her eyes and blew her nose. She sat on the bed, looking so sad while I just stood there, unable to move or say anything, my mind all stirred up. Then she sort of roused herself and got up and looked in the mirror and started to turn her head this way and that. At the time she wore her hair in a very short and curly Afro, and she had just had it cut. I knew she was trying to gain time. When she spoke again it was in a much quieter, thoughtful voice.

"I'm glad I've got to know Celia now we're older. Otherwise I would have gone through life hating her. She's my best buddy now. But how do you think I felt, all of us felt, when we were growing up to have everything we did compared to her?

Knowing there was room in your heart for only one person. Have you any idea what that did to us?"

I was trying to think, having no recollection of ever calling Celia's name aloud, once she left home. Where did Shirley get this from? Maybe when I got a letter I would read it out loud to the others, and her father of course would tell us all about her after he'd been to visit. But me holding up Celia as a model to them? How could I have done that, since I hardly saw her? I suppose I might have mentioned how well she was doing when Shirley or Junior failed something in school. Or what new things she had just accomplished. But it wasn't as if I was going on about her all the time. That was unfair and I told Shirley so.

"Ha," she said, "not to mention you sneaking off to visit her all those times and leaving us alone in the house. With nothing to eat all day. Me and Junior and Lise. Alone in the dark. What kind of mother is that? And you carry on about Pops leaving us."

"Me?" I said. For I was truly confused. I never "carried on" about their father leaving. Never. That was untrue. As far as I recall, I left them only the one time. I never tried to visit Celia again. At least, I don't think I did. So how did this get multiplied in Shirley's mind to the point where she was recalling several visits so many years later? And how could she have known of that one abortive visit when I hadn't told anyone? She soon answered that question. Millie — to whom I had given a not very truthful account of my day, since I had to tell her something. As far as she was concerned, I had gone to take Celia something, something she urgently needed. Millie for once didn't ask questions, and I could see she didn't believe a word of it, but I didn't care. The whole experience left me feeling so ashamed that I vowed never to tell anyone.

"I heard you talking," Shirley said, "the first time you left us. Talking the next day to Millie. So I knew you had gone to Kingston. To see her."

"But that was the only time."

"Mama." She turned to look at me fully and spoke extra slowly as if to an idiot. "It wasn't one time. It was many. You just left. You never said where you were going. Never. But I knew, didn't I? Where else did you have to go?"

That shut me up then, for it so encapsulated my narrow little life. The woman with nowhere to go and nothing to do but beat herself against the cage holding a daughter captive. Only to return defeated time and again. I was so busy with that thought that I never got around to challenging Shirley about all these other phantom visits she had me making. She no doubt took that belief to her grave. I have thought a lot about this, don't think I haven't. But I can truly recall only the one time.

25

MAYBE IT DID GRIND us down as a family, after all, caused the first fracture that broke us apart. Shirley's strange behaviour the day they drove off with her older sister should have been a sign. This was meant to be just another visit with those people, it had been going on for a year or two now, their taking her for the holidays. She always came back for school. But after this time, she never came back, for they offered to send her to boarding school, and paid for it, so it seemed natural that she should spend most of her holidays with them and often the holidays were spent abroad. How could we deny her the opportunity? And so it went. I never saw her as property, no I never did, but they came to own her more and more.

On this occasion the Reverend Doctor and his wife came in their jolly way, all charms and smiles and lollipops and colouring books for the other three, sometimes more substantial gifts, clothes, shoes, and games. Gifts for the ones they hadn't chosen. Celia as usual was packed and waiting, as if she couldn't wait to leave.

The goodbyes were said. He opened the back door of his big American car and she got in without a backward glance. He shut the door. She was so tiny she vanished from sight. He went around to the other side to open the door for his wife. The wife looked over at us and smiled and got into the passenger seat. He returned to the driver's side, got in, and started the car. They both stuck their hands out the windows and waved to us — me, Shirley, and Junior and my husband with Lise on his shoulder.

The car had already started to move slowly down the road when I heard a wail from behind me and saw this little figure running after it, crying out, her arms outstretched. "No no no," she was calling, "Junie, Junie," as she stumbled along, her little feet pumping as she tried to keep up, calling her sister by the name we used at home. Suddenly through the rear window I saw Celia's face, she must have climbed up onto the seat to look out. She wasn't waving or smiling or anything, just staring at Shirley running after the car, her round face getting smaller and smaller as it picked up speed. As it disappeared round the bend, Shirley threw herself down in the middle of the road and howled with sorrow. I hardly noticed as her father picked her up and tried to comfort her, the blood beginning to ooze from her cheek where she had bruised it on a stone. For all my consciousness was travelling in that car. It was dragging me along until I felt stretched to breaking.

Why Shirley was so upset this time I did not know. Whenever Celia left in the past I would tell the others "Soon come" until "soon come" became a kind of mantra for anything promised. Did Shirley pick up subliminal signals we missed? It took us a while to get her to calm down. I guess I did not understand her heart was breaking. The thing is, Shirley in turn broke little Junior's heart, you might say. I can see that now. For up to then they were inseparable, almost like twins. But from that day she began to turn against him, showing him an angry face more often than not, choosing to ignore him or show her impatience, for no apparent reason. You could see the boy's bewilderment, the hurt at these times. He, too, became withdrawn. But after a while this period of estrangement seems to have worn off, and I heaved a sigh of relief that everything was back to normal.

26

I WANT TO TELL her — tell Celia — some of this for she never knew, did she? At least about that one time I went to take her home. Maybe we could have a good laugh about it, for my actions seem so silly now. I could tell her about Shirley lying in the middle of the road and howling when she left. Does she have any recollection of such things?

Here at Ellesmere Lodge, displaced and far away from everything I have known, the past rises in front of me like a hill to be climbed, for there is no other way through. I'm thinking there's so much I would like to tell her. We have never talked about the past, she and I. Though now I'm wondering if she never spoke about her other life because she didn't want to hurt me. Did she sense how much I resented the Reverend Doctor and his wife? It must have been clear to her even when she was little that I didn't want to hear about them. But did I actually say that to her, in so many words? I don't remember. But I didn't have to, not really. Children pick up these things easily, don't they? The clever ones know just what to do to survive.

In my saner moments I long to tell her, "I did love you. I do love you." That would be something, wouldn't it? But it's probably too late. I wouldn't know how. I see it on TV all the time, people doing that sort of thing, flinging their arms around each other and bawling and begging each other's forgiveness, saying "I love you" over and over. But is it real? How does one just come out and say a thing like that?

27

SHIRLEY WOULD HAVE, THOUGH, wouldn't she? Shirley was like that. The expansive one in a family where we didn't much show our feelings for each other. The good feelings, that is. She was the one who would hug and touch and say "I love you" and throw her arms around you. The one who would come into my room at night when I was reading, when they were supposed to be sleeping, and throw her body across mine. Just for the contact, I think. Just for the warmth. She would say nothing and fall asleep there, her head on my bosom. She hugged her father when he came home and twined her arms around him. She always had her arms around Junior's shoulders or those of her chums. She walked arm in arm with her girlfriends to school. It was as if she was perpetually thirsty for human contact, in need of love and reassurance through touch. Eager to give, too. I don't know, though, maybe I misread Shirley and her needs. I think it is so sad that in the last picture I have of her she is standing in a street all by herself. Just herself and some tall buildings behind.

Shirley in the picture is not herself. She is gaunt, with an underwater smile and wild looking hair, and she is squinting as if the sun is in her eyes. She does not look like the Shirley I know. Shirley came out the darkest of the children with hair that was thick and hard to comb, like mine, so she was glad when it became stylish for her to chop it off and she continued to wear it short and curly like that for many years. I didn't know this Shirley with the wild hair. The short style suited her, for she had a beautifully shaped head and well-defined

features with my high cheekbones. And though she was
not beautiful — she was the one who looked most like me
in every way — she had her father's light coloured eyes,
which gave her an exotic cast. She was the kind of girl who
attracted second looks wherever she went, as if people were
perpetually trying to figure out what combination of parents
could have produced her. She had lots of personality too,
too much perhaps, because she had a big mouth she was not
afraid of using.

28

IT WAS CELIA WHO brought me the news. Stale news, as it
turned out, but I didn't know it then. It was the middle of
the week. Her husband drove her. As soon as Celia stepped
out of the car wearing huge dark glasses, I knew right away
something was wrong. Herman quickly went around to her
side and put his arm around her and gave her a hug and
said something. He kept his arm around her shoulder as they
walked towards the house. All this I saw as I watched from
behind the curtain. I was moved by the tenderness he always
showed towards her, even though they had been married
almost four years by then. I felt anxiety as to what had happened to bring them down in the middle of the week and
immediately thought it was something to do with one of their
children. I never thought it could be one of mine.

We greeted each other and Celia smiled and tried to look
normal, but I couldn't hold my own anxiety in.

"Celia, what's wrong?" I asked as soon as they sat down.

"It's bad news, Mom. It's Shirley."

"Shirley! What happened?"

Celia started crying then, and it was Herman who told me Shirley was dead, shot to death on a New York street.

At first I didn't even take it in, for there were so many questions to be asked. But not many answers were forthcoming, for they didn't seem to know much themselves.

"She was just in the wrong place at the wrong time," was the only explanation I got.

"So, what are we going to do?" I asked. "When are we bringing home the body?"

And this was the most painful part of the whole thing, when Celia told me Shirley was already buried. The shooting had happened some time before.

My anger overcame my grief then, because I couldn't understand how my child could be not just dead but buried without my knowing. I probably took my anger out on Celia, for I can't remember all that was said. It was only later that I understood why she had brought Herman, for he was the one who managed to calm things down, explain as best he could. Shirley seemed to have been caught in crossfire between two rival gangs, he said. He and Celia hadn't known anything about it for a while because they had been away in Europe on holiday and it wasn't until they returned home that they'd found out. By this time, Shirley had been buried. Her friends over there had taken care of everything.

"Friends?" I remember crying. "What kind of friends that they couldn't inform her own mother? Where is Junior, why didn't he tell me? Where is Lise? Does she know? She couldn't tell me?"

I could feel tears welling up, but they weren't tears for Shirley. Her death hadn't sunk in. They were tears for what I saw as the indignity done to me. A reversal of the right order of things. What kind of friends did Shirley have, in truth, that they knew so little about proper conduct? I was raving, but not so I didn't see the looks passing between Celia and Herman all this while, looks that were both embarrassed and wary. I felt that they knew far more than they were telling.

"Why didn't Junior tell me?" I asked again, for Shirley and Junior had always been tight. Celia and Herman had no answer to that either, they just looked more uncomfortable.

"I don't know, Mom, I don't even know where Junior is at the moment," Celia said, her voice flat and dull. She suddenly looked incredibly weary to me.

I felt guilty then that they had travelled all that way and I had treated them so badly. I remember bustling into the kitchen, offering them food and drink, trying to act normal, but apart from coffee none of us could take anything. By the time the coffee was ready, we seemed to have run out of things to say. We sat there in embarrassed silence until Herman stood up and said he was terribly sorry but they had to go, he had to get back to the office. They promised they would let me know everything as soon as they found out. Celia hugged me and I hugged her back. I'm afraid I must have felt cold and unyielding to her, for I was already blaming the bringer of bad news, angry with her, with myself, with everybody.

After they left I couldn't keep still, couldn't focus on anything. I remember that I kept walking up and down, up and down like a mad woman, feeling stunned, as if I had been hit over the head and was no longer fully conscious. After a while, I called Ken and asked him to go get Millie, as I had to talk to somebody.

Millie came over and acted surprised when I told her. She had all the right responses, she screamed, she groaned and moaned, she raised her hands to high heaven to think my daughter could be dead and buried without my knowing. But I remember that I had the same feeling that I had had with Celia and Herman, that there was something here that other people knew that I didn't and that Millie was one of those people. It was as if she was acting out a performance just for me.

"You hear anything from Junior?" she asked. I shook my head. "Well, if anybody should know anything it's Junior."

I was taken aback by her tone, how aggressive she sounded when she said this, for Junior was a favourite of hers. She knew me and my family better than anyone else.

Then she asked suddenly, "Them catch the boy them yet?"

"Who?" I asked. "What boys?"

"The ones that shoot her."

"How you know they are boys?"

"Then how! Don't is shoot them shoot her? Right there in cold blood! Don't is pure little youth them use to do that sort of thing?"

"What sort of thing? Celia said it was an accident, she was just in the wrong place at the wrong time."

"Oh! Is so?"

Millie's tone was so skeptical I looked hard at her, and she looked away from me. To my eyes she had a guilty look.

"Millie, tell me the truth," I pleaded. "You always know everything. You know something I should know? Please tell me if you hear anything."

"Me, Miss G?" This in her self-righteous tone. Millie was protean in her reactions and expressions. "Why you think I would know something and not tell you? Believe me, my heart really grieving for you. Little Shirley! Lawd. Ah can't believe it. Ah can't believe it."

Instead of making me feel better, Millie's presence was making me feel worse. I could not stop myself walking up and down, ceaselessly. I felt hot and cold at the same time. My hands seemed to take on a life of their own, holding on to my body as if for warmth, clutching each other. Millie took hold of me and led me to my bed. She sat with me for a long time that day, sopping Bay Rum on my forehead to cool me down and brewing fever grass tea. She made me sit up in bed and sip the tea. After a while I began to take hold of myself. But I felt haunted by that great gap of my ignorance. What had really happened to Shirley? I remember saying over and over, "Millie, I have to know. I just have to know. Oh God, what am I to do?"

Millie didn't answer, but I already knew it was a useless question for it only made me feel my poverty more acutely, recognize my lowly place in the world, my inability to act. I had never travelled. I didn't have a passport. I didn't have money. What could I do? Nothing but wait on Celia to bring further news. Or for Junior to turn up. I thought of turning to Sam then, but my pride held me back. After all, he was the one in touch with them all, he probably knew long before I did. He hadn't contacted me.

The funny thing is I did get a letter from Sam, the day after Celia's visit, so they must have stopped at his house too. It was a nice letter, and it touched me for it seemed sincere, though it failed to yield any information. He said he knew Celia had told me the news and he just wanted to let me know he was thinking of me. He wanted to come and see me but he wasn't able to drive at this time, nothing serious but he had just had an eye operation. But if I needed anything or if there was anything he could do, I should let him know. He signed it, *Yours ever, Sam*. Well! I turned the letter over and over, staring at it as if I could force it to yield some meaning beyond the bare words. It was the first letter of a personal nature Sam had written to me, one in which we were not dryly exchanging information about Junior's schooling, and it woke in me all the complex feelings I had ever felt for him. Instead of comforting me as I am sure he intended, it just added to my overall misery. My sense of everything that mattered slipping away from me.

29

I HAVEN'T SEEN MUCH of Celia recently, but that might be a sign that I'm behaving myself at last and Matron has no need to summon her to report on my bad conduct. I have to admit I did miss her phone calls. So I was pleased when she called to say she was back from a trip and would I like to go for a drive. Instead of saying no as I usually did, I remembered I wanted to buy notebooks. I said I would like to go into town to the bookstore. In her typical way, she didn't ask questions, she just said, "Sure." She knew that I didn't like going into the city. It was hot and crowded with people, noisy and dirty, something I wasn't used to. But I had to go to the bookstore myself to get exactly the right kind of notebook; I couldn't leave it up to her.

Once we were beyond the fancy cast-iron gates of Ellesmere Lodge, I was amazed at the world beyond those gates. It shocked me that I had so easily left it behind. For that was a world where lawns weren't always manicured and hedges not always trimmed, where sticks and the bare earth and cardboard were home for many in a city that was full of poor people, people who looked like me and acted more like me, I'm sure, than that little corner of the Empire that I was leaving. The world outside these gates was full of dark-skinned people, while back there Matron and I and now Mr. Bridges were the darkest people, and we were more brown than black. All the domestic staff were dark, so was the gardener, the workmen who came to fix things, the drivers, the deliverymen, the little hairdresser and manicurist, all the people who did the hard, heavy, low-paying work.

I don't think I really noticed these things until I came to Ellesmere Lodge, which was like taking me back to the world of my childhood. Some of the people inside acted like that too, like Miss Celia and Aunt Zena, as if their pale colour gave them a right to lord it over everyone who was darker than they. Which is probably why I so wanted to get my own back at them. For now I was grown up and not scared. I had a physical advantage, too. I was younger than most of them, except Miss Loony if she is to be believed. I was taller, too, and now that I had taken to eating most heartily, I was bigger as well. No shrinking with old age for me. I had no idea being big could give one such a sense of being formidable, but that is what it was doing for me. I could feel them shrink away if I sat down on a couch beside them, shrivel up if we had to pass in the corridors or squeeze through the same door. Big. Silent and big was even better.

But big and a murderer was even worse. Months later Matron was still going on about my almost killing Mr. Bridges. I heard her remarking on it to someone on the veranda the other day, though I couldn't see who it was from the other side of the latticework. So it's still there, that feeling of being in the wrong hanging over my head, though Mr. Bridges is looking more and more like an upstanding gentleman to me. He likes his food, and I admire someone who does, and he cleans his plate at every meal. He likes to walk briskly around the grounds, as I do, and he has taken to playing music again in his room, though now it's classical stuff. When he plays dance-type romantic tunes he makes sure to lock his door. The key turning in his lock is like a dagger in my heart. I'm really sorry I started out on such a wrong footing with him, for of all the people here, he is the one I would like to get to know.

I already know a lot about him, from listening to the talk. He's a retired director of a very big firm; his wife is dead, his children all live abroad. He used to keep racehorses and was a noted tennis player. Nothing bad about him so far, but give them time. He's brown-skinned, darker than me, and well set up financially. Much discussion about how much he is worth. Quite respectable, thank you. Most people here seem to have already known him so he's settled in quite well, unlike some of us. Mr. Levy and Miss Pitt-Grainger and old Mr. McNab are overjoyed to have him, for he makes up a fourth at bridge, the other player having recently passed on, as Matron describes death. He and Ruby knock their heads together over the racing form. I've seen him in earnest conversation with Mrs. Holier-than-Thou Humphrey, with Miss Loony looking as if she is about to warble at him, and at the chessboard with Heathcliff, so a most versatile gentleman is he.

He reads books too, and has similar tastes to mine as I have sussed from checking his titles. This gives him something in common with me, the only other reader at Ellesmere Lodge. I assume we are ignoring the Pancakes and their Mills and Boon and Harlequins and Mrs. Humphrey with her Daily Word and her bodice rippers disguised in hand-sewn book cover. Even Miss Pitt-Bull with her crosswords and even crosser books, for I am sure she chews them up and eats them when she's done. But how will I find a way to get into his good books when I am sure by now the rest of them have defamed me?

I lean back in Celia's lovely car and smell the leather. Think of all the paper and pencils I will buy. Maybe a book or two, a special, desirable book, perhaps one on the bestseller list that I will wave around like a hook, to bring him around to me. I know exactly which one he would like.

30

IT'S A LONG DRIVE, and after a while I am no longer with my thoughts at Ellesmere Lodge, I am increasingly conscious of being in the car, alone with Celia. I look at her sideways, at her thin, manicured hands on the steering wheel, at her face, all bones and angles, her beautiful hair that is honey coloured and crisp and crinkled like her father's, but which like her skin now looks dried out as straw. I can tell she is trying to think of something to say to me, for I am trying to think of something to say to her. The way it always is between us. My throat is dry as I try to speak and I know the same things will be uttered. Me: "Are you okay, dear?" "How is work?" She: "Is everything okay?" "Need anything?" I am sad that all we ever do is go around in these circles. I'm angry too that she makes me feel inadequate. Even as a small child she would just stand her ground, her little legs braced, and stare me down. She was a sturdy little girl and her feet seemed to take root when she didn't want to do something. Now I wonder where this sturdy little girl has gone, as all of a sudden she seems so brittle to me, so delicate, as if a light wind would blow her over. I know she works too hard and probably doesn't take care of herself, but is something else the matter? Is her thinness saying something else?

Perhaps I wouldn't have been so conscious of this if I hadn't had imprinted on my mind all these years the image of that gaunt-looking Shirley in the photograph taken a few weeks before her death. Although I knew it was a gunshot that killed her, that last image made me feel as if she was already facing death, the thin body under the baggy clothes, the starkness of her facial bones, her shadowed eyes. I didn't conjure these thoughts up, they forced themselves on me. Which is why I can't stop worrying about Celia now.

I wouldn't have thought Celia's thinness was anything if I hadn't seen this headline and the awful picture staring at me from the cover of a *TIME* magazine someone had left on a chair in the lounge. It's the sort of thing that sets us all off nowadays, isn't it, seeing something in print or on TV and allowing it to percolate in our brains until it embeds itself there and refuses to let go. The latest thing to worry about. So I suppose I am getting as bad as everyone else. I was caught by the cover picture and garish caption, so I picked up the magazine and started reading the article then and there. I became so engrossed that without thinking I walked with it to my bedroom and shut the door and sat on the bed and finished reading. Which of course brought another charge against me, for the magazine was the Pitt-Bull's and I forgot to return it, forgot I had it even, when she was turning the place upside down in search of it. Well, to show I hadn't stolen it, as she was to allege, hadn't I left it right there on my bedside table, to be found by Matron as she stalked the corridors, doing her daily checks as she called them. I normally keep my room door closed, and locked, not that that would stop her with her bunch of keys, but that day I had left it open and gone off, to show the state my mind was in, having just read the article again. She didn't have to go inside to see it on the bed.

I did try to apologize to Miss P, but it came out the same as all my other efforts at communicating with that formidable lady, "Sorryididntknoitwuzyursmeanttoreturnsorry," which made her toss her head and walk away from me. She didn't speak to me, aside from a curt greeting, or a mini-lecture now and then, in that upmarket English voice of hers, so her withdrawal of speech wasn't very noticeable. It made the Pancake Sisters ever so nice to me, for a day or two, since they disliked the Pitt-Bull even more than I did. On one thing I could agree with them, that we were ever so thankful we were never at her school.

Of course the Pancake Sisters don't believe I ever went to school. "What school?" was the first question they barked at me, the day Matron seated me at their table and introduced me. From the way they pulled back from the table over which they were leaning and sat up straight in their chairs, I could tell they were shocked to see someone like me there. But it was the only vacant place at the five round tables that served the Home's twenty current residents. The gentleman who previously occupied it had just passed — Matron's word. Never having heard that expression before, I looked around to see where he had gotten to and couldn't understand how he could have passed so quickly. The three women at the table mumbled hello in various tones and smiled with their teeth and looked me up and down.

On approaching, I had thought they were much younger for it seemed like a table of colourful, noisy birds. But up close I could see they were not only old, like me, but very old. Not that they were like any old ladies I had ever seen or heard; clearly someone had forgotten to give them their age paper. I mean, they were so made up and dressed up and loaded down with jewellery — rings and things that were jangling and earrings and bangles and bracelets and ropes of pearl necklaces. I thought maybe they were dressed up for a party, but I soon realized this was their normal gear. They wore the most extraordinary colours too, especially the one I came to know as Ruby.

I took them all in, even as they were raking me over themselves. They greeted me politely enough, but didn't relax in their seats until Matron told them whose mother I was. Oh, they said then, collectively, leaning forward and raving to Matron, not to me, about Her and how wonderful she was, only last night on TV blah blah, with three pairs of eyes still scrutinizing me so closely I could feel my newly bestowed curls uncurling under their gaze, rivulets of unladylike sweat cutting furrows down the unfamiliar makeup and powder on my face.

"What school?" was the question that came as soon as Matron left, before I had finished unfolding my napkin. This from the one thin as a razor blade who said I was to call her Ruby, who wore lipstick of that colour caked into the creases of her lips and surrounds, and rings the size of birds eggs on gnarled fingers stained brown from the cigarette that was never far from her hand, lit, even at the table and between courses and while she checked the racing form which I came to discover was her main diversion.

I didn't understand what she said at first for Ruby spoke in a deep rasping voice and mangled her words, so it came out as "wazhul?" But even when the others, Babe, with a long face with glasses, and Birdie who was plump, with a sweet round face, repeated the question in increasing loudness, "What school?" I still didn't understand, for such a question had never been addressed to me before. So I had no idea that it was part of the social code, knowing if a new acquaintance had gone to one of the right schools or not and so was worthy of one's attention. You can see how far removed from present-day reality these ladies are. By this time I was so confused by the attention I could feel my usual shyness coming over me, shutting me down like a crab in its shell, so all I could manage was "zntcathrycadmy" under my breath before falling on the soup that had mercifully, been placed before me.

"What? Where? What did you say?" my table-mates cried, but I kept my head down. They got no more out of me. By then they had decided that I was someone to be ignored. They'd gone back to their chattering.

Ignore it, is what I was telling myself as the car sailed so smoothly down the hill. I have never interfered. From childhood She has always gone her own way and I've had little to do with the shaping. So I can't take any credit for the admirable things about her, and there are plenty I have to admit. But I don't know how she came by her achievements. The thought brings tears to my eyes, this not-knowing. I steal another look and wonder again, what drives her, this stranger? There's this public self that's vocal and courageous and then there's this private self that's guarded and watchful. She knows everyone, but who knows her?

I blink and wet my lips, for I am thinking this would be a good time to broach the subject that's uppermost in my mind right now, to ask her outright: My daughter, are you starving yourself to death? Is this anorexia? Bulimia? Are you one of those women? Or are you simply like the Rubys of this world, fashionably thin to the point of emaciation? Can't you put some flesh on your bones? It's not a look I'm familiar with, or one I could ever get used to, though more and more it's the look I see on so-called celebrities. But you are not their age, my love, you are at the time of life when you should have some flesh on you. Is something the matter? Cancer? Something else?

But try as I might, I can't get the words out. Something flashes into my mind that I had never thought about, in all these years. My husband Sam's sister, Jean, who lived at home with her mother and weekend husband. How thin she was, skeletal even, in a country where the norm was well-padded women. I knew nothing of these illnesses then, of course, I just thought the thinness went with her absent personality, her listlessness, her lank hair, her bloodless lips. She had had no children and died fairly young, in her thirties, but her passing made as small a ripple on my mind as her life had. Is this how it was to be with my daughter? I stifle the thought, and try again to speak, but I have never learned how, and nothing at all is said between us as she swings the car into the shopping centre and we find ourselves walking in step to the bookshop.

Walking in step with my daughter! In all our lives this has never happened before. Walking in step together, even to a place as ordinary as a bookshop. If only we could walk backwards together, undoing the miles, unravelling the web, starting all over.

31

WHEN DID IT BEGIN, this separation, this distance between us?

You weren't there the first time they came, for you had already left for school, neat in your uniform of navy blue pleated pinafore and yellow blouse, your hair in two plaits tied in blue ribbons from which wiry golden strands were already escaping. The neighbour's big children were happy to take you to and from school, and to tie and retie your ribbons, the laces of your white crepe-soled shoes, for to them you were like a little doll. So you weren't there to hear how these people spoke of you, the little prodigy, how you had been the star of the summer camp, what a brilliant child you were.

I remember I was hanging out clothes on the line, and had clothespins in my mouth, the bucket at my feet, filled with the children's garments already wrung out, several more loads waiting for me in the washing basin out back. Shirley was scratching around in the yard with a stick, already covered in dirt though the day had just begun. Junior, like his sister, naked except for underpants, was standing braced against my bare leg, holding on. He followed me with every step as he was at that stage where he couldn't bear to let me out of his sight. We were both standing still, Junior stuck to me tight, when a large black American car stopped at our gate.

I jabbed the clothespins onto the line and used my hand to shield my eyes from the morning sun in order to see who it was. Two people came out of the car, strangers, a man and a woman, and I thought they had stopped to ask for directions. I moved from around the side of the house where I was and started walking towards them, picking up Junior and carrying him. I was surprised when, before I even reached the gate, the woman called me by name, "Mrs. Samphire?" And when I nodded asked, "May we speak with you for a moment?" I could tell right away they were Americans.

He came around from the other side of the car and stood beside her, and I took a good look at them then. They were white people, of that flat chalky whiteness that is hardly ever exposed to the sun, so although they were both fleshy with strong features, their faces looked pale and indistinct, almost nebulous, shadowed under their hats. Hers was a rolled-brim cream leghorn with a blue band around it so tightly fitted that none of her hair showed, his a white Panama which he took off and held in his left hand as he extended his right to shake mine. He was wearing a plain white long-sleeved cotton shirt buttoned at the wrists and neck, a black string tie, and grey woollen slacks with turned up cuffs, a bit too short for him as I could see the green and yellow pattern of his argyle socks peeping above the oxblood oxfords. She was in a blue and white long-sleeved seersucker shirtwaist with a white Peter Pan collar, crisp and simple, which is indeed how both of them struck me, standing there looking as scrubbed if they had both been spat out by a washing machine.

Her face looked as shining as his and she wore no makeup. Their only jewellery, matching gold wedding bands. She had a square face, a broad jawbone and regular features that didn't add up to anything one way or another, nothing memorable, and washed-out blue eyes with lines around them that hinted at something both shrewd and kind. His eyes were a much darker blue and piercing under large glasses in black frames. His hair was light coloured and very thick though cut in a crew-cut. He seemed a much more hearty specimen than his wife, towering above her by at least a foot, for he was well over six feet and well built, with a booming loud voice to match.

By this time they had introduced themselves, but their names meant nothing to me, until they said that my daughter had probably mentioned them from her time at Maryfield Camp. And they both proceeded to speak of you for a good few minutes, smiling all the time.

That gave me time to think and realize that they were referring to the camp your teacher had taken you to over the summer holidays, two whole weeks of it, run by American missionaries. So these were they? That cleared up my initial confusion, but I was always flustered by strange people, by most people actually, so I didn't tell them you hadn't spoken of the camp at all. I said nothing, my heart fluttering with anxiety, unsure what these people wanted or what I was expected to do. In the silence I became suddenly aware of how I must have looked to them, my head wrapped in an old cloth for my morning's labours, my face already dripping with sweat, my old house dress patched under the arms and damp from the washing, my feet pushed into a pair of broken-down old shoes of my husband's that I wore around the yard.

I had put Junior down and I could feel him pressing against the back of my legs, probably exposing only one eye to peek out at the strangers, for at that stage he was as timid as I was. Shirley had no such inhibitions. She marched right up to inspect them, her face and body streaked with dirt.

The woman smiled at the children. "Oh, these are the other two," she said. Then she bent down and simpered at Shirley and held out her hand, which Shirley took willingly, though still wide-eyed. "You must be Shirley."

Shirley nodded.

"Your sister told me all about you."

Shirley looked pleased at that and pulled away and did a somersault right there on the grass which made them laugh. Even Junior was giggling behind me. The woman reached into an embroidered straw bag that she was carrying over one arm, the kind of fancy bag they sold to tourists at the straw market, and took out two huge lollipops with swirly colours. Peeling off the cellophane, which to my amazement she neatly crushed and kept in her hand, she offered one to each of the children. Well, that certainly pulled Junior from his hiding place.

I didn't smile, for already I was hardening my heart against them, already jealous that they were claiming even a little part of my child.

I felt foolish, embarrassed, not knowing what to do, wishing my husband was at home. He had all the social skills, he was good in any situation. They must have felt my discomfort, for I noticed them glancing at the laundry bucket, the washing on the line, taking me in, all of my dishevelled, incompetent self. Finally, the man said, "Look, we know you are busy and we won't take up your time. But my wife and I really were enchanted with your daughter at camp, and since we were passing by ... well, we were wondering ..." He paused then, as if unsure how to go on, but she chimed right in.

"Our own children are grown up, the last one just went

back to the States, you see, and we are going to be alone over Christmas, for the very first time. So we were wondering if you would allow your daughter to come and spend a little time with us. Over the holidays? We would love to have her and it would mean so much to us, to have a child in the house."

"Otherwise we won't even feel like decorating the tree. Will we, Mother?" He moved to put his arm around her. He was full of voice and authority all right, but I realized then and there that she was the cleverer and more dangerous of the two. For what she said next was, "It would give you more time to spend with these other two, wouldn't it?" And then she looked down at my belly in a meaningful way, as if she knew before anyone else what I was carrying there.

It was only afterwards when I replayed the scene in my head to my total embarrassment — at the state they found me in, at my lack of manners, for I knew I should at least have offered to invite them in, offered them some refreshment — that I realized that I had not spoken a word. So it was my silence that was making them trip over themselves to find even more elaborate means of persuasion, for they kept talking, on and on. But they needn't have bothered. I was so uncomfortable I wasn't even thinking about what they were saying. I was simply itching for them to leave.

"Of course we know you need to discuss this with your husband," he wound up.

I nodded then, for that was something that made sense. Then he got brisk. "Listen, Mrs. Samphire, we won't keep you any longer. Here's my card." He handed me a white rectangle. "That's our address there. Why don't you or your husband drop us a line when you have decided. We hope you will say yes. We could come right back down to collect her as soon as the holidays begin. You can talk to Mrs. Johnston at the school, and her husband for that matter. They can vouch for us."

I clutched the card tightly and nodded, and they said goodbye and walked backwards for a bit before turning around and getting into the car. "Goodbye Shirley, goodbye Junior," she gaily called out and waved as they moved off.

Shirley stood smiling and waving and ran to the road to watch them disappear in the direction in which they were headed, the direction of the school, while Junior clung to me and sucked his lollipop, his hands and face already sticky and streaked with colour. As I heard the car wheels crunch, crunch on the gravel as it moved off, in my mind's eye it was no longer a car but a hideous black beetle, intent on grinding down every foolish stone in the road. The most foolish one of all was me.

32

"HEY MOM! G! HEL-LO!"

It was like coming up from a deep dive. I'd been so into my thoughts I had to shake my head to clear it. I was embarrassed to find Celia standing with a tray in her hand and smiling down at me. It took me a moment to realize where we were. It was the coffee shop in which we had ended up after our book buying spree and our stroll around the shopping centre, which, I have to confess, I quite enjoyed. She put the tray down on the table and sat across from me and, still smiling, started to unload from it the teapot and cups and cake she had gone to the counter for. She was smiling and energetic and looked nothing at all like the hollow-eyed skeletonized girls in the pictures. Why had I made that association? While she laid out the tea things I looked around, and the bright colours of the place, the plants hanging in pots, the painted tabletops and chairs, lifted my spirits. Every table was taken, the occupants for the most part stylishly dressed women like my daughter, many of whom had greeted her as she entered. I settled my body in the chair and brought my mind back to the present. It immediately focused, I have to confess, on the huge slice of chocolate cake that Celia put in front of me. I could hardly wait for her to pour tea for us both before starting on it. She dug her fork into her cake and after sampling the first mouthful I think we both said "Mmm" at the same time, which made us smile at each other.

"Devil's food, my favourite," she said after we'd been silent for a few mouthfuls. "It's what Auntie used to make for my birthday. She was a great baker but she never made this any other time so I spent a whole year looking forward to it."

I paused with my fork halfway to my mouth. Celia must have realized what she'd said, for she suddenly looked down at her plate. "Sorry. That just slipped out. I know you don't like to hear me talk about them." Instead of the unconcealed enjoyment of a moment ago, her face started to close in and she was using her fork to play with the cake.

I felt awful then, as if I was the one denying her joy. And I realized that I really wanted to hear what she had to say. It is true that I have never wanted to hear anything of these people before, but now I found I was curious.

"No, please," I said. "Did you have a party on your birthday?"

"Yes. They always made a big fuss. Invited the neighbours' and their friends' children."

She seemed reluctant to go on, so I asked, "So what was the party like? What did you all do?"

She smiled a bit. "We wore paper hats and played games. The cake had candles, which I blew out. All the children took home presents. I had lots of presents too. Uncle would put on a fake moustache and a funny hat with stars on it and entertain us with magic tricks. I was so happy my birthday fell in the summer holidays so I was at home, not like some of the poor girls at boarding school whose birthdays fell during term. Some of the parents did send cake and arranged for ice cream, but it wasn't the same, was it?"

I wouldn't know, I thought, never having had a birthday party myself, nor for that matter having ever organized one for my children. We would note the date and try to give the child a little present, something special. But organizing a party is not something I would have thought of doing. I don't know anyone in our part of the country who did.

Celia had fallen silent and was putting cake in her mouth, but not with the previous enjoyment. I could feel a kind of sadness creeping up on us that I wanted to head off; I desperately didn't want us to fall back into our usual silence.

"Well, you certainly seem to have enjoyed yourselves. I'm surprised!" I know I sounded silly and my voice seemed false to me. "The Reverend Doctor doing magic tricks even. I thought ministers were supposed to be sort of serious and sing hymns and pray all the time."

Celia surprised me by breaking into a genuine laugh. "Well, yes, I guess there was a lot of that, but it wasn't what people imagined. Remember, these were quite sophisticated and well educated Americans. I mean, they were serious, diehard Christians determined to win souls for Christ, or whatever, but they were quite liberal in some ways."

She paused to sip her tea and gaze out the window, but I didn't feel threatened by this silence. I could feel a relaxing of the tension.

I thought of the Reverend Doctor the times I had seen him and how hearty he had seemed. I could imagine his great booming voice swaying souls in the large white tent they had pitched on an open lot. I had passed by once and seen it, the place where they started their first church in what was to become a well-established business. The Reverend Doctor must have worked a lot of magic from such humble beginnings. The church had grown to the point where there were now handsome concrete structures bearing the name "Church of the Living Bible" the length and breadth of the country, each one looking like the first, differing only in size, each with a main door on which was painted an open Bible. They had also established schools, a hospital, and a radio show on Sunday mornings, *Spiritual Breakfast Time*, which for a few years had the ears and pocketbooks of the converted all to itself until competition directly from America began, and nowadays of course from our own homegrown Reverends.

Celia was staring out the window, but with a little smile on her face. "I guess if they were around today I would find myself disagreeing with them on a lot of issues, as I do with the so-called religious right. But when I was growing up, I adopted their point of view on everything. I mean, they did encourage me intellectually. They wanted me to think for myself so they encouraged discussion, but there wasn't any clash in terms of moral values. I didn't start thinking differently until I went to the States and entered university. That is what opened my eyes to a lot of things, I can tell you."

I nodded and poured more tea.

"Plus," and she seemed terribly embarrassed, "it's when I really discovered that I was Black."

For a moment I didn't quite know what she meant, but I didn't interrupt, for she was talking in a rush that surprised me.

"Not that the non-white girls weren't segregated at boarding school. The point of those schools was to ensure that we knew our places in the hierarchy, wasn't it? So" — and she gave a funny little laugh — "I was always somewhere in the middle. Of course the fact that my adopted parents were white and considered rich counted for something with the headmistress and teachers, who were mainly all English themselves. Though their respect was somewhat tempered by the fact that they were Americans. Still, looking back, I suppose I was somewhat indulged. But when it came to things like sleeping arrangement in the dormitories, you can be sure I was safely tucked in with the brown and black girls in our little side room. The main dormitories had to remain untainted."

"What!" I said. I was truly indignant. I had known nothing about this. "You mean you went to a school where they behaved like that? Here? In this country?" I thought of the Pitt-Bull. Is that how she conducted her school? Wait until I got back to Ellesmere Lodge and that woman. I would certainly have it out with her!

I might even have said this last part aloud. Celia laughed in an indulgent kind of way. "Oh G! Of course that's how it was before Independence. Remember, I was still a tiny girl when I started boarding. Of course things changed a lot afterwards. By the time I was ready to leave school there was none of that foolishness. At least not on the surface. But that sort of thinking was everywhere. Poor black people couldn't afford to send their children to those schools anyway. And the ones who could afford it were so pleased to get their daughters into this elite, snobbish institution they certainly weren't going to listen to any complaints from their little ones about how they were treated. Nobody listened to children then anyway. No one wanted to hear anything about race. Certainly not those who considered themselves respectable. Remember how it was? And it's still that way in some places, if you ask me."

The thought of my child being treated like a second-class citizen was still burning me up, so I wasn't paying much attention to her next remark until it bounced back and hit me.

"You of all people should know what that was like anyway. Didn't your father's family treat you like a second-class citizen?"

"What?" I was so startled I nearly fell off my chair. I had never discussed my father's family or my upbringing with any of my children. Or with anyone for that matter. "What? How — who told you that?" I babbled.

Celia showed nothing on her face. But I was learning to read her body language, and though she was still smiling she was twisting a lock of hair round and round her finger, which signalled embarrassment to me.

"Oh. Sorry. I might have been wrong. I just gathered that from some things Dad might have said."

"What? What did he tell you?"

"Nothing really, just that they always referred to you as 'the little outside girl.'"

I sat back in my chair and said nothing, amazed that I could still feel crushed by the indignities of the past, by hearing that hateful phrase from the mouth of my own child. It had been such a way of reducing me to nothing that I had pushed it to some forgotten corner of my mind. I was surprised that Sam knew it and that he would have mentioned it to Celia.

"How did Sam know? What did he tell you?" My knowing that suddenly seemed important.

"He didn't tell me anything; occasionally he would mention how they treated you. I mean, they were his family too, weren't they? So I guess he knew what they were like. They just came into the conversation sometimes, that's all. It wasn't like we were discussing you or anything ..."

O yes, I thought, you did discuss me with your father. One day I'll find out what was said. I realized this wasn't the right time. Instead I smiled, remembering how Miss Celia and Aunt Zena would puff up and get angry at any mention of the

Samphire boys. Was it the hint of danger they represented that had pulled me to Sam?

"They said Sam and his brothers would never be allowed to cross their threshold. This was long before I even knew Sam, so I have no idea what that was all about."

"He was a lot older than you."

"Fifteen years. Nowadays I suppose that's nothing, but when you're young …" I was suddenly thinking of how much I had in fact told Sam in the early days of our marriage when I thought that was what intimacy is about. A way of pulling him closer. Instead, it exposed my neediness.

I didn't say any more because I was thinking that Celia was as entrapped by the past as I was and I genuinely wanted to hear her tell me more.

"So what happened at university?" I asked her. "You said that's when you discovered you were Black."

"Oh well, that's what everyone was doing in America then. It was the 'Black is Beautiful' phase, so I suddenly became conscious of what I was in relation to these white people who had raised me. I don't know, it's hard to explain without going into a lot of detail. I was suddenly questioning a lot of things I had never noticed before. And not in a very subtle way, I'm afraid. I was used to being obedient, so it was a painful time for me — and them too. Regardless, they were awfully good to me. Probably treated me much better than I deserved."

"Oh, don't say a thing like that," I said for want of something to say. In my heart I wanted to hear that those people had gotten their comeuppance.

She suddenly laughed. "You know, the first thing I did was

loosen my hair from all the clips and ribbons they got me used to, to hold it down, keep it neat and looking as straight as possible. I turned this nayga hair loose and began to look like a wild woman. Later on I was into headwraps, African style. My flag of liberation was flying from my head. I was hot in the Women's Lib movement too."

Celia seemed to be enjoying this vision of her younger self, wild and free, and I was trying to envision it, too. But apart from the hair, still loose and curly, I didn't feel that I had been exposed to anything else that was wild about her. She seemed as buttoned up as always, controlled, the voice of reason and the personification of the woman who was always well pulled together. But then, of course, I was coming to realize that there were so many other Celias to be discovered and that I had never given her a chance to reveal those selves to me. I let her keep talking.

"I feel terrible because after that it was as if I turned my back on them. I didn't really, but I was no longer their little girl and I got impatient with their protection. By this time, of course, they'd retired and moved back to the States, so I was still living with them when I started university. By my second year I'd moved out, and after that, though we still saw a lot of each other, I got caught up in my own life that was taking a different turn. Uncle died around the time I was entering grad school and Auntie moved to California to live with her eldest daughter. I kept in touch but, you know, not the way I should have, after all they had done for me. I still feel guilty that I was so neglectful of her."

I sensed her sadness and I instinctively reached across and

placed my hand on hers. She smiled at me and placed her other hand on top of mine and held it there for a while till the warmth spread to my heart. Her eyes glittered as if there were tears in them and I let my hand rest where it was, between hers, really surprised at myself. I guess she was surprised too, being unused to any such gestures from me. She moved her hand then and the moment passed and neither of us said anything for a while. There was really so much I wanted to ask her, but my words had dried up. I no longer knew if I should feel happy or sad at anything she had said.

"Well, Mo — G — I guess we should be getting back," she said rather brightly, looking at her watch and reaching for her bag. Then she looked at me. "Here I am calling you G. Impertinent, eh? But I feel much too old to be calling you Mom. You don't mind?"

"No, of course not," I said as I rose from the table and picked up my packages. I was actually quite pleased. I couldn't help thinking that though much hadn't been said, it was as if Celia and I had crossed some sort of bridge and were walking in the same direction. On the drive back to Ellesmere Lodge neither of us said much, but the silence felt companionable rather than forced. For the first time in months, my body didn't feel rigid with the rage I'd brought with me.

33

RED LETTER DAY. DEAR Diary, ha-ha. I was wearing red, a colour I would never have chosen for myself, but it was one of the dresses Celia had bought me that was hanging brand new in the closet, and I had put it on to go into town with her, a red linen two-piece with the cutwork embroidery at the collar. I'd worn it just to show her I was not an ingrate. I always made an effort to tidy myself nicely whenever she took me out, which was the only time the smart clothes got worn. Otherwise I just slopped around. Today I dressed with care, even put some powder on my face and wore a pair of new shoes, smart black leather court shoes with tiny heels. I carried the red and white handbag that matched the dress. I hated wearing closed-up shoes, anything dressy, but since I wasn't sure I was out of the woods yet, in terms of trouble with Matron, I got it into my head to make the effort to please Celia. I'm glad I did, for she had remarked on it when I got in the car, how nice I looked.

But that was as nothing compared to what happened when we returned home from the bookshop and she pulled into the porte cochere at the entrance. For who was standing right there, having just come out of another car that was driving off, but Mr. Bridges, him that I had murdered. Looking back, I am amazed that the first thought that came into my head when I saw him was pleasure because I was looking so smart. Then reality overtook me. I wanted to sink into the ground as he turned towards us. He frowned when he saw me, and then he looked at Celia and his face lit up. She was already walking towards him and extending her hand. They knew each other? Who didn't know her? They were greeting each other as old friends and then she turned to me and said, "I believe you have met my mother, Mrs. Samphire?"

I could see the various emotions washing over his face, for he had made a special effort to avoid me since that fateful day, barely nodding if we happened to cross each other's path. But good breeding won out and he extended his hand and said, "Well yes, under rather curious circumstances but never mind, now I know who she is …" and me not looking but stretching out my hand and muttering "pleds2meetusorryaboutheother dayidon'tknowwhati …"

Barely touching my fingertips, he turned away from me and was saying to her, "Samphire? I had no idea that was your maiden name. I'm sure I know your relatives, there's only one set that I know of, used to play cricket with them when we were boys, me and my brother though we were a lot younger … our uncle had a property near theirs and we spent our holidays … George, no, what was his name, he was the most brilliant fast bowler we had ever seen, blasted my stumps every time. No, not George, it was …"

"Geoff," she said. "That's my uncle. My father's youngest brother. He was known all over …" and they were away at it. Cricket… and what had happened to Uncle Geoff … and his children … one of whom she saw all the time and …

I just gaped at her, shocked. How did she know this? But of course she was her father's daughter, wasn't she? I had made a point of never taking them to their father's home. His mother understood, especially since she was the one who had seen to it that Sam and I moved away after we were married. She visited us from time to time, but she never once suggested that we visit her. I can't remember if Sam's brothers visited much, he was more likely to go back to visit them. So how could Celia now be talking about her Uncle Geoff in this familiar way?

Before I had time to consider this, Mr. Bridges was turning to me again, and in my agitation the two packages I had been holding slipped. I caught them just in time, but before I righted them a book fell out, the very one I had bought to tempt him! He bent and picked it up and the title caught his eye as he handed it to me. "Oh, the latest Martha Grimes," he said with pleased surprise, pulling back his hand and gazing at the front cover and then turning it over and passing his eye over the back. "You are a fan?"

He looked at me properly then, for the first time, I think, and I managed to smile and croak out, "Yes. Are you?"

"Wonderful," he said. "I've read all her books and I've been meaning to get this one."

Before I even knew it, I was handing the book back, saying, "Please, why don't you keep it and give it back when you've read it?"

"That's very kind, but I can't deprive you of the pleasure. I'd be happy to borrow it when you are through, though."

"Don't worry, go ahead," I said, fishing in the bag. "I have two more of hers to get through." I held them up in triumph.

"Oh, I have read those," he said. I already knew this, as I'd seen him with them in the lounge.

He looked at the new book he was still holding. "Well ... if you're sure?" His voice was quizzical, but I could see the book lover's greed in his eyes.

I nodded. He looked pleased, paying more attention to the book than to me. "If that's all right, I'd be delighted." Then he added, looking at me again, "Good to know there's another reader with my taste around, Mrs. Samphire. Perhaps we can do a little book exchange from time to time."

"Certainly, Mr. Bridges. And" — I was into this without even thinking — "I'm sorry I was so rude to you the first time we met. I don't know what came over me, it was the music ..."

But by the time I got there I'd lost that surprising burst of confidence that had so carried me along, for it came out as "whtcmeovermeitwasthemuzik ..." and my voice faded to nothing. I studied the toes of my new shoes.

Celia wasn't a top-flight interviewer for nothing. She was right there with, "Lovely seeing you, Mr. Bridges." He smiled, inclined his head, and headed into the house.

We stood there for a moment then, she and I. I expected her to say something. I was full to bursting. I thought she had noticed it, the way I had managed to carry on a real conversation with Mr. Bridges, knocking the ball back and forth. I felt like a child, wanting her to praise me. But I don't think she noticed. She leaned over and brushed my cheek with hers, got into the car, and drove off. I stood there for a while wondering why I was feeling so let down after my high a moment ago, how the feeling of warmth we had captured at the coffee shop could have vanished so quickly. I couldn't help thinking, and not for the first time, how animated she seemed when we were with other people, how lacklustre with me, as if I was always the pinprick that deflated her.

34

BUT IT'S HER FATHER all over again, isn't it, always putting me down, as if everything I did interfered with his pleasure: "Don't be a spoilsport." "Don't cling." "Don't bother me with that now." Though I never did learn the ways in which I transgressed. He never said, "Don't nag," for I didn't, if nagging is purely verbal; we never spoke beyond the most basic acts of communication necessary for two people to get married, have children, and run a household. I ran the household, cutting and pasting, turning inside out and basting. He ran me, just as I imagine it had been with his parents. I thought then, and for a long time after, it was my fault, for he was the outgoing one, the talkative one — with everyone but me.

To this day, I have no idea what it was about me that attracted him in the first place. He never said. Not like they do in the books, where the loved one is told something specific and thrilling. Something to make her feel womanly and beautiful, for beauty exists, after all, only in the eyes of the beholder. Why hadn't he followed up and simply seduced me, as he had countless women? Was I so lacking in charm that a noted womanizer disdained me? This is something that bothered me a great deal. Not then, for I wasn't so aware, but later, when I had a great deal of time to think, and wonder. It finally shamed me, defeated me. The thought of being so lacking in attraction.

Once he got me, he treated me with such bemused disinterest that I can only assume his original intention was simply a desire to see how quickly he could bind me to him. Or perhaps

I was a ripening fruit to be plucked — and discarded for being too green. Or it could have been that I was simply a victim of a silly schoolboy joke, a way of annoying those complacent and self-righteous relatives, Miss Celia and Aunt Zena. He came from a line of cruel people, I was to learn, people who joked and tormented. I don't know what I did or failed to do, but he was bored with me from the start, for after he took me to his mother and left me there, I hardly ever saw him.

Wasn't his whole family something else! Tropical Gothic, I would have named it, had I known then what that was. Sam's father was dead and his mother lived in the old family house she shared with a married daughter whose husband worked as an accountant and came home on weekends, while the boys — there were three unmarried sons in all — lived together in another house nearby. This was a house of bachelors: "the Bull Pen" the locals called it, for all the Samphire men were noted womanizers, including the father, as I was to learn.

They were a breed of countrymen who were as bold and lusty as their animals. They had some colour and some property; when they took women in whatever way they wanted, usually girls of poor families, it was simply regarded as their due. Nothing had changed since slavery, except the tint of the master. But of course these thoughts never occurred to me then. I was just like the daughters of the field labourers: I too was up for grabs. I questioned nothing.

We women were never allowed in the bachelor house, and from all the sounds, they lived a raucous, drunken life. A frequent visitor was the fourth brother, Johnnie, who was married and had children but seemed hardly to have spent time at his own home, which was about a mile away. It was only after arriving there that I understood what would have driven Aunt Zena's disapproval of Sam, of all the Samphire men.

35

SAM'S MOTHER, DAISY, CALLED Ma D by everyone including her own children, was a small, lopsided, sweet woman who simply took me over when he brought me to her. When, late that afternoon, he handed me down from the horse, I was trembling, aching, tired, and ready to weep from the numbness and confusion that had begun to overwhelm me from the time we left the river and set out for the unknown. On that journey I can truly say I lost track of time, as I clung tightly to him, my lifeline, my fog of confusion lifting occasionally to focus on this romantic dream I had of what awaited us, the two of us, when we were alone together at last.

When we stopped at this huge, sprawling, unpainted wooden house that didn't seem at all ramshackle to me — rather a filigree of wood sun-baked silver and magical — and he lifted me down, I could barely stand. He had to steady me as my knees buckled; but, even in my confused state, I sensed the lack of contact, the impatience, as he held me. He did smile at me as he said "Whoa," and O how that smile lifted me, for my emotions were oscillating like a toy windmill in the breeze. For a moment, smiling into his face, losing myself in the blue-green eyes that seemed to warm me, I did feel that everything would be all right. Until he turned his head and I turned too to look at the house that should have been empty, like the landscape, with no other actors but us two, playing out our roles, to see this figure filling the doorway. She came out onto the veranda and looked over at us, shading her eyes as if to see better. And then she came down the steps, crablike, and headed in our direction. I could see she was a small woman dressed in a house dress — a collarless short-sleeved shift of dark blue cotton, her feet pushed into ankle socks and house slippers, a hairnet holding down her steely white hair, her dark brown face surprisingly seamless, though pulled to one side by a nasty scar. I was further confused as to who she was by the fact that Sam looked nothing at all like her.

As soon as she appeared, Sam let go of me so quickly that I lost my centre of gravity and stumbled and I had to shake my head to clear it. I watched him stride quickly to meet her. I could tell he was already speaking and gesturing as he neared, but moving too far away for me to hear what was being said. I stood there, feeling foolish, not knowing what to do. They faced each other and talked for a while. I could see her looking over at me, shaking her head and throwing up her hands, palms facing inwards. He threw up his hands — a different gesture, palms up and out — and I could imagine his ingratiating smile. I could see she wasn't smiling. She shook her head many times. From her hand gestures, I could tell she was angry. But Sam with his talk and gestures became even more persuasive, and she threw up her hands one last time and headed in my direction.

I felt true terror then, for I had no idea who this woman was or where Sam had brought me. I felt both threatened and guilty, as if I had transcended some boundaries, but what these were I had no idea. I was overcome by the same kind of shyness and embarrassment I felt at meeting anyone strange, the shyness that made me want to run and hide when even relatives came to visit Miss Celia. But now there was nowhere to hide, for I was exposed by this new landscape that was tree-less and flat and open as far as the eye could see. The only movement was the john crows wheeling far above in the seam-less blue sky that couldn't care less but was simply allowing the heat to pour down like rain. I was damp with sweat, and I felt my legs, my whole body turn to jelly as the woman neared. Sam, behind her, smiling, hat in hand, didn't make me feel any more assured. More than anything, that smile, that overarching confidence reduced me, making me feel as if I had done something shameful and had no right to be in this place.

Although I kept my head down, I could see her scrutinizing me as she came on. When she reached me, she stood close, so close that I was forced to lift my eyes up to hers and I was embarrassed to be staring at the deep gouge on her left cheek that pulled the lid of her eye down so I could see more of the white than I wanted. I quickly looked down again. She didn't move an inch. I could feel her staring, until I was forced to raise my eyes. She locked me in a gaze I couldn't break. She seemed to study every inch of my face for a very long time. And then she nodded her head and smiled, a smile that trans-formed her whole being from scary to sweet.

"Fabian's girl," she said.

I burst into tears then. I couldn't help it. Deep horrible sobs, tears of relief. She knew my father! It was the nicest thing anyone had ever said to me in my whole life. And this woman, whom I had never seen before, did something strange. She reached out and put her arms around me and held me close. It made me never want to move. I couldn't name what I felt as I bent my head to lean my forehead on the shoulder of this tiny person who seemed so capable of bearing me up, to a place I had never been before, where my tears could fall freely, without scrutiny, in the open light of day.

36

SHE FINALLY DISENGAGED HERSELF and said, "Come child. You can call me Ma D." She held my hand and led me towards the house, calling over her shoulder, "Sam, you want some dinner?"

"No," he said, and I turned to see him put his hat back on. "See you later." He inclined his head towards us both, so I never knew to whom this promise was addressed. I assumed it was to me. I didn't know where he was going, why he wasn't coming with us, but how could he not return?

At first I thought that Ma D's children were so indifferent to her that she served as nothing more than a food factory for them, sending cooked meals and cakes over to the Bull Pen, leaving food for her daughter in the kitchen for whenever she chose to eat. She never ate with us. Hardly spoke to us at all.

It was only after I was there for a while that I realized Ma D was still the powerful matriarch, for they deferred to her on everything important in their lives.

That day, Ma D took me in and tried to feed me, though the lump in my throat prevented me from swallowing. She made me wash up and she gave me a white cotton nightie and a cup of cocoa and put me to bed, asking no questions, murmuring nothing but comforting words all the while. She opened a big chest to take out clean sheets and pillowcases, releasing into the air the familiar aroma of dried khus khus root that scented the linen and left me aching even more, as if I had lost something precious but didn't know what it was. "Don't worry, my dear, everything will seem better in the morning," Ma D murmured as she bustled about. "It will work out, you'll see. It's not the end of the world." But it was for me. He hadn't returned. That was all I could think of as I spent the night trying to choke down my sobs. That was all that drummed in my head until near morning when I fell into a restless sleep.

I don't know what Sam told his mother, but the first thing she did, I learned later, was to write to Miss Celia. By the time the messenger arrived, they already knew who I had run off with, and how. Aunt Zena returned a note to say on behalf of her mother and the rest of the Richards family, they never wanted to see me again as long as I lived. I was an ungrateful wretch, and a thief to boot.

Ma D was more disturbed by this last piece of news than all the rest, for she didn't immediately show me the letter. She only said she had a note from Aunt Zena to say I had stolen something from her. Had I taken anything? All this in a very gentle voice, and perhaps surprised, too, for she could see I had come empty-handed. It was only then that I remembered the grocery money in my pinafore pocket still, along with the list for Mr. Lue. It didn't matter that Ma D returned the money the very next day, with an explanation, I was forever tarred with the designation of thief. My family declared that nothing on earth would move them to take me back. The messenger was given a cardboard box — Drax Soap — packed with all my worldly goods. It was addressed to "Mrs. Daisy Samphire," for they never communicated directly with me.

Once I settled in, I was so glad to be away from their constricting care that it took me a while to realize the enormity of what I had done. They were the only family I had. With a child's optimism I thought their anger would never last, they would come around, I would be able at least to visit again, but to the day she died, Aunt Zena did not speak to me. Miss Celia never did either, her head as high as Aunt Zena's when they passed my house. But when my first child was born, someone sent me a beautiful piece of linen and a five-pound note. Although the bearer said she couldn't reveal who it was, I knew it could be no one but Miss Celia. I was so touched, I gave my baby the middle name Celia and I saved up the linen until she and my second daughter, Shirley, were old enough and I made it into dresses for them one Christmas.

The day the bearer came I was sitting on the veranda with my baby in the cradle beside me, studying her sleeping face, my feelings oscillating between elation and utter despair from the first moment I looked at her, wondering if I would ever be up to the task. From the kitchen I could vaguely hear the sounds of Millie as she cleaned up and prepared to leave for home. Out of the corner of my eye I thought I saw a patch of blue sticking out from behind the cedar tree near the road and my heart leapt, but when I stared it vanished and just then I was distracted by Millie's shout from the back to tell me she was going.

As soon as Millie disappeared down the road, a figure in navy blue emerged from behind the tree and approached me, fingers to her lips. I nearly died laughing. It was Miss McDonald, the village dressmaker, a lady so full of secrets and so scared of spilling any that she spent her days entirely buttoned up. Literally. Though she was renowned for making the most exquisite dresses, she herself affected plainness of garment; her only concessions to adornment were the buttons that she liberally added to her own clothing. She was wearing a simple paisley print shirtwaist with a self-made belt, and matching covered buttons marching in close order all the way up the front, right to the high neck she affected. There were buttons in tight rows holding the cuffs of the long sleeves together. She never exposed more flesh than she could help. Miss Mac was childless, tall and thin, so of course all the children called her Macaroni, though she wasn't round but totally flat from whatever angle she was viewed. As she approached I smiled at a vision that floated into my head of her lying on her back with the row of buttons showing above her supine body like a second backbone. Her own backbone she carried very straight from the tips of her sensible laced-up shoes and thick stockings to her greying hair. Miss Mac was noted for her dignity.

Her hair was the one thing she could not control. She pulled it severely back into a little bun and wore a hairnet, but wiry wisps always haloed around her head and softened her rather hawkish features. The source of these very European features and brown skin was the only thing Miss Mac never wanted kept secret. Everyone knew her father was a Staunton, the white Busha of the property where her mother worked as a field labourer, who never acknowledged the child. But that mattered little to Miss Mac's mother, who had rejoiced in her brown-skin girl and passed on to her ridiculous notions of her genealogy. Poor Miss Mac acted as if she were way above the group she rightly belonged to, yet she was constantly rebuffed by the one to which she yearned to belong. Such as never once being allowed to enter the Richardses' house through the front door. Of all the people I knew in my childhood, Miss Mac for all her silliness was the one with whom I could feel an affinity, for I sensed she was as out of place in the world as I was.

"My dear Miss G," she greeted me, like everyone else acknowledging my newly married status by giving a handle to my name. She moved to bend over the cradle and smiled and cooed. "How you keeping? How is the little one?"

"Fine, Miss Mac."

She looked around. "You one here?"

I nodded. She was fishing in her large cloth bag with the wooden handles at the same time she was looking around in all directions. Satisfied that we were not overheard, she brought out a parcel in brown paper tied with string.

"Take it," she whispered. "Don't tell a soul."

"Thank you, Miss Mac," I muttered and took the parcel, wondering why all the secrecy.

"No, no, don't thank me, child," she whispered. "Someone asked me to bring it to you." And then, I swear, she winked and tapped her nose with her finger as she took a seat on the bench beside me.

"Someone? Who? What is it?" I was so mystified that I made no attempt to open the package.

"Someone who wish you well. But don't want other people to know she send you anything. She don't want a fuss so she ask me to bring it. Our little secret. But go on, open it," she urged. "There's a nice piece of cloth that I will make into a lovely dress for you, as soon as you get back your figure you can wear it to the christening. A five-pound note to buy something for baby."

Five pounds! That seemed such a fortune I knew it couldn't have come from Miss Mac herself.

"Miss Mac, who?" My mind was racing as I feverishly tore the parcel apart and found inside the piece of yellow linen, neatly folded, and a white envelope with the money inside. To my great disappointment, no note or anything written on the envelope. I put the money back inside the envelope and held it in my hand, my heart thumping in my chest. The only person I could think of was Miss Celia, but why couldn't she have sent it to me openly, or even brought it herself? Didn't she want to see her great-grandchild?

Miss Mac might have been reading my thoughts. "It's the other one," she whispered. "She still vex. She don't want them to have nothing to do with you." She must have noticed that my eyes were filling with tears, for she patted my hand. "Just wait, my child. Time longer than rope. One day they will come around. You can't do anything for now."

When I said nothing she added, "Just remember, she don't want anyone to know, especially certain people. I will tell her you send thanks. But this is a secret between the three of us. Not even Sam to know." Miss Mac actually took my hand as she said this and held it against her bony chest as if she were forcing me to seal a pact. I almost laughed at the conspiratorial look in her eyes.

"Okay, Miss Mac," I mumbled. "Please tell her thanks for me. And tell her if — if she wanted to see —" but I got so choked up, I could go no further.

"Never mind, my child."

Miss Mac and I sat there for a while, neither of us speaking, and then she patted my knee and got up to go. She was halfway to the gate when she turned back and said in a rush, "Miss G, you have to learn patience. Sometime you have to wait a whole lifetime for someone to acknowledge you, you know. And then they could die and it would never happen." She had a strange bitterness in her voice as she said the last part in a rush. She turned quickly and set off with a firm stride, her straight nose leading the way.

I hid the parcel under the mattress. When Sam came home I told him I wanted to name the baby Celia, but he didn't seem very keen. "Why," he asked, "after the way they treat you?" I didn't answer and he didn't pursue it, knowing full well it was a story that didn't show him in a particularly good light. We ended up calling the baby June — Sam's choice, with Celia as her middle name. But Celia is the name she came to be known by.

Shirley, our second daughter, had Daisy as her middle name after Sam's mother. I wanted to name one of my daughters after my mother too, only to realize that I did not know my own mother's name. I had never even seen my own birth certificate. It had remained the property of those whose property I became — Miss Celia and then my husband, for they would have needed one when I got married. But I never thought to ask Ma D or Sam for it. At the time everything was arranged for me, I didn't need it myself, and it never occurred to me that my mother's name would have been on it. No one had ever spoken of my mother in my hearing, except to name her a slut. How could it be that I knew nothing at all about her, this woman who bore me? How could she have so offended the Richards women, apart from being, as I suspected, black, poor, without family, and forcing them to take an unwanted orphan into their care?

Of course I never thought of asking Ma D or anyone from my district. Even my father's other brothers and sisters, who came to visit their mother and sister from time to time. I was too cowed by the Richards women to think other people would have known what I most wanted to know. But could it also have been that they had made me so ashamed of her I was afraid of catching the disease of her poverty, her lowly origins, her blackness, her inability to survive? For how many times had I created a fantasy mother — echoes of a white pre-Raphaelite woman, I later realized — that bore no relation to the real? How many times did I hate her for leaving me? How much grief and guilt did I feel in the certain knowledge that it was I who had caused her to go?

37

THE WAY THEY TALKED about me when I got married and moved back into the district with Sam, two years after I left! Think I didn't know? Think I didn't know how they passed by and called out, stopped to visit, all the women I'd known all my life, so they could smile to my face and snicker behind my back? Because after all I had been tossed out by the district's leading family, the arbiters of manners and good taste, and serve me right, what would I do now I'd been cast down low? Sam's little child-bride. As if they knew more than I did what that meant. Good old Sam! The women all hugged him and the men slapped him on the back as if he had gotten into the henhouse by stealth and snatched something away from the hens. Sly mongoose! Was that saying something about their attitude to the hens? Or did they know that the treasure was not a pretty little chick but an unhatched egg? Not one of them hugged me. But then, I wasn't huggable, I was already folded into myself, and the prickly stuff that Ma D had managed to smooth away was bursting into growth again as if the egg was turning into a spiny sea urchin. I didn't speak to them either. Opened and closed my mouth just enough so I would not seem rude. Not from malice, as they thought. Or false pride. Though pride enough I had. The smile was always just hovering behind my lips, the words on the tip of my tongue.

I couldn't get them out. They must have remembered how I was from before. It wasn't that long ago, and they could go away with the thought that marriage hadn't changed me and wonder why that was so. Hadn't I achieved the status that was every girl's dream? A man every woman wanted? After a time they couldn't be bothered and left me more or less alone, which suited me fine. It made my sorrow invisible and more easily borne if there was no one to remark on it. No one to spread it abroad as news. All I ever made them see was my garden flourishing, my laundry out every Monday like every good wife's, and, too soon, nappies on the line forever.

Things might have turned out differently if we hadn't gone back there, living just a mile away from the Richards house with Aunt Zena throwing out words and poisoning the atmosphere. If we'd gone to a place that was new to both of us. Or even if we had stayed down on the family property with Ma D to support me. But I had nothing to do with any of it. Nor did Sam, I think. It was all Ma D's doing. I got the feeling she wanted me and Sam to get away from there, as far from the rest of them as we could. A cousin of theirs who was living in what was to become our little house moved out just then and left it empty. A sign, as far as Ma D was concerned.

She managed my life so well I often wondered how she seemed to have failed at managing everything else, including her own. She was born in the city and her family was well off. Her father was said to have made a fortune working on the Panama Canal. She was sent abroad to be educated, something almost unheard of for girls in those days. How could she have ended up marrying such a man as Sam's father? All I know is she came down to teach at the girls' boarding school and met him and fell in love. More than that I don't know, but I can guess, can't I? At least I knew all about falling in love. It was the falling out that I couldn't manage.

Sam was never in love with me. That must have been obvious to Ma D, but it didn't stop her. She went ahead and got us married and sent us off. She made me a beautiful wedding dress. We made a special trip to Kingston to buy the material, a full floor-length skirt of Alençon lace over white peau de soie, the fitted bodice embroidered with seed pearls that she sewed on herself, one by one, taking her glasses off and holding the fabric and bead up to her one good eye, her hand trembling as she pushed the needle through each bead and tacked it onto the fabric. I was so afraid to watch her. I held my breath each time. I was not surprised at the perfection of her work, every bead in place. The preparations made me feel excited, but uncomfortable at the amount of trouble I saw Ma D taking for me. I didn't feel I was worthy of this kind of care, as if I had not earned it and had no right to it. But Ma D seemed happy with all the preparations, happy to be kept so busy getting rid of another of her troublesome sons.

She arranged it all, the church and everything. I had no family present. The doctor, a friend of Ma D's, assumed the role of father and gave me away. It should have been the happiest day of my life, but I wasn't happy at all. I remember so little of it. I was steeped in misery because all my consciousness, my entire being, was focused on my longing for Sam. Nothing else mattered except Sam showing no longing for me.

Back at the house, Ma D had arranged quite a spread with

the help of various aunts and cousins who had mysteriously appeared a few days before. They slept in all the beds, on couches and mattresses on the floor. There was a lot of teasing and gaiety and laughter in that house, the first in a long time, I think, but I didn't feel it had anything to do with me. At the reception, they made me and Sam cut the cake, feed it to each other, link arms, and drink a toast. Sam was laughing the whole time. So was everyone else as they put us both in the back of the car in which one of Sam's cousins was driving us to our two-day honeymoon at a hotel on the coast.

As soon as the car was out of sight of the house, Sam said, "Stop" and climbed out. The cousin climbed out too. I stayed in the car, listening as they laughingly removed the *Just Married* signs and old shoes and tin cans that had been attached. Sam took a bottle out of his bag in the trunk of the car. He and the driver had a drink, there by the side of the road. And then they turned their backs to me and pissed. And instead of returning to sit with me in the back seat as I expected, Sam got into the front seat and they both carried on drinking from that bottle, laughing and joking. Before we arrived at our destination, I had willed myself to sleep.

38

AFTER THAT DAY WITH Mr. Bridges and the book began the happiest time of my life. Not the heart-thumping disturbance I felt when I first fell in love with Sam, but a warm glow that came from finding someone, a companion, whom I felt comfortable with. I think the change in me began that very day, with me in my red dress. When I got back to my room, I looked at myself in the mirror, and I decided not to change into my house dress after all, but to wear my red dress to dinner. I put on lipstick and, just for good measure, a pair of clip-on earrings. I made sure to comb my hair and style it carefully. Well! You can't imagine what an impact a simple thing like that had, perhaps not exactly where I wanted it, but I enjoyed seeing the Sisters' eyes pop when I came in, and even the Pitt-Bull at the far end of the dining room leaned over to gaze.

"Wow, G! You look fabulous!" Birdie gushed before I even sat down.

"Hey! What happened?" from Babe.

"Díos mío! You have a hot date, chiquita?" growled Ruby, who littered her speech with Spanish phrases in memory of her last and favourite husband, who was from the Dominican Republic.

Even Annie, who was serving at dinner that evening, looked across at me as she placed a dish on the table and stood back, one arm akimbo, and mimicked shock: "Miss Sam, w'appen? You look great, man, look like you going out on the town."

I was too dark-skinned to blush, but I could feel my face growing hot. I flapped my napkin open and placed it on my lap and said nothing, but I was secretly pleased. Throughout the meal and their usual chattering I could sense the Sisters' distraction, their eyes floating over me, and then meeting each other's in speculation. The crowning moment came when Heathcliff came over while dessert was being served, kneaded my shoulders from behind, and said, showing his profile to Babe I know, for he always did, ever hopeful: "My dear Sammy, what has come over you? You look absolutely ravishing." Then he gave another squeeze, winked at Birdie, and scurried back to his seat in time to dig into the custard tart just as it was placed before him. Babe rolled her eyes at me, and I wondered if anyone else in the room thought I was ravishing. I wasn't sure what had gotten into me, but at least I was giving them something new to talk about.

39

I'VE BEEN PAYING ATTENTION to the way I dress and groom and carry myself. Celia's investment in me is paying off. I hope it will pay off for me too, but what payoff I am after, I'm not sure. Even Matron has noticed: she comments on each new outfit I wear, more impressed by the fact that Celia chose it than anything else. But after the initial surprise, people have stopped paying attention to the "new me," as Babe said. Now Mr. Bridges speaks to me occasionally. He returned the first book and borrowed others and lent me some of his; we exchange a few brief words about them, or the weather, or something equally inane. He speaks and I mumble. Each time, after the initial thrill, I mentally berate myself for being so tongue-tied and sounding so foolish, though I am usually unable to remember afterwards even the few words I speak. I have no idea, of course, that in my sixties I am going through a phase that girls normally go through at sixteen. So we never had a real conversation until yesterday afternoon when he came upon me at the back of the house, where the gardener, Winston, and I are preparing beds to grow vegetables. Yes, I've gone back to farming.

I couldn't imagine why a place with so much land didn't grow its own vegetables and had no fruit trees apart from a few mangoes and citrus fruits and some wild guava trees at the back fence. It all seemed so wasteful to me. I was missing my little farm, missed getting my hands in the dirt and pruning and reaping and watching things grow. I'd been missing all this from the time I left home, but the need to get back to the soil had grown in me so much that I was willing to struggle, first with Matron, who was thrown into such a tizzy for no one had ever wanted to do such a thing before. She had to consult with the board of management first. And then it was with that most difficult of men, Winston, to get a little plot going. I had gotten the seeds and sowed them in makeshift flats myself, simple things like carrots, cabbages, beans, tomatoes, peppers. But now they were ready to be planted out, and Winston had failed to get the beds ready, though he had assured me up to the day before not to worry, no problem, Miss. Everything right as rain, Miss. Though if ever there was a man who should have problems, it was Winston.

The only reason I could get Winston going at all is that I was the only one of the residents who walked the grounds, and he knew that I knew about his flourishing plot of ganja at the back. And then I had totally confused him because instead of reporting it, as he expected — and I kept him dangling on that one for a few sweet weeks — I had given him advice on the best fertilizer to use. That got him so confused he then turned around and offered me a present of some of his finest product, which I regretfully refused. So now he doesn't know where he stands with me. I wasn't like the others who simply stood from afar and gave orders. Part of his grudging respect comes from the fact that he knows that I know what I am talking about when it comes to plants, and I know that his own knowledge, apart from the ganja, is of asphalt-farming. Winston is a city boy, born and bred, growing up in the little shantytown only a few hundred yards from the Ellesmere Lodge gates. He only got the job as gardener many years ago through proximity to the previous private owners of the house and the attrition of their old retainers.

Winston's idea of gardening is to ride around on the power mower cutting the huge lawns and climbing a ladder and slashing away at the top of the thick sweet lime hedge with his cutlass. This hedge grows along the frontage, so he chops at a little piece each day until he gets to the end and then it's time to start over again. This way, he can always say when asked by Matron to do some other task, "I have to cut the hedge, Miss," and that is that. Oh, he does set out the sprinklers to water the lawn after it has dried down to nothing. And, very grudgingly, when the flowers are too limp to be ignored, he will turn the hose on the two round beds of canna lilies in front of the porte cochere. This is the extent of the official garden on at least two acres of grounds that wander away at the back into terra incognita.

Winston in fact spends more time cleaning the cars of staff and visitors and running their little errands than he does gardening, but then he has a lot of need for extra cash. I know, because in spite of all the extra earnings, he is always touching me for a loan, which he scrupulously repays at payday, grudgingly though, hanging on to the notes to the last minute, hoping I'll refuse to take them. Which I won't, of course, for I don't see why I should support Winston as a one-man population explosion unit.

Winston certainly doesn't have the look of a Romeo; he isn't a youth, he is in his forties or older. His face is squashed down and full of wrinkles and his shaved head is as much fashion statement as disguise for grey hairs. He is short, not very well built, doesn't have a particularly sunny disposition, and has lost a lot of his teeth. Still, a procession of baby-mothers turn up at Winston's door as often as he turns up at mine begging a loan, and they are all attractive, very young girls. I suppose in a poverty-stricken country any man who has a steady job is king, even though the coffers are depleted by each addition to the royal family. That Winston was even willing to consider helping me with the vegetable patch owed something to my suggestion that he would be able to offer the baby-mothers some of the crop. Though the alacrity with which he disappears around the corner into his room each time one of these visitors arrives suggests he has more on offer than vegetables.

Anyway, here we were yesterday, Winston and I, both mucking about. He rather unwillingly double digging, I on my knees mixing manure and compost into the bed he had already dug. I didn't know Mr. Bridges was anywhere near until he spoke.

"What will it be, flowers or vegetables?"

I was so lost in thought, in the sheer enjoyment of the task, that I jumped at the sound of his voice.

It was Winston who answered, "Vegetables, sir" and stopped his digging, glad for the diversion. I was surprised when Mr. Bridges bent down, picked up some of the soil, and ran it through his fingers. "Not bad," he said, "a bit on the clayey side."

"Uh-huh," I said, standing up to ease the strain on my back and wipe the sweat from my face. "I'm adding some sand and lime to lighten it. And Winston has a nice compost heap going."

"Oh, that's good. What are you planting?"

So I told him, surprised that one I took for a city gent could be so knowledgeable. It turned out he had been a keen vegetable gardener, his wife being the one for flowers. He too missed his garden, he said, and starting one here was an excellent idea. He wasn't dressed for it today, but would I like him to give me a hand? Did I come every day? Tomorrow? Of course I said yes. I hoped to start the planting out then and could do with some help.

"Fine," said Mr. Bridges, but he didn't go, he stood watching us for a while, and I turned back to my labours. Winston too I could see was impressed, for he returned to digging with an enthusiasm that had been lacking, and I could see him mentally figuring out if Mr. Bridges would be a soft touch for loans. Or maybe it was just the fact that it was a man showing an interest in gardening that spurred him on. I got so caught up with my work that I didn't even notice when Mr. Bridges left. It wasn't until I got back to my room and showered and dressed for dinner that I realized that despite all my well-laid plans, he had caught me looking my worst — my hands covered in dirt, my grimy face streaked with sweat, my headband soiled. I was wearing an old T-shirt, my washed-out pants, and ugly black water boots. But somehow it didn't seem wrong to have him see me like this, for who am I fooling? This is truly who I am.

40

IT WAS MA D who turned me into a farmer, who turned me into something, though she seemed to have failed with her own children. I was such a child that when Sam brought me there, and it became clear to me that he and I were not going to live together — at least not for now, as I told myself — I became quite content to stay alone in the house with her, for her presence was light and she seemed glad of my company. I never went back to school, but she was the best education I had. She had been a schoolteacher. Her house was full of books: novels, dictionaries and encyclopedias, and how-to manuals. I spent much of my time devouring them, not noticing that everything was at least thirty years out of date. At first she tried to quiz me on what I had read, but when she realized I was too shy to say anything, she gave me paper and pen and made me write book reports and essays, which she carefully corrected, giving me high praise from time to time, something I was not used to. She taught me French and Latin, and botany, making me do all the drawings and label them. How to embroider and sew and cook. She taught me a million things. She understood my inability to express myself out loud and she worked around that, never calling me dummy and treating me like a fool as others had.

She had a kitchen garden that fed her household and the bachelors as well. I marvelled at how this educated woman had slipped so easily into the mould of countrywoman, for apart from the help of an old man and woman — Mass Ephraim and Miss Gem, who lived in a little cottage at the back — she did all the hard work herself. Her skin was like old leather, dry and weathered from the sun. She wore a broad straw hat when she was out in the sun and she never seemed to take care of herself as Aunt Zena did with her gardening gloves and skin creams and potions.

Soon my own face, my hands Aunt Zena had made me keep covered with long sleeves, so I wouldn't get any darker, were black from the sun; my palms coarse and scratched from planting and digging and mulching. We raised chickens and rabbits for food. Mass Ephraim had his flock of goats that seemed to live on nothing but rocks and air and kitchen peelings, though there was strong competition for the latter between them and Ma D's compost heap that was guarded by a high chicken-wire fence. We worked all the time, but this was work I did willingly, because I wanted to, not like the make-work inside the house that Aunt Zena had forced on me.

I would hitch up my skirt and tie it at the waist, as the countrywomen did, and show my legs, my hair still in school-girl plaits. I would push my hands into this thin and battered soil and learn from Mass Ephraim and Ma D how to make it rich with mulch and compost and manure so it would spring to life again and bear fruit. I thought that year and a half I spent there, learning about soil, the effects of wind, how to conserve moisture, how to conserve everything, from these two country people, one of them unlettered, was the best time of my life. The only thing I could never get up the nerve to handle was extracting honey from the hives, for Ma D kept bees that produced from the fragrant logwood blossoms the most exquisite honey.

The Samphires had a large spread, hundreds of acres, much bigger than the Richardses, but I could see that the family had come down in the world, for the house was badly in need of repair and the yard, like Ma D, had an air of neglect. Besides the main house and cottage there was a huge barn-like building, with a dry shingle roof and much of the walls caved in, and several outhouses that had been stables, for this had been a livestock pen for several generations. They too had been allowed to fall apart, though enough remained for them to serve as night residences for Mass Ephraim's goats. Another stable had been crudely patched up and was home to a horse that Ma D kept for the occasional rides she took around the property. She didn't have a car. The stable was also home to a milk cow Mass Ephraim fed by hand, travelling miles on his donkey to bring back fresh grass. Mass Ephraim and his donkey were in fact our main means of contact with the outside world. He rode off frequently to collect groceries and packages at the railway station or post office and was Ma D's all-round messenger. He never returned without the hampers on both sides loaded down with goods for Ma D or grass or fruit he'd collected on the way, his small wiry body seeming to fit perfectly with the energetic little animal that always burst into a gallop the minute it sighted its home.

The land immediately beyond the house was nothing but dry packed red earth, not a blade of grass. It was criss-crossed by a lot of fenced-off areas. Whatever purpose these had once served was no longer apparent; the wires sagged and the fence posts leaned crazily. There were no flowers or plants in front of the house, it was just that hard packed earth right up to the three broad steps of cut-stone that led up to the veranda. The same type of cut-stone blocks were used to raise the house slightly off the ground, the space underneath providing a dark and cool refuge for the mongrel dogs that hid there from the midday sun. The veranda was my favourite place: it was wide and cool and went three-quarters of the way around the house and was well served by deep, comfortable old wicker chairs. At the back there was another porch enclosed in wire mesh to keep the insects out, the coolest part of the house, for against it grew an enormous passion fruit vine. It was at the back, too, that Ma D kept her flourishing garden, where her pumpkins and melons grew rampant and her tomatoes and green peppers and carrots thrived in the thick mulch. There was a large tank to catch rainwater, but there was so little of that we had to conserve every drop and reuse it on the plants.

Apart from the garden, everything about the old homestead seemed dispirited and sad, in sharp contrast to the Bull Pen and its noisy occupants and visitors. The boys, as Ma D referred to them, raised beef cattle and horses somewhere on the backlands, but I never saw them. They cut logwood for cash. Outside of Ma D's plot, no crops were cultivated, and the land as far as the eye could see was just scrub and logwood and dildo cactus. After a while I understood why, for though they lived only about ten miles from where I came from, which was an area of lush vegetation, they were the other side of the mountains, in the rain shadow, so they received hardly any. On these savannas when the rivers and springs dried up, as they sometimes did, there was no water. There were years, Ma D said, when they had to butcher all the cattle and virtually give the beef away. The horses wandered off and died, as they could not keep them alive.

I only understood the strangeness of this land in which I found myself when I wandered away from the yard one day and kept walking on and on and nearly died of terror when I came across the barbed wire fences with the bleached white skulls of horses and cows staring back at me from the top of every fence post. More than anything else, it made me feel that I had wandered into a territory far more demanding and cruel than the safe, protected haven of the world I had left behind. This was a world that mocked me. I had never seen skulls of large animals before and the sight of so many gave me a feeling of having fallen into a pit. I ran back home as fast as I could, my head spinning. I said nothing to Ma D, but after that I was always afraid to go out of sight of the house on my own. So many worlds out there I didn't know. So much darkness.

Ma D never spoke of her husband, but I knew he had died some years back and there was something very strange about the atmosphere of that house, secretive and claustrophobic. The sister and her husband, who had a job on one of the sugar estates and came home on weekends, kept mainly to themselves on one side of the house, hardly speaking to me or Ma D. Fairly soon I realized that Ma D herself was strange, as if two people resided in her. One was the sweet school-teacher who was kind and careful with me, a woman who without fuss took charge of everything that needed doing, was the model of competence. The other was a woman who seemed at times without warning to sink into a fuzzy haze of forgetfulness, to shrink at the slightest touch or sound, and to not know anyone around her. She had horrible nightmares too, and I would sit up in bed in the room next to hers and pull the pillow over my head to block out the awful sounds of her wrestling with the Devil, as Aunt Zena would have called it. These spells or turns only lasted a day or two, or even hours, and then she would return to normal as if nothing had happened. At first I was worried that she would go mad like my father, but she was never frightening or threatening at those times. Since her two old helpers seemed to take her spells for granted, I learned to do so too.

But then I noticed that in those times of her distress, for that is the only word I could use to describe the expression on her face, her bodily afflictions seemed to stand out more, for she looked like a battered chicken in a way, like some of the men of our district who had returned from the War. She had one arm slightly bent at the elbow, as if it had been broken and not properly set; she walked with a limp; she had that deep gouge on one cheek which pulled down one eye so that the lower lid always seemed red and exposed; and she had a useless thumb on one hand. She also had various scars on her body that had healed into unsightly lumps. She didn't try to hide them, as if she no longer noticed them or cared. Maybe it was my imagination or I studied her more at these times as she paid no attention to me, but all these wounds on her body seemed to jump out at me, and I would look at them afresh and wonder.

Her husband had been a respectable man in the community, I was to learn much later, a justice of the peace and a charmer, if loud and boisterous like his sons, a man's man, hard riding, hard shooting, hard drinking. So who would have believed what went on inside his house, how he viciously beat his wife and children, raped his own daughter? No one would have talked about any of it if he hadn't been killed in his own house one night — beaten to death, some said. At that time the boys were all still living at home, the move to the Bull Pen taking place after that event. No one was ever charged, there were no outside witnesses, no evidence that could link any one family member to the crime, and none of them would say more than the story they had all agreed upon, that some stranger had obviously broken in. Rumours and finger-pointing had followed the family for a while, then the hand of guilt was settled alternately on the daughter or the wife. Though why them, I don't know, except that the boys were men's men and popular, and drank and went bird shooting with the policemen and lawyers and judges and politicians. I heard this story long after I left there, and so when I saw Ma D in one of her moods, little did I know how close I could have come to emulating her.

41

SOMETIMES WHEN I WASN'T too overwhelmed, I would feel sad about my constant sadness, guilt that I was giving in to something soft, rotten even. For, after all, I hadn't been scarred on my body with beatings from parents or men. Not like Ma D, not like many of the women and girls I knew. I hadn't been raped by father, uncle, or brother. Up to the time I left home, I had had a soft life, a substantial roof over my head, a room to myself, a comfortable bed to sleep in, three meals at least each day. So much more than the majority of the people who shared my world. So what was there to be sad about? Did I have a right to be sad? How much are you expected to bear before you allow yourself to be weighed down? To abandon yourself to the pain of indignity? The toll of indifference?

42

ONCE SAM TOOK ME and left me with his mother, I hardly ever saw him, and when he did come to the house it was for the briefest of visits, usually with some request, some matter to do with the property, and he usually spoke to her standing on the steps leading up to the veranda, hat in hand. I noticed that neither he nor any of his brothers ever came inside that house if they could help it. Ma D would go out to meet him, with me like some shadow at her back, smiling shyly at him, and he would lift his hat and smile broadly at both of us, but he never took any further notice of me. I would lurk then, first on the veranda, then, as I was ignored, retreat until I was at the doorway, backing off until I was fully inside the dark hall. Sometimes Ma D followed him out into the yard and they would talk. I could hear the murmur of their voices but not what was said. When they were finished, he would mount his horse and ride away. I would stand there with my head pressed against the wall until I heard him go, trying not to cry, trying to force down the lump in my throat so that when Ma D came back inside and found me by the doorway, I would be looking not at all concerned.

She never said anything, but I knew she understood my pain, for those were always the times that she kept me most busy, usually finding something new and complicated to teach me.

"Come," she would say, "Ephraim brought us lots of lemons. Let me show you how to make lemon meringue pie."

Or it would be cutwork embroidery. Or how to debone and stuff a chicken. I would go and apply myself to the complicated task at hand, for it kept the pain at bay, and it compressed time, so that another day of my life would pass without my noticing the emptiness. It was as if the pastry that I rolled out, the bread dough I thumped down, the cutting of an intricate pattern for a dress, the carving up of a chicken the proper way, provided solace. It was only later, looking back, that I realized how Ma D had worked out these ways of coping for herself, and I was always thankful that she had taught me not just the intricacies of domesticity, but how to use them as a way of smoothing over the hurt.

I wonder now about my own children, how they could have been sending out distress signals all the time that I was too ignorant to read. For I never seemed to have passed down to them the strategies for survival that Ma D taught me.

43

WHEN I MOVED BACK to live in the district, a married woman, I was a different person from the one who had flown away in that scandalous fashion. I was now a woman of accomplishment, a woman capable of coping with whatever life threw at her. A woman of strategy. Or so I thought. But what is the use of knowing how to debone and stuff chickens if there are no chickens to stuff? Still, I would have made it, you know, I would have opened up to the world, become my grown-up self, if only I knew that he loved me. But finding out so soon into our married life that he didn't care one bit drained me of whatever confidence I had managed to gain under Ma D's tutelage. Drained me so quickly that by the time I came to take up residence in our own house I had turned back into that silent, withdrawn girl. Hopeless.

44

ONCE MR. BRIDGES AND Winston and I got our garden going — and within weeks it was already a beautiful sight — you would have thought that everyone at Ellesmere Lodge had once been a farmer. Even Ruby came tottering out in her high-heeled gilt sandals, with matching toenail polish, not to praise but to announce that Winston's next task would be to dig a bed for roses, the planting of which she would supervise, for her rose garden had been such a showplace, rose growers from all over the world had come to admire it. And then like a poem she proceeded to reel off the names of the roses she had grown — Etoile de France, Paul Neyron, La Tosca, Else Poulson, Gertrude Jekyll, Queen Elizabeth. It went on and on, with her flashing her cigarette like a conductor's baton. Between puffs and French pronunciation she told us how difficult it was to grow roses here in the tropics, unless one had the expertise. The performance was so impressive that even Winston, who made a point of putting on his surliest face in the presence of any of the residents unless they were asking him to do a paid favour, stopped what he was doing and gazed at her open-mouthed, nodding his head to the cadence of the rose call.

Ruby was an impressive if incongruous sight in the garden, the gold chains around her freckled and wattled neck glinting through the V-neck of her cream silk blouse with the billowy sleeves, her wrists and fingers flashing with jewellery, her fake fingernails long and ruby red, her stork-like legs emerging from her too-short linen skirt to totter on the heels. Her make-up was bold and already running, masking the strong features of what must have once been a beautiful face, the forehead high, the nose straight, the mouth a natural Cupid's bow. Ruby probably didn't know that all this had changed into carica-ture. Ruby was then well over eighty.

Fortunately, she never visited too often, she was such a distraction, but garden talk more and more did come to occupy our table in the dining room, and that of the others. Although not one of them knew what it was to put their hands into the ground or dirty them in any form of manual labour, it turned out that they had all had gardens. Except for Heathcliff, who had always occupied a house provided by his school and left that sort of thing up to the agricultural teacher, and Mr. Levy, who said he left it all up to his wife. Miss Loony's contribution was that music was the food not only of love but of plants and she would come and sing to ours.

A nice garden, as opposed to gardening, I discovered, was another mark of the social elite, the kemptness of their acreage a source of judgment and competitiveness as much as the grandeur of the house or the size of the husband's car and investments. This came out even among the best of friends, the Pancake Sisters, who began to argue now about the respective merits of their ginger lilies and Ixora, the rarity of their orchids and the size of their bird's nest ferns. Until it finally came down to the nitty-gritty: who had had the better gardener. I discovered too that a good gardener, one who really knew what he was doing, was a priceless acquisition, and that these folks were not above poaching each other's. Everyone rated a gardener with Indian blood as the best.

Even Miss Pitt-Grainger came out to our vegetable garden from time to time to offer instructions, for it turned out that the kitchen garden she started at her school had produced so prolifically under her guidance, it could have fed nations. Though I was sure the poor plants, like everything else under her care, sprouted from sheer fright. A visit to our plot was about the only time she went outside the shelter of the lounge, as it was in shouting distance of the kitchen for ice cubes and limes for her gin and tonic, the gin stashed in the capacious carpetbag that never left her side, jostling with the needlepoint and crossword and pencil which she never let out of her sight.

On these occasions she wore what could only be construed as her gardening costume. Her massive legs white and hairy beneath a pair of tailored khaki shorts that bulged in the wrong places, despite the pleats, nicely turned down white socks, and sparkling white tennis shoes that instantly turned nasty from the wet soil, as Winston always seemed to need to turn on the hose for some watering as soon as she hove into view. A sleeveless white cotton blouse from which flabby arms protruded and a stiff and spotless Jippi Jappa hat with a fluttering blue ribbon completed the ensemble, so she looked more like a dry-land tourist than a formidable moulder of thousands of young minds. Never mind, she had come to mould ours, and Mr. Bridges and I would spend the next fifteen minutes or so rolling our eyes at each other. She didn't stay long, because she could not abide the sun, but she would continue talking as she walked off, snatches of words coming back to us fainter and fainter on the breeze as she disappeared inside to her favourite pastimes.

All of this interest, of course, is because of Mr. Bridges. Had I been working there alone with Winston, few would have bothered to notice our efforts. Or perhaps I should say the interest is in Mr. Bridges and me. That combination is as incongruous to them, I'm sure, as a tuna cactus and a rose growing together in the same bed. No guesses as to which of us is which.

45

THERE MUST HAVE BEEN so much talk about me and Mr. Bridges, even my daughter heard about it, for she teased me the next time she came around. The teasing, not the knowledge of my growing friendship with Mr. Bridges, surprised me. This was a side of her I had not seen before. I wonder how much more I don't know about my Celia.

It's as if everything around me is in some sort of flux, and the changes I am feeling are not just in myself but in other people as well. Or perhaps it is my own changing life that is altering my perception of everyone and everything. I know it isn't my change of life, for I went through that a long time ago. Suddenly I feel I am on shifting ground.

Take the case of Miss Pitt-Grainger. A woman who delights in alienating everyone with her superior airs and attitudes. And yet, when she collapsed and had to be taken to the hospital, we all felt, I think, genuinely concerned. When the ambulance pulled out from the porte cochere, it was as if the little group of us standing there moved closer together, to prevent the hand of time from plucking the next one from our midst. Matron kept us up-to-date with bulletins from the hospital and soon Miss Pitt-Grainger was home, recuperating. She had had some sort of seizure and fallen, breaking her right wrist. On returning to Ellesmere Lodge, she was confined to bed. But it never occurred to me not to visit her and offer my help, for that is how it had always been with me and my neighbours at home.

I was amazed to find her room full of flowers, and at first

I thought they were from some of her ex-students, many now famous women, as she liked to boast. But when later I offered to freshen them up and looked at the cards, I saw they were all from residents of the home. Even the Pancake Sisters, her most ferocious critics and who had had to endure her a lot longer than I, had sent her a dozen yellow roses. Like many of the other residents, they came to visit. I passed by one day to find the sick woman and Ruby nattering away — in Spanish! Languages, it seems, had been Miss Pitt-Grainger's special subjects.

Although Miss Pitt-Grainger had always appeared larger than life, lying in the bed she seemed shrunken, her face hollow and grey. I realized she was much older than I thought. She was anxious about how long she would have to stay in bed. I understood her concern. It was one all the residents shared, the fear that the day would come when they would no longer be able to stay at Ellesmere Lodge. I excluded myself, for I still wanted to leave. Ellesmere Lodge catered only to those old people who were able-bodied and capable of taking care of themselves. When they could no longer do so, they had to move on. Since I'd been there, two residents had sunk into increasing senility and had disappeared from our midst. I wondered where Miss Pitt-Grainger would move to. Unlike most of the other folk, who had younger family members or friends to take care of arrangements, she seemed to have no one.

I suddenly felt a wave of sympathy for her that I had never thought possible, the fact that here was someone who seemed even less connected than I was. I asked about her family and whether she would like me to write some letters for her, but she said there was no one. Except for some distant cousins in England, she had lost touch. She was one of those who had come out to the colonies, in her case fresh out of university in the post-war years, youthful and optimistic. The experience had ruined her forever. She had never returned to live in England and yet was never able to settle. She had moved from one tropical country to another, her visits back home growing fewer and her connections becoming less and less. She would probably die here, a place she had never really put down roots. She was as much a castaway as Heathcliff.

I could see that over the years she had accumulated little, for I knew how to read those signs, having been there myself. Her room revealed a few clothes, some books, a painting or two, some photographs. I cut her nails and trimmed her hair, which was falling into her eyes — it was pure white, dead straight, thin and silky. It reminded me of Miss Celia's. I used to think Miss Pitt-Grainger refused to avail herself of any of the services offered at the Home because she was too mean, but now, looking around her room, seeing the dark skeins of worry crisscrossing her face, I realized it was because she was too poor.

I can't say I grew to love Miss Pitt-Grainger, but I did feel ashamed of some of the things I had thought about her, and even about the Pancake Sisters, whom I considered selfish and shallow. They are all of that still, but they are also kind and generous. They couldn't have been nicer or more helpful to the sick woman, Ruby especially smuggling ice and lime for at least one drink a day against doctor's orders. Since they were probably also seeing her room for the first time, they must have had the same thoughts as me, for presents kept appearing

— soaps, body lotions and powders, books and magazines and classical music CDs for her little player.

I was there the day Ruby arrived with a present in a large white box tied with a bright pink ribbon. "From the three of us," she announced as she dramatically untied it. I almost laughed out loud when she unfolded the tissue paper and held up a kimono in bright salmon pink silk splashed all over with green and blue flowers. Just the kind of thing Ruby herself would wear, but a more incongruous gift for the Pitt-Bull I could not imagine. To my surprise, the patient looked pleased, despite her protests, and flushed as pink as the present when Ruby insisted she try it on then and there. She helped her out of her washed-out plain cotton housecoat and into the new. Every day after that I would come and find Miss Pitt-Grainger wrapped up in this luxurious garment, looking like a somewhat bedraggled kitten.

Miss Pitt-Grainger did get better. Her sickness softened but did not alter her. She is as autocratic as ever. But somehow, the beam of her critical eye is not as piercing, her verbal blows no longer sting, perhaps because she herself seems to have grown smaller, more fragile. I also think my rosier view on things is a result of Mr. Bridges' benign influence, like some sweet anodyne working its way through me.

46

I THINK THE SECRET of Mr. Bridges' charm is that he is the most uncomplicated of human beings. This is the reason everyone finds it so easy to like him. Unlike some people, there are no hidden edges or dark corners in his psyche, no quicksand or murderous shoals or dangerous waters, though I keep looking for them, for that is what I'm used to in people. He is even-tempered, polite, considerate, never raises his voice, and never seems to get into a fuss about anything. Over the months of our acquaintance, I have learnt that he had a happy childhood, enjoyed his boarding school where he excelled at sports and mathematics, enjoyed his time at a Canadian university, loved his job, had a good marriage, enjoyed a good relationship with his children, and still has a wide circle of friends and many activities. His only regret now is that he allowed his children to persuade him to give up his house. After his second heart attack, they insisted that he should not stay there alone. The choices were to go and live with one of them in the United States or move into a residential home. There was no question of his going abroad to live, he says, so he chose Ellesmere Lodge. At the time he had been willing to make the move, to have someone come and take care of all the arrangements, as his daughter had, in order to move into a place where all his daily wants would be met. But now he was feeling healthy again, he was wishing himself back in the house he had lived in for thirty years. He missed the vines on his veranda, the fruit trees he had planted, his fish pond, the cool breeze blowing down the valley at night, and the view of the mountains. He was glad that he had dug his heels in and refused to sell the place; a cousin lived there now and took care of things. So the possibility of going back was always open.

The way he talks about it makes me realize that this is the only thing that bothers him, the indecision he feels about the house. I marvel that he seems otherwise to have lived a life without regret. How is that possible? Sometimes he says, "It would be easy to go back to the house if I had someone to go with me." He never says anything direct, and I am not presumptuous enough to think a hint is being thrown at me. I have lived in hope only twice in my life and it never worked out, so I'm not going to develop new longings now, though in my insane moments I find the idea appealing and I fantasize a bit about me and Mr. Bridges in his house, in cosy domesticity, until I summon up enough common sense to clobber the image.

Yet, perhaps a hint is being thrown, for Mr. Bridges is one of those men who left everything domestic up to his wife, and she not only ran the household but dealt with all matters pertaining to the physical property as well. He merely signed the cheques for the carpenters and masons, plumbers and decorators, he told me; he had no idea how or why they came or went. His vegetable garden was his only claim to domesticity. She was the kind of wife, he said, who even laid out his clothes for him to wear each morning.

I have to wonder at that, for he seems to manage perfectly on his own. Mr. Bridges' looks are a mirror of his personality. He is compact but well built, no stoop in his posture even now, for though he no longer plays sports, he is disciplined at using the exercise bike in his room and does his push-ups regularly. He has a rather large head and big ears, which I like, but his other features I would describe as regular, an attractive rather than a handsome face that has aged well, his eyes that might have been dark brown lightened with age to the colour of his skin. I suspect he's the kind of man who is more handsome in old age than in youth, and in my more playful moments I think of Mr. Bridges as a charming little brown mouse. But that would make me a cat. It is when I am near him that I am conscious of the enormous size to which I have grown, and I have vowed to cut back on my eating. Not as hard as it sounds, as the intense desire for food which came upon me when I first arrived here gets less and less the longer I stay. In truth, without any great effort on my part, I am getting back to where I was. I'm now working backwards in my wardrobe.

I think of time spent with Mr. Bridges as a way of reducing many things to more manageable proportions, including my anxieties. He has such a calming way of looking at life. Even Winston seems tamed under his influence, for he is so much more amenable now to gardening work. On his own initiative, he has forked up several more beds for planting. The fact that the land, the seeds, the plants, the tools, fertilizers, the sprays, even the water is provided by others, and that his labour alone can yield such bounty, must strike him as a good bargain, for much of the harvest seems now to be going to his baby-mothers.

But it is to Mr. Bridges that I attribute this tenderness that is taking root in me. To tell the truth, I am afraid of it. I don't know if I was tender with my children. I have never thought of it. I mothered them, but I don't know what that meant beyond looking after their needs. I don't know if I had time to be tender, they came so fast, three before I was of legal age, and I had not just the children and the house to look after but the fields as well, the goats, the chickens, the eggs we sold. I didn't do it all by myself, I always had someone to help in the fields, but I was the one who had to see that everything got done. I sewed all our clothes, mended them, stitched sheets from flour bags and salted down beef when we got some, for we were awfully poor the first few years since neither of us had brought anything to the table except for the land and the little house that he had fixed up. Everything was cut and carve and worrying about the next meal. I don't remember he was at home much, even at the start, and I was too timid to ask where he went though, my God, how I longed to know. How I longed to turn him inside out, know everything about him. And how he twisted and turned, slipped away from me so that I could never truly say I had caught him.

It was an uneven yoke, one he never wanted. It was his mother who expected us to get married. She wanted all her sons married. She thought they needed to settle down. Though her eldest and only married son, John, was hardly a shining example of being settled. I also thought she believed that Sam had wronged me and should pay for what he had done, marriage being the only possible payment.

While I was living with her, I don't know what kind of conversations she was having with Sam, but she was writing to the Richardses from time to time asking them to give their permission for me to marry, for of course I was well under legal age. They did not reply, but she never stopped trying.

Things only came to a head because of that married John

attacking me one day. I was alone in the house, Ma D having left that morning to accompany her daughter, Jean, to town, I don't know what for, and Miss Gem had gone along too. I don't know where Mass Ephraim was, I didn't see him around, and undoubtedly John had not either, but he is the one who came running when he heard my screams.

I was so angry that day that I could easily have killed this man myself, and little Mass Ephraim, who must have been in his sixties at the time, would probably have done so, had John not been so much younger and stronger that he easily disarmed him of the cutlass he came flying through the door with. But it was enough to prevent him from carrying through with his intentions. Before leaving, he looked at the old man on the floor where he had flung him, after the cutlass, and I could still hear the sound of that body striking the wall.

"Oh Ephraim, Ephraim, Ephraim," he said, shaking his head and laughing, "I would never have taken you for such a gallant. Well done, my man. We'll knock back a quart in celebration. Later."

He had the nerve to give a V for Victory sign and smile at me before leaving. But I could see the angry purple scratches that were breaking out on his cheeks where I had scratched him and the redness of his ears.

The door slammed behind him. Mass Ephraim got up very slowly, as if in shock, walked over and leaned against that same door, and then, to my immense alarm, burst into tears and sank slowly down onto his heels, holding his hands over his face and howling. I stood helpless, trying to murmur words of comfort. When his sobs finally ceased, he let his hands drop and held up his face as if waiting for the air to dry his tears, and then he just got up and took up his cutlass, as if everything had returned to normal. He smiled sadly at me and shook his head.

"Miss G," he said, "you don't know, young miss, you just don't know what this house pass through. Is only because of the Missis why me and Gem stay. As long as breath in mi body I wi' stay with Missis. But I pray you don't tarry here long." And with that he went through the door. Then he popped his head back in and shook his cutlass at me. "Don't worry, little miss, me and the 'las still here. We and Massa God will protek you."

Left alone, I backed into a chair and eased myself down. My body was shaking uncontrollably. From fright, from anger, from relief. When I had calmed down I began to feel proud of myself too, for I had inflicted some slight damage on the beast, as I thought of him, and an even greater wound to his pride, no matter his taunt to Mass Ephraim.

Now that I had escaped serious hurt, I realized what really annoyed me was how he had crept up on me and frightened me, ripped a strip off my privacy, seen a part of me no one ever saw. I had been sitting at the sewing machine in a corner of the covered porch overlooking the backyard where nothing moved except a hen and her chicks, stitching a new dress that Ma D had helped me cut out, my feet working away at the treadle and singing loudly to myself. I thought I was alone. What was I singing? That same song my father taught me, one I never forgot and sang to myself sometimes, but only when I was sure I was alone, moving my upper body to the rhythm as I was doing now as I fed the material through.

If you don't have love songs to fit my key
Baby don't you sing your blues to me.
That's YOUR RED WAGON,
So just keep dragging YOUR RED WAGON along.

I was in my own private world, one that no one else had ever seen, so it was embarrassment more than fright I felt when I suddenly heard steps behind me. I stopped singing instantly and before I could turn to look, I felt two arms kneading my shoulders and a hot breath on the back of my neck. It was strange that I never thought it was Sam. From the first touch, I felt it was dangerous and dirty. Before I realized who it was, I screamed with fright and tried to jump out of the chair. But by then he had already moved and was on his knees burying his head in my belly, his hands kneading my breasts, hurting me, unbuttoning my blouse.

I screamed louder then, a proper scream this time, and tried to free myself, knocking the chair over. My feet got entangled and I fell. He was instantly on top of me. I was murderously angry, and eyed the scissors on the machine above me, for I wanted to plunge them into him. When I realized that I couldn't reach them, I screamed again, and he put his hand over my mouth. I tasted the blood as I bit my own lip. I could feel his anger as I fought against him. It was strange to think afterwards that he never said anything, he just grunted as he struggled to control me. But each time he took his hand from my mouth I screamed again. So then he slammed my head against the floor and put his hand against my neck to pin me there. From the look in his eyes I truly thought he was going to kill me.

He was breathing heavily and moaning. He removed his hand from my neck and placed it on the floor to balance himself, while trying to unbutton his trousers with the other. I closed my eyes then, trying to think my way through this, praying to a God I only called upon in times of crisis. It was then that I heard someone slamming the kitchen door and Mass Ephraim calling out, "Miss G, Miss G, you aright?"

I found the courage to open my mouth and scream again. He got up quickly, my assailant, straightening his clothes just as Mass Ephraim came running into the room, cutlass raised, his normally placid face distorted with rage. I pulled myself up and buttoned my blouse, my hands trembling, feeling ashamed as I did so, wondering if Mass Ephraim would think I had invited this on myself. But there was no doubt what he thought, for he swung at John, who was on his feet now and who laughed as he easily shifted out of range and parried the blows until he got into position to grab the old man's hand on an upswing and twist it until he winced with pain and dropped the weapon.

By this time they had both backed into the kitchen. I got up and followed them in time to see John toss the old man against the wall like a sack of cornmeal. I don't know that I have ever hated anyone in my life as much as I hated that man then. I never spoke to him again, though he had the nerve to attend my wedding with his wife and children, looking scrubbed and neat and so respectable.

She was a poor white girl from German town, with lank pale blond hair and a manner to match. But she had three of the most beautiful children I have ever seen, and Ma D praised her as a wonderful mother. I always wondered what she made of the scratches on her husband's face that day, but that perhaps was a normal occurrence.

When Ma D got home and heard what had happened from Ephraim before she even came inside the house, she didn't write this time, she went in person to see Miss Celia. I don't know what she told her, but she returned in triumph with her written permission for me to marry. The day she went, Gem never left my side, but we needn't have worried. Sam had given John a thorough beating, we heard, with a few blows thrown in by the other brothers, and it was some time before he started showing his face around the Bull Pen again. At the time, Sam's actions made me feel so proud, a sign that I mattered to him. Only later, of course, would I realize that John had not been chastised because of the injury he had done me, but for his disrespect of another man's property.

47

PROPERTY! NOW I CAN laugh about it, but at the time the realization just added to my bitterness. Not long after he left me for good, Sam and his brothers sold the family property to a bauxite mining company, for an enormous sum, I am told, shared between the four of them. By this time both Ma D and their sister, Jean, had died. That bare-boned soil was found to be full of aluminium, and he was rich. I was still scratching around in the dirt, with two children at home. Never once did he offer us anything. At least not to me, but it was strange that as the children grew up and left home it was to him that they gravitated, or so I heard, for they lost no time in cutting me off.

No wonder he looked so smug and prosperous when he came to Celia's wedding. Paid for it too, I was to learn. I can still remember how I shrivelled up inside myself when I saw him. Here I was, Mother of the Bride dressed all in blue, for she had chosen my outfit down to my dyed satin shoes. I was glad my hat had a little brim I could hide under, hide my plain face, sunburned black, and my silk gloves would hide my work hands that one quick manicure couldn't disguise. Hands that spent the entire ceremony clutching and unclutching the beaded silk purse in my lap. When I stood up, the beads that I had worked loose fell to the ground, and I was trailed thereafter by a dribble of tiny pink and blue beads that got crushed underfoot. By the end of the day, the purse itself was as bare as my soul.

Celia hadn't told me he was coming. To give her away. As if we hadn't both done that a long time ago. Up to that moment in the church I had sat there feeling proud of her, though she was not at all famous then. I was proud of the good match she seemed to be making. Her husband, Herman, came from a well-to-do family of legal luminaries. He was an up-and-coming lawyer himself. The few times I had seen them together, I was touched by how he seemed to care for her.

It wasn't a large wedding, but as the church filled up with fashionable people, the groom's family, their friends, the more dowdy and awkward I felt, sitting there beside my son, Junior, who was assigned to escort me but who maintained such a space between us on the pew I knew he had no desire to be there with me. Though he was pleasant enough when he came to collect me, I have to say, bending down to kiss me on my cheek, smiling and telling me how well I looked. I didn't say much to him in the car, for there were other guests present, but the lingering smell of his aftershave made my heart ache. I remembered how even as a small boy he would help himself to his father's, mimicking him in all his masculine ways.

I looked out the corner of my eye at him, for I was too self-conscious to turn my head and look at my own son whom I hadn't seen for some years, now fully grown. Over six feet tall and handsome, looking like none of us really, more Indian than anything with his beautiful chocolate skin and curly black hair and, unlike the others, my brown eyes.

The last time I'd seen him was when he came home to collect his things after he'd been expelled from school. My prediction then, loudly flung at him as he left, was that he'd come to a bad end. But here he was at twenty looking quite prosperous, if the beautifully cut silk suit, the expensive watch, and the way he carried himself were saying anything. Of course it might have been his father's doing, but I had heard that Junior had gone into business with his old schoolmates, Michael Evans or whatever his name was and that Pinto boy — with the help of their rich fathers, no doubt — and they were doing well. Exactly what the business was I didn't know, and I didn't get the chance to ask Junior that day.

His father was the focus of all my agitation and anger and resentment. When the wedding march started and I looked down the aisle and I saw Celia on his arm, my stomach turned somersaults and I blanked out the rest of the ceremony, consumed by the unfairness of it all.

48

JUNIOR WASN'T THE ONLY one of my children in the church that day. I'd forgotten Lise was there too. To that Lise would have said in her sharp little voice, "So, what else is new?" She claimed she always came last with me. That could well be true. She was an impossible child from birth. From the time she was implanted in my womb, sorrow, anger, bereavement, and regret were stalking me. I knew it was all over between me and Sam, that nothing had gone right and nothing would ever be fixed between us. Another child I didn't want, I have to admit that. And it was while I was pregnant that we allowed those people to take Celia. Would I have allowed Sam to persuade me it was the best thing for her if I myself wasn't in what people used to call a "delicate way"? Did I allow my heightened emotional state at the time to cloud my judgment?

On top of it all, Ma D, who had been ill with cancer, died. I had gone to stay with her from time to time, though it was hard for me to leave my home. She had her other daughters-in-law to take care of her, for all her sons were married by then and living nearby. Then one day they took her to the hospital for treatment that didn't work. I never saw her again. Losing Ma D was like losing a part of myself, for though after I married and moved away we didn't see each other that often, just knowing she was there was good enough for me. I went to her funeral and wore black and bawled like a baby, not caring what anyone thought — in those days pregnant women were not supposed to go to funerals or wear black or bawl their heads off. But this was one time I got my own way with Sam. He didn't want me to go, but I simply got dressed and seated myself in the car and refused to get out until he finally gave up and drove.

I suppose I was in mourning for a lot of things by the time Lise came, not least for the death of something I couldn't even name, for some spark that I thought would come and live inside me the day I rode off with Sam, that would keep the darkness at bay. It's not that I turned away from the baby. At least I don't think so. She was breast-fed like the others. But they say babies can sense things even in the womb. She must have felt chilly winds blowing. I suppose I should accept some blame for the way Lise turned out. Loud and demanding, selfish and mean-spirited. I know it's bad to say such things about one's child, but really, she had none of the sweetness or charm of the others. Which is probably why she felt she had to grab all the attention. She wasn't an attractive child, definitely shortchanged as far as looks were concerned, though by the time she was in her early teens she certainly had learnt to make the most of what she had. Don't ask me where she got it, that thing called sexiness, but you should have seen her at the wedding — sixteen looking twenty-five, with her overripe breasts falling out of her frock, and behaving like forty, drinking champagne and carrying on with all the men. I have to say she did look fantastic as Celia's bridesmaid. I know Celia wanted Shirley as her maid of honour, but Shirley had gone to New York by then and didn't come for the wedding. I'm not sure I ever knew the reason why, except that Celia was terribly upset about it. Young as Lise was, she carried it off. I had to admire her.

At the reception, she barely deigned to notice me. She was hooked up under her father's arm the whole time, which is probably where she felt she belonged. I spent my time avoiding them. As far as I was concerned she was her father's responsibility. So why did I feel shame every time news of one of Lise's scandalous affairs reached me?

49

IT'S WHEN I LOOK at people like Miss Pitt-Grainger and one or two of the other folk at Ellesmere Lodge who never seem to have visitors, who clearly have no one, that I have come to appreciate how much Celia has done for me. I wonder why, for apart from life, what have I really given her? She's given me so much. For one thing, she gave me status among my neighbours once she started to get her name and picture in the papers. You wouldn't believe how important people considered this. Well, I was proud of her too, of course, every step of the way, but I certainly wouldn't have gone around the place boasting about her the way everyone else did. As for when she started to host one of those television talk shows. Well, you'd have thought she was the Queen and I the Queen Mother.

Of course, by this time people in the district had begun

to benefit from having children abroad or themselves going overseas as farm workers; foreign travel was now the norm rather than the exception. Many homes boasted large TV sets and a few had satellite dishes on the roofs. Quite a difference from when I was a child and we seemed so cut off from the rest of the world. I was still cut off in a way, for apart from my radio all I had was an old black and white TV. Until Junior turned up at my house one day with this big colour one. Of course it didn't mean very much, as I didn't have a satellite dish, so it was still just the local station I could watch. But that's what she was on, this talk show. So at least I could watch her. Mark you, Junior did say he would see about getting me a dish, but I absolutely refused it, I thought the whole thing was too ostentatious and far too much money to spend, though I was pleased that he was being so thoughtful.

It was after Celia's wedding that Junior got into the habit of dropping by. He never stayed long, but I was happy to see him. He stayed long enough to eat, as he missed my cooking, or so he said, and I usually rushed to the kitchen to rustle up something. Junior always loved his food and now I could see it showing. I teased him, for he was certainly filling out. I kept asking him about Shirley. I had had no reply to any of the letters I wrote to her in New York and I was getting seriously worried. Junior assured me she was all right, they often spoke on the phone and she always asked for me, she was just too busy; studying and working at the same time. I believed him, but I still fretted over Shirley, wondering why she never answered any of my letters.

I was always glad when any of the children came by —

though, if truth be told, Lise and I couldn't be together for five minutes before we fell out. Or at least, she argued and shouted and I said little, but she knew how to read my body language and my silence itself enraged her. After my first few words and her reaction I would just give up in disgust and let her rant. Almost every visit ended with her slamming the door and leaving in a huff. And then I would heave a sigh and say, "Good riddance." But really, it would take me hours and sometimes days to get over the disturbance she left in her wake. What did we argue about? Maybe the same things all mothers argue with their teenage girls about. The way she dressed and carried herself, her behaviour, her school work, boys, her lack of consideration. Her lying. I caught her out so many times. Maybe we would have resolved our differences in time. I was not to find out because, as it was with Junior, she didn't have to stay around and take it from me. She had her father to run to.

As the youngest, I suppose she was always Daddy's girl. She was the only one who asked after her father when he left us for good.

She just came right out and asked, "Where's Papa?"

We were all sitting at the table having dinner, stew peas and rice. To this day I remember that moment and the turmoil I felt. Her question forced me to face up to something I wanted to pretend wasn't happening. Although he had been gone over a week, I hadn't prepared an answer to that question, not even for myself. I never answered her; I was too afraid of bursting into tears. But I could feel the silence around the table getting longer and longer, as if all of us were collectively holding our breath. I gave Lise a look that normally would silence her. It did, but it didn't stop her playing with the empty spoon in her wide open mouth and gazing at me with what I called her mongoose look. The one the mongoose gave to the boa constrictor to stop it in its tracks. Even then, at eight or nine, Lise was already tough. My God! She had her father's face and eyes and red colouring, but not his good looks, and at this moment with her coarse little plaits unravelling and her face covered in freckles she was an awkward, plain-looking child, her eyelashes stubby and almost white, her eyes pale and disconcerting. Her looks brought her plenty of teasing. "Mongoose," the children called her, "Muss-Muss." "Quaw." "Redibo." If they did this in my hearing, I would tell them to stop; but I didn't worry about it, for I really didn't see it as anything more than what children did to each other. So I guess Lise learnt at an early age to fight her own fights.

At first the teasing would make her cry, but then she got more and more aggressive: throwing sticks, stones, whatever there was to hand, fearlessly launching her skinny self at children much bigger, trying to scratch their eyes out. She was fierce. Where she got this from, God only knows. To me she was just the bad seed. And didn't she prove it? But that was still to come.

At the table that day her question went unanswered, and not another word was uttered for the rest of the meal, not even by talkative Shirley. I could feel the tension, though, growing and growing from the day I sent off their father's clothes. Maybe I was the one generating it, for I felt brittle and stretched. So now the question hung in the air, tantalizing, unsettling, as mysteries are. We sat there, trying to eat, but overly conscious of each other, of every movement, the slightest little sound. For once, I couldn't wait for them to leave the table. They couldn't wait either, and as soon as I said they could go they jumped up and cleared the table with great eagerness while I just sat for a long long time till darkness fell. For once I didn't check on them or the house. I got up and flung myself down on my bed and fell fast asleep.

But Lise refused to let it go. For more than once after that she asked, without getting any answer from me, "When's Papa coming back?" And whenever she got into a real temper, which she did more and more, lying on the floor kicking and screaming, scratching her own face and tearing out her hair in clumps, inevitably the tantrum would end up with her falling quiet, gulping in air along with huge sobs, and muttering "Papa, Papa," half swallowing the words until she fell silent. After a while I paid her no mind; I just left her to sleep it off wherever she had thrown herself. I had decided that I would not allow this child to rule me. I had too many other things to worry about.

But don't think I didn't notice the two older ones those times, how they exchanged looks between them, secret guilty looks as if they were in some grand conspiracy. They always were, weren't they, Shirley and Junior. They must have let Lise in on the mystery, however they saw it, for after a while she stopped mentioning her father. To me, that was all to the good.

50

EIGHT YEARS LATER AND Lise was living with him, in his nice posh house on the outskirts of town, where the rich people lived, with his new woman. Lise left home as soon as she finished her exams. She didn't wait on the results, probably because she knew she had done so badly. She stayed in the town to get a job for the summer, she said, sharing with Shirley, who by then had a little apartment of her own on the side of someone's house. Lise used to come home for weekends quite often, for I insisted, and then it got less and less. She was such a liar that it was some time before I knew that she was no longer living with Shirley but had moved in with her father. It wasn't "a big ting" as she put it, she had her own room and she wasn't paying rent, and though it was a bit out of town Dad — as he had become — drove her to and from work for she had no intention of going back to school.

Next thing I knew, she was having a baby. Some married man she had taken up with. Lise always worried about her looks, considered herself ugly, which is probably why from an early age she was so determined to attract attention from boys. I could see it in the way she sexed up her clothes, puffed up the hair, dyed it, pouted her lips, invested in looks rather than books until she did become in time quite glamorous looking, in the way of teenagers then, tight skirts, little tops, cleavage, and endless costume jewellery and makeup. An earlier version of my hairdresser Morveen. But what the hell was she doing at eighteen with this hard-back businessman even though he drove a Mercedes-Benz? His wife rammed her car into their apartment building at one time and grabbed Lise on the street one day and gave her a good box, though of course Lise retaliated. Next thing she's up on an assault charge, though I guess wiser heads prevailed and the charge was dropped. Ostrich-like, I kept my head down and pretended it had nothing to do with me each time a new scandal reached my ears. Millie or someone else in the district would be sure to bring me the news. They all professed sympathy at those times, but I could see their eyes glittering with the excitement of the scandal, hoping to get some extra tidbit from me. They never did, for my only reaction was, "I don't business."

That was only the beginning. Lise got into any number of scrapes and ended up having two other children by two different men. She had moved to some other part of the island and for a long time I neither saw nor heard from her. Junior told me she had settled down and taken some business courses and had gone into real estate and was doing quite well. That part didn't surprise me. Lise was so good at getting what she wanted she probably twisted the arms of her clients till they signed.

Some years later who should turn up driving this posh new gold-coloured car and looking rather grand but Miss Lise herself. I almost didn't recognize her as she stepped out of what Ken assured me later with awe in his voice was a BMW. She looked completely different, really glamorous, like a movie star. She had managed to smooth out her complexion so her skin looked golden, to match the hair that was plentiful and straight and reddish blond, whether her own or a wig I don't know. Makeup and her long mascaraed lashes gave her eyes colour and depth, so they looked challenging rather than weak. Her lips, which were rather large to begin with, were emphasized with a pale orange glossy lipstick. She looked very fit, as if she spent all her time at a gym, and the dress, a plain white linen sheath, wasn't tight but showed all her curves. The black and strappy heels were high, the pearly orange nails were out to here, and the rings and necklaces and bracelets looked expensive and real. Her manner had changed to match the exterior gloss. All smiles and charm and beautifully modulated voice, as if she couldn't mash ants. But underneath tough as nails still, you could feel it, for she exuded a kind of powerful energy, as if she had finally found a way of channelling her ferocity. I was genuinely glad to see her, glad that she had turned into someone, even though that someone frightened me a bit.

She pretended to be happy to see me and promised to bring the children to visit as soon as school was out. But she never did, and I thought afterwards that she only came to show off on me, to show me how wonderful she had turned out. She was that kind of person.

Never another word did I hear from her again until some years later she began to send me Christmas cards from America. No message except *Love, Lise and the kids*. No return address. I didn't know she had left. By this time, Shirley had died, which is probably why the news for some reason upset me when Junior told me that Lise had moved to New York. What's this New York thing, I thought then. Is there some kind of homing call that they have to respond to, as birds to their instincts, to go to that place, to die — or vanish, as Lise seemed to have done. She vanished to me, though I have no doubt she was in touch with her father. They all were. So what did that make me? I wondered sometimes. A monster who ate her children?

No, I was simply eating myself up with jealousy of their father, as Lise in another of her own bitter moments had told me. Or maybe that was Shirley. I was the one who was full of anger and hatred: "No fun to be with." Yet, in all honesty, wasn't it that same grin, that powerful charisma that had also drawn me to him? So why did I condemn them for falling for it? It's all such a long time in the past anyway, and he is the past too. Died quite a few years back.

I was surprised that I didn't feel anything when I heard the news. At least not at first. And, I'm ashamed now to admit, I said no words of comfort to Celia when she came to tell me her father had died, nor to Junior. I just said, "Oh," asked a few practical questions like "What happened?" or "What did he die of?" as if they were talking about a stranger. I honestly didn't think at the time how much their father meant to them. Or, for that matter, what he had meant to me. Yes, I suppose I was jealous. Jealous of the way he displaced me in my children's lives. And angry. Angry even now. For I still feel this man stole a whole part of my own life. Diverted me from some other road I might have taken.

And yet (to borrow Mr. Bridge's technique) if I hadn't run away with Sam, what would have become of me?

51

SOME WEEKS AFTER SHE brought the news of Shirley's death, Celia came, by herself this time, but she had very little to add. The police thought the man responsible had been killed in another shootout. I felt I would never hear the truth. Celia did bring me the picture, though. It was Shirley all right, but not the Shirley that I knew, for she looked old, thin, and faded, only the smile remaining like a ghost of her former self. Or was it just my imagination that had already turned her into a ghost, a spirit child? A spiritless child?

I studied that picture so much it got cracked and worn. I kept trying to superimpose on it this vision of a child who in my mind was always vital, happy, larger than life. Noisy, irrepressible Shirley coming home from school bursting through the door, slamming down her school bag on the floor as she tore off her shoes and uniform and wriggled into her house dress almost at the same time as she was rushing through the kitchen asking, "What's for dinner?", grabbing an orange or banana, recounting some event from school, and dashing out the door to play before I could get a word in. No matter how hard I tried, I could never slow her down, and it wasn't surprising that she was the queen of the fifty-yard dash at her school's sports day.

I couldn't reconcile that Shirley of my mind with the woman in the picture, Shirley slowed down to a dead halt. I wanted to cry every time I looked at it. Then one day I put it away in the old biscuit tin where I kept the few things that were important to me. It was many years before I looked at it again.

What I couldn't face was the chasm that had opened up between us, Shirley and me, before she left home. I hardly heard directly from her once she went away. Lise had done the same, once she moved to her father's, but with Lise it didn't matter that much. Shirley's silence was really painful since we never had the history of antagonism that Lise and I had. Shirley and I always got on well, she got on well with everyone. She began to change the year or so before she went to America. She got these terrible mood swings, almost as if she was two different people. In a way I was glad when she told me she was going away. I thought she needed a change of scene, she needed to do more with her life than be a typist in somebody's office. She was thrilled when she got into university. Things seemed to have worked out for the first year or two. But I really didn't know any details, for I relied mainly on Junior and Celia for news of her. Not that there was much forthcoming, and I was disappointed that she never came home on a visit, but at least I knew she was all right.

When I thought about it afterwards, though, I realized I didn't know if she was all right for I knew virtually nothing about Shirley's life in the five years she was away. Yet it was that very knowledge I needed to make the leap between the Shirley I had known and the one in the picture. Shirley silent and still. I think the image of Shirley in that picture disturbed me so much because I got the feeling that she was lonely, and Shirley was never cut out to be alone.

52

I KEPT WAITING FOR Junior to come and see me because he was the one I expected to fill in the gaps, tell me everything about Shirley, but he too seemed to have vanished, for not a word did I hear from him. That made me realize something very strange that had not struck me before. In all the years Junior was visiting, he had never given me his phone number or address. I didn't even think about it until I was the one who desperately wanted to contact him. Then I realized how empty was my knowledge of him, how evasive he was if I asked him anything personal. After Shirley's death it was as if I was suddenly opening up a box marked "Junior," to find there was nothing inside.

Once I did say to him, jokingly, "So, Junior, why don't you bring some of your friends to visit? Why you always come alone? You don't have a girlfriend? Man, you don't think it's time you settled down and got married?"

Junior just laughed. When it came to himself, he was the most closed-mouth, though he was quite affable about everything else. He hadn't forgotten his roots, either; everyone passing by who saw his car parked outside the house would call out some friendly greeting or come inside to shake his hand. He would always stop to chat with people on the road, the guys he'd gone to elementary school with. Although he had done so well for himself and gone way beyond them, there was nothing high and mighty about Junior. He was the same guy he always was. Generous too. I knew that, but I was quite surprised that Millie could cite chapter and verse of people whose children Junior was sending to school. He had never given me the slightest hint of this and I never let on that I knew. I laughed when Millie called Junior the Godfather, but only because for me that image was of a much older man, and though he was very mature for his age, Junior was still a boy to me. When I said that, she said quite seriously, "No, is true, Miss Sam. You don't know how many people him help. If it wasn't for Junior, plenty families wouldn't eat."

This side of him was really news to me, but I had never doubted his popularity. I guess there was a lot of his father in him, though Junior was much more a man of substance in every way.

"Junior," one day I teased him, "it looks like you're planning to run for election. Millie says if they put you up as a candidate, not even a dog would vote for the opposition."

Junior laughed heartily and his eyes crinkled up and vanished inside his face till they could hardly be seen, for though he had started out with his father's face, long and narrow, over the years both his face and body had filled out. Junior was a walking advertisement for the good life.

"No, not me," he said. "You think I would be crazy enough to go into politics?" But everybody knew he was an active supporter of the party in power and a friend of some powerful politicians, including our very own MP.

Once when I complained that I knew nothing about him, he said, quite seriously, "Sometimes it's best not to know. What you don't know can't hurt you."

He had a faraway look in his eyes when he said it, but I remember laughing to myself at his use of the saying, one more likely to come out of the mouth of some old person like me than this youth.

It was only after Shirley's death when I so desperately wanted to get in touch with him that I remembered that he had in fact given me an address. Not a home address, but one of his business cards. "Samjam Enterprises," it read, with an address in Montego Bay, a phone and fax number. He hadn't wanted to give it to me, but I had begged him. "Suppose there is an emergency or something," I remember saying, "how on earth would I contact you?"

He took the card out of his wallet then and handed it over, saying, "If I'm not there they will always know where to find me."

So now when I so desperately wanted to find him, I dug up the card and dressed and took the bus to town, determined to phone him, for these were the days before cell phones and there were no call boxes in the remote country where I lived.

You can guess how the story ends, can't you? After a lot of trying and frustration and grief, I ended up knowing that phone was no longer in service. Ditto fax, for I went over to the hardware store where I knew the owner and he tried to send a message for me. Nothing going through. I went home and wrote Junior care of the company address but no answer came back.

I then started to think of all the people Junior knew in the district, since some of them were bound to know how to get in touch, especially if he was helping them out. But I was too ashamed to ask, for it would have been admitting that I didn't know anything about my own son. There was one person, though, Bertie. He was older than Junior, but they were good friends.

Bert was one of the young men from around who was born with nothing but had suddenly blossomed into the wealthiest man in the district. A show-off one too, so people had a lot to say. He built himself this huge house on the hill, a white palace with many arches that could be seen for miles, with a huge satellite dish on the roof. He owned several trucks, huge refrigerated things, not to mention matching Volvos for himself and his wife. Bert used to hang around with Junior when he was a little boy, but I hardly saw him these days, the most I got was a wave as he sped past. People had a lot to say about the source of his sudden wealth, but I thought a lot of it was envy. Bert had gone away as a farm worker, and unlike many of the others had saved his money. He continued to go, year after year. When I mentioned this to Millie, who was always throwing word after him, she laughed long and loud.

"You really believe is so farm worker can get rich quick, Miss G? Well, if that was the case I would send my Roy over there to pick apples in Canada long time. I would even go myself." She walked off laughing, perhaps at the idea of her husband — a hard-working mechanic — working for someone else. I suppose I was being naïve, because by this time the drug trade was big business and there were whispers everywhere about who was the Mister Big behind it. Or rather several Mister Bigs. Our own MP was rumoured to be one, though at the time the air was so polluted with politics, drugs, and gun violence there were rumours about everybody. All I wanted from Bert was to find out if he knew anything about Junior or had heard from him or knew where I could find him. But I was shocked to discover Bert too had gone away, his cousin was running the trucking company, the Volvos had disappeared, and his wife and children had departed overnight.

After that I gave up on Junior. I got to a point where I decided to forget I ever had children, for all I ever got from them was ingratitude. Even Shirley, how dare she go and die? Leaving me to the blankness of questions with no answers. To the emptiness.

Long after this, Celia told me Junior was in Canada, but he didn't want anyone to know. I kept my mouth shut, though I couldn't believe he could have left without telling me. But this was a time when politics had tainted everything, had split the country. People were dying for it, and so many who had been involved in even the most marginal way were running scared, leaving the country without telling their closest friends. Most of the business people were running, afraid of Castro and communism. Another set was running because they feared the opposition coming to power in the election that was imminent. So I thought it was something like that with Junior. Part of that exodus, when bumper stickers were reading, *Will the last person to leave please turn off the lights*. I don't know if Junior might have been involved in politics far deeper than I knew, and it was to be some years before I actually got a letter from him. I didn't think of Junior and Lise too often then, but I couldn't get Shirley out of my mind.

53

MR. BRIDGES' STYLE IS to ask a question as a way of finding an answer, and I'm trying to adopt it rather than leap to conclusions. He certainly asks me a lot of questions, and I am flattered, for no one has ever shown this sort of interest in me before. I have come to open up to him, a little bit. He is so comfortable to be with, he seems to draw things out of me like a conjurer. I hadn't spoken much about the other children, but one day we were talking about Celia. So when I told him Celia hadn't grown up with me, which made me feel guilty to this day, he asked me to tell him how that had come about and then he posed the question: "What would she have been if you hadn't done what you did? Have you thought of that?"

It is late afternoon and we are sitting by ourselves in comfortable wicker chairs in a corner of the veranda over-looking the lawn, our words unheard by a bunch of noisy Scrabble players at the next table. Mr. Bridges is making the one whiskey and soda he permits himself last as long as possible. I am struggling with needlepoint.

But, perhaps what is really making me uncomfortable is not the needlework but Mr. Bridges, because it is not always that we want friends to be so reasonable and rational about things. Sometimes we want people we like to agree with us, to say yes, you have been hard done by, regardless. But Mr. Bridges is not like that; in his gentle way he always looks at both sides and in the process is forcing me to confront some hard truths. So now when he asks me if I have thought about it, I want to snap at him, "Of course I have."

What else have I had to do these days but think about things, especially the last twenty-odd years when I was there by myself with nothing for company but my chickens, my rabbits, my goats, and my books? I only moved out, Celia came and moved me out, because the place was so badly damaged by the hurricane, half the roof gone or leaking, the guttering to the tank blown away, the electricity cut off.

It was meant to be only for a time, while Celia arranged to get the house fixed, but despite her promises I have heard nothing further on that score. I know she sends money down regularly to Millie, who watches over things. But it is my house and I would like to have it back, I tell Mr. Bridges, just as he would like to go back to his. He doesn't see it like that. He doesn't see how I can go back there on my own, even if the place is fixed up. What would I do with myself, he asks. And with the state the country is in, how could I feel safe, a woman on my own? Besides, he says, and here is the clincher that really, really annoys me, it is probably costing Celia less to keep me at Ellesmere Lodge than to undertake the rebuilding of a house, especially down there in the country. "That requires substantial capital," he says, his accountant self, "while keeping you here is a monthly outlay." If I didn't know him well enough to know he is without guile, I would have thought Celia put him up to it, for he knows by now that the word *expense* is the one thing that will stop me in my tracks.

But I don't snap or show my annoyance; I haven't changed in that respect, showing feelings. I pause in my labours and I look up and catch his eyes on me, eyes the same colour as his skin, which is so even-textured, so soft I want to stroke it. I smile and look away. I say yes, in response to his question, I have thought about it many times. But I say no more, for I am not ready to share with him what my true thoughts are. I like it that he never presses me. So we just sit there in companionable silence for a while, me stabbing away with the needle again, he turning his glass round and round, staring into space. I often wonder what he is thinking at those times, but I am too shy to ask.

54

THERE'S A LOT OF interest in me and Mr. Bridges, but then people around here have nothing to do and will latch on to anything that passes for diversion. A lot of teasing goes on that I do my best to ignore. People seem to think of us as a couple, though there certainly has been no coupling. Might never be. He has shown no interest in that side of things, and I myself am too scared to contemplate it, having been alone so long. Nor are my memories of lovemaking pleasant ones, for it was more coupling than love. My husband took me when he wanted and I yielded because I thought it was my duty, but the warmth, the love, the foreplay and the mutual pleasing, all the things they openly talk about nowadays, everywhere, without shame, were certainly not part of my experience. Our marriage was a dreary triumph of duty over Eros. Of course I could have gotten married again had I wanted to, there was no shortage of men making me offers, for a single woman alone is fair game for even the most unsuitable. Though there might have been mild interest here and there on my part, I can't say I ever felt attracted enough to anyone to take it beyond some mild flirtation. I was enjoying my freedom too much, the notion that I was — finally — in charge of my own life.

But I'm thinking that I'm missing something, especially here, for I am amazed at how all these old people are still maintaining a lascivious interest in the opposite sex, even the ones who can barely walk. It's as if keeping up the pretence is a bulwark against that dark threshold we are all facing. Why else does Ruby bother with her makeup, even when her hands are so shaky she can barely hold the mascara brush or the lipstick? She brightened up considerably when Mr. Bridges came on the scene, but now I think she is fluttering her mascara at the charming Mr. Levy. Even Babe, who has been married three times and has had a double mastectomy, is not averse to a little archness, though she deigns to ignore her chief admirer, Heathcliff. Poor Heathcliff doesn't stand a chance, as Babe believes the only marriageable man is one with money. That rules out our ex-schoolmaster. Though Birdie claims that teaching was a front and that he really is a Remittance Man. She had to explain to me that a Remittance Man is a black sheep from a good English family to whom they pay a regular allowance just to stay away.

"Oh Birdie," laughed Babe. "They don't have such things anymore. Good families today are proud of their black sheep! It gives them a certain cachet."

Heathcliff really does have that haw-haw accent and rather fancies himself, always with a rather rakish smile and lively eyes, seeming perpetually pleased as he slinks around the place, walking with a bit of a limp that is quite pronounced sometimes. He seems to pop up everywhere and he loves to hold on to people, especially women, and chat some nonsense in their ears.

He is a man who has shrunk. He must have had a large frame, as he is a bit stooped. He wears clothes that seem too large for him, as if they belonged to an earlier period in his life. His belt is drawn tightly to hold up his pleated trousers. Everything he wears is old, but of good quality and well made, though his everyday shirts of heavy linen or cotton have been worn to pale, washed-out colours. His face is quite handsome still, or perhaps distinguished, a large face that fits his body and has worn well, with regular features and startling blue eyes. He seems to have acquired a permanent tan over the years. But, as if to show that he has renounced schoolmastering, he no longer wears his hair short, as I imagine he once did, but long and brushed back into a ponytail, except for Sundays when he wears it untied and hanging down, looking quite silly in my estimation since the hair is stringy and white and he's balding on top. Every time I see him I want to take my scissors to that silly hank of hair, for he'd look so much better without it.

The thing about Heathcliff is that one can't dislike him, no matter how annoying he becomes, for one gets the sense that he is rather aimless and harmless and entirely without guile. Or even much sense, for that matter, he is so silly sometimes. How on earth he could have been a school principal is beyond me, though it is probably saying a lot about that private school, which, according to the Sisters, was founded as a kind of up-market reformatory for the rich to park their children who were too wicked or too dumb or too lazy to make it in an academically challenging place. He is the biggest flirt among the men, probably because he is the least battered and the most ambulatory, forever passing little flattering, and sometimes quite suggestive, remarks to all the women on the premises from kitchen to office as he hobbles about. Even to the good Mrs. Humphrey. He avoids Miss Pitt-Grainger like the plague, though, which only gives credence to Birdie's theory because she says it takes one English person to know another.

But Heathcliff is truest to Miss Loony Tune, frequently playing adoring swain to her nymph. We are sometimes drawn to the window to watch them sitting under the shade of the almond tree on the lawn, in canvas chairs, their knees unable to meet the challenge of sitting on the red blanket they take along and spread for theatrical effect, he playing the flute and she warbling away.

All the men actually salivate over Miss Dune, because she really is beautiful still and must have been stunning in her youth. She has a classical Greek face, all carved features, angles and planes and high cheekbones, which she is certainly aware of as she is constantly thrusting them at you, first one side and then the other, and huge dark eyes surrounded by long, unmascaraed lashes. Miss Dune doesn't have to wear anything on her face to be beautiful and can even bring off the short mannish haircut she favours, the white hair offset by her sultana skin, which is largely unwrinkled.

I'm not sure of Miss Dune's ancestry, she tends to give everything such romantic twists that pursuit of truth is difficult. She does look Latin. Though Ruby swears she is nothing but a little hurry-come-up Coolie gal from the canefields. Although I'm not a big fan of Miss Loony, when I heard that jibe it was like a dagger in my heart: Miss Celia's remark about my mother all over again. I left the table without even waiting to finish the meal and took to my bed and slept until morning. For weeks after that I refused to speak to Ruby, though of course she did not notice as I hardly spoke anyway. I was angry, too, because I had learnt by then it was the canefields — and the people who toiled there — that gave Ruby such privilege, for her family had been big sugar estate owners.

Miss Loony spent many years abroad training and had an impressive concert career if she is to be believed. She has albums of clippings. She taught music after her return home, before ending up at Ellesmere. Why, I don't know, but she doesn't seem to have any family. At least none of them come to visit. She entertains us at the piano sometimes, though I for one could do without her singing, all tremolo and soulfulness and much writhing of her exquisite hands. Miss Loony is thin and flat and has no body to speak of, which ruins my fantasy of all trained singers having to be as upholstered as couches. She does give off a certain *je ne sais quoi*, as Babe calls it, and she should know, so that she is always surrounded by a little claque of those men capable of walking, sitting, or even just smiling.

I know I am being unkind, but Miss Loony is the most shallow, silly, irritating woman I have ever met. Maybe that is the secret of her charm. Even Mr. Bridges says he finds her charming, provoking the first of what I am alarmed to find are jealous twinges.

55

"SO DID YOU EVER see your father again?" This is Mr. Bridges asking me.

I have to stop and gather my thoughts on the subject. I am ambushed by the question. I told Mr. Bridges about my father one day in his room when I had asked him for the umpteenth time to play that song for me, "Your Red Wagon," and he'd refused. He kept saying, "No, I don't want you to assault me again," mimicking Matron's words that I had repeated to him, holding up his hands in mock surrender, so I knew he was joking about the incident and I no longer felt ashamed.

This was when we had moved to another stage, me in Mr. Bridges' room, door wide open, nothing untoward, listening to music. He had a collection of CDs and a very expensive looking, very tiny player, the speakers no bigger than his ears. But the most astonishing sounds came out of them. He invited me over sometimes to come and listen, especially when he'd gone out and added something new to his collection, as excited as a boy as he handed me the spare set of headphones.

"Listen to this now," he'd say, holding up his hand or conducing in time to the music. "Listen to that."

I'm afraid he had to educate me. His taste was very catholic, so there were some things I enjoyed immensely and others I didn't. But it wasn't so much the music as the comfort I felt sitting in the armchair listening and watching the pleasure on his face. Just as I think he simply wanted someone, anyone, to share his thrill of discovery.

I couldn't understand why he wouldn't play the song when I'd asked him to so many times, or any of the blues that he had. But one day, when he seemed in a particularly playful mood, he said, "Okay, I'll play your song if you tell me why it is so important to you."

So I told him the entire story of how I'd stayed home one Sunday hoping to get to know my father better, how he had played music for me and how we danced. Until Miss Celia and Aunt Zena came home and caught us at it. How Aunt Zena tossed out of the window my father's gramophone and records, smashing them on the rocks below. How my father was carted off to the lunatic asylum and I never saw him again. How I blamed myself.

It was a long recital, and I found it harder and harder to speak as I went along. I was drained when it ended and felt cocooned in the silence that fell.

"My dear G, what a terrible time you've had," he finally said. "But you shouldn't continue to blame yourself for everything that happens in life. Here, dry your eyes." He handed me a Kleenex. I blew my nose and sat there with my eyes closed for a while. Then I got up and left without saying anything. He let me go, as if he too was feeling the atmosphere in the room.

I didn't find his response very comforting, for reliving that day with my father made me feel no less guilty. Though in my heart of hearts I knew what happened would have happened anyway, if not that day, in response to that trigger point, then some other. But I didn't feel like staying in that room any longer. It wasn't until afterwards that I realized he had made no move to play that song for me.

56

THERE IS ONE THING I didn't tell Mr. Bridges. I didn't think of it until I went back to my room and was overcome by the sadness I always felt when I conjured up my father. I probably wouldn't have shared this with him anyway: the black hole I fell into the day they took my father away.

Miss Celia and Aunt Zena were standing with all the neighbours in the front yard to watch the Black Maria drive off. I hadn't watched. I had crept away and found myself at the side of the house that my father's room overlooked. This is where Aunt Zena had thrown his Victrola and the records. Here the yard sloped down to the gully and was full of sharp limestone rocks swathed in a jungle of wild foliage — huge ferns and wild coco leaves and convolvulus. I had no thought in my head as I waded into this vegetation. Anansi webs wreathed my face and arms as I tore a path through the dew-wet leaves. I could see pieces of the records Aunt Zena had smashed, black shards on top of the rocks that rose above the plants, others lodged inside the coco leaves. Farther on, I found the turntable sitting on top of a rock, right side up. I forced the branches aside to reach it and stood there looking at it for a long time. I reached out my hand and gave it a slight push, which set it spinning. But only for a short time, for it was well and truly broken. Each time the spinning stopped I pushed it again, and I kept on doing that, over and over, until I couldn't stop. From it I was hearing a faint music that was made up of sadness, all the tears shed by all the sorrowful people in the world. By my father on his way to the asylum. It was as if I had to keep it going, this sad ribbon of music that was coming up from the turntable and running through my head, keep it going so that my father would never reach his destination. He'd keep on going and going until he came back round to me. I kept looking down and spinning with my hand and hearing that music. Until I could feel it pulling me down into this vortex, into this place where all the sad people were, and I wanted to go and join them. But it seemed with all the spinning the world was expanding, moving so swiftly, everything amplified. Tears were falling out of my eyes and onto the turntable, tears as big as the dewdrops that still clung to the coco leaves, for we were on the shaded side of the house and the sun hadn't yet penetrated. I could hear the sound of my tears falling, the drops speeding up to match the speeding of my heart until it became a solid wall of noise like a huge wave breaking over me. I remember feeling my bare feet sink into the damp earth, and I must have fainted, for when they found me some time later I was lying on the ground, unconscious.

I lay in bed for a long time, not saying or doing anything. They had the doctor in. Their biggest concern, I could tell from the snatches of conversation that broke through my fog, was that I was *going off*. Just like my father.

I don't know how long I stayed like that. Until Aunt Zena

got angry enough. One morning she came in, whipped the sheet off me, and hauled me out of bed.

"Get up, get up," she said. "This has gone on long enough. School starts next week and you are going to go. So, Missy, you had better get yourself ready."

She forced me out of my nightgown and into clothes and pushed me out the door. She did it so fast, I had no time to think. From that day, I simply went along with what they said I should do, who I should be. I felt as if my head was stuffed with cotton wool, that cobweb still clung to me. They took care to knock the stuffing out of the rest of me then tie me up tight, after I had been purged with castor oil and bitterwood drink. By the time I turned into a young lady, as they expressed it, I was bursting out. I was forced into brassieres and corsets and stockings and tight shoes, my hair pulled back so tightly and tied that my forehead hurt. It was as if Aunt Zena and Miss Celia were determined to rein me in, squeeze out vulgarity — madness and sluttishness. Which they did, for my feelings were locked down too. I never thought of my father. Never conjured up my mother. Never felt anything at all until that day Charles Leacroft Samphire came into my life. I certainly threw off the reins then. Or so I thought.

57

SOME WEEKS LATER, MR. BRIDGES came back to the question of my father. We were sitting on the veranda, he sipping his Scotch and soda and I sitting, doing nothing. Out of the blue he brought up the subject. He's funny like that, he'll let things slide and then he'll reintroduce the topic when you've forgotten, as if he'd been turning the whole thing over in his mind. This time when he mentioned my father I didn't get all choked up as I had before. I had in fact seen my father one more time and my heart was broken all over again. But I was much older then, hugely pregnant with my first child, with Celia.

"It all came and went so quickly that it's almost a dream. His coming back," I told Mr. Bridges, fishing in my mind for the details of that day. "In all the excitement my waters broke and the baby came so quickly, I didn't have time to think about anything else. It was only afterwards, that I started to worry and wonder ..."

"What happened?"

"He just vanished again."

"Vanished?"

"Yes. Sam was at home that day, as I was due. He had sent to call the midwife. I don't know where he was exactly when my father suddenly appeared, but I remember afterwards hearing their voices out in the yard, Sam and Georgie, a cousin of his who was visiting."

"Your father just came back? After all those years?"

"Yes. I had no idea where he'd been. I suppose he was in Kingston in Bellevue but I really didn't know. His name was never mentioned by Miss Celia or Aunt Zena, at least not in front of me. To tell you the truth, after he left, I only thought about him occasionally. Those thoughts were so painful I always forced them back down. I didn't want to know."

"So how did he find you?"

"That's just it, I don't know if he knew that it was me living there or if he was just wandering around and turned into our yard by chance."

Talking about it now, I could still see the scene so vividly, me standing on our veranda, my hands on my big belly, sort of dreaming about this baby ready to pop out. I was not afraid at all. I probably had a smile on my face, when this apparition, I can only call it that, came through the gate.

"The minute I saw him I knew, I just knew it was my father." I had to pause to slow myself down, for I was feeling as excited as I did that day. "I wanted to run to him, but of course I couldn't move very fast. When I got up closer I could see it was him in truth. But I was so shocked. He was such an old man, filthy, thin to the point of vanishing, his hair long and uncombed, most of his teeth gone. But I already had my arms open. 'Papa,' I cried.

"He had this silly grin on his face the whole time, but when he heard me call out he stopped and looked at me. A smile broke on his face. I thought he recognized me. He held out his arms to embrace me, or so I thought, and I moved towards him. I didn't care what state he was in, I was just happy to see him."

I paused, envisaging the scene again. How my father held out his arms and I thought it was to greet me, but then he clapped his hands together and opened them and looked at his palms and laughed and then he spun around and did the same thing, clapped his hands together before opening them, looking and laughing in glee. As he continued to turn round and round, over and over, reaching up high sometimes, first one side then the other, I realized he hadn't recognized me at all, he was chasing and killing mosquitoes or some other flying insect that only he could see.

I think at some point I must have cried out, for I remember hearing the voices of Sam and Georgie and then Sam holding me and getting me into my room and onto the bed. After that I remember very little except the baby coming in a great rush.

After telling this to Mr. Bridges, I must have sat there with a smile on my face, lost in the miracle of the moment, the birth of my child, for I was startled by his voice asking, "But what happened to him?"

I had to pull myself back to the thread of this other story.

"Well, yes, that's the strangest thing. When I finally asked about him, Sam said that after the midwife came and they knew the baby and I were all right, he and Georgie put him in Georgie's car and took him to the Richards house — Georgie was, like Sam, a relative on that side of the family. The Richardses claimed he never turned up, though Sam swears he opened the gate and they left him inside. Nobody seems to have seen him from that day to this. If Sam had not been there as a witness I would have thought I had dreamt the whole thing."

"So that was it then? Nobody reported it to the police or anything?"

"I don't know, I guess the Richardses might have done that. By this time everybody in the district knew he'd turned up again because Sam would have talked about it, I'm sure. But people just saw him as a madman anyway, so who would have cared about him?"

I paused then, thinking, and we sat in silence for a while. "It's just that I would give anything to know what happened to him. You know, it's like a hole in my heart. Of course when they found the skeleton, I thought about him all over again."

I wasn't looking at Mr. Bridges when I said this, I was so focused on the past, but I could sense him turning to stare at me and his voice seemed a bit sharp when he said, "My dear G, this is getting too dramatic. What skeleton?"

"Oh, this was a long time after, Celia was a big girl then, maybe four or five. Anyway, this man — a neighbour of ours — was bringing some new land under cultivation, on a little side track off the main road, nobody ever went down there really. It was all rocky stuff, bush, and he was working down the gully, very steep-sided, clearing it by burning, when he came across this skull. Well! You can imagine the excitement that caused. The police came and dug around and they found bones strewn all over that gully, probably scattered by animals, but when they assembled it, it was all the bones of one person."

"And you think …?"

"I don't know what to think. But no one else went missing in those parts, as far as I know. Of course it wasn't like now when they have all sorts of fancy ways of making identification. DNA and that sort of thing."

"So did you tell the police about your father?"

"Well, I wanted to, but Sam was dead set against it, I didn't dare. He just kept saying we didn't want to get involved. I guess he was anxious about the baby too. 'Just imagine what he could have done to you. To the baby,' he kept saying. 'That madman. You didn't see how he was behaving when you were in labour. Me and Georgie had to tie him up. You were crazy to go out there to him. He could have killed you. He could have knocked you down.' Of course I knew that he wouldn't have. But Sam never listened to me. He was always saying I was lucky the baby didn't come out with a madman's mark."

That made me smile, for I remember the midwife agreeing with him about that.

"Madman's mark?" Mr. Bridges raised his eyebrows.

"You know how country people are," I explained. "They think shocks to the system of the pregnant mother will mark the baby in some physical way, though I can't imagine what a madman's mark would look like. Of course it was all nonsense, for the baby was perfect. I don't know if anyone else mentioned my father to the police but it was a nine days' wonder. They carted the bones away and we never heard anything more about it."

"You don't think …?"

"No, I don't think," I said firmly. I suddenly felt tired and headachy and I didn't want to pursue the matter any further. Thankfully, the dinner bell saved me.

58

IT WAS AS IF everyone from my past vanished the years I was having my children. When Junior was two, Aunt Zena died, much to everyone's surprise, for up to then she had been a hale and hearty woman. She had a massive stroke that took her off quite suddenly. I went to her funeral and stood at the back in both the church and the graveyard, not wanting to disturb any ghosts. She had never reconciled herself to me, though it wasn't for lack of trying on my part. I left without speaking to any of the family. After that, I did summon up my courage and for the first time in eight years walked up the front steps of their house, determined to see Miss Celia as she hadn't been at the funeral. I did see her, but it was as I had heard. She no longer recognized anyone. I still felt it as a blow that she didn't remember me. She otherwise seemed the same, older and more frail. She sat up in bed and chattered away while I was there, giving instructions to her helpers and behaving as if everything was quite normal. I tried to smile. But really, I wanted to weep, for looking on the spotted white skin now fragile as parchment, the straight fleshy nose, the silky white hair, the realization came to me that this woman was really my grandmother. My flesh and blood. For the first time it seemed real. In the years that I lived with them, I had never been encouraged to act as if this was so. No connections were ever made for me. But there she was, my father's mother. When I was leaving, I wanted to throw myself on the bed beside her and take her in my arms, but all I dared to do was bend down and touch my lips to her cheek. Surprisingly, she reached up her frail arms and put them around my neck and hugged me. I'm not sure who she thought I was. The gesture only pained me more, as if it were a mockery.

On leaving the house, I stood on the front steps and looked across at the faraway blue hills as I used to do as a child, believing then that they formed the rim of the world, a world that was nevertheless boundless. My own world had so narrowed, I could no longer fantasize about the pull of adventure out there. It was as if I'd found my place at last. Down to earth. Grounded.

I took a deep breath to steady myself, for I felt a kind of numbness creeping over me. I wasn't grounded at all. I was terrified by the knowledge that there was nothing to hold on to, all that had shored me up had crumbled, for Aunt Zena and Miss Celia were my last links to that past. And though they were the ones who refused to acknowledge my existence after I had run away, I still felt guilt for what I had done, for they had after all taken me in and cared for me in their own way. Whether they liked it or not, I was their child. They were the ones who had made me.

59

OF ALL THE PEOPLE at Ellesmere Lodge, Mr. Bridges goes out the most. He has lots of friends and relatives who come and take him out, and, although he says he hates travelling, he goes to Miami from time to time. That is as far as he will go, to stay with a sister. His children must travel from other parts of the States to come and see him. He gets lots of mail too, much of it with U.S. stamps, which is all I ever manage to glimpse. More and more he talks of moving back to his house. This makes sense since he is still quite fit and active, especially compared to most of the people at Ellesmere Lodge. Indeed, for an active person, as I am too, contemplation of the residents collectively is sometimes a depressing prospect, all white hair and glasses and walkers and orthopedic shoes — except for the high-heeled Pancake Sisters, of course — and snoozes and snores mid-morning and afternoon and drooling. There is probably a lot more life here than at similar places; still, the illnesses and operations, the life-sustaining medical interventions, and the endless discussions surrounding them are quite depressing. So are the vanishings, as I think of them — the people who are too ill or frail to stay at Ellesmere Lodge and who disappear, shifted elsewhere to places with hospital beds and bed pans and professional nursing care.

Equally distressing are the deaths, Babe's being the most shocking one. She took ill one day, was taken to the hospital, and was gone within a week. Ruby was to say later Babe had had so many medical interventions she was living on borrowed time. In our dismay at the suddenness of it all, I could see the other two, Ruby and Birdie, eyeing each other in a speculative way, as if to say, who will be next? Babe had a lovely funeral, her three children, grandchildren, and great-grands all came from abroad and saw to that, but apart from them and some of the Ellesmere Lodge residents and staff, the turnout was scanty. Like the rest of us, she had outlasted most of her contemporaries.

Shortly after Babe's death, Mr. Bridges said, out of the blue, "I am thinking of getting married again."

I looked at him, startled, my heart beating so fast I'm sure he could hear it, though on my face I never showed a thing. Is this a proposal, I thought? Should I say something? What should I do? I looked quizzically at him, hoping my face showed nothing but interest at the news. But he just turned his glass round and round and looked at it and smiled and said, "I really need to get back to my house. I was over there on Sunday and though Gerald does try, things are really in a mess."

I expected him to go on from there, back to the bit about marriage, wondering if I was up to the task of taking care of the house itself as well as things domestic, but then hadn't I done all these things on my own? But when I saw he planned to say nothing more, I turned back to my book to hide my confusion. I can't say I read a single word.

He never broached the subject again, though now he had planted the idea in my head, my fantasies began to get the better of me. It was at times like this that I truly wished that I had a friend, someone to share secrets with as the Pancake Sisters had done all their lives. Someone to bounce this one off to see if a ball had really been thrown into my court. I was so lacking in social skills I couldn't figure out a simple thing like that. I went to my room feeling the lowest I had felt for a long time: it made me realize how poverty-stricken I truly was.

60

I WONDER WHAT CELIA would say if I told her? I can't help turning this idea over in my mind. Would she laugh scornfully, be happy, disapproving? Or would she sit there, old stone face, with that slight natural upturn to the corners of her mouth — just like Shirley — that makes her expression seem so pleasant all the while, masking an interior life I know nothing about? I always wondered where she and Shirley got this lovely little feature that no one else in the family has. Was it perhaps something passed down from my mother? Was Shirley smiling when they shot her? Laughing with her big mouth in that joyful way of hers? What really happened to my daughter?

What was Shirley doing in New York, anyway? A mother should know a thing like that. But I seem to have lost my children like the mother hen is destined to lose her chicks. Only I could never replace mine over and over.

The day Shirley came to tell me she was going, she was so happy, in her usual excited manner. I was happy for her. I thought she had gotten a scholarship, for I knew she had applied. Until she told me her father was paying for it. I don't know. Just the mention of their father in those days was enough to drive me crazy — it drew out of me all the pent-up anger, the words I never spoke otherwise, and unfortunately my children were the ones those words fell on. It wasn't because he was paying, I wanted him to pay and pay and pay. It was just the way she spoke of him, Shirley who had hated him as much as I did, the way she said "Pops" now in this loving tender manner, which let me know that to her he was more than a bank account. I just stood there and said "Pops?" Something in the tone of my voice triggered that angry reaction in her. For she immediately launched into such a defence of him. Which of course ended up with a devastating attack on me. My God! What did that man do to earn such a whitewash?

Silence. Silence can sever as effectively as a knife. I never once told my children about my own childhood, my past, my relationship to the Richardses, they only knew that we were somehow related. So when Shirley flung at me that day to conclude her narrative of my bad qualities, "Not even your own family would talk to you!" I should have realized the power of that silence, its potential to surround the heart and squeeze it dry. In knowing nothing about me, Shirley knew nothing about her own past; she was as lacking in anchorage as I was. How was I different from the Richardses and their refusal to speak of anything to do with my history, of my mother?

61

SOMETIMES I WISH I had someone to talk to, especially now, when I am forced to think about these things, for one can't live in the world today without becoming aware of one's own shortcomings, of how the past loops around to choke off the present. Or, perhaps, of how one can undo the knots, set the past free. I am confronted with all of them, the advice-givers, whichever way I turn, the Oprahs and the Doctor Phils. If these oh-so-confident talkers are to be believed, by facing the past we can find our own strengths in the present, to overcome the mountains to be climbed and conquered. Or in my case the pit to crawl out of. I try not to put too much trust in these people; they are foreign and get rich from this sort of thing, so how can they be trusted. But I'm a majority of one, it seems, for their aura, their authority penetrates even into the kitchen.

Even the two young beauticians, Morveen and Kyisha, are constantly quoting psychobabble though I'm not sure they understand what it means. I can't escape it in the glamour and beauty magazines the Pancake Sisters pass on to me.

Shirley was beautiful enough, in her own way, but she wasn't obsessed with her looks, like Lise. Shirley was more into herself, I think now, into finding out who she was. Did she? Was that what it was all about? Every time I think of Shirley I'm tempted to pick up her picture and wonder. Try not to open the old biscuit tin and look.

I never gave them much of an anchor, did I? I launched them on the great sea of life and then I just let them drift off until they disappeared beyond the horizon.

62

SOMETIMES I ASK MYSELF, now that my heart seems to be opening wider, did I really love any of them? And when I am feeling sorry for myself: Did anyone ever love me? And now sometimes I ask: Why am I feeling like this? Is it love?

63

MATRON IS ALL EXCITEMENT these days, I don't know what's gotten into her, but she's more fluttery and buttery than usual. Ruby swears she's got a man, which leads Birdie to question in her sweet way, "What ever did she do with the first one?"

For Matron is Mrs. Spence. She is the Director, as she keeps telling me, for I am the only one who calls her Matron. The rest who've been here a long time call her by her first name: Delice, pronounced De-Lees. Which I think is much too nice a name for her: Delice Spence. But I have to confess she's been awfully nice to me lately, always stopping to exchange a few words, to rave about our latest vegetables, to compliment me on a dress or a new hairstyle, for I've gotten quite vain and experimental, I must confess, to Morveen's delight. Not a single complaint from Matron in months. I think it's all because of Mr. Bridges. Matron is a romantic at heart. Romance is all she ever reads, and she rushes to her cottage every evening to watch the soaps. She is very caught up in them, if her avid discussion with the other fans at our residence, including those in the kitchen, is anything to go by. Even Winston surprises me sometimes with his knowledge of these matters, as I learn from overhearing the post-lunch conversation of the domestic staff when they are relaxing outside the kitchen.

I think all of this soap opera business has given Matron the idea that something is going on between me and Mr. Bridges and marriage is imminent, which explains her breathlessness, for nothing untoward seems to be happening in her life. She keeps telling me about that old couple in their eighties who met at a retirement home in the city and how they got married and had their pictures in the papers. "On TV, Mrs. Samphire, imagine!" Of course she didn't tell me, as Ruby did, referring to them as "silly old fools," that neither survived the shock of new-found love longer than six months. I just smile at Matron and everyone else, for the only evidence they have is that

Mr. Bridges and I spend an awful lot of time together, but all of it in the open.

What do we do in this time? We garden, we sit companionably and read, we listen to music occasionally, we go for walks around the grounds, we talk. Mr. Bridges is impeccable in his politeness, and says nothing more of marriage, although he still talks of going back to his house. Why he hesitates to make that move I don't know since there is nothing stopping him that I can see. But of late I've noticed a restlessness in him, a subtle ruffling of the surface, a slight shifting of his attention from the matter at hand, as if he is not quite as focused as he used to be. And I wonder what is the matter, is he feeling unwell? But I dare not ask. And soon off he goes to Miami again, as he seems to be doing more and more.

64

I AM PLEASED TO see that Mr. Bridges has come back from his latest trip seeming like his old self, all confidence and smiles, his distracted air vanished. He's gone over to his old house several times in the past week, to take an inventory, he says, of what work needs to be done. I'm a little disappointed that he doesn't invite me to go along at some point, as I feel I could be useful, but I guess he knows what's best. He has roped in a young relative, an architect, to help him. In any event, he has not invited me to go on any of his forays outside of Ellesmere Lodge, so this is nothing unusual. But he does report back to me when he returns.

What an appalling recital his inventory is. What an awfully long time it will take to put things right, I'm thinking. My heart sinks. For Mr. Bridges is the kind of perfectionist, in his person and his home, who will do nothing until everything is arranged to his complete satisfaction.

65

MAYBE THE WORD HAS gotten to me, but last night after dinner, back in my room, I took an inventory of myself. I laughed at my foolishness when I was finished and vowed to tear the page out, but it's still here and I think I'll leave it to remind myself how silly I've become.

My own personal inventory:

Body: in quite good shape for a woman my age, I would say, especially one who has been so battered about by life. I've always had good posture, drummed into me by Aunt Zena. I hold myself straight, and while I'm not fashionably slim, I've got myself back down to what one might call nicely uphol-stered. Not too stuffed. Or, maybe pleasingly plump? It helps to be tall, for the weight is quite evenly distributed. I would say I'm well proportioned. So I wear clothes well. It helps to have such nice things too. I mean, I have big breasts and I do have a bit of a bottom. A belly, too, if I am perfectly honest, but it's okay with the right clothes.

Face: Well, there's where I think I would score myself much higher now than I would have done in the past. Paying attention to my skin and hair does make a difference. My hair is thick, extremely coarse and curly, and I've always worn it pulled back from my head and tied in a knot. But a nicely shaped cut that frames my face has done wonders, as has a little straightening and the light henna that Morveen insisted that I try. The colour sits much better with my skin tone, she says, which she brightens up with foundation and highlighter.

With all the gardening my skin has gone from the colour of putty back to sultana raisin. Some people might consider that too dark, but that's their problem. Dark is now beautiful. Not that I would ever call myself beautiful, but I am saved by my high cheekbones, which give my broad face character. At least I think so now. Not too many wrinkles. Well, that's a matter of opinion, but when I smile I do look quite nice. Even to myself. Note: Smile more!

My eyes, which have always been a muddy brown colour, are beginning to look a bit washed out, but I think that's just old age. The touch of blue shadow does help to bring them out, and they are a nice size and properly spaced, though when Morveen told me that I told her she was talking foolishness. How vain I've become. I only wear glasses for reading and close work, but I could do with a more fashionable pair. My hearing is okay, I think. Well, excellent, I'd say. If only some people knew!

My nose, oh my nose, it is still too big and flat, I wish I had inherited my father's, but I guess it goes with my face, which is rather large, and what the fashion magazines would call triangular shape. Too large, maybe. I don't know, sometimes it looks just too big to me, with those cheekbones. It goes with the rest. Like my lips. Much too big, but Morveen has shown me how to reduce the effect with lipstick and lipliner, if you please. I haven't paid this much attention to myself since Charles Samphire first started to gaze at me. But what he saw I will never know. I wonder what Mr. B sees?

I can't do much about the size of my hands and feet, but after the monthly attention from the manicurist, my hands and nails would be rated passable, even at elegant dinner parties, I would say.

In addition, I tick off: I am intelligent, well-spoken, very well read, a good listener, willing to learn new things, know how to set and eat at a good table. Thank you, Aunt Zena. I could tackle the repair of a house or just about anything else if I had to, and I have all my own teeth, thanks to my mother, I think. Very healthy, with no scars visible unless I take off all my clothes. Must make a note to do so only when other people take off their glasses.

66

I HAVEN'T OPENED THIS notebook for such a long time. I don't want to open my eyes ever but I promised her and I will I will maybe tomorrow.

67

WHO ARE WE TO question the will of the gods???? (William Shakespeare or maybe Sophocles.)

68

I'VE TOLD HER I really must go back home I can't stay here one minute longer and she says she understands and she has promised and this time she really means it I think but says they have to finish the repairs first. I feel guilty because I know it's going to cost a lot and I haven't a red cent of my own. I tell her that she doesn't have to do everything at once I just need one sound room to live in. She tells me not to worry it's all being taken care of. I don't know if I should believe her or not. These days I don't know what to believe.

69

SHE DID SAY I could come and live with them in the meantime if I wanted to. They'd love to have me. Well, that's a new one. Nearly two years too late. Thanks but no thanks. I've had enough of people.

70

WHAT I CAN'T STAND is everyone being so bloody cheerful with me. Even that bloody Matron. She keeps popping in, in her breezy little way. "And how are we today?" We???? God, I could strangle that woman.

71

LOTS OF VISITORS COME, at least the ones whose immune systems won't be compromised by a sickroom. But I don't want them here. I don't want anyone. The only one I can stand is Ruby, who arrives in the afternoon wearing some outlandish outfit. I can hear her coming down the passage, signalled by the tinkling of ice cubes in her cocktail shaker of dry martini. In her other hand she bears a martini glass with two olives and a cigarette pack with her gold Ronson lighter pushed inside it and exactly two cigarettes, for since Babe's death she has been good at rationing herself. She bangs on the door with the hand holding the shaker, enters, and uses her bony hip to push the door shut.

Without saying anything, but smiling and waving the shaker, the diamonds surrounding her large sapphire ring almost blinding me, she totters grandly to the armchair where she lowers herself carefully. She puts her burdens down on the small side table and then crosses her legs at the knees, leaving me to wonder how on earth she manages that at her age. She pours herself a drink, dropping one of the olives back into the shaker for the second glass, and with glass in one hand, cigarette in the other, and one shoe dangling, she salutes me. And then, between sips and puffs, she talks non-stop about herself or whatever else she is interested in at the moment. None of this "and how are we today" foolishness.

Sometimes she comes with Birdie and they spend their entire time arguing about the name of some girl they knew in school seventy years ago, totally ignoring me, which I like.

Poor Birdie is getting so shaky she can't always manage the stairs. This afternoon Ruby comes alone, a vision in silk capri pants with matching pink wedge-heeled mules, and a swirly chiffon top that would outdo any of Matron's for colour and floatability. I don't even bother to listen to Ruby, but I like to watch her, a beautiful, wind-battered macaw, and after her visit I always feel a little better.

I'm actually sick, not pretending as some who know my circumstances might think, a bad flu that I seemed to have got over but which then knocked me down again with a touch of bronchitis thrown in. Now I sound like a macaw. Yet people would expect me to be feeling a lot worse, if only they knew.

72

Even though I was feeling physically okay, except for a little chestiness, I probably would never have gotten out of that bed, could easily have just given up and died, if I hadn't had another visitor that same day. It was Annie who serves in the dining room and brings my dinner up on a tray for me, so she wasn't a real visitor as she does that every day.

Annie usually lingers, and chatters a bit in a cheerful kind of way, as she goes about adjusting the drapes, checking my bathroom for clean towels, straightening out the room, and generally looking around to see that everything is right, even though it isn't her job. She's good that way. Annie is at least in her thirties, if her fifteen-year-old daughter is anything to go by, but she looks like a teenager herself with her smart little cane rows or intricate locks, tied back on the job, out and flashing once she's changed into fashionable spandex street wear and headed for the bus stop, or waiting for her current taxi driver boyfriend. Annie has delicate features and a trim body that looks stylish even in the ugly green or pink uniform dresses. She is cheerful and cheeky, and often manages to coax a smile out of the most miserable, as if getting smiles all round was part of her duty. I could never understand how anyone with a life so hard could be so consistently cheerful. Three children and a bedridden grandmother to look after. No male help in sight. I guess it's just a question of personality.

I really like Annie, but during the time that I've been lying here, feeling miserable, I've been annoyed by her presence as I have been by everyone's. So whenever she came I would close my eyes and ignore her. Never mind, she always had some sass on her lips before leaving, often along the lines of, "You'd better eat something today, Miss Sam, or you draw down to nutten. See if any of your nice clothes can fit you then. You might have to give them to me." This was a laugh, as everything I owned would go twice around Annie. I imagined her rolling her eyes and chuckling as she closed the door. Even though I ignored her, Annie's coming was something I looked forward to.

But that evening I heard Annie's soft opening of the door as usual. I shut my eyes and waited for her usual greeting. It never came. I could hear the sounds that told me she had come inside and was pulling up the small table and placing the tray on it, unrolling the napkin from the ring and flapping it open to tie around my neck — for she ignored my protests and insisted on the niceties. But apart from what sounded like a sniffle, not a sound came, and I wondered who it was if not Annie. So I opened my eyes just as she reached towards me with the napkin. I was startled to see such a different Annie from the one I was used to, for her face was puffy and her eyes were red and filled with tears. Our eyes locked as I opened mine and I was so shocked at her state that I spoke. I croaked out "Annie?" before she burst into tears.

"Oh Miss Sam," she wailed. "You up here. You don't know what is happening out there in the world. You just don't know."

I had no idea what she was talking about, but her agony actually made me sit up in the bed. When she continued to sob, I found myself swinging around to put my feet on the floor and patting a place on the bed beside me.

"Annie, look," I said. "Leave that." For she had moved to take the covers off the dishes. "Sit down. Sit here and tell me about it. What is happening? What are you talking about?"

She perched on the edge of the chair, but it took some time to get the story out of her. It was Cookie she said, Cookie's grandson, Trevor, had been shot. By the police.

"Shot dead, you mean?"

"Yes'm. Him and three other youth. In a house over where they live. In Cumberland."

That name meant nothing to me, but I knew the boy, Trevor. A bright, tall young man who was going to a good high school, was on the athletics and the debating teams, and was the pride of his grandmother who was raising him as his mother lived abroad and had not been heard from in years.

Cookie's real name was Icilda Samms, as I discovered when I helped her to fill out a form, but she was called "Cookie" by everyone. She introduced herself that way, with pride, for she was undisputed mistress of catering at Ellesmere Lodge.

Cookie's forty or so years as a servant in other people's kitchens had taken their toll, for she was overweight, bulbous in shape, and diabetic, her legs wormy with huge varicose veins, bunions peeping out of the men's brown sandals she slopped around in, her round face constantly shiny from kitchen grease. Her snowy white hair under her cap was unstraightened and braided in fat, unfashionable little plaits. Every cent she earned went to keep Trevor and his two younger sisters. Cookie was the opposite of Annie, of a serious and unsmiling disposition, unless the subject was Trevor, when her face became transformed as the frowns creased upwards into smiles. Poor Cookie! The news of this young boy's death was so shocking it pushed everything else from my mind.

"But how? What were they doing?"

"Nothing, Miss. They weren't doing nothing."

Annie sounded defensive, and I realized why. I had automatically assumed that the boys had to be guilty. I was right, for her voice was rising. "Miss Sam, you know how the police stay aready. Them is murderer! Kill the poor boys them in cold blood!"

"But what was Trevor doing there?" I asked, for I was still trying to sort this out in a rational kind of way. As far as I knew Trevor lived with his grandmother, but where that was in relation to the place where the killings took place I didn't know, for I was not familiar with the city.

"Is Trevor cousin live there, and some other boys. Trevor was visiting his cousin. Police say is bad man living there in the house, druggist, and that one of them shoot a policeman, but nutten nuh go so. Is pure young fellows. The house belong to one of them mother that abroad right now. In New York. She just gone last week to earn a little money to finish the tiling. And now this is what happen."

Yes, there we go again, I thought. The earthly paradise. That is also where Trevor's mother was last heard from.

"Miss Sam, they just surround the house on every side, with their M16 and then the one name Samson, the bad-man Inspector, just hail them up over the loudspeaker and tell them to come out." Annie's voice was passionate with conviction. "And everybody say they were coming out with their hands up when the police just rain bullets down on the house. Through the door, the windows, everywhere. Trevor and his cousin was on the front porch already with their hands in the air when they cut them down."

She stopped then, and I could feel my heart hammering as I tried to visualize the horror of the scene.

"Now the police saying is the boys shoot first. Miss Sam, they go in afterwards and plant gun on them."

"When was this, Annie?"

She paused to pluck another tissue from the bedside table to wipe her eyes.

"Three days ago, mam. Matron said not to tell you. She going to vex with me. For she say right now your system can't take anything more. I didn't mean to cry, but I can't stop for I thinking, suppose those children was any of mine? But I know how you stay, Miss Sam. You would want to know."

"You're right, Annie. I'm okay now." I tried to work my stiff mouth into a smile for her sake. "So where is Cookie now?"

"She just finish up dinner so she must be gone home by now. Still have the little ones to look after."

"You mean, she didn't take any time off?"

"She take the one day off to go and identify Trevor body. That's all she could do. Mrs. Spence say she should go but she don't want to stop work for she say she would die if she just sit down and do nothing. They wouldn't even let her talk to anybody in authority down there. Mr. Levy trying to help her find out what is what. But nobody not saying nothing. And what the police saying is pure pure lie. Everybody know it."

She paused for a bit of nose blowing and then seemed to get up some steam, for she waved her hands about and her voice rose higher. "Big big thing, you know, Miss Sam! People talking bout nothing else. How them gun down the poor black people pikni in cold blood. Nothing else on the news but that. Cookie all pon television and everything. When she did go down to view the body."

Despite the grimness of the story, Annie couldn't keep the excitement out of her voice at the mention of television. She was even smiling a bit, as she replayed the scene. "Same way she leave here you know, Miss Sam, when them come tell her the news. The people from her yard come up in taxi for her for they never want to phone. Same way she on television in her uniform and apron and everything as she rush down there. Don't even take time to tidy herself. Right on the seven o'clock news."

Then Annie turned serious again and wiped her eyes as the tears flowed afresh. "God know when they will release Trevor body for burial. Post-mortem and all them ting. You wonder why when everybody know what happen already. Is that really burning her up now. When she will ever get Trevor body to bury."

It was at the word *body* that I burst into tears.

73

WHO WAS I CRYING for then? Trevor? Cookie? Myself? I asked myself that question as I lay awake all night, turning it over and over in my mind, refusing to face up to the real reason. It was the first time I had cried, and it had taken me a long time to convince poor Annie that she could leave me, it wasn't her fault, she hadn't upset me, I was upset for Trevor and Cookie. Crying was good for me, as it was for her, for all of us. I told her this, over and over. Then I had to make her swear that she would say nothing to Matron before I could get her to leave. It was true, crying was good, for the next day it got me out of bed and on my feet, though I was still a bit shaky.

But it wasn't the crying that got me up the next morning. It was admitting to myself that I had been living a lie for so long, pretending I was this bona fide lady. Cushioned in this little cocoon my daughter had prepared for me. Buying into the notion that somehow I belonged here in this closed little world. That it was my birthright and the rest was all a mistake. For though I had kept saying I wanted to go back home, in truth the longer I stayed the more I was seduced by the ease of living in a place where people were there to meet my needs. Poor people. Like those I came from. The ones who couldn't afford to take too much time off from work even when their children were killed. A place where comfort and safety could be bought by high walls and wired gates and floodlights and alarms and security systems.

Comfort and security had made me forget about a real world out there, where children are dying every day from drugs or gang warfare, abandonment to the streets or police brutality. That wasn't my world, it is true, that world of urban violence and anarchy. Like many country folk I have been untouched by the violence, viewing it as a city affair, but when I think back to my own little corner of the world, I can see it was there too, waiting to burst out. Hadn't I seen the seeds of rage even in my own son so many years ago? I see it festering in a new generation of children who sit idly on the bridge, watching the world go by, smoking ganja. Armed with guns now, not knives. Just weeks before I left home, our local shopkeeper was shot, and the post office had been held up by armed men more than once. There were rumours of cocaine use and crack houses nearby. Burglar bars were beginning to go up in even the humblest of houses. People no longer sat out on their verandas at night.

When Mr. Bridges said it would be dangerous for me to return home, a woman alone, he was not being sensational. Elderly women who live alone are now prime targets, if the record number killed in the last few years is anything to go by. Many were women of distinction, women of prominence living on their own. Their years of service to the nation, to education or social work, medicine or politics, provided no more immunity to being shot or battered to death than the poor widow living on her mite in the shantytowns.

But that night, following Annie's news, I wasn't thinking of how vulnerable I myself would be back home. I was thinking about how vulnerable I had allowed myself to become, once the hurricane had swept my old life away and deposited me here like flotsam. I had come close to losing the one thing that had kept me going all these years, that had stiffened me against apathy and despair. And that, simply, was rage. After the first few years of my marriage it was a silent rage against my husband and everything that flowed from my connection with him, but over the years since then I have come to learn it was a rage that was probably always in me. Rage perhaps born from that moment my mother ceased to hold me to her breast — or is that too fanciful? Ceased to let me feel her warmth, hear the sound of her voice. Throughout my life I have experienced loneliness, anger, guilt, shame, remorse, and shame again. But only in recent times have I allowed these feelings to overwhelm me, for I have lost my backbone, undermined by the seduction of the soft life, the promise of comfort. The things that I now know were never meant for me.

The next day, after some fitful sleep towards morning, I got out of bed at my usual hour and got dressed and went down to the kitchen. Later, at what I considered a decent hour

I phoned my daughter. But all I got was a recording, so I left a message asking if she had heard about Cookie's grandson being shot. I knew that she already would have known and no doubt sprung into action, for she was like that. I said nothing in the message about myself, but I knew that it would be enough of a signal that I was getting back to normal.

74

MARK YOU, NORMAL IS not a word I should ever use again in relation to myself, for the events of the last few weeks have convinced me more than ever that I have no idea what normal is. Normal is a universe that is predictable and trustworthy. But I now know that my own understanding of people, of life, is abnormal and deficient. That the life I have lived so far is narrow to a fault, and that insular though the life of Ellesmere Lodge is, it has taught me more in the time I have been here than all the previous years had. Take even the response of the domestic staff when I came into the kitchen, and I'd come specially early to avoid the other residents and Matron. I had gone there to commiserate with Cookie, but it was they who were busily comforting me. As I walked in and gave Cookie a hug, I was truly amazed by the warmth of their greetings, their questions about how I was feeling. As if that mattered now in the wider scheme of things. I asked Maisie if she could bring breakfast to my room as usual, I wasn't yet ready to face the dining room. But really, I was feeling so humbled, it made me decide to face my demons and write down everything that has occurred to so disturb what I had considered to be my new-found equilibrium.

75

I HAD TO ASK Maisie when she came what the date was. Then I had to check the calendar for myself, for I didn't believe it. I have no idea where three weeks of my life went. Three weeks to the day! Which started off so normal. Nothing untoward. No hint of summer lightning. A bit of time in the garden, mainly just standing and looking things over. It's the height of summer, hot and dry. There is little work to be done. I did a bit of reading. At lunchtime I endured our new table-mate, who was foisted on us following Babe's death. He waxed long and boringly on the subject of double indemnity. He was an ex–insurance man, light brown, huge shock of white hair, black horn-rimmed glasses, full of himself. Talk talk. Lecture the little ladies. Then back to my room where I was taking in some of my dresses, using a little hand machine Matron has released into my care.

I hadn't seen Mr. Bridges at all since I glimpsed him at breakfast and I assumed he was once again off to do battle with his house or the architect nephew. I was sort of lost in the sewing, in the afternoon lull, a sleepiness that seemed to fall over everything in the hours after lunch, for I found myself nodding off. I'd just decided to give up on the sewing and have a little rest when there was a tap on my door. I knew right away it was Mr. Bridges. A very discreet "rat-tat." Pause.

"Rat-tat." I took off the glasses I wear for close work, and I rushed to primp in the mirror and straighten my dress before I opened the door.

As usual, my eyes, all my senses, took Mr. Bridges in, every inch of him, from his sparse salt and pepper hair, meticulously cut very, very low, almost disguising the balding at the top, to his thin but attractive raisin brown face, with the two vertical creases on either side of his nose, to his equally familiar everyday attire: brown tasselled loafers without socks, chinos, plaited brown leather belt, short-sleeved white cotton shirt or — today — white Lacoste shirt, neatly tucked in. Everything looking as neat and pressed and perfect on him as if he had stepped out of a magazine. Even his glasses appear to have been designed just for him, rimless, feather-light with no bifocal lines, looking as if they are hardly there so his eyes come through clearly. Bright as a mouse.

"Hello G," he said, and I noticed he had his mail and some CDs in his hand. He smiled and asked, "How are you?" And when I smiled and said, "Fine," he said, "Can you come across for a minute?" He waved the packet to indicate his door. "There's something I want to say to you." Say? I didn't know why, but though nothing showed, I felt some kind of current, a slight stumbling of the air between us.

"Sure," I said. Leaving my door wide open, I moved with him to his room. There seems to be some sort of unspoken etiquette that while I may go into Mr. Bridges' room, it would not do for him to cross the threshold of mine.

76

I DON'T KNOW WHAT I expected when I went into Mr. Bridges' room. Probably just hearing some new music he was excited about, for that is usually what a summons meant, and he had that same air of gaiety about him as he did when he brought home something new. But this time he didn't head for the stereo as he usually did, inviting me with a wave of the hand to sit on the couch. As soon as we got inside he closed the door — most unusual! — and he turned to me.

"G," he said, "there's something I want to tell you. Nobody else, for now."

He was smiling, with an air of suppressed excitement when he said it, which made me feel almost faint, I was so sure what was to come. But then, instead of continuing, he went to the player and said, in a jocular kind of way, "Let's have a little music then." He looked at the CDs he had bought and read off the names of the performers of each one: "Buddy Holly" — whom I had never heard of — "Ray Charles, the Temptations. Let's see. How about a little Buddy Holly — I used to be crazy about him — just when I first started going to dances and of course I was too shy to dance. But he's so great. He's stood the test of time."

He put on the CD and I put on the headphones as the music came pouring out. It was music that I liked. I automatically started tapping my feet and moving my shoulders to it. The music played on, and I guess we both would have looked comical to an observer, two oldsters wearing headphones and tapping our feet and moving our bodies, I sitting on the couch and Mr. Bridges standing and waving both hands about, swaying his head and singing along. I was so caught up in the silliness of it all I forgot for a moment the important news that Mr. Bridges said he had to impart. He stopped that song and waved another of the CDs at me. "The Temptations," he said. "Songs of our misspent youth. The sixties. Remember?"

I smiled and nodded, but of course I had no pleasant memory of the sixties, it had all passed me by in a haze of loneliness. So I was surprised to hear the soulful outpouring of men's voices in beautiful harmony. I smiled more broadly at Mr. Bridges, but again he seemed lost in the music, moving his upper body, singing the words. This was a new Mr. Bridges to me, relaxed, almost boyish. I took that for such a good sign I found myself caught up in the rhythms of this music too, for my whole body started swaying.

Suddenly he said, "Come, G, let's dance," and he held out his arms to me. "You've been dying to dance with me from my very first day here," he added, but he laughed when he said it. "Now's your chance."

I laughed, too, as I moved where he led, for though it was not the song I had waited for so long to hear, it was as if destiny was at work and we had moved, he and I, into a complete circle. He drew me close but not tight, and my feet and body seemed to move as light as the wind over wynne grass as I followed him.

"You're a good natural dancer," he said after a while. I was surprised to find I was. I had no difficulty following him. One more thing to add to my inventory.

The song ended and another began, but I hardly noticed

the break I was so happy to be in a place where I felt I was meant to be. This transition from friend to Mr. Bridges' arms seemed so natural that I must have entered a dream state because I was jerked back to the moment when he suddenly stopped dancing and I stumbled. I opened my eyes and I saw that he had turned serious again, and he was looking into the distance with a rather strained expression. Again I felt that slight displacement in the atmosphere, like a night hawk or a bat flying at dusk so it is barely seen, just a flash of something not quite as it should be, but so slight it is difficult to tell if it is really there. He seemed to pull himself back from whatever place he had momentarily gone to and we started to move again. After a few minutes he started talking while we kept moving to the beat.

"G, you of all people know how I've wanted to move back to my house." Was it my heart that went *dah dah dah* along with the Temptations? "But not alone." *Dah dah*. "Well," he laughed, "my children would not let me, even if I wanted to." *Dah dah dah dah dah*. "Now, I've finally found the right …"

Even now I'm wondering if I missed something here, if my thoughts were so focused on what I thought Mr. Bridges was going to say that I missed that beat of his own heart, out of sync. It was all so sudden. He stopped speaking as if he had choked on the last word, made one little gasp, and slumped against me. I moved to hold him up as he swayed. He made another kind of choking sound as I half-carried him over to the bed and lay him down, put his feet up, but by then his body was as unresponsive as a sack.

I'm writing about this now in a rational kind of way, but it happened so fast that all I felt was blind panic. I didn't know what to do, for I had never been confronted by this kind of situation before. I lightly slapped his cheek and called his name, as if he was a child in a faint, then I thought, water, and then I remembered about the tablets he told me he had to take. I dashed for the bathroom and the medicine cabinet, but I got no further than the door, for the bathroom counter itself was covered in pill bottles, an enormous number of them, many with prescription labels. I picked one or two up and tried to read the labels, but they meant nothing to me, for I had paid no attention when the other residents talked about their ailments and medications.

I went back to the bedroom and Mr. Bridges hadn't moved from where I had placed him. I put my hand on his heart and felt nothing, and it seemed to me that he wasn't breathing. He's dead, I thought, my own heart fluttering so wildly I thought it would burst. I had the insane idea that I needed to hold a mirror up to see if he was breathing. The next thought that flashed into my head was, I've killed him. It was like my father all over again. My fatal curse. I must have wrung my hands and spun around a few times and whimpered and then I opened the door and dashed out of the room, uncertain what to do. I don't remember pounding on the door of the next room, not even conscious of whose room it was. But I did recognize Mr. Levy's voice when he called out, "Who is it?"

"Please, Mr. Levy," I said, "it's Mr. Bridges. I've killed him. You have to come. Do something." I know my voice was rising higher and higher and my hysteria must have conveyed itself to the old gentleman. For in short order he was there, shirtless in his merino, zipping up his pants, concern on his face.

"Mrs. Samphire, what is it?"

I could only point to Mr. Bridges' room, I was so frightened that no words came and the sound of my own heart was now so loud it was drowning out everything else.

I made to follow Mr. Levy in, but he stopped me at the door. "Wait here, please." I instinctively reacted to the voice of authority and leaned against the wall, feeling faint, distanced, as if my head was filling up with cotton wool. Mr. Levy was in the room for a long time. I heard his voice and at first I thought he had roused Mr. Bridges, but realized he was speaking on the phone. When he came out the door he seemed surprised to see me still standing there. He put his hands on my shoulders, steadying me. The way he said, "My dear Mrs. Samphire," I knew, and I got hysterical all over again.

"Oh my god, I killed him, I killed him," I kept on saying over and over. Mr. Levy in his calm, old-world manner, soothing me, trying to calm me, then pulling me to him and putting my head on his shoulder, putting his arms around me and patting me. "Mrs. Samphire, you haven't killed anyone, Mr. Bridges has probably had a heart attack ..."

"No," I shouted, pulling myself away. "You don't understand. We were dancing and ... I did ... whatever it was, I caused it. Don't you understand?"

Now it was I holding on to Mr. Levy and shaking him. He

gently disengaged my hands and steered me towards my room door and marched me backwards until I was forced to sit on my bed. He held one hand out, as if to keep me in place, as he sat in the chair beside the bed, and then he leaned towards me, like a doctor. Unlike my doctor, who brayed, he did not raise his voice one whit but spoke in his usual soft, melodious way. But it was full of the lawyer's steel.

"Mrs. Samphire. G. Listen to me, please. Are you listening?" My eyes were closed, but I nodded.

"Mrs. Spence is on her way up here. We're waiting on the doctor. I am going to leave you in this room and I'm going to shut the door when I leave. And you are going to stay inside this room, do you hear me?" I nodded.

"Do you understand?"

"Yes." I could barely get the word out.

He paused for a few seconds, and then he said, "You were never in Mr. Bridges' room. You haven't killed him or hurt him in any way. Correct?" He was articulating very clearly, as if I were stupid or a child.

I nodded.

"Good." He patted me on the shoulder and then stood up. "I'll call your daughter for you. Promise you won't leave your room. You won't say anything to anyone until she comes. Right?" I nodded yes to everything, for I was suddenly numb, already retreating to a place where I'd want to stay for some time to come. I heard him leave and the click of the lock as the door closed behind him.

I lay in bed, my hand pressed across my forehead to cool it, for I felt I was burning up. I heard sounds in the corridor, footsteps coming and going. Voices. After a while they seemed to fade out until a non-human sound, the screeching of an ungreased stretcher wheel, made me sit up and really listen. But I never heard it wheeled back out, for I was blasted by the ringing of the phone. I automatically reached out and picked it up, and before I could say anything Celia said, "Mom, are you all right?"

Why did she ask? "I killed him," I said.

"Mom. Don't talk nonsense." The voice was strong, though she never changed her tone.

"Yes, I did."

Pause. "Mom." I could hear her pause, summoning her patience as if for a child. "Listen, I'm really really sorry. I know it's a shock. But please don't say something that you know is not true. Mr. Bridges died from a heart attack."

Died? So he was really dead then? The silence must have finally hit her, for she said, almost in a hurry, "Listen, I'm just finishing up here and then I'll come right over. Be there soon as I can. Please stay in your room until I get there, okay?"

I don't remember hanging up but I got under the covers, for I was shivering, although it was the height of summer and well into the nineties. I was truly sick, I swear. I already had a raging fever.

77

TRY AS I MIGHT I could not sleep, though it was quite dark by the time Celia came. She switched on the lamp when she entered. Turned it off again, as I was pretending to be sleeping. Then she did a surprising thing. She came to the bed and lay down beside me and put her arms around me and held me.

78

I DON'T KNOW HOW much holding you ever got as a child, but I say it softly to myself, for I think you have fallen asleep, your thin arm still around me, resting lightly as a bird. Within three months I was pregnant again. They say it can't happen while you are nursing, but it's not true. So by the time you were one, there was Shirley, and at two there was Charles Junior. You had left home by the time Lise was on the way four years later. I don't know what came first — my not holding you enough or your not wanting to be held. You almost walked out of my womb, you came so fast. You kept going, creeping, standing, toddling, then striding along by your lonely little self. It was as if we were all afraid of you, you so perfect, with the round face and plump cheeks like a little china doll, bisque coloured, so beautiful, so self-contained, so distant. Even Shirley and Junior, they made a pair, from the start they clung to each other, never to big sister.

Maybe it was that self-sufficiency in you those people saw when you went away to camp that year you were almost five. It was the principal at the infant school who took you. Her husband was headmaster of the primary school and their daughter was the same age as you. You had both just started school and the wife was going as a camp counsellor so she asked us to let you go with them. Two whole weeks at this Christian camp, some American denomination, children 5 to 15. It was free.

You came back the way you left, not saying a word, but plumper, the bisque darkened to caramel, wearing shorts and a T-shirt and a cloth cap that both read MARYFIELD CAMP. It was your teacher who told us what a wonderful time you had, playing games, learning to swim in the pool, singing around the campfire, learning to plait straw and finger paint and memorize Bible verses. To us you said nothing. You just came out of Teacher's car carrying your little bag and smiled. You went straight to your room. It was only after talking with your teacher that we could question you about the time you'd had.

No coaxing could ever get you to sing or talk about anything you had done. You just shook your head with your mouth compressed in that funny little smile, as if it was a game with you, this determination to keep all information from us. But you did share with your little brother and sister your coloured cards of scenes from the Bible, the packets of sticky stars, the paper dolls, your new crayons, and the coloured cartridge paper they had given you. You supervised their colouring. You even allowed them to take turns wearing your cap and T-shirt. You were generous that way. With your things. It was with yourself that you were stingy. Lying here now in the bed, your body fragile but warm against mine for the first time in over forty years, I have to wonder how much I ever spoke to you.

79

I SPOKE TO YOU when I carried you in my belly, but silently, for you were so much a part of me I knew you understood my every heartbeat, my entire life opening up to you. You understood that it was now up to you, the you in whom I was investing everything, all else in my life having failed, for he was already running around. When you were born I played with you a lot, moving your tiny feet up and down as I sang, over and over: "Bye baby bunting / papa's gone a hunting / gonna get a rabbit skin / to wrap my baby bunting in." I'd have tears in my eyes, for that was the only song I remembered from my own childhood. But who sang it to me, I don't know. As you got older, I'd fall into the curvature of your smile. But my belly was big again by then, and there was always so much to do. After the washing of nappies and the cleaning and cooking and ironing I would lie exhausted on my side with you beside me on the bed, and I would study the perfection of your little hands and feet, smile at the fragility of your eyelashes, your nails, feel your tiny hand clutch mine and wish I could hold on to you forever. But I never said these things out loud, and already, although I did not know it, you were slipping away from me.

80

WE DIDN'T TALK AT all that night, Celia and I. I couldn't sleep, but I let her until she woke as day was breaking, came fully awake the minute she opened her eyes, peered at her watch and jumped up.

"Omigod, I have to go. I have a class first thing this morning." Putting on her shoes and taking up her handbag, taking out her cell phone. She paused and looked at me. "Mom, sorry I have to rush. Will you be okay?"

I nodded, surprised that while she was there with me I was feeling perfectly fine, but now I could feel the heat rising again inside me.

"I'll call you and come by later. Okay?"

I nodded and closed my eyes as I heard the door shut, ever so carefully, behind her.

81

MATRON CAME WHEN I didn't appear for breakfast, cooing, "Mrs. Samphire. Miss Sam. I am soooo sorry," as she walked in. She threw open all the windows, for I guess the room was stifling hot, though I was shivering under the cover. Then she took a good look at me. She leaned over to place her hand against my cheek, took hold of my wrist to feel my pulse. Then she called the doctor. After that I don't remember very much of the next few days. By the time I came down off that high of fever and medical cocktails, Mr. Bridges was well and truly buried.

I remember Ruby and Birdie coming into my room looking like kling-kling birds in their funeral black — jet beads, even — and just as noisy. I suppose by then I was lucid enough to want to hear something of the event. But after telling me that the church was full, and about the soloist and the flowers and all the children and grandchildren present, they both got so caught up in arguing about the relationship between this person and that, and who came from what side of the family and what was their name again, that I fell asleep before they sorted it out.

82

IT WAS MATRON WHO unwittingly introduced the second act in this drama, though to this day I am unaware of how much she knows. But I do think the motive behind her invitation was innocence rather than malice. For the more I've come to know her the more I think there's more to Delice Spence than I first credited. Or maybe it's just that my own state of mind has undergone so many spins, I no longer know what is what.

She must have sensed that I was feeling so much better, almost myself, that day she came to my room. For though I was spending most of the day out of bed, I still hadn't gathered up the courage to go down to the dining room. I have to grant Matron credit for sensitivity, for although she must have known the state of affairs, she made no fuss about the room service she had to provide.

I was still feeling fragile, both mentally and physically. As with other people who are hardly ever ill, the shock of being incapacitated and dependent on others frightened me, and for the first time I began to feel my age, indeed felt much older than my years. It was if I had suddenly skipped a decade or two and metamorphosed into a really old woman, like one of those downstairs who spent her days drooling and nodding in front of the TV, waiting to be transited from Ellesmere Lodge to an Old People's Home. I was still floating on cotton wool, studiously avoiding thinking of Mr. Bridges or anything else. I engaged in the most mindless of activities — watching the soaps in my room, leafing through the fashion magazines, *TIME*, *National Geographic*, and Jehovah's Witnesses' *Awake!* that various visitors brought. Listening, with only half an ear, to the visitors.

But I really perked up, without showing it, of course, when Matron introduced the topic of her visit. She breezed into my room one morning just as Maisie had finished cleaning, in brisk mode as ever, asking how I was feeling while plumping up the pillows, adjusting the venetian blinds, before looking hard at me in a fashion I assume was dictated by the Holloway Nursing Manual. She seemed satisfied by the whites of my eyes, or whatever, but instead of rushing off then, as she usually did, she fluttered around for so long in blinding lime green and cerise that I finally asked her if she would like to sit. To my great surprise, she sat in the chair beside the bed, crossing her legs — orange wedgies, so now I know who her fashion icon is — and arranging her bat sleeves in a way that suggested she had something of importance to say.

My hackles rose, for it reminded me of my early days at Ellesmere Lodge and those endless office grillings. But then I relaxed, for I sensed here less of the tyrant and more of someone who had information of some slight embarrassment to convey. Or someone who wanted to ask a favour. I was steeling myself for her usual whimsical and winding and annoying approach to the subject when she surprised me by coming straight to the point.

"Listen, Mrs. Samphire. I wonder if. You can help me. Your daughter ... I can tell you are feeling. Ever so much better ... Bit of a jam. New resident to be settled in ... and then it's the board meeting tomorrow and everything and I'm up to my ears. Minutes and reports ... So. I was wondering?"

She paused then. I looked blankly at her, as I had no idea where this was leading. But then I almost jumped at the mention of his name.

"Mr. Bridges. Daughter just phoned. Supposed to come over to clear out his room. But now. She says. Been so tied up with other things. Can't. Flying. Back to the States tonight. Well. So inconsiderate. Since we have a new resident. Arriving. For the room. On Monday."

Matron's voice fluted up on the last note, and she drummed her fingers on the wooden armrest and paused, as if she expected me to genuflect to the economics of keeping the rooms at Ellesmere Lodge filled. I showed nothing on my face, which encouraged her to go on. And was I surprised! For Mr. Bridges' daughter had asked Matron to just go ahead and pack everything up.

"She says I should take what we can use here. Give the rest away. To the staff. Or whoever. Imagine that!"

Matron said this in a rather disapproving tone, and I have to confess to sharing her amazement at the casual way the rich could toss things out! A sure sign that in our earlier years, Matron and I had been spun out of the same frugal cloth.

The cousin who was looking after Mr. Bridges' house would come over to collect his personal stuff — his papers, jewellery, cufflinks, that sort of thing, and an oil painting he had brought with him. She had a list. But they didn't want to be bothered with anything else.

"She said," Matron reported, unconsciously mimicking the daughter's voice, "'Can you imagine how much stuff we already have to sort out at the house? Daddy was such a collector.' Didn't sound too pleased, I can tell you."

I wondered what all of this had to do with me, though the cotton wool in my head was beginning to clear. And it floated away entirely when Matron explained, or rather, asked, in a very sweet voice, the bat sleeves fluttering and the wedgies twisting together in a girlish way: Would I feel up to sorting out Mr. Bridge's room? She had spoken to my daughter and she said as long as it was fine with me.

"Normally, I would never ever ask a resident to do this, Miss Sam … Never, in all my years … but this is a special case, and I know you are, well, not like … I know how close … I mean how you were such a friend of his here … I mean … I think you wouldn't mind …?"

The request was so unexpected that I didn't have time to enjoy Matron's discomfiture. What amazed me is that I didn't have to think about it. For my heart was already pounding out, yes, yes. As if I'd won the lottery. I truly don't know why. But the thought of going into Mr. Bridges' room one more time excited me, as if that was where I needed to go to find a lingering presence, in the scent of his aftershave, the rustle of his silk shirts, the warmth of his suits. As if this contact with the atoms of his living self, no matter how fugitive, would enable me to exorcise his ghost. For part of my grief was being a player in what had turned into a truncated drama, a word unspoken, a dream deferred.

I no longer thought of his room as the scene of my crime. Subconsciously, I had accepted the diagnosis of heart attack as the cause of his death, though the conjunction of circumstances between him and my father would always disturb me. Nor did I think of entering his room as spying, or prying, just the chance to say goodbye in a way I wasn't able to do before. In fact, I thought the gods had smiled on me to give me this opportunity. But of course I revealed nothing of this to Matron. I just sat there looking as if I was considering, for a very long time, enjoying her anxiety, and then I quietly said yes, I'd be willing to do it.

All I wanted then was for her to hand over the keys and go so I could step across the corridor. But she wasn't called Matron for nothing, for she lingered, to give instructions. I just needed to go through and sort things into piles, and let her know when I was done so she could send up bags and boxes and someone to do the packing. And would I mind labelling them — she'd send up tape and markers. Winston would come and collect and store them until she had the time to go through and decide what was to be done.

I heaved a sigh of relief when she got up to leave, dangling keys in her hand, though I noticed that instead of his usual bundle on the large ring she carried, there were just two keys on a small ring, similar to mine, one for the front door and one for his room, to be handed over to the next occupant, no doubt. It made me sad, for it seemed to signify such a swift diminution of one's presence here on this earth.

I was now consumed with anxiety to get going when she paused to say, "Don't tire yourself, though." Then, "Are you sure? I could send Annie or one of the girls to help you?"

I wanted to wring her neck. But I gave her my brightest smile and assured her I'd be fine on my own. At least for the start. I'd let her know when I needed help. Then, in case she changed her mind, as now I was desperate to get the job, I assured her I would let her know the minute I felt it was too much for me. Really, I wanted to beat her over the head to make her hand over the keys. Thankfully, I didn't have to, for she did so, and I greedily closed my hand over them, imagining the warmth they yielded was from him. As soon as she left and closed the door, I held them up to my lips and kissed them. Then hastily put them down again, for she came charging back in.

"Oh, Miss Sam," she said, her expression hovering between a frown and a smile. "Perhaps you would like to take something for yourself? A memento? Anything you would like."

I looked at her and nodded and she left, for good this time. I threw up the keys and caught them. A sign of my complete restoration to life.

83

ENTERING MR. BRIDGES' ROOM was not as hard as I thought it would be, nor was going through his possessions. I felt rather at peace the whole time, as I placed his suits in the garment bags I found with a cedar hanger to repel moths in each one — the first I had seen. As I folded and placed his shirts, his socks and underwear, his dressing gowns, his ties, his cashmere sweaters, in piles on the bed, I couldn't help remarking how new everything appeared. Even the clothes he wore for gardening — his Tilley shorts and hat, his Lacoste shirts — were washed and neatly folded with the rest, nothing on them to show they had ever come in contact with dirt. I'm sure he must have had a much stronger influence over Mavis the laundress than I had, if she indeed was the one who looked after his clothes. I doubted it, for no such attention was paid to mine.

Didn't some people wear things out, I wondered? He certainly didn't need a wife who could mend. Or one who could pack, for that matter, for every item, in the drawers, the closet, was meticulously arranged. In the bathroom, towels were symmetrically aligned on the towel rack, as were his shoes on trees. Mr. Bridges was nothing if not consistent — everything in his room was as neat and ordered as his person had been. I wondered now, could he have been as dependent on his wife for domestic comforts as he claimed? For the state of his possessions certainly didn't reveal a man in need of anyone.

Even without considering the stuff he must have had at his own house, I was amazed at just how much of everything Mr. Bridges possessed. It was an extraordinary windfall for Matron to dispose of. I thought of how she could use it to buy compliance and favours from the staff, tradesmen, for years to come. And then I suppressed that thought, for I was beginning to think of myself, and Matron, as entirely nice people after all. Perhaps something of the unruffled nature of Mr. Bridges' life was rubbing off on me.

In the bathroom, I bagged up his medicines for disposal, again alarmed by the quantity of both prescription and non-prescription items. Had he needed all of these? It seemed extraordinary. Was he that sick? Was my amazement at such an arsenal of goods simply due to my ignorance of things medical, because, apart from this past week, my own cupboard held nothing but the most basic of first aids?

The medicine collection was the only sign perhaps of a slight disorder, for the bottles on the surface of the counter around the sink were placed there helter-skelter, in no special arrangement, some even turned over on their sides. The medicine cabinet also yielded lots of items, but no surprises.

Mr. Bridges had an equally large quantity of grooming aids, expensive like his clothes. Six or seven bottles each of things like shampoo, conditioner, aftershave, and things I never knew men used: moisturizer, concealer, face wash, cologne. I was beginning to think the owner of this cache might have been slightly vain, but then I replaced that thought with one that this kind of excess was probably perfectly natural for people with plenty of money. Then I backtracked on excess, for I didn't want to be critical, but perhaps his list of basic necessities was longer than my own. What did I know? I felt the first twinge then of being out of sync with a world that was not now meant to be mine. I was not used to excess. Until I came to live at Ellesmere Lodge, my own cupboard was entirely bare. I wondered then what commentary on one's life did possessions make. Was mine as threadbare as it seemed? In comparison with someone like Mr. Bridges — or Ruby, for one could hardly move around in her room for the trunks and boxes, for her things — was my life to be judged as empty?

Having come along this route, I slid from thinking of these people's lives as models of excess to mine as an example of deficiency. Of carelessness. Of loss. Didn't I always manage to let slip away anything of value?

Contemplation of this state must have induced some kind of trance, for when Maisie banged on the door I'd left open to ask if I wanted her to put my lunch in my room, I jumped. I was surprised to find myself standing in front of the bathroom mirror holding plastic bottles of shampoo in both hands and squeezing them.

Once I took that break for lunch I found the morning's work had worn me out. I decided to leave the rest of the task for the following day. This was mainly the clearing out of the other items — the top drawer of the chest that held jewellery and odds and ends, and the two drawers of his bedside table. I thought that task would take me no more than an hour or two. I vowed that after I was finished there, I would make my way downstairs and face the world.

84

WHEN CELIA CAME OVER that night, I don't know why I didn't tell her about what had happened with Mr. Bridges that last day, for I wanted to. I wanted to tell her about what might have been, about the circumstances of his death, that breathless word withheld. How my heart was pounding, longing so hard to hear it, I sent such a powerful signal to his own that it was shell-shock all over again, a short-circuiting of the body's electricity.

Instead, I found myself telling her about my day, sorting out his things, and how I was bothered that I didn't feel sad at the death of my friend but rather detached — as if I was clearing out a stranger's room.

"Was that natural, do you think?" I asked.

She said, "Yes, it takes time for grief to develop fully, and sometimes activity to displace that grief, at least for a while, is just what is needed." She paused, and then she added, smiling at me, "Perhaps that is why Mrs. Spence asked you to do it."

What! I thought, but didn't say, Matron with insight?

"She knew," she said, "as I did, how much he meant to you."

I mentally retorted, Of course you do not know. No one will ever know.

As she continued to talk, I turned to marvelling as I always did at how even in tone her voice is, almost without inflection, unlike mine, unlike most of the rest of her countrymen and women, for we are all given to voices that play up and down the scale to reflect the high drama, the low moments of our lives. And yet that modulated voice was commanding, one that I, like her students, her television viewers, could have confidence in. For like Mr. Levy she spoke with the voice of authority. Looking at her, lying stretched out on the bed, shoes off, in a simple pink cotton dress that made her look girlish and pretty, I couldn't help wondering, what were the high dramas, the low moments of your life?

I was never there to share them, not really. Though when you came home on your visits you might have been telling me much more than I realized at the time. I used to eavesdrop on your play sometimes, when you had all the little children under your spell, not just your brother and sisters but often the neighbours as well. You were their Pied Piper, as they hardly ever had visitors. How exciting and glamorous you must have seemed to them, with your beautiful clothes, your books and your toys that you willingly shared. But it was the stories you told that I listened to, the way you kept them in line with your rules and your instructions. You were as open and alive with them as you were like a clam with me. I listened as often as I could, pausing to eavesdrop as I went about my day's work, especially if you were at your favourite spot, which was under the big poinciana tree at the back, with the swings and the bench or exposed roots that were perfect for sitting. You would have the bench, of course, because you were not used to slumming. I would watch how carefully you would first dust it off, then arrange your skirt before sitting down so it would not get crushed or dirty. How unchild-like these gestures were. I suddenly recalled the very first time I saw her, this woman you came to call "Auntie," how she had peeled the cellophane off the lollipops she brought for Shirley and Junior and how, instead of discarding the paper there on the roadside as any normal human being would have done, she kept the wrappers in her hand the whole time, taking them back to the car with her, no doubt to be properly disposed of. Was it that carefulness that was rubbing off on you? Was her vocabulary becoming yours, peppered now with words like *satan, sin* and *Jesus, Heaven* and *Hell*, words you had never heard around my house, well, not outside the goodnight prayers I encouraged the children to make. My one concession to churchiness. You were so kind to the other children, but so strict, with all your rules and regulations, with your punishments for infringement, which they happily complied with, thinking it all a game. "You, Shirley. Into the corner with you, miss. Think about what you have done and don't come out until I say." And Shirley would go and stand in the designated space and turn her back, while the rest of the children giggled. At the time, such actions made me smile, too, because it seemed so incongruous coming from such a little one. And, because you were small, never once did I think of my own constricted childhood in the thrall of adults.

85

I WAS SITTING UP in bed with my back resting against the headboard, letting my thoughts roam, for Celia had fallen asleep beside me. I didn't wake her, for I knew she had some sort of built-in clock that would suddenly propel her awake and into movement. But while she was asleep, I could talk to her the way I couldn't otherwise. I turned to gaze at her closed eyes, her eyelashes still long, but fuller with mascara. You are like a doll still, I thought, but one much emaciated, the cheeks no longer plump, the skin no longer bisque. If I shook you like a doll, would your bones rattle? Would your eyes, not earthy like mine but water-signed like your father's, fill with tears? You hardly ever cried as a child. So I never wanted to shake you, as I wanted to shake the others sometimes, especially Lise who was so filled with temper. What wounds to her soul had transmitted such agony that she in turn inflicted on others? Had I conveyed my own unhappiness to her when I carried her? Did the blows I received when she was already inside my belly create a disturbance that registered inside her tiny brain? Is there already a functioning brain at that stage? How little I know.

I do know that's the last time we had our drunken dance at night, he and I, the last time he laid hands on me, in any sense of the word. For it was only the next morning in the pristine light of day, as he sat on the bench on the veranda and pulled on his boots before leaving for work, that I told him I was expecting. I have to admit, it hit him hard. I could see by the blood rushing to his face and his hands falling from tying the laces. He lifted his head and looked out at the yard, his expression bleak. I wasn't sure what disturbed him really, the prospect of another child, or the balling up of the fist to hit me the previous night. He didn't look at me and my swollen mouth. He looked at his hands. He clenched and unclenched them. He didn't say anything for a long time while I stood, in my kitchen apron, my hands unconsciously curled around my belly. He resumed tying his laces, and he got up and put on his hat and he mumbled something as he turned and walked away. I still am not sure if it was "Sorry." It would have been the only time the word was ever said.

86

IT IS TO YOU I've wanted to say sorry, those other evenings when I was ill and you dropped by on a quick visit and you lay beside me on the bed, dressed in your business suit, which signified you hadn't gone home yet after your day's labour, your high heels off, your feet stretched out though not reaching as far as mine at the bottom of the bed, for you didn't inherit my height. Rangy, like your father, your body, your arms, your little legs sturdy from the start, and strong, well able to carry you as you left me. For that is what was hurtful, your eagerness to leave, to find another home away from us. Was it the crowded room you shared with your brother and sister, the skimpiness of everything? Our meals, our clothing, our toys and playthings. Our threadbare lives?

That day you walked away, you didn't wave when you looked back. You didn't cry.

Suddenly I'm startled, for out of nowhere, as if you were reading my mind, you ask, "G," — for so you have taken to calling me from that day at the coffee shop — "why did I end up living with Aunt Phil and Uncle Ted? You know, I've been trying to remember, but nothing comes back at all."

It takes me a long time to reply to your question. For since our talk in the coffee shop you have showed no further interest in the subject. Nor have you ever shown interest before in discussing anything about our lives. I'm stunned to hear you say you don't remember anything about leaving home when it is so engraved on my heart. Your calling them "Aunt Phil" and "Uncle Ted" still makes me want to grind my teeth in a jealous rage, for they were not related to you at all. Yet in all these years it is them you related to.

I wet my lips that are suddenly dry and I open my mouth several times without getting the words out, for it is as if the shyness that had been gradually leaving me during my time at Ellesmere Lodge, the inability to speak that plagued me all those years, has returned. I glance at you and am glad that you are still lying there with your eyes closed and not witnessing my confusion. But I am conscious of your waiting on my answer, and I feel the moments stretching between us. Finally I mumble, just as I pull the blanket up to my neck and bury half of my face, like a child, so you can't hear me properly, nor suspect the reason for the telltale tremor in my voice, "You know, I can't remember now either. Isn't that strange? But I'll think about it; it will come back, I'm sure."

And you say, "Oh, don't worry. It's just that there are so many things that I wonder about, that I would like to ask you now that I have you here." You chuckle. "Maybe it's the age thing. This looking back."

You softly pat my shoulder that is already burning up under the blanket, my whole body, from cowardice, from sadness, from denial.

"But," you say, "things can wait. We have lots of time."

87

I DID NOT MAKE it downstairs for the next few weeks. After the equanimity of the previous day, clearing out Mr. Bridges' room, who could have guessed what surprises awaited? I cleared out all the bits and pieces. I retrieved the jewellery boxes, placed the rings and cufflinks inside them, and set them along with some odds and ends from the chest of drawers into a box and labelled it for the cousin to take away. Then I started on the bedside table. There wasn't much in the large bottom drawer, just a few fat file envelopes. I didn't open any of this, feeling respectful of Mr. Bridges' privacy.

After that task, I decided to take a break and I spent some time looking through his CD collection before packing that away. Since Matron had offered me a memento, I was strongly tempted to take his miniature stereo and some music to go with it. For that was not on the list of things the family wanted. But then I thought it was much too extravagant for me, as I'd seen similar sets advertised in American magazines for thousands of dollars. I was intimidated by its endless array of buttons. How would I ever understand them? The red and green and yellow lights that raced along a track or blinked softly, even now. Should I unplug it? Turn it off? Where was the CD he had been playing that day? I looked at the little player, willing it to defeat me, but when I found the button marked STOP and I pressed it and it did so, I smiled in my moment of triumph.

On the floor, between the chair and the stand holding the player, I found the empty case together with the other CDs he had brought home that day. They had probably been placed there by someone else, as I remember now his putting them down in the chair when he entered the room with me. I reached down to pick up the CDs and brought up the mail he had carried in that day. Most of the envelopes were unopened, but as I walked over to drop them in the carton with the papers, I came to one that had been torn open, and I stopped. Unlike the others that were clearly official, with typed addresses, this address was handwritten, in flowing black ink. It had come from the U.S.A. I squinted at the return address, which was on a little printed label. Mrs. Margo Haynes-Crosswell and a Florida address. My first thought was that it was from one of his children, then I remembered they did not live in Florida. Then I thought, well, it's a cousin, it's a married woman, so that's okay then. But instead of throwing it into the box, I held on to it, a feeling compounded of fear and jealousy growing in my heart. I truly didn't know why I had such a strong reaction to this letter, which could have been of the most innocent sort. But I felt the envelope burning my hand and without any further thought I extracted sheets of airmail paper so fine they crackled.

Well, isn't this proceeding just like your typical Mills and Boon or Harlequin novel? Or maybe more like Victorian romance, or one of Mrs. Revd. Humphrey's bodice rippers. The device of the letter! That fatal letter by which lies are finally ripped away and truth is unmasked. It was like that for me. Though it took more than one letter to convince me of the enormity of this lie — the ignominy of something much, much worse. It wasn't that here was revealed the romance conducted on those Miami visits, an old flame rekindled, that here — finally — was the woman he intended to marry. Far worse was to come. For I would discover that I had all along been playing a starring role in their little drama: the Little Country Mouse, or LCM to use their playful shorthand.

That first letter was only the beginning of what I was to find out. I read it as my face burned and my body shook so much I had to sit down. And then I read it over and over again. She was obviously returning home to marry him, to be the chatelaine of the mansion he was restoring. That much was evident, but now she had finally given him a date, assuming all the work was finished by then. Was this what he had rat-tatted on my door to tell me? The source of his secret, inward smile, his playfulness that day? The fact that nothing I thought of as a relationship with him ever existed. Not even that most basic of connections, mutual friendship, respect, loyalty?

I came to this conclusion after sitting down in the armchair to read the stack of letters from her that were in the top drawer, for I went looking for them, neat packs in order of arrival, each set bound with coloured rubber bands. There was no reference to me in the first letter I read, and so my initial reaction to the shock was shame at my own poor deluded self. Shame at my foolishness. Thankfulness that I had confided in no one. Shame at how I had mentally elevated myself into a sphere that I was so clueless about, for this was one in which a woman would get down to brass tacks immediately after the endearments and the pledge.

For dear Margo was dictating the terms from the start, with the whip hand holding *Architectural Digest* to beat the rat that was running around in the cage. Inventory, inventory. These types of windows. This type of flooring for the living room and hallway. Carpets? Question? Back patio ripped up and replaced with terrazzo tiles. Relined swimming pool, a gazebo at the far end. Paint chips, catalogues, estimates for designer sanitary fixtures coming by courier. And when next would he be up so they could consult?

I guess I'm being facetious about this now because I really don't want to talk about the other bit, the part so painful that it scored my heart more than anything had ever done. It was so cruel. So gratuitous. So indecent.

I spent the rest of the day in that room reading those letters. I had to. I didn't leave the room to eat the lunch brought up for me. After Maisie knocked on Mr. Bridges' door to let me know she had left it in my room, I got up and turned the lock in the door. I could not trust myself to speak to anyone.

I focused on the discussion of the china, the throwing out of the old — his, Spode, too old-fashioned — a suggested list of the new that was to be bought. Perhaps they could have a look on his next trip, or should they wait until Europe and see what they had in Florence? She was thinking she would get rid of her silver tea set, for she seemed to recall his was much nicer. They didn't want two, did they?

I kept thinking, china? New tea service? At her age? I didn't know her age, but from the large photograph in the drawer — much handled, I now noticed — and the smaller one among the many framed photos in the room that I had never actually scrutinized before, she had that seamless, elegant, bland look that denoted age erased by plastic surgery, the tight smile a tribute to expensive orthodontics. Her hair and her face had that finished, polished look that rich people who take care of themselves seem to have, but the eyes behind the mascara looked tired and washed out. Or maybe the image was simply dissolving into my own raddled, washed-out, washed-up self.

88

I READ ALL THE letters. I now know the worst that can befall a human being. But I also finished off my job in Mr. Bridges' room, left everything neatly packaged and labelled and tied up for Matron. The CDs in racks fitted into cartons. The stereo in the very box it had come in, which I found stored flat in the top of the clothes closet. The framed photos all carefully wrapped before packing, to go with the other carton for the cousin. I turned back to survey the room before I closed the door. Good job! Every scrap and speck accounted for. No broken hearts lying on the floor. Not a shred of trampled reputation or skewered loyalty. Those were tightly bound up in the stack of letters, which I clutched firmly in my hand as I exited. My precious souvenirs.

89

I HID THEM IN the same place I used to hide the pens and pencils I borrowed when I first came to Ellesmere Lodge. None of that foolishness anymore. All the pens and pencils have been liberated, restored to some owner, if not the rightful one. But that whole subject is making me think that perhaps if paper and pens and pencils had not been invented, typewriters or printing presses or computers, there would be a lot less misery in the world. Though I'm not sure how I've arrived at this argument, which jerks me from the sleep I have been trying all night to fall into. The ink that wrote those letters is black and

rich, the hand is firm. The recipient is dead. The current reader
is dying. Well, not quite, not yet.

… *just keep dragging YOUR RED WAGON along.*

90

SLEEPLESS, I GET UP in the middle of the night. I switch on the
light and retrieve the letters. I have another read. A sampling
only this time. Already I have engraved on my heart the phrases
that will now forever jump out at me, ambush me like a fist
in black leather gloves. I'm grateful for Mr. Bridges' sense of
order, for the letters are arranged to be read chronologically.
I start at the back. So what becomes accessible is a history of
our relationship, or, rather, a history of a relationship that was
not. It was an amusement for two people.

It was clear from reading her remarks just what it was he
told her. Everything. I didn't start off as LCM — Little Country
Mouse. For remember, the mouse first roared at him. So at
the beginning I was MCC — Mad Country Cow. The Mouse
only came much later, when he realized how shy I was really,
and how much he had to coax me to get the words out. Little
Country Mouse meeting Town Rat.

My face burned with flame afresh, feeling as red as the
dress I wore the day I first signalled my interest in him; for
from then on he was reading me like a book. Writing me like
one too. For soon Miss Margo gets all cutesy about *her rival*.
About him coming perhaps to prefer women with *clodhopper
feet* over one *clad in Manolo Blahnik American size six. Triple*

A. Underlined. The bitch! Enquired about my growing trans-formation into a *glamour puss*, commented on the hennaed hair! (*So out it's in again*, she hissed. *Bravo LCM!*). Worried about the two of us *getting hot and sweaty together in the garden.* Warning him not to introduce me to *the practice of taking showers together to cool off. Reserved strictly for size six tennis-playing non-gardeners.* Many exclamation points topped with cute little hearts.

I stopped reading then, taking my only consolation from the fact that he had written to her about some of the other residents of Ellesmere Lodge, though perhaps not with the malice he reserved for me. For regardless, they were all more or less of his own social group and perhaps not suitable targets. Still, I don't know what he had actually said, perhaps it was only her pen that dripped with vitriol. *What! Old Ruby de la Whats-her-face still alive? My God, she must be a hundred years old. Still grasping at youth and wearing those awful shades of eyeshadow? Well, at least they match her jewellery. I wonder who gets them when she pops off?* What was with this woman? Perhaps I wouldn't have felt so badly if she hadn't come across as such a perfectly awful human being. I wondered how Mr. Bridges could stand her. Then I reminded myself that he was an awful human being himself. Now I wish he hadn't gone and died, for I would prefer to think of him living with this woman as a punishment worse than death. The thought made me giggle, but the next minute I was retching with pain.

Ever since I fished out that first letter from its envelope, my feelings were running up and down. Sometimes I thought it served me right, the gods were paying me back for my curiosity. I didn't regret my actions, for the thought of those letters falling into someone else's hands was even more chilling. Though I hadn't been named in any of them, anyone familiar with Ellesmere Lodge would have easily identified the creature who came to figure as LCM. I hastily suppressed the thought that Matron perhaps had taken a look at them?

I put the letters back in their hiding place and crawled into the cave of my bed, which was to become my hiding place, every bone in my body aching. But before I switched off the light, I got out my notebook and found the page where I had made my Inventory, and I crossed out *intelligent*. I also crossed out *well read*. I had been read too well. And I wrote *Knowledge Is Power*. And then I crossed that out too.

91

I NEVER WANTED TO get out of bed again. I felt so rotten I couldn't take satisfaction from Matron's discomfiture. She thought it was her fault that I had overexerted myself the previous day. I assured her that it was simply my flu returning. She watched me like a hawk for the next few weeks, came in person to administer medicines or take my temperature, little knowing that the germ that had been implanted in me had no cure, for it was called shame, one that I had to hide from the world. Or maybe what I was doing was wallowing in it, for almost every night I found myself tottering out of bed to fetch the stack of letters and read portions of them. Then I had nightmares about what would happen to them if I died and they were found. I tried to think of sensible means of disposing of them. But really, I didn't want to destroy them, I wanted to wear the wounds they inflicted as my stigmata. Punishment for my gall, my prideful self.

It seemed to me so bizarre that to this woman I had never met, my life was a soap opera, for so she came to call it. *What! Murderous Husband on top of Mad Father!!! How would you solve this one you great reader of mysteries? Do you think the husband and cousin really killed the old man and deposed of the body?* (I took great satisfaction in the "*deposed.*") And then: *Skulls? Skeletons? Give me a break! Tell her to stick to reading Martha Grimes and stop lending her your Patricia Cornwells.*

One or two paragraphs quite interested me, despite myself, such as this one: *You mean she was married to one of those Mad Samphires?* ("*Those*" underlined.) *Weren't you at school with them? I seem to remember us St. Dorothy girls quivering in our loins at the mention of their names. Bad Boys! But sexy! Though one didn't even breathe that word in those days. How amazing. Hardly seems the type. But aren't they the ones who murdered their parents in cold blood and got off on a technicality? God, my sweetie, aren't you lucky she didn't murder you?* I took great satisfaction from the fact that her mention of the Samphire boys suggested she was much older than me. And him. But as I read on, any small glimmer of self-satisfaction would be skewered by the next barb.

There were times when I truly didn't want to live. On the days when I didn't feel physically ill, all I wanted was to get out of there, to return to my own little place in the country, the space where I now knew I belonged.

92

I LAY AWAKE AT nights thinking about belonging. About going back. What ties me to that place? The earth and its bounties, the trees, the mountains, the heartbreaking landscape, the charting of the moon's traverses, the sky that I watched every night from the darkness of my veranda till its arc is drawn on my retina? People there do not belong to me nor I to them, not even Ken who's lived with me on and off since he was a child or Millie my neighbour or old Maud who has been peeling ginger and making cassava bread forever or one or two of the others. When I vanished so suddenly from that place, did anyone miss me? In my misery here, did I ever think of them? Is it that misguided search for belonging that makes me act so unthinking sometimes? Or am I just plain crazy, like my father? Stones belong, like the big smooth rock sitting in my backyard all by its lonesome. I have no idea how it got there, so out of place, but we use it for everything: for sitting on, bleaching clothes, spreading out ginger or coffee or cocoa beans to dry, using as a chopping board or a work table. Maybe it really is in its place, something solid and dependable around which everything revolves. Perhaps that's what I shall be in my next life. A rock.

93

AS LONG AS I was suffering and sulking in my room, each day seemed to bring a new surprise, as if the gods were determined to shock me out of my misery. One day Celia told me repairs to my house were almost done. I could set a date for moving back. Then she added, "If you really want to."

I bristled, for it sounded as if she doubted my resolve. "Don't you think I want to go back?"

I was aware of how sharp my voice was, and I was instantly ashamed. She smiled and said something that surprised me then. "It's just that I've got so used to having you around. It would be so nice if you could stay."

I didn't say anything. I needed time to examine that statement.

"I thought you had finally settled down here," she continued. "I know it was rough at first, I know you are not used to living with other people. But everyone likes you."

I couldn't help feeling that she was talking about me as if I were a child she had settled in boarding school. Which, considering all the nonsense I have been through, wasn't far wrong.

"They can't stop talking about what you've done to the garden." She was raving now. "Mrs. Spence says she wishes she had more residents like you, taking an active part in things."

That old hypocrite, I thought, but inwardly I smiled, pleased despite myself, for in the new mould that I'd been recasting Matron she might well have said it.

I was lying on top of the bed cover, my back propped up

by several pillows. I was finally wearing a dress instead of my nightie and housecoat, though I planned to go nowhere. I had my eyes half-closed, so I could shut them quickly if need be. I wasn't sure how to deal with the emotions that were being stirred up in me, especially by her, by her nearness; every time she sat beside me on that bed I felt such a surge of tenderness, it brought tears too close to the surface. Crying was something I'd banished along with a lot of other feelings following the first years of disillusionment of life with Sam. But now, once I started, tears seemed forever threatening.

Out of the corner of my eye I watched her pick at a thread dangling from the hem of her cotton blouse and play with it, winding it around her finger. She was wearing linen pants of the same colour as the blouse, a beautiful tamarind shade.

"Listen, I know this business of Mr. Bridges is upsetting you, but are you sure you don't want to give it a few more months here at least?"

"No," I said. "You've gone to all the expense of fixing the house. The sooner I get out of here the better. I don't want you to have to keep on paying for me here as well. I feel guilty enough as it is."

"That's not the point, really. It's not a question of expense, it's what will make you happy." She paused then, for so long that I turned my head to look fully at her. She had stopped playing with the thread and was holding her body perfectly still as if she was bracing herself for something. I automatically prepared myself, too, for more bad news. I was surprised when she said, "Of course now Gabriel is gone, we have lots of room. You could come and live with us." She paused. "If you wanted to. Herman thinks it's a great idea. You know he likes you."

She had made this offer before, but I hadn't taken it seriously. I was surprised she'd gone as far as discussing it with her husband. Where had her children gone to? Gabriel and Ashley. I had to struggle to recall their names. I felt ashamed that I had shown so little interest in her affairs, that I was in fact such a terrible mother. Grandmother. But now of course I was too ashamed to ask the questions I wanted to, for a caring, loving mother would not need to ask them. I wonder how close her children would have been to her other mother, her "Auntie," had she lived to see them. What kind of grandmother would she have been? But I knew. I didn't have to ask. I could see that Phil had all the equipment for child seduction from the very first moment I set eyes on her.

Celia was saying something else, but I wasn't listening, for suddenly I was jerked back to another day, seeing in my mind's eye the Reverend Doctor that first time he arrived at our house. To steal my child.

94

I'M WONDERING NOW, AS I have wondered many times, what made us say yes, and keep on saying yes to them. Was it the burden of another child expected that swung the balance? For Sam thought your going that Christmas was a great idea. He was the one who got to know them, who visited from time to time. He always told me about the visit afterwards, making out that he had made a detour on the way to somewhere else, a last-minute decision, but I knew it was because he never wanted to take me. You duly went for the Christmas holidays, that first time, and then it was for Easter and then it was for the whole of the summer that somehow merged into the following school year. You were taking piano lessons and tennis lessons and holidays with them abroad. Somehow, it became forever. They moved away, to the other side of the island. By then you were a boarder at school, so naturally you spent most of the holidays with them. We caught brief glimpses of you after that, for a week, two weeks at most out of the year. By the time you grew up and were on your own, it was a weekend snatched here and there, then years before you came back from university. Even then I saw you no more than a few hours, occasionally, when you drove down to see me and back in the same day. I can't remember the last time you spent a night in our house.

In all of this I remember nothing but your remoteness from me, your distance. So at what stage, I'm asking myself now, did you get so close to your father's family, to your brother and sisters?

I was so lost in thought, or perhaps I had fallen asleep, that I was shocked to find myself back in the present. With Celia gently shaking me.

"G, gosh, were you sleeping? Sorry. Listen, got to go. I'll talk to Junior later and see what he says about the electricians. They were supposed to finish the wiring this week."

"Junior?" I came wide awake then. "Junior?" That made me sit up. "What's Junior got to do with it?"

I must have looked out of it, for she said, "You really were sleeping! You haven't heard a word I said."

"Sorry," I muttered, "it's these pills. They tire me out." I don't know why I couldn't have come right out and told her what I had been thinking, for she herself had quizzed me on the topic only days before. I had tried, I'd really tried to talk about it then, before I hemmed and hawed and faked tiredness, so I wouldn't have to answer. I was feeling ashamed of myself, I have to admit, but I couldn't throw over a lifetime of subterfuge. Of shutting down like a crab the minute anything threatened to probe soft and tender places.

Celia was standing up, straightening her clothes and searching with her foot for her shoe, and I found I wanted so much to keep her, to bind her to me, to tell her … So I licked my lips and said in as casual a voice as I could muster, "You know what, I just remembered about you and the — and those people. About how you came to live with them? Remember you were asking me?"

"Great," she said, fluffing her hair in front of the mirror, not even looking at me. "Don't forget to tell me next time. But now" — looking at her watch — "must run." I felt let down by the casual way she was treating this, as if it was of no importance at all.

"Yes," I said, "but listen." I sat up. "What about Junior, you haven't told me anything."

She was already opening the door. "Sorry, can't stop now. Talk to you. Later." She was gone.

I was left totally puzzled about Junior and what he had to do with anything, for I hadn't heard from him in years. But isn't that a boy for you? As a child, it hadn't taken him long to stop clinging to me. As soon as Lise was born and started crawling around, he metamorphosed into a boy's boy, old enough to wander around with the other boys from the area and to stay away all day long if I let him. But what turned him into a real little man was getting his own bicycle, an old Raleigh that his father got from somewhere and fixed up for him. Once he got his own wheels he could ride away, and he did.

Somehow, Junior wasn't someone I wanted to think about at all, especially when he left in such a hurry after Shirley's death without telling me. That really hurt, for I thought we had gotten over our early difficulties and were friends again. He could at least have placed a little of his trust in me, his mother. Not that I put the two things together — his leaving and Shirley's death — though I know it must have hit him hard, for they were very close. But the fact that he put up such a block between us meant that for me, the blockage was still there, preventing me from seeing him clearly. Or perhaps nothing about Junior was ever clear. I couldn't wait to talk to Celia again to find out what this son of mine was doing in my business.

95

NEXT TIME CELIA CAME she told me she had nothing to do with the fixing up of the house, that Junior was taking care of everything. I didn't know how to take this news at all, I felt trapped between anger and helplessness, as if I were being stripped by my children of all my decision-making powers. For that is how Celia got me here to Ellesmere Lodge in the first place: she had simply made the arrangements without consulting me and then swooped down and swept me off. At the time I didn't know what I was getting into, but in a way I was glad to get away from my broken-down house. The hurricane and its aftermath had left me dispirited, as it did all of us, in the dark, without electricity or running water, the fields virtually gone. No fresh vegetables or fruit. Downed trees and detritus everywhere, waiting to be cleared. At least Celia was someone who was continuously in my life, unlike the others. She came down to check on me the minute the roads were cleared and wanted to take me back with her that very day. I wouldn't leave the house the way it was, not until some temporary patching-up was done. Then Ken miraculously reappeared from one of his walkabouts, as I called them, for he would leave without warning and reappear months or years later just as suddenly, without any explanation of where he had been. Over the years, I had grown used to this behaviour, so I just took him as I found him. Ken didn't talk much, perhaps one of the reasons we got on well together. He said he had come to check that I was all right after the storm and promised to stay put for a while and look after my house. I had no further excuse for not going with Celia. At the time I thought it would be for a few weeks at the most while the roof was repaired, so I didn't feel resentment at her taking charge like that — at least I didn't until I found out what kind of place Ellesmere Lodge was, though that's all water under the bridge now. But to be told that Junior had taken charge of my house and is doing as he likes is an entirely different matter.

It must be twenty years since Junior went to Canada and I don't think he ever came back, or he never got in touch if he did. Some years after he left, I got a card and a picture of him and this blond girl to tell me that they were married. No mention of Shirley, his leaving, or anything else. No apology or expression of regret. It was like a communication between people who knew each other vaguely. After that, I got the occasional card from his wife, Dolly, with a note and sometimes some money from Junior. Over the years she sent me photos and news of their growing family, their two children Charlene and Mark, but it was all rather hit-and-miss. She kept saying they were hoping to visit, but it was always next year. Then a few years back, the letters and cards stopped coming, and there was no reply to the letters I sent. I interpreted this as their loss of interest in me, so I stopped writing. To hear from Celia now in this casual way that Junior had been down here all along fixing up my house was a shock to me.

"Well, he wanted to do this, from the time of the hurricane, but he was having chemo at the time and couldn't come out then ..."

"He was having what?"

"Didn't he tell you?"

"No."

"What?" She seemed taken aback by this. "I thought ... I guess I misunderstood."

"Celia, it's been donkey's years since I've heard from Junior and you know that."

She frowned a bit then, as if thinking, and then her voice got brisk again. "Well, he probably didn't want to alarm you. I can tell you because it's all over now. Prostate cancer. He was diagnosed a while back. But he's fine. Trying to change his lifestyle, though, after all he's been through."

"Been through?" I was getting a little annoyed.

"Well, you know. About his daughter. Charlene. Then his marriage breaking up."

"What about his daughter?"

"You know, G," she said, as if I really knew. When I looked blank, she asked, "You mean you really didn't know? They didn't tell you?"

"Tell me what?"

"The terrible trouble with Charlene? Years and years of it. Drugs, bad company. On her sixteenth birthday she took off and not a word have they heard from her since. I can't tell you how much Junior has spent trying to find her, in both time and money. Dolly couldn't take it. She walked out. Well, I don't know, perhaps things were rocky with them to begin with …"

It was hard to take in so much information at once. I remember how much I liked Dolly from her pictures, a big blond girl always laughing with what I imagined was a happy kind of laughter, head thrown back, silver-blond hair. I remember now she wrote to me that her parents were Norwegian. I thought of the two children, Mark and Charlene, whom I had only seen in photos that had stopped coming when they were probably just entering their teens. It was hard to envisage them as grown-up people. In the pictures, their bright blond hair and white skin looked foreign to me. I couldn't see anything of Junior in them.

This is making me think of all my grandchildren that I do not know — Celia's two, Junior's two, Lise's how many? Here they are, like a potential but unharvested seed crop now wasted and scattered to the four winds. All the time, all those years, I had done nothing to reach out and capture some of this crop, for I had always found it safest to pretend I didn't care.

Celia must have seen the look on my face, but she misinterpreted it, for she said, "Oh, don't worry about Junior. Right now, he's happy as Larry, back down there in the country, supervising the contractor, catching up with the fellows from his youth, letting his big businessman trappings fall away. Getting back to his roots, man."

"But why didn't you tell me. About the house?"

"We wanted it to be a big surprise, that's all. You make it so hard for anyone to do anything for you." She smiled when she said it. "So now you will get even more annoyed when I tell you Lise says she wants to buy all new stuff for you. Furniture and whatever you need to replace what you lost. We can go shopping. Isn't that great! When you feel better. Lise says as soon as the house is ready she's coming to visit."

"Lise?"

I said it as if I didn't know who Celia was talking about. Not once in recent years had she mentioned anything about Lise or Junior. Though now that I think of it, I probably never gave her the opportunity. For after so much silence on their part, at some point I just decided never to speak of them, never to ask about them, never to show the slightest interest in their doings. One thing I have learned about Celia over the years is how sensitive she is to other people's feelings; at least, she has always been sensitive to mine. That's one of the things I like about her. Unlike her television persona, where she deals with other people's business, in real life she never seems to press mentally or force anything, she never belabours the point. At the slightest hint of trouble, of nearing deep waters, she will drop the subject. That doesn't mean she won't sneak up from another direction to get her own way, as she did in getting me to Ellesmere Lodge.

Yet, listening to her talk about Junior and Lise in this casual way, as if there isn't an ocean of bad blood between us, makes me wonder what it is really saying about her. Emotional cowardice? An unwillingness to get involved? Navigational expertise? I'm sure I would have been more interested in my family if she had taken the trouble to persist with me. That was what I needed, wasn't it? Someone like Ma D to take me firmly in hand and drag me out of my self-absorption, take me away from that house and all its sadness and expose me to another world. And then I thought, in all fairness, isn't that exactly what she did in bringing me here to Ellesmere Lodge? Yes, the other me answered, and look at what that has brought down on my head.

All these warring emotions brought out the meanness in me. I wanted to dig at her, break through that facade, shatter her complacency.

"So since when have you become so friendly with Lise and Junior?" I tried to keep my voice neutral.

"What do you mean?" She seemed genuinely surprised. "We've always been friends."

I didn't respond to that, which was perhaps unwise, as her next remark skewered me. "Mom, just because you gave up on us doesn't mean we gave up on each other."

I opened my mouth to speak, but nothing came out. I felt I was treading on dangerous ground because I was close to admitting that I had no conception of how she or any of my children lived their lives. I had always thought she was the one who never cared about the rest of us. The one that was distanced. That the attention she paid to me was born of duty and guilt maybe, but not family feeling or love. But now, I thought, what do I know? I didn't want to think this was saying a lot more about me than it was about her.

We parted on that note, bristling, though we sensed rather than showed it. I tried to bury myself in the sleep that now constantly eluded me. All this information about my children, the house, instead of making me feel better, as it should have, was merely adding to my feeling of despair. For the knowledge I had gained over the last few weeks — of an entirely different type of human nature, it is true — merely reinforced my growing awareness of my own blind ignorance.

The Slough of Despond from which Annie dragged me with the news of Cookie's grandson's death was not just brought on by physical debility. It is also what others more sophisticated would choose to call Information Overload. Knowledge had entrapped and wrestled me to the ground.

96

ONCE ROUSED BY THE news of the killings, I never turned back. I started to watch the news on TV and listen to the radio talk shows. As Annie said, the shootings were all people were talking about. As with everything, there were two versions, that of the police and their supporters and that of everyone else. But none of the talk and the anger was going to bring Cookie's grandson back.

Still, she soldiered on. Just a few days after the shootings, and before I had moved back to the dining room for my meals, she sent me a huge slice of lemon meringue pie, something I had taught her to make. I'd had to sneak into the kitchen to do it, on a day when we knew Matron was away, for residents were strictly forbidden to enter into those hallowed grounds. But I couldn't stand the waste from the lemon tree right outside the kitchen door, the fruit falling and left to rot. This was because everyone swore by limes, and that tree in bearing never lacked for patronage. It was the same where I grew up. Lemons were regarded as a pale cousin of the more powerfully acidic green fruit. It was Sam's mother, Ma D, who had introduced me to lemons and taught me to make the pie, one of the times I suspect she was trying to take my mind off Sam, though I remember I only mastered the meringue after several tries.

When I suggested to Cookie that she use up the lemons in this way, she said she always wanted to make that pie, would I show her how to do it. So I did. After that it was her biggest dessert hit with residents, and from the start her pies were infinitely superior to mine. Cookie was truly a natural, masterful baker, though her repertoire was fairly limited.

At the time she asked me to show her how to make the pie, I wondered why she hadn't simply taken down one of the many cookbooks on a shelf in the alcove off the kitchen and looked up the recipe. I'm glad I didn't ask out loud, for it was some time before I figured out that Cookie couldn't read. And yet she really ran the place. She managed the domestic staff, all the cooking with very little assistance, kept the kitchen inventory, and followed the week's menus, which Matron wrote out, taking into account some of the specialized needs of residents who numbered no fewer than twenty at a time. I think she relied a great deal on Annie, who had had some years of secondary school, and perhaps Maisie and one or two of the others who had some modicum of education. They obviously never questioned her little subterfuge, which always took the form of, "Read this for me nuh? I forgot my glasses." Though no one had ever seen her with a pair. No wonder, I thought now, she was so proud of Trevor's achievements, the fact that he had planned to study medicine. But now there would be no one to rescue her from the daily grind in someone else's kitchen. And grief made no difference to the sweetness of her pies.

97

I FORGOT THAT BEFORE I was up and about, Winston had sent me Bombay mangoes, from Matron's tree no doubt, for Maisie had brought them in a covered shoebox one day, disguised by the clean towels on top, the whole package clutched to her body like some secret ready to explode.

"Winston send these for you," she whispered, even though there was no one else within shouting distance. "They green, but they soon ripe. A going to put them here for you." And she opened my clothes closet and made room for the box on the top shelf.

I murmured thanks, but, to show how sick I was feeling at the time, the gift did not really register. Until this morning, when I woke up to the distinct smell of mangoes on the air, wafting into my room from outside, I thought. Mango season. Another reason for me to get going, for I had several trees of my own in the country and they would be bearing.

When Matron came by to check on me I noticed her sniffing too, but she didn't say anything. It was right in the middle of her visit that I remembered my hidden cache, and I wondered how she hadn't seen the light bulb going off over my head. As soon as she left, I went and turned the lock in my room door. I carefully lifted down the box. Three Bombays, fully ripe. The smell was divine, it instantly cleared my brain, wiped out all the bad thoughts. I couldn't wait to bite into the first one as I headed for the bathroom and sat on the side of the bath and leaned over as I ate, greedily, messily. I sat and ate those three mangoes, licked the insides of the skins before discarding them, and sucked the seeds until they were white. And for all the time I did that, I became like that greedy child again, I didn't think about a single thing but their ambrosial presence. After that, I had a leisurely bath and combed my hair and dressed. For the first time in weeks I began to feel human. I went downstairs, to join the rest of the residents, as if nothing had ever happened.

98

THERE IS ONE OTHER thing I forgot to mention earlier. The night after I discovered the letters in Mr. Bridges' room, I was so angry that at some point I got up and marched back over there and I took up the box with the stereo set and I brought it back to my room, feeling triumphant. The bastard, I thought. Then after a few minutes I started to have second thoughts. I was so bothered by having taken it that I marched back over there and put it back. Then as I read something else in the letters that angered me, or thought some more, I went back and brought it over to my room again. This time, I also looked for and found the jazz and blues CDs, including the one he never played for me as well as the music he had bought that day — Buddy Holly, Ray Charles, the Temptations. Once I had the stuff in my room, I began to feel awkward about it again, though I wondered who it would end up with if I didn't take it. My feelings went back and forth all night. The stereo and CDs ended up staying with me, for I think I just got too tired of getting out of bed. After that, I forgot about them because someone tidying up my sick room had stuck them in a cupboard. I only came across them again when I started to pack. Which is what I am doing, for I know it is time to go.

99

THIS MORNING THERE WAS an unfamiliar knock on my door. I had just come back from breakfast, intending to get on with sorting out my stuff, amazed at how much I had accumulated in the time I had occupied the room. When I opened the door I was surprised to see it was Morveen, the hairdresser, and her sidekick, Kyisha. I'd forgotten about them and their weekly visits. Morveen was looking more than ever like a walking advertisement for everything that was the latest. This time she had shoulder-length straight red hair with bangs across her forehead — she later confessed it was a wig, as if I wouldn't have known — and long silver nails with a red star painted in the middle of each. How on earth she — or more likely Kyisha — managed that I made a mental note to find out. Kyisha's nails were bright pink with silver half moons; I guess they had been experimenting as usual.

Kyisha reminded me of Lise, as she had the same sort of colouring and the pale, weak-seeming eyes that made her look timid. She was never as outrageous in her dress as Morveen and today she was fairly sober-looking in a short black skirt, a simple sleeveless knit top in purple and green stripes, and little black Chinese cloth slippers. She didn't wear a lot of make-up, just lip gloss, but she made up for the lack in the size and quantity of gold-like jewellery, starting with earrings the size of cartwheels.

"Miss Sam, how you doing?" Morveen greeted me. Scrutinizing me at the same time, taking in, I'm sure, every inch of my sartorial deterioration. Well yes, for next came the anguished cry, "Miss Sam, look at you! No, man, this won't do." Almost a wail, as she touched my hair, my skin, and clicked her tongue over my chipped and broken nails. "Kyisha, look here," she said, taking possession of my hand as if it was no longer attached to me.

"Miss Sam, this is bad," was that child's contribution.

Up to then I hadn't been able to get a word in, and I was trying not to laugh, for although Morveen was a teenager, or so I believed, she was behaving like my grandmother.

"Come in, girls," I said.

"Oh Miss Sam," said Morveen as she entered and gazed around my room. She had probably never been outside of the room downstairs with the mirror, basin, and professional dryer that served as her parlour. "I know you been sick and all and that nice gentleman your friend die I really sorry to hear and the two of you look so lovely together. You wouldn't believe I scream with fright when Annie phone to tell me, Miss, and how you take to your bed with a broken heart. But Time Waits for No Man, Miss Sam, you can't let yourself go like this. Eh, Kyisha?"

Before I could say anything to this, the open suitcases and general signs of packing must have registered. "Miss Sam, you not going away?" she wailed.

I told her yes, I was going back to my home in the country.

"Country?" Kyisha piped up, as if I had said the General Penitentiary. "Country, Miss? But how you can leave Kingston to go a country? You mean to live? Forever?"

This time I couldn't control my smile. But, before I could say anything, Morveen jumped right in to chastise her. "What

you know about country, Kyisha? It can be nice, you know."
And she sounded almost dreamy. "One time I did go to
country to visit my Grannie, somewhere far, I don't remember
where now. I was little and my mother did take me. It was
sweet you see! I eat cane the whole time, cane that mi Grannie
cut for me. Right from the tree!"

"Well, I did go country one time," said Kyisha, not to be
outdone. "And my Grannie pick mango for me. And starapple.
Right off the tree. But when night come, it was dark, man. I
fraid you see. I wanted to go to the toilet bad bad, but you
think I was going to go outside in that darkness. So I ..."

"Kyisha," said Morveen sharply, "Miss Sam don't want to
hear your business."

Kyisha looked suitably cowed, as she probably was all the
time by Morveen, who then turned her attention back to me,
all business.

"Now, Miss Sam, we come to take you downstairs. For
you must be forget. You need a good haircut and some nice
colouring." She had taken hold of my hair again as if she
was sampling the quality before purchase. "Maybe we'll try a
new relaxer this time. And Kyisha, you have to well try with
these nails, yu know." She seized both my hands again and
held them out for viewing.

I untangled myself from Morveen's probing grasp and
decided enough was enough. "Morveen, Kyisha, I'm really
glad to see you, but I really don't have time these days for all
that foolishness."

"Foolishness, Miss?" They spoke simultaneously, in
anguished tones, as if I had shattered the very altar at which

they worshipped. "Miss Sam, you can't mean that." Now it was Kyisha's turn to wail. "And yu was loooking so criss and stylish up to the other day. Everybody in the kitchen was talking about it. They even saying ..."

"Miss Sam is when your man gone you must take care of yourself," Morveen interrupted sharply, giving Kyisha a cut-eye. "For is them time everybody looking at you see how you draw down. Take me now, when my last baby faada did leave, him send the new matey him tek up with come dare walk down my street to check out how me look. But when she come, you know, me was ready for is them time when him leave that me a bus style, you know. A tek up mi celli and call mi auntie a Miami beg her courier down some supplies for me quick. So when the jezebel come, I just flick my hundred-dollar U.S. weave and step out in my new gold lace-up bootie and mek out like a risto. You should see how that skettle turn tail and run."

I was as mesmerized by her language as by the revelation of her "baby faadas." Good grief! How many children did she have? No wonder she was so free with advice. She wasn't finished with me yet. Not that I understood half of what she'd just said, for Morveen seemed to switch into a different language when she was excited.

"No, no Miss. Is when your heart is low that you must have high ambition. And I know you is no paa-paa, you is the kind of lady that pick up yourself when you batter down and rise again in glory."

The two of them were so earnest that I didn't have the heart to turn them away completely, and they had made me aware for the first time in weeks of how awful I really looked, as I'd barely glanced in the mirror.

"Okay," I said in my firmest voice. They broke into smiles. "But none of this hair colouring business and all that fancy stuff, Morveen. I won't have anyone to look after it once I get back to the country. So there's no point in starting now. And Kyisha, all I want is for you to cut my nails short short short. Nothing more."

They both nodded and left smiling happily. A few minutes later I had my head bent over Morveen's basin downstairs. At lunchtime, I came out of their little room with my hair in a very short, stylish shag with blond highlights, my nails painted cappuccino and my face fully made up and tingling with pleasure after a steaming and facial.

I knew that once I put myself in the hands of those two there was no turning back. And I didn't want to. Morveen was right. I was the type of woman who picked herself up again when battered down. Now I couldn't wait to rise in glory.

Though I wasn't sure how to take Kyisha's parting remarks as she gazed at my hair. "Lord, Miss, you look like that singer there, what she name again, Morveen? She have hair just like Miss Sam. You know, she very old ..."

I saw Morveen's elbow snake out to give her a hard nudge, before she said, "You mean Tina Turner. And she not so old ..."

"Thank you, Morveen," I said.

But Kyisha would have the last word. "Well, she not so old as Miss Sam, but is same so her hair stay ..."

"And you, too, Kyisha."

As I entered the dining room all eyes swivelled in my direction. I thought, Mrs. Margo Haynes-Crosswell-Bitch, eat your heart out.

100

I WAS SHOCKED AT how upset Ruby was when I told her I was leaving. Her eyes actually filled with tears that spilled over, making no difference to that mascara that was already smudged over half her face. She blinked and tried for something of her old bullying tone: "Of course you can't go." But, as I passed her a tissue, we both knew it was a done deed.

"They've finally repaired my house, Ruby. From the hurricane. Almost two years. I can't stay away forever. You know I was only stopping here for a while." I couldn't resist saying with some pride, "My son's down there looking after it for me, he's finally found the time," although I hadn't heard anything further about Junior's involvement.

I'd pulled up a chair beside hers on the veranda where she was sitting alone playing solitaire, the cards spread out on a tray across her lap. Poor Birdie was so decrepit she could no longer hold the cards and her eyesight was almost gone. There were times when she couldn't hold her spoon or fork at table, her hands shook so much. Ruby had to take over and feed her like a child, Ruby herself having difficulty manipulating knife and fork. Now Birdie sat nodding in an armchair slightly to the left of Ruby, and I had to go right up to her so she could see who I was when I greeted her. It was clear that Birdie should be in a place where she would get nursing care, but Ruby was determined to soldier on for the two of them. She walked now with her arm around Birdie's waist, almost dragging her along, though she herself was tottering. Watching the two of them slowly making their way down the corridor was the most powerful signal that as long as Ruby was alive, Birdie would never pass on alone to an Old People's Home. In the middle of our little chat, Ruby leaned over and confided that she and Birdie had made a pact. She gave me an arch look, as if I should know what she meant. But I hadn't a clue.

"A pack of what?" I leaned over and whispered back.

"No, no! Caramba! Are you deaf? Pact! Agreement. You know. Together." And she used her index finger to made a cutting motion across her throat.

"What! You wouldn't!" I was truly aghast. For her gesture had conjured up an insane image of throat slitting and blood spurting, though between them they could hardly hold a table knife steady.

"Pills," she croaked. "We're saving up."

I sat there with my mouth open, trying to get my head around the idea. I truly didn't know what to think, it was so foreign to me.

"Best thing for both of us. Look at her!"

We both looked at Birdie, who was now loudly snoring with her head on her chest, her mouth wide open. Unlike Ruby, she no longer bothered about her appearance, and her pink scalp showed through her snowy white hair, cut short and feathered around her head. Her face was sunken in, pale and colourless. I was amazed at how quickly she had passed to this stage.

"You think I want to be left alone with the likes of that Running Water?" Ruby asked, for so she referred to our talkative table-mate. "I'd rather die first." She paused to light a cigarette, although she already had one burning in the ashtray, and she gave her little signature cough after the first puff.

She looked defiant, then just old and sad as she angrily stubbed out the butt of the old one. "Life's no fun anymore." Then, recovering some of her old feistiness in a more accusing tone, "And now you say you are going too."

I didn't respond. She took that as a sign to continue. "At least you brought a little life to the place. All your vegetables. Now I won't get a chance to plant my roses."

"Winston ..." I began.

"Winston!" she said. "That ram goat! All that man knows to plant is one thing. I'm amazed he hasn't worn it out by now!"

"Ruby!"

"You and that Ralph Bridges made such a pair, brought a little excitement to the place. You know Matron ..."

"But Ruby, we were not a pair," I protested. "We were just ..."

I was glad that she interrupted. for I found I was having difficulty getting the word *friends* out of my mouth.

"Oh, I know that, dear," Ruby said airily. "But I wouldn't make anyone the wiser. Their silly speculation was so delicious."

I didn't quite know how to take that remark, so I fumed

for a few seconds, until the next one brought me fully back to listening.

"I think it was so stupid of him wanting to marry that awful Margo Frome, or Cresswell, or whatever she calls herself. A little hurry-come-up, she's done more climbing than a passion fruit vine. She'd have sucked him dry, for that's her style, for God's sake. Two down so far, he'd have been the third. But then men …"

I didn't even bother to listen to Ruby's little diatribe, I was both shocked at her knowledge and elated at her description.

"Ruby," I interrupted. "How did you know? About Mr. Bridges and this lady?"

"Oh, sweetheart, just because you see me here looking like an old cabbage, doesn't mean I don't know what goes on. I'm still plugged into that Florida circuit, you know. For months she's been busily telling everyone about her trousseau, at her age, for God's sake! And pestering them with her plans for home decorating. Why she would want to come back here …"

"Mr. Bridges didn't want to go and live in the States," I said and almost bit my tongue, for I had vowed to forget about the two of them.

"Well, if he knew what was good for him, he would have been much better off with you, my dear."

Despite myself, I felt a wave of gratitude to Ruby for her endorsement. "Except," she continued, "I don't know about you, but the idea of living with a man with a brain like a filing cabinet is too appalling. Like Birdie's first husband." She leaned over and whispered this, though Birdie was still asleep. "He used to run a factory so everything with him was assembly line. He had to take off every item of clothing and neatly fold or put away each piece before jumping on top of her. You can imagine how exciting that was." Ruby cackled loudly at the thought. "My Jorge, now, was a man of terrific spontaneity. I can't tell you all the places we tried it. Caramba!"

"Ruby!"

"Okay, okay, I won't shock you. But you yourself could loosen up a bit you know, Mrs. Samphire. Although I have to say you've made a three-hundred-degree improvement in your social skills since you came here. You really couldn't stand us, could you? I could see you mentally wanting to chew us up and spit us out."

I didn't say anything to that, I just smiled, amazed how over the time I had come to know her I had had to constantly revise my opinion of Ruby.

"I don't know," she said, changing tack. "The turnover in this place is getting too fast for my liking. First Bridges, then that old man Turner, then the Pitts. Now you leaving ..."

"Miss Pitt-Grainger?"

"Yes, didn't you know? Just keeled over one day. They all seem to be doing that. No lingering anymore. Nowadays, everything quick, quick. Not like my Jorge." She cackled at my raised eyebrows. "Geez, when was it? Quite a few weeks now. It must have been when you were sick, so I guess no one told you. She had this huge write-up in the papers and everything and you should see the turnout at her funeral. Still, I wonder where all those Old Girls were when the old girl herself was sitting here, so lonely."

"Yes," I said, for I'd had the same thought when she was sick, and I felt guilty now that I had been so full of myself I hadn't even noticed her absence.

"She wasn't a bad old sort really. Just set in her ways. But boy did we love to tease her!"

Ruby picked up her cigarette that had been burning in the ashtray and waved it around, dropping ash everywhere. She suddenly looked happy. "That's what the three of us always loved to do, Birdie, Babe, and me. Take the mickey out of people. The Three Musketeers, they called us. Until we got married, we were always together, hatching up plots. Birdie and I have been friends since we were born. Our families lived next door to each other. Babe was my cousin. We were always in and out of each other's houses. I don't know why we hit it off so well, we three were closer than they were to their own sisters. I was an only child, so you bet your life I wasn't going to let go. I have to say, I have been so fortunate to have had such good friends. There's nothing to replace that, really."

She fell silent, and I said nothing, weighing my life against hers and finding it wanting, for I have never had a single friend. I was never allowed to have friends in my childhood, and by the time I was married and having children, there was no one around to be friends with. Well, nobody around that was good enough, for I certainly considered myself a cut above the women in our neck of the woods. Never mind our poverty, they all knew where I was coming from. Or so I thought, though I am a little embarrassed when I consider that self now. But I had certainly been injected with pride and prejudice by my father's family. Those were the very elements of my upbringing that I hadn't managed to shell off. I had friendly encounters and neighbourly exchanges, all right, but nothing that went beyond that, except perhaps with Millie — though the social divide was always there. Never mind that Millie was one of the women whose children had done so well she has not only taken to travelling but has learned to drive and has her own car to boot. Now she's way ahead of me. Of course, I never went out socially or to church, which is where women seemed to get to know one another. Marriage did not bring the opening up of my life that I expected. All it did was reinforce my isolation.

I looked at Ruby again and I thought, this is the closest I have come to having a friend. She must have picked up something of my mood, for she stretched across the tray, scattering her cards, and took my hand in hers. Then she turned it over and began a fake reading of my palm. "I see a road. I see a house. I see a tall, dark, handsome stranger." She must have felt my hand tighten up, for she quickly added, "'Tall,' I said. Tall handsome stranger."

Still holding my hand, she peered at me and said, "You really liked him, eh, chiquita?"

I nodded and felt tears come to my eyes. I thought, this is the moment, this is where I confess to someone and shed my pain. But I couldn't bring myself to do it. Ruby held on to my hand without speaking, then she squeezed it and smiled at me. I knew she understood.

She turned my hand over again and said, her voice bright and teasing again, "What happened to your rings?"

"Rings?" I laughed. "I've never had any. I lost my wedding band years ago."

"You know," she said, "in the old days men left rings to their male friends in their wills. Mourning rings they called them. Even that old pirate Henry Morgan did it. I am not quite done for yet, but I know that once you leave here I won't see you again, so I am going to give you my friendship ring now." And much to my astonishment, she eased off one of her rings, the very one that I had so secretly admired from my first day at her table, and she took my hand and placed it on my finger. It was the large sapphire surrounded by a circle of tiny diamonds, the whole seeming to form a strange constellation of tiny stars in the blue night sky like the one I used to gaze at. How had Ruby, whose hands were covered with rings, known that this was the one that always caught my eye?

It slipped off her finger easily, for she was mostly skin and bone, and it slipped easily onto mine, which made me realize she must have been a large woman in her time. The gesture made me too stunned to speak. But I finally did, and I pulled the ring back off.

"Ruby, no. I am utterly grateful. But I couldn't accept something so valuable. I really couldn't."

"Of course you could," she said, waving her hand at me. "And you will. It's mine to give, and I want you to have it to remember me by."

"Ruby!"

She sat back and paid no more attention to me. She had this little smile on her face, and I knew she had wandered away from the present, as she sometimes did. I held on to the ring and turned it over and over, admiring its sparkle.

"It was my grandmother's ring," she said. "All the ones I like to wear were." She turned both hands over and over to look at the glint of diamonds, rubies, emeralds. "But that one was the first one my grandfather gave her, she told me, so it was very special. She gave it to me because she couldn't stand my mother. But I don't have a daughter or a grand-daughter and my son is about to get divorced from a wife whom I couldn't stand myself. So I'd rather give it to someone I like."

I was mesmerized by the ring and still trying feebly to protest, but Ruby was paying no attention to me.

"It was funny about my grandmother, my father's mother," she said. "She was just a little coolie girl from the canefield, you know."

I jumped as if she had sent a jolt of electricity up my spine. But she wasn't paying any attention to me.

"Well, her father came over from India as an indentured worker, as they did in those days, so he was in the canefields. My grandfather saw her one day and they fell instantly in love and that was that. You can imagine the scandal; he the scion of the plantation owner. Of course, the scandal wasn't that he had taken up with this little Indian girl, for that would have been seen as him exercising his droit du seigneur, you know. But when he insisted that he wanted to marry her! His family literally threw him out of the house. They ran off together anyway. His parents eventually came round to forgiving them, for they were the only ones to produce grandchildren. Very important in the planting classes, my dear. And his mother took her under her wing and trained her up and she became this very grand chatelaine. Actually, she looked a bit like Louella Dune, but much grander. And nowhere as silly. She was a very smart woman. Her husband showered her with love and jewels. The story had a happy ending."

I'm glad that Ruby didn't seem to expect any kind of response from me, for I would have found it difficult to speak. That she had used the exact phrase "from the canefields" to describe her own grandmother, as my mother had been described, but in so loving a fashion, with none of the scornful implications of the Richardses, was a revelation. I had no difficulty about accepting the ring then, for it took on a whole new meaning for me. I put the ring on my finger and I got up and leaned over and kissed Ruby on her cheek.

"Thank you, I will treasure this, and wear it to remember you always."

Ruby seemed pleased at this. I wished I could have told her what I was really thanking her for, about my own mother. But, despite Mr. Bridges' attempts to unravel me, the knots that bound up the secrets of my heart hadn't been loosened enough.

101

SHORTLY AFTER THIS, I had an unexpected visitor. I was out in the garden with Winston when Maisie called out from the back of the house, "Someone to you, Miss Sam. I tell her to come round there."

I called out, "Who?" but she didn't answer, so I started walking around to the front of the house, quite curious.

I saw this young girl walking towards me, at first glance not too different from Morveen, very slim as they all seemed to be these days, with very long legs and a very short skirt, a tiny blouse, and — as she came closer — several earrings in each ear. But there the resemblance ended, for even at a glance I could tell this was a child from a different background entirely, just from the way she moved, as if she owned the world. As she approached, something about her looked vaguely familiar, and my attention was caught by her hair, which was long and very, very curly, its lightness contrasting with her cocoa brown skin. She gave me a brilliant smile as she came nearer, and from the way her mouth turned up at the corners, I knew right away who she was.

"Grandma," she said, and leaned in to give me a kiss on the cheek. Her name didn't come to me right away, but she helped me immediately.

"Ashley," she said.

"Of course," I said as if I had known, for she truly had grown out of my sight. "How are you, dear?"

"Fine, Grandma, how are you? You're looking awesome. Love your hair," and that brilliant smile again. Then, without waiting for me to answer, she hurried on. "Mom had to go away, so she asked me to pop by. I would have come anyway, now that exams are over. I hope you are feeling better. Anyway, I came by to see if you needed anything. I have Mom's car, so I could take you someplace. But I don't know what you'd like to do."

"Whoa!" I had to laugh, for she hadn't paused for breath. Unlike her mother, she was very animated. "Let's go in for a moment and sit down."

On the way to the lounge I got caught up on her doings and the doings of her brother, who was at Harvard. She had just finished high school and had been accepted at the University of the West Indies. I was really happy to see this girl. I couldn't stop looking at her, trying to unravel the combination she revealed of her father — nose, dark skin, dark eyes — and her mother — mouth, hair. Her high spirits enchanted me. I didn't even have time to revisit my guilt at how my own blindness in the past had prevented me from my really seeing her and my other grandchildren. Though if truth be told, the few times I had been to Celia's house the place always seemed filled with young people who all looked the same to me and who never seemed to stop talking or moving long enough for me to figure out who was who.

When Ashley leaned over and said, "Grandma, let's go out and do something. Let's go to a movie," I said yes without thinking. As I stood to go upstairs to change, she lightly took hold of my hand.

"Love your ring. Wicked!" she said.

"Thank you," I said, "it was my mother's."

I honestly don't know where that came from, and as soon as I said it I could have bitten off my tongue, but I didn't want to break the mood of the moment. I thought: I'll explain to her some other time. As I walked up the stairs, I couldn't understand why I was feeling elated, whether it was from my granddaughter's presence or the fact that I was about to visit a cinema for the first time in my life. Of course, I would never have shared that fact with her or anyone else, for wasn't it a shameful thing?

Had they known, people would be surprised at how little practical experience of life I had, though I had a vast knowledge from reading and just paying attention to what was happening around me. I had never travelled abroad, for instance, never until I came to town eaten in a real restaurant — meaning not an ice cream parlour — never worn a bathing suit or sat on a beach. That's so astonishing now, when I think of it, but that's what living in the country was about for me.

I knew that all the other women with children in town or overseas had readily taken to the latest of everything, like Millie. Even the old grannies would be seen wearing Jheri curls or bright red wigs or whatever was the fashion of the moment, sporting cell phones and designer track shoes. They had been to Disney World and New York City and Toronto. Ridden trains and roller coasters. Flown on airplanes. But I had so buried myself that I knew nothing of the things that made the modern world go round. I averted my eyes when people flaunted them at me, worse when they flaunted the children and grandchildren who came to visit. I had stayed deliberately ignorant of makeup and the latest fashions, though these were the things I had yearned for in my early life. If I couldn't have them, I didn't want them, I decided; my decision, like everything else, hardening into a kind of scorn for those who did. But I was a fast learner. For once I was exposed to all the fashion or home decor magazines lying around Ellesmere Lodge, I began to treat them with the same studious attention

I gave to everything. I became knowledgeable about brand names and the latest styles, and quite curious about people's choices in scent, makeup, or lipstick, even the colours, because of what I felt these choices were saying about them.

Listening to the Pancake Sisters, of course, was an education in itself as to what was fashionable and what was not — at least in their eyes, which was at least one generation removed from reality. I was lucky that this was counterbalanced by the endless information on the topic of fashion and makeup imparted by Morveen and Kyisha when they worked on me. It was from them that I also managed to extract information on their other clients' preferences, including Matron, who apparently went to a real beauty parlour where the girls normally worked, as they came to Ellesmere Lodge on Mondays when the parlour was closed. All of this was when I first came and had the feeling that knowledge was power and that the more I knew about my enemies — Matron, the Pancake Sisters — the more I could prepare myself against attack. Those days are long gone, of course, but what I haven't lost is the insecurity, the fear of being found out as an ignoramus.

My husband never took me anywhere, preferring to escort other lady loves even before he bought a car. I wasn't one of those mothers who did things with their children; it was as if they walked away from me once they left to go away to secondary school. After that, they did things with their friends, occupying a world in which I had no place. I might have had to visit their schools once or twice on business. I went to the town at least once a term to buy school supplies and whatever else I needed, but entertainment was never a part of these.

Money was always tight, but it really was that I had a profound fear of going out, of being in crowds, surrounded by or interacting with other people. I think it was always because I felt too ashamed of how I looked, how far my clothes, my hair, fell from the internal standards I had set myself. For, thanks to my grandmother and Aunt Zena, I knew what I was supposed to be. But it seemed I had fallen a long way.

It was as if I was always two people. The one who was visible: plain, awkward, and shy. And the other inside my head: well-dressed, fashionable, and in command. For that, at least, is what Aunt Zena always was, which makes me think now that the scenario of her having travelled, living in the United States, having a husband and a fashionable wedding dress, seems plausible. Having heard some of her story from Ma D I could think of her in another way, as a woman who, in another life, would have been attractive. She wore makeup — at least by the modified standards of the country, powder and lipstick — and who knows what else in the jars I saw sitting on her vanity top when I scouted it out. There was, hidden in her clothes cupboard, a curling iron — which, by the time I came along, she probably never used — jewellery never worn, smart hats in boxes, and beautifully pleated and beaded dresses I never saw her put on. But there must have been considerable vanity in her makeup that I hadn't recognized, of a woman who saw herself as attractive and attracting male attention, or who had at some time in the past.

"Oh, Zena was quite the girl," Ma D had laughed another time when I questioned her. I noticed that she had this peculiar little laugh she only gave when Zena's name was mentioned.

"She was attractive and stylish. She had a way about her. She liked other women's husbands, that's for sure. Once I caught her kissing mine." My eyes popped then, but, instead of continuing, Ma D suddenly pinched her mouth shut as if she'd said too much. Over time I was to learn more about Zena, as I kept on bringing up her name. It turned out that Zena was the scandal of her generation, for she had run off to America with some married man. He had eventually left her, but she stayed on, getting married to a man no one ever met. He too seemed to have wandered on. Zena came home when her father got ill, meaning to stay for only a short time, but she had ended up staying for a long time to nurse him and then forever after he died, trapped by family obligations.

I remembered other photographs. Her alone looking rather glamorous in a fur collar and a cloche hat. Her with others — male and female — in winter coats and boots with a backdrop of tall buildings and high steps leading up to them. In these photos she was always smiling.

So what had happened to turn her into such a shrew? Why had she reacted to me, her brother's child in such a manner? Was it because I was illegitimate? For such things mattered a great deal then to such people. Was it because of my colour? I was so much darker than they with what they would have called "bad" or "tough" hair. Was it because my mother came from a dark-skinned family that they, of English origin, refused to recognize? Was it because of my mother's moral qualities — "the slug"? Or was it because of my father — the madman — and the embarrassment to the leading family of the district? Or was it simply that Zena herself had skidded to such a dead end in her own life she was forced to take out her anger and frustration on the most vulnerable member of the family, me?

But she did give me one thing, and that was the image of how smart a woman could be. Although that image never left me, I made no attempt to make myself into that person. Perversely, I courted plainness, as punishment, perhaps, for the bad choices I had made in life. If I went out at all, my one objective was to get my errands done and return home as quickly as possible.

So how did I get here then, so quickly transiting that space? Sitting comfortably in my daughter's grand car. My smart beige two-piece linen dress, my pointy-toed high-heeled pink shoes, my leather handbag, my feather-cut hair with the blond highlights, my lipstick — Revlon Super Lustrous in flesh tone. Ruby's ring! Whence this new feeling of confidence, riding down this hill into the city with my eighteen-year-old granddaughter, a competent driver down to her lacquered fingernails — Poster Pink nail polish, for I asked her.

With all these thoughts flying through my head as swiftly as the miles, of past, of present, and — for the very first time in my life — of future, it seemed that I had come such a long way since that hurricane blew my roof off.

102

I WENT TO MY room in a state of high excitement after Ashley dropped me off at Ellesmere Lodge. I couldn't remember the name of the film or what it was about, for too many images from the big screen were sliding around and colliding inside my head. I was drunk with new wine — the images of other worlds. The film was a silly comedy, but silly is a place I had never been before and where I wanted to be right now, for I felt giggly and foolish like a young girl.

Normally I would have slipped off my high heels the minute I came through the door, then stripped down to get into something comfortable, as if I couldn't wait to take off the face and finery I put on for the world. But this time I didn't bother. Still fully dressed and without any consciousness of what I was doing, I reached for the box in which I had packed Mr. Bridges' CD player and headphones and took them out. Then I fished around for the CDs he had brought home and played that last day and which I had taken from his room. I had no desire to play the blues or "Your Red Wagon" or any of that music I had so yearned to hear. What I wanted was the music of a later time, the music of the fifties and sixties that Mr. Bridges had played for me that day.

It's funny that the yearning I felt was not for him or those last moments we spent together but for the sweetness of that music as I remembered it, the bearer of memories of a vanished time in which I had never shared. Then I decided I didn't want the music that we danced to, the mellow tones of the Temptations or Ray Charles. What I wanted was something heard only once but which I remembered as joyous and — yes — silly. Buddy Holly is what had had me tapping my feet and swaying my body before Mr. Bridges had put on that other CD and asked me to dance. In retrospect, it seemed a silly kind of music for Mr. Bridges, too. Was its purchase a last bid to recapture his lost youth before he signed himself on to a life sentence with a gorgon? Perhaps he was really bothered after all; perhaps he was having second thoughts that day. I batted the idea and the image of Ralph Bridges out of the way. What do I know? What do I care? I plugged in the player and the earphones, not feeling in the least bit intimidated by all the buttons and flashing lights. How difficult could it be for an intelligent woman if a Rat could manipulate it? I slipped in the CD and pressed PLAY. Looking at the liner notes, I pressed the number of the tune I wanted. Number seven. I put on the earphones and felt the groove bounce through me.

Suddenly I was dancing in my room, by myself, all dressed up and wearing my pink high-heeled shoes. Dancing to the music of a young boy who was born the same year I was born and died at twenty-two, as the liner notes told me, around the same time my youthful self had died. I let the rest of the record play, not listening so much as feeling the changing moods, letting the images from the film of my life run through my head as I danced, trying to let each image fade out like a ghost, snatching from the air the few words here and there that I caught, hanging on to these fragments of self-assertiveness and belting them out to the last. "It doesn't matter anymore." And truly, for that one night, it didn't.

103

ASHLEY CAME AROUND QUITE a bit after that, while her mother was away, and she seemed to like my company, which surprised me. I went with her to all the places her mother had offered to take me when I first came, but which in my state of misery and anger and frustration I had not wanted to go to. Ashley and I went to the movies again and to the beach and to the mountains, and we ate at roadside shacks and fast food restaurants. I think Ashley loved to be my guide, and I loved everything about Ashley, except the music she played in the car the minute she started driving, slipping in a tape from the stack she seemed to travel with. She shouted above the music as we talked or turned the volume down as needed, which made me nervous no matter how skilful a driver she was. The reggae she played was not the music of Bob Marley or Toots, which I was familiar with and rather liked, but some awful stuff that could not be classified as music in my book. Dancehall, dub, rap, whatever. The pounding in my head! One day I decided to take some of my CDs along.

"Have you ever heard of Buddy Holly?" I asked as I got into the car, fishing the CD out of my handbag and holding it up before she even started the engine.

"Oh my God!" she said, laughing and covering her mouth with her hands in mock horror. "I don't believe it, Grandma. You too?"

"What?" I was taken aback.

"My parents. Well, my dad actually. He's always playing stuff like that. He's into all this stuff about the history of music and who was the greatest and what have you. Buddy Holly! Gosh, I never knew he had got to you."

"No," I said, laughing. "Herman and I have never talked about music. But I'm surprised, this was long before his time.

I thought he would be strictly into classical."

"You don't know him. Sure, he plays the classical stuff. But he's also into all kinds of popular stuff, not just Jamaican music but rhythm and blues, rock and roll, everything. He fancies himself as this historian of music. Which is so bor-ing! When we were little, he was always trying to get Gaby and me to listen to that stuff. We used to creep around the house when he was in one of these moods so he wouldn't grab us for a lesson." She shook her head and laughed. "Both my parents think the fifties and sixties were the greatest times for the music. They dig all that early ska and rock steady. But they also like that American stuff, like these old hippies, you know. Bob Dylan, Joan Baez, Crosby Stills —"

"Come on! I know your mom was into Black Power and the women's movement and all that sort of thing when she was in college in the States, but wouldn't she have been a little young to be a flower child?" I was pleased to sound so knowledgeable about Celia.

"Yeah, but she likes to pretend she had this carefree, hippy youth all the same. Like she was once on this big radical kick, throwing off the traces of society or some such thing. My mom! Can you imagine?" With her hands on the wheel, Ashley turned to face me, rolling her eyes.

I smiled back. "Well, I can't imagine your father into that sort of thing either." From the first, Herman to me was always the proper, straight-laced lawyer who chose his words as carefully as his ties.

Ashley laughed as she turned the key and started the engine. She kept on laughing and tapping the wheel for emphasis as she drove, as if amused by the vision of her parents my question had brought to mind. "Oh, you really don't know about my dad? His Rasta phase? What! You've never seen the pictures of him in his wild youth, in his dreadlocks and tam?"

"No!" My tone reflected my absolute disbelief.

"Don't tell me Mom never told you. It's their big party piece. How Herman Alphonso Jerome, Queen's Counsel, once grew his hair and smoked ganja and dropped out of school to go and join some Rasta commune. The Bobos or something like that. You know the ones that walk around the place with their hair wrapped in these glorious tams, wearing long white robes and selling brooms? Apparently that is what all those middle-class boys were doing then, all his friends. Dropping out to turn Rasta. Like Jeff Markle that everybody says will be the next prime minister. You didn't know? Gran! He was at school with my dad. Might even have been the one that inveigled him into it. Can you imagine? And he's such an old stuffed shirt now!"

"Who, your dad?"

"No, that Markle. Dad's all right. We argue a lot, but he still has some kind of social conscience, I have to say. Not like those fat-cat politicians."

Although it was hard to imagine Herman as a Rasta, I did have first-hand knowledge about these middle-class youths dropping out to join the brethren, for it was something that my own son, Junior, had tried to do. He came home from that first holiday he spent with his school friends wearing a tam, and when I dragged it off his head, I was appalled to see what was underneath, for Junior had always been so vain about his hair. Now it was long and natty and unkempt. Well, I let him know right away I wasn't going to put up with that and it was off with that tam and hair if he wanted to stay in my house. He didn't try any of it as long as he was with me, though I don't know what happened after he left to join his father. But it was a sign, wasn't it, of the rebellion all these boys were undergoing at the time, the desire to shed their privileged trappings and become one with the so-called sufferers. Or maybe they just wanted to go and smoke ganja. Not that Junior was privileged, like those others, but he was certainly a lot better off than most of the boys around. I thought with Junior I had nipped it in the bud, just as I refused to let him bring that I-man and Selassie-I talk to me. But it was soon after that he left home to live with his father, and I remember now that he was wearing the tam the day he came back to pick up his things. To tell me how my authority now counted for nothing, I suppose. But Herman's father was a high court judge and from all accounts very proper. They certainly seemed like that, he and his wife, the one time I met them at the wedding.

Ashley was still chattering away. "Imagine, I could have been born a Rasta Queen. Hail me up, nuh Sista! But guess what? Dad's father had a heart attack or something, the poor man was so mortified, and my little old Gran — did you ever meet her — a proper little lady with her gloves and hats and all, like the Queen Mum, you know — well, Grandmama just marched on right up there to that commune and dragged her son back home." She paused. "Actually, I don't know if that's exactly how it happened. But ol' Herms gave up all that nonsense and went back home and settled down to being the nice little middle-class boy." I could hear the satirical note creeping into her voice. "Who in time met your nice little middle-class daughter and married her. And here I am. Miss Criss!"

Half the time I wasn't sure whether Ashley was being serious or mocking, but right now, she seemed to find the whole thing incredibly funny and was giggling so much she even forgot to turn on any music at all, for which I was very grateful.

If I hang around Ashley I'll find out everything. All the things Celia would never tell me. Or would she? If I asked her?

104

ISN'T MY LIFE JUST like our country, hills and gullies, up dale and down, like riding on the true-true natural version of a mechanical roller coaster? So it was this plunge into the trough with Celia when she came back, and she ended up telling me far more than I wanted to hear. She came at night, as she usually did, after her day's work, so she found me up in my room, back at the sewing machine, altering some clothes. That in itself was probably a reflection of the mood that persisted after my granddaughter started to visit, for before that I had decided to give most of these clothes away. Ashley was shocked when I told her that, and urged me to do no such thing. For she is as confident in her opinions as Morveen is in hers and not at all hesitant about giving me advice. She went straight to my wardrobe when I told her I had to decide what to take, a few things only was all I would need in the country, for — though I didn't tell her this — I was still in that mood of wanting to shed my new-found vanity. She ignored what I said and started to take out dresses, holding them up against me and saying, "Oh, Grandma, you have to take this. The green is awesome. It looks great against your skin ... Where's that blue scarf again, see, it goes perfectly with these beads ... awesome with your beige dress, and this striped blouse too. These shoes, oh, you can't leave them behind ... neutral colour ... go with everything." Exactly as if she was my fashion consultant.

Ashley wore the most extraordinary high-heeled sandals, the type you see on models coming down the runway, the type that makes you wonder how on earth they walk in them. But she had no difficulty whatsoever. She had the body of a model, too, but covered, not like some of the ones who are all skin and bones. Not like her mother. I banished that thought. I let her prattle on, for she was making me smile inwardly. I was beginning to enjoy the attention of someone else in my business. How easy it is for these young people to cut through all the nonsense and get straight to the point.

Like the day she was occupying herself, colour-coordinating my wardrobe, moving her body to a beat only she could hear as she hauled out beads and shoes and scarves and laid them out on the bed, standing back to look at them, holding something up against her body and looking in the mirror, snatching up a belt and choosing something else to lay down beside the pants. She stopped suddenly and looked at me and said, out of nowhere, "Hey, Gran. Mom said you ran away from home when you were fifteen and rode off with Grandpa on horseback. Is that true?" She turned to me, her eyes sparkling, but in her usual way not waiting for an answer. She had turned back to her task and continued to shift my wardrobe around as she spoke, putting to one side those items she thought I could dispose of. "That is way, way too cool. I want to hear all about it. Every single detail. My girl-friends think it is so awesome. Like the movies. *Gone With the Wind* or something like that. They're dying to meet you. What was Grandpa like? I don't remember him at all. I guess he died when I was little. From his photos he was one handsome dude. Mom said he sure had an eye for the girls, but … oops!" She caught herself there but recovered without missing a beat, "You were divorced by then."

I didn't say anything, keeping pasted on my face the smile that her first words had evoked, thinking how different people's visions can be of the same event.

I had learnt that when Ashley asked questions, she didn't expect answers right away. But she would come back to those questions, so that sooner or later she would be asking me about Sam and myself and really listening this time. I knew that while she acted like the butterfly, flitting from one thing to the next, at heart she was really like her mother, more like a tick, never letting go once she had attached her mind to something. I knew I should start preparing answers on the subject of Sam and me. Prepare, for there was no way I would be telling this child any of the truth surrounding our so-called romance and marriage. Mark you, I rather liked the idea of seeming a romantic figure myself to this generation. O the things I could think of telling Ashley! Perhaps after all, half a lifetime spent reading romances would not be wasted.

But, as it turned out, it was Celia who found the way to shatter my new-found sense of self and silliness.

105

THE FUSS WITH CELIA — which I haven't talked about yet — at least brought one good thing in its wake: it gave me back my ability to sleep. I mean just plunging into sleep as a way of getting away from the world. Ever since Mr. Bridges' death, I've had great difficulty sleeping. Now I'm willing myself into sleep again. Willing myself back home, really, but we still have a few weeks to go. When Celia came back, she told me most of the work on the house was finished, the electricity was connected, but Junior wanted to paint, inside and out, a house that had never had a coat of paint in its life. I was secretly pleased to hear it, though — a sign of my continuing vanity, as if a painted house was more in keeping with the new way of viewing the world that I'd grown accustomed to.

I was seated at the machine, bent over a hem I was basting. Celia was sitting in the armchair beside me. She reached for her handbag. "Junior wants you to choose the colours, he sent a whole bag of paint chips. I have them somewhere ..." She kept on talking as she bent over and dug around in the bag. "I could take you one day next week to buy material for curtains and cushions and stuff. That should be fun."

As she bent down all I could see of her was the hair like a golden, wiry halo that hid her face from me. She was dressed in clothes that did not reveal much either, a creamy silk blouse with a high round neck and long sleeves and tailored trousers that fitted loosely, so it was hard to see anything of her body but her thin brown hands and her half-hidden face. I thought back to the times I had seen her and realized that she was wearing clothes as a disguise, to create the illusion that someone of far more substance occupied them. In a way she was like Ruby inside her clothes now, but Ruby was an old woman.

She broke into my thoughts as she held up her hand triumphantly and shook something that made a racheting, clicking sound. I now know rationally that it was only a heavy ring with plastic cards attached with the different paint colour samples, but at the sound of them clicking together, something seemed to burst in my mind.

Bones, I thought. A feeling of horror and revulsion sweeping over me. Why is she carrying bones around? I couldn't help it, I had this vision of bones — Mr. Bridges, my father's, all the dead people in my life — and bones that were hers lying among them. I was seeing her now as nothing but skin and bones. I couldn't stand it. All my years of keeping silent fled in this one flash of the irrational, for her movement made me jump.

"Bones," I said aloud. I might have shouted it, for I remember her eyes opening wide as she sat up and looked at me, the ring with the paint chips dangling from her hand.

I don't remember all the things that were said after that, I guess I was babbling, but I know I finally said, "What are you doing to yourself? Why are you killing yourself?"

She tried to calm me down then, I could see she was genuinely shocked at my outburst, it was so unlike me, like my rushing into Mr. Bridges' room to ask him to dance. But I didn't want to be calmed or reassured. It was if some other self had taken over.

"Look at you," I said. "What is it? Anorexia? Bulimia? What exactly is your problem? Why are you doing this to yourself?"

She was immediately defensive, I could tell, but she never raised her voice. "Doing what to myself?"

"Oh please. Don't do this to me. I'm your mother. Can't you be honest with me, just this once?"

She laughed then, not her usual modulated laugh but a high, artificial laugh.

"Me," she said, "be honest with you? Now isn't that a joke."

"What? What do you mean?"

"Exactly when have you ever been honest with me? With any of us? I don't think you have been honest with me since the day of my birth."

I looked at her, stunned, thinking, where is this coming from? Why are we discussing me? I couldn't bring myself to speak. It was she who finally broke the silence that stretched between us.

"Do you know how uncommunicative you have been to me throughout my whole life? How you have told me nothing, given me nothing. Even now, you cannot bring yourself to speak to me. Even something as simple as telling me why I went to live with the Frasers that I asked about the other day. All the things I have been trying to puzzle out, my whole life." She paused, then flung out, "I don't know why you ever bothered to have children, you cared so little for any of us."

She broke down then, crying silently, burying her head in her hands while the clicking of bones turned into the beating of my own heart against my ribs.

"Junie, Junie," I said, dropping the garment and turning around to face her fully. I wanted to reach out to her and hold her, but I was too terrified to move.

She took her hands from her face and looked at me, her face puffy, her eyes red and spilling over. The image of perfection shattered.

"Junie?" she said in a wondering sort of voice. "No one called me that since you sent me away." She was silent for a while, her eyes looking faraway, her face indescribably lonely. Then it was as if she was getting up steam again, for I could feel the heat in her voice, "You never even bothered to tell them what name I answered to. They didn't know that name. They didn't like the name I answered to at school, my first name. So I became Celia then, my middle name, a name I have always hated. And I heard Celia so often that when I went back to visit you, I told you I was no longer Junie, I was Celia now. I wasn't really, I wanted to go back to being Junie, if only you had let me. But you started calling me Celia, too. That's how I knew then that you didn't care. Only Papa ... Papa still called me Junie ... when it was just the two of us together ..." She broke down into tears again. I didn't say anything, there was nothing I could say. My mind was too churned up.

I did care, I wanted to say out loud. I did care, but I could never find ways to show it. It was as if I myself was always on the edge of things, barely managing to hold on. The first time you came back after you'd been away for a year and they were sending you to that expensive school, you were so much bigger that I hardly recognized you when you came out of the car. They had cut your hair too, very short. It curled all over your head. You looked so different from the child who had left. Polished. Your clothes were expensive. A crisp little white organdy blouse with blue forget-me-nots embroidered on, puff sleeves and a Peter Pan collar, a plaid pleated skirt held up with two broad straps, white socks, and sensible-looking brown oxford shoes. I remember you had a tiny handbag of your own, which made me smile, a yellow fabric one with green plastic handles that you gripped tightly in your right hand, like a grown woman. You were already beginning to look as cleanly washed and ironed as your keepers.

The Reverend Doctor came out of the car carrying a nice little brown grip. His wife held your Jippi Jappa hat dangling by the elastic. This time they came onto the veranda and I offered them lemonade, as we had been expecting them. Sam was home to do the greeting and talking. He took them around, past the granadilla arbour and down to the cocoa walk to show them "our little plantation," as he humorously called it, letting them think all the while I'm sure that it was his doing.

I didn't mind; I stayed behind watching them, holding the baby Lise. I didn't want to talk to them. It's you I wanted to talk to. But you were gone, too, your left hand in your father's, your right still clutching your handbag, Junior and Shirley excitedly following behind, chattering, skipping, laughing. As you vanished into the cocoa walk, the sounds of your voices came and went, all of you together in this joyous group. I stood there, feeling not that you all were moving ahead, but that I was falling, falling further and further behind.

106

I DON'T THINK I would have been able to write any more if Celia hadn't come back the following night, to "have it out." But she said it in a playful way, and I could see she was in a far different mood from the one in which she'd left. She had abruptly taken up her bag and gone through the door, without another word. I was left to sit all night, the words she threw at me clicking around inside my head — "cold," "indifferent," "spiteful," "don't care." I was so taken aback that I resorted to my former technique. I said nothing. I had nothing to say.

In the morning, I was still feeling rotten, but I did something I would never have done in the past. I phoned her. I only got her answering machine, but at least I was able to leave a message to say how sorry I was. I apologized. I wasn't sure what I was apologizing for, but at least I was taking some responsibility for my actions and not simply getting into a huff.

Our outburst, hers and mine, must have stirred up something, for she came over later that day, threw her handbag on the bed, and, smiling, stood with both hands up like a boxer and said, "Okay G. No more tears. Let's have it out."

I was feeling humble and still confused about a lot of things, but that stance made me laugh. We both laughed. I no longer felt hopeless. When she sat down in the chair and kicked off her shoes, I felt even better. I took that as a sign that she was staying for a while.

"Well, first of all, let's get one thing clear, G," she said. "I don't know where on earth you've got this idea that I've got an eating disorder. That's just not so. I'm thin, yes, but I can assure you I am perfectly healthy. I go to the gym every day — well, as often as I can. I can't help it that I'm the type who doesn't put on weight. I take after Papa's family, I guess." She laughed, "You have no idea how envious some people are of me."

"I'm sorry," I mumbled, "I honestly don't know where it came from." But I was mentally seeing the cover of Miss Pitt-Grainger's magazine in my head and feeling quite foolish. How could I have thought Celia looked like those skeletal creatures? What was wrong with me that I could so easily fall victim to every passing trend?

"All of us on that side of the family are skinnies, all of my cousins — Gina and Simone and Uncle Jeff's daughter, Janice, and Uncle Mark's as well."

She must have seen the blank look on my face, for she said, "I keep forgetting you never kept up with any of Papa's family."

"You seem to know them all."

"Well, Janice and Uncle Mark's daughter, Kayla, came as boarders when I was in high school and we are still close. You must have known Gina and Simone, though. They were at your wedding. I remember them telling me that, though they would have been little at the time. They're the oldest of the lot. Uncle Johnnie's girls."

John, I thought, the man who tried to rape me. I said nothing, but Celia must have picked up something from my face, for she said, "G, what happened with you and that family? Between you and Dad for that matter; I mean, why did you split?"

"He never told you?"

"Not really. I don't think I ever asked him. But I always got the impression that you were the one that —"

"That what?"

"Wanted out, I guess. I mean, you never even told me that you had separated. It was some time before I found out. Papa never told me, either. At least not directly. He wrote and told me he had a new address and I was to write him there. When I wrote and asked him why, he only wrote you had finally got fed up and kicked him. But he wrote 'smile' after it, so I was never sure. I mean, did you kick him out?"

"No, I didn't."

"What happened?"

"Your father walked out and left me with three children to look after. He never gave me a reason. He never told me to my face. He simply sent someone to come and collect his things."

"That can't be true!"

"Why?"

"I can't believe Papa would do a thing like that. He wasn't that kind of person."

"Oh really? What kind of person was he?" Not the type, I

said to myself, to slam my head against the wall, not the type to beat me when I was pregnant, not the type to humiliate me with other women from the moment we were married. Not the type to leave me and his children with nothing.

"Mom?"

I was standing in the middle of the room holding an empty hanger in my hand. I realized I hadn't spoken aloud, for which I was truly thankful. The rage was all in my head. A good sign, I thought wryly, because it used to be all in my heart. But it was the same rage I knew, for as usual it was succeeded by sadness. I don't know if I showed any of this, for when I looked at Celia she only smiled a rueful little smile and shook her head as if she had nothing further to say. Finally she said, "I would like to understand, you know. But you give me so little to go on. By the time I was grown up enough to be conscious, I saw a lot of my father but never anything of you." She paused, not looking at me but somewhere far in the distance. Then she said softly, "You have no idea how hard it was, do you?"

"What was?"

"Doing everything right. Being perfect. That's what you all wanted, isn't it?"

You all? I said nothing, feeling she had more to say. But she kept quiet. Sitting curled up in the chair like that, twisting a lock of hair around her finger, she looked so small and lonely I lost my fear of her.

I could see her, neat in the pretty new clothes, out in the yard with the other children, my own and the neighbours', directing their play, teaching them things, but never herself fully involved in the action, never getting dirty, always seeming somehow apart. My heart ached for her then, though I didn't know why, as it ached for her now. Always there was this barrier between us. I did not touch her, for I thought she didn't want to be touched. Hugged or held. She was always such a world unto herself.

"You don't know, do you, how hard it is to live up to someone else's ideals," she said, very softly. "They did not let me breathe. All along I kept looking down that road, for I expected you to come for me. To take me home. But you never came."

Now, I thought, as if preparing myself for a race. Now is the time to do it. Go on, tell her. Tell her you do know. It was like that for you, too. Tell her about your feelings. About going to fetch her back and not having the courage. Tell her what it was like, what living with Sam was like. About your own childhood. Spill everything. Spare nothing. Pour out your guts. Don't let them keep walking around with this distorted image of you. But I couldn't do it. I stayed silent.

So we didn't have it out, Celia and I. But at least she didn't leave angry with me. I could feel her frustration.

The problem is that I can talk to Celia, really talk, inside my head only, when she isn't there, the way as a child I talked to my imaginary mother, my absent father. That's how I am talking to her now.

Why did I let you go? Because I thought you deserved better. No, that is such a lie. The awful truth is that I thought I deserved better. I wanted for you what I thought I should have had for myself, the good life, with tablecloths and napkins in rings and polished mahogany floors. A life where people spoke properly and read books. This is the life I had lived for my first fifteen years, the life I threw over. And how I resented and disdained that other. The one I fell into, poverty and humiliation, my books, my reading, the only bulwark against the encroachment of squalor. Poor as we were, I did join a subscription library that had started, for there was no public library in our parish as yet. I earmarked the sale of the eggs of one hen as stamp money to pay for the books and magazines I shipped back as soon as I read them, eagerly awaiting the next batch. I called that hen Mrs. Rochester, and she brought me comfort for many years. I told myself I was not entirely selfish, as I got books for the children too.

The most precious moment of my existence became the evening, when the dinner things were washed and put away and you were all in bed, your uniforms ready for the next day, the ironing and other chores done, for I was careful not to be a slug. I got into bed then, and read, by lamplight, until I fell asleep, the book clutched in my hand.

When I was first married it was hard to concentrate, for I spent so many nights waiting for his footsteps crunching on the gravel path leading to the veranda. At the sound I would whip the book under the bed, jump up, and rush with the lamp to greet him at the door. But those moments became fewer and fewer as he came home later and later, long after I had fallen asleep.

I have to plead that I had no defences against these people when they came, wanting you. You have to understand this. I was ashamed for them to see me the way I was, the squalor of my surroundings. I could find no way to tell them, then or later, that I was used to better. It wasn't that I wanted to be grand. Just a cut above my neighbours, so they wouldn't look down on me, for they all knew where I was coming from and how far I had fallen. It was this that made me so ungracious to those people, the first time I met them, an ungraciousness that continued over the years, because I could never reverse the way I felt they perceived me, our status unequal at that meeting.

They were not to know that it was my own ignorance and folly that had reduced me. It was a way to avoid such ignorance and folly that I sought for you. No, I am lying. I didn't seek anything, for that implies thinking and I didn't think. My days were already passing in a blur of unhappiness and resentment. Sometimes I could remember nothing that had happened only a moment before. I was frightened of another baby on the way. How would I manage? Already I knew that in the world I was entirely on my own.

107

I AM LOOKING FORWARD to going home, yet there's a part of me that is decidedly uneasy. The more I think about Junior and the house the more I feel my heart hardening against him. I don't feel that I can just go back there and greet Junior as if nothing has happened. I can't do it. I need to know the truth once and for all of what happened to Shirley and why he had to run away. Everything. I need him to face me squarely and tell me the truth. But first, I want Celia to tell me what she knows. It is time she came clean.

I was trying to find a way of broaching the subject when she invited me to come and spend the long weekend with them. In my new frame of mind, I accepted, I thought it would be a good occasion to bring up the subject, since Herman's calm presence might keep Celia and me from bristling at each other. They lived up in the hills above the city, and this time as we turned into the driveway I didn't see the house as the pretentious monstrosity I had in the past but as a rather charming, restful, tasteful modern house set on a hillside with a spectacular view. Celia said it would be a good time for me to visit because she and Herman planned to stay home and relax for the weekend. Their helper, Mae, had gone home to the country. I was surprised to see how Herman pitched in. In fact he was the cook that night, a barbecue on the terrace. Ashley assisted him and did the cleanup afterwards. They refused any offer of help from me or Celia, so we sat there in a rather companionable silence, listening to the tree frogs and enjoying the view and the luxury of sitting outdoors at night, something I hadn't done since I left home. Later, Ashley went out with her friends we three watched a movie. Celia and Herman slept through most of it. Once in bed, I read for some hours before I fell asleep. I felt very relaxed in a way I had never felt in Celia's house before. But I vowed that no matter what, I would bring up the subject of Shirley the very next day.

It was Herman himself who unwittingly introduced the subject that Sunday morning. We had eaten breakfast out on the terrace and were sitting idly around the table having more coffee, reading the Sunday papers, when Herman started to comment on an article he was reading. It was about the connection between Jamaican drug posses in Kingston and New York. At first I didn't pay much attention, but my ears perked up as he read a bit about how easy it was for innocent bystanders to get shot since the drug enforcers had no qualms about spraying bullets at their target on a busy street. Without thinking, I blurted out, "So that is what happened to Shirley then?"

This was greeted with dead silence. I could see Celia and Herman exchanging glances and then looking away as if something appalling had just occurred. I didn't care. This time I wanted answers.

"Look," I said, addressing each in turn. "Don't you think I deserve the truth?" And when there was still no response, I said, "I can't live with this any longer." I could hear my voice breaking. It was over twenty years since Shirley's death, but I was surprised at the pain I was still feeling.

It was Celia who spoke first. "We thought we were protecting you. Well, it was my idea. I didn't want you to know the truth. I think I was hoping you'd hear it from someone else. Oh God! I was such a coward, and then time passed —"

"That's okay," I mumbled. I picked up the spoon and started stirring my coffee.

"It's not," Celia said, shaking her head.

Herman cleared his throat and said in a very gentle voice, "G, you did know Shirley was a heavy user. A drug addict. Right?"

"Shirley?" That shocked me, as I truly had no idea. I said so.

"But you must have suspected something," Celia said. "Even before Shirley left home. Didn't you notice how she'd changed? From the time she took up with that Pinto fellow she was a different person."

"Who? Pinto? You mean Junior's friend?"

"The same one. Shirley was madly in love from the moment she clapped eyes on him. When they were still at school. I mean the kind of blind, foolish love that would have made her do anything for him. Everybody warned her. Even Papa. He was the one who was busily encouraging her to go to New York, hoping that would get her away from him. Little did he know!"

"But isn't he the one they busted for drugs in Miami or somewhere?"

"Yes."

"Murder, extortion, and racketeering. Among a few other things," Herman broke in, and they both laughed, though I couldn't see the humour.

"But ... what would Shirley be doing with someone like that?"

"Oh G!" Celia's tone was exasperated, as if one could question the ways of love. Or maybe it was because she thought I was being deliberately obtuse. I thought of the Pinto boy and the times he had been to the house. He was a year older than Junior, so he would have been Shirley's age. I recall now he was a rather tall, good-looking boy with just the self-confidence and the cheek that an innocent girl would fall for. I had in fact liked him at first, before he started leading Junior astray, as I saw it, and I don't think I was far wrong with that. Even then he struck me as being far more mature and knowing than the other boys. I had no idea he had anything to do with Shirley.

Apparently he had Shirley on a string, on and off, while she was crazy about him, and the drugs were just part of his lifestyle. First ganja, then cocaine. By the time Shirley got to New York, she had started using crack. All the stories she told me about going to university were just that, lies. She was simply following this man to New York, where he was setting up his operation. God! No wonder she never wrote. Now her anger the last time we met was becoming clear.

"Remember how I wanted her to be my maid of honour?"

I nodded and started moving the sugar bowl around. I had to focus on something. I didn't want to look at Celia.

"By then, of course, I had some idea what was happening. Before she left I tried to talk to her, many times, but I never dreamed how far gone she was. Well, you don't really want to know, do you, if it's happening to someone you love. When she first went to New York I saw her once or twice, but after a time it was clear she didn't want to see me. We'd talk on the phone and arrange to meet if I happened to be passing through, but she'd never turn up and she would never give me an address. She was always very secretive — well, paranoid — though looking back perhaps they were really under all kinds of surveillance since Pinto by then was some sort of go-between for the Colombian cartel and the Jamaican posses. It made me laugh, but Junior said Pinto's one qualification was that he was fluent in Spanish, English, and Patwa. I think his mother was from Venezuela or the Dom Rep or somewhere. Spanish is the only subject he ever managed to pass."

Celia chuckled and then was quiet for a while. I could see that she too was seeking distraction, for she was using her finger to trace the flower pattern on the placemat. Herman sat there, both hands on the table, his eyes behind his glasses steady like a wise owl. And though Ashley, who was sitting beside me, never said a word, I could tell she was mesmerized. She was waiting for her friend to collect her for tennis, and under the glass top of the table I could see her twisting her sneakers together this way and that, like a little girl.

"I couldn't imagine getting married without Shirley there," Celia continued. "Junior told me I was a fool to think she would come. He was the one who was in touch with her. I guess I was fooling myself. When he saw how determined I was, he took me to New York to see her. He wouldn't let me go alone. By this time Pinto was out of the picture, or so it seemed; I think he was on the run then, and Shirley was living in a nasty smelly squat in Brooklyn Heights with a bunch of people like herself. Dedicated addicts. G, you would not have believed the place. Dirty, smelly, no running water, no electricity, and they all slept around wherever, on these old mattresses and broken-down furniture. It was unbelievable. Weirdos wandering in and out, muttering to themselves. I take a much more charitable view of things now, but at the time I was amazed that my own sister could be part of this filth and squalor. Shirley had given up on everything. She was living for the drugs."

Celia stopped and shook her head, and then she looked straight at me.

"You know what, G? I'm glad I went. She was so happy to see me. Really, really happy. So was I. When she saw me she screamed for joy and the two of us grabbed each other and started hugging and dancing around and yelling and crying. Poor Junior! I'm sure he was embarrassed, but of course no one else was paying us the slightest attention.

"Once I got a good look at her, though, I was hoping my face didn't show how shocked I was. She just wasn't bothering anymore to take care of herself. She was thin and dirty, full of old scabs, and her hair was out to here, like a wild woman. It was the middle of summer, a real New York scorcher, and she was wearing these big boots and combat pants — you know the real army ones with these huge pockets everywhere, sort of barely hanging on her hips even with a belt, and a skimpy little T-shirt and an old leather waistcoat which she wore open, like some Western marshal. Pockets, pockets everywhere, and all seemed full of stuff."

Celia paused then. None of us said a word. I was suddenly feeling so breathless I wondered if I was having a heart attack.

Celia gave a half-smile and shook her head. "Junior told me afterwards she also carried a Glock 9-mil stuffed down her boots, but I never believed him."

"A Glock?"

It was Herman who replied. "A handgun, G. The fave accessory of the posses."

I opened my mouth but no words came out.

"You know what?" Celia smiled again, but this time as if recalling something pleasant. "The one thing that remained of the old Shirley was her big laugh and kind of energy. While we were there, she was behaving like the mama of that squat, calling out and joking with everyone, bussing that huge laugh. The laugh is what made me fool myself into thinking hey, it's still there. We just need to get her away from here, get her cleaned up, get her to a doctor, get her dried out. Get the old Shirley back.

"Of course Junior had warned me from the start not to bother; he had been down that road many times. 'She has to want it, Sis,' he kept saying. 'She has to decide she wants help. Don't even bother to take this on your head, please. You are just setting up yourself to get run over.'

"But of course I thought I knew better. When Shirley took us down the street to a West Indian club to eat, I thought we were halfway there. It was a grotty little place with a memorable name — Sunshine Stables — isn't that great? Well, inside was kind of scary for it was dark and smoky with a funky smell and full of rough-looking guys playing dominoes and pool. Everybody called out to Shirley as she came in and she was calling greetings right back — she seemed to know all their names. We sat in a little room at the back and Sugar Baby — this little man-woman who ran it, a former jockey wouldn't you know, and who obviously adored Shirley, brought us curry goat and rice and peas. We ate and drank Red Stripe and chatted and laughed and believe me, it was almost like old times. But by the end of the meal I could see Shirley getting anxious and then frantic and her eyes suddenly sort of retreated in her head, as if we were no longer there. She was scratching away at her skin and patting her pockets in a crazy kind of way and then she turned to Junior as if to a stranger and said, 'You have change for a phone call?'

"Junior just rolled his eyes and fished out some dollars from his wallet and gave it to her. She grabbed it like it was a lifeline. I was such a fool that by this time I had my wallet out too. Shirley didn't say anything, she just stuck out her hand, and I opened the wallet and handed her a wad of notes, I don't even know how much it was. I remembered noticing the dry, ashy skin on the back of her hand and her broken fingernails. By the time I looked up she was gone. Not a word of thanks or anything. Junior just looked at me and shook his head and smiled and he stood up and said, 'All right, we can go now.'

"'What? Aren't we waiting for Shirley?' I asked. You know, I was that foolish. Junior said in his deadpan voice — you know Junior and his cool — 'Yeah, you can stay here if you want to wait forever, Sis. You've just given Shirley enough for a few big hits.' I felt so awful then. We left, Junior and I, and we never talked about it again. I hadn't even got around to mentioning the wedding to her. Junior had made me take off my engagement ring and all my jewellery before we set out. That was the last time I saw Shirley."

Herman got up from the table while she was speaking, and as he came back and handed her a tissue I realized Celia was crying. No expression on her face, just the tears streaming down. Herman stood behind her and she leaned against him, and he had both arms around her in a loose hug as she wiped her eyes and blew her nose. Across from them, I was blinking, trying hard to keep my own tears in. Ashley, who was sitting beside me, had her elbow on the table and was leaning her cheek on her arm, looking from her parents to me, her eyes wide. She seemed terribly young and vulnerable, not the bold high-heel-wearer I'd gotten used to.

I raised my eyes and met Herman's. He gave a small smile and said, "G, you might as well hear the whole truth. Shirley was killed, but it was no accident: she was a small-time dealer and seemed to have crossed her supplier so he had her taken out. At least that's the official version of events. She — well, this is the awful part. Her body was found in a Dumpster on the other side of the city with no clothes, no identification on her, so it was some time — months — before they found out who she was."

Ashley gave a little gasp, as I did.

"Even when the police identified her we still wouldn't have known who she was," Celia continued. "It turned out, she was married to Pinto. Not a word to any of us. And that wasn't even his real name. Well, it was his mother's name and he used it, as the Spanish do, but her name was given as Shirley Aguilar. It was probably carried in the papers here, no doubt in the *Star*. But even if we saw it, we wouldn't have known it was our Shirley."

I could see Ashley screwing up her mouth as if she wanted to say something, and I fully expected "Awesome!" to come out. But it was Herman who spoke.

"Shirley wasn't a bad kid, but her life went off the rails."

I was tensing myself to hear the rest of it, but just then there was a loud halloing at the front door and the grim atmosphere dissolved. Ashley's friends had arrived. Celia dabbed at her eyes and immediately turned into her smiling, gracious self as she greeted the youngsters and introduced them to me. Herman looked at his watch and said he had promised to drop by his parents. "We'll talk later," he said, looking over at me. I nodded, feeling that we had made a breakthrough. Somehow I knew this time I would hear the truth. Celia and the youngsters trooped out, and I was left alone. I sat and then I got up from the table and was surprised at how weak and confused I felt. I tottered out into the garden and sat on a bench that overlooked the city and the sea and I took deep breaths and allowed the beauty of the morning to pull me away from the darkness of Shirley's last days. I forced myself not to think of that.

I was truthful when I said I didn't know about Shirley's drug use or her relationship with Pinto, but somehow I wasn't all that surprised at what I had just learned. Did I already know it, at least subconsciously? Had I heard rumours? Was it a mother's intuition? Or was it that I already knew the narrative so well? So many other children had fallen victims to violence in the years since then, to drugs and guns, perhaps we had simply lost the capacity to feel anything but helplessness.

I couldn't help myself from asking, why? What had turned Shirley so weak and foolish in the first place? What signals had I missed? What signals had I failed to give? Was it the way she was raised or some internal flaw she was born with that had widened over the years? I didn't have the photo with me, but I didn't need to look at it now to understand the depth of the sadness in her eyes.

108

WE CONTINUED TO TALK about Shirley on and off over the weekend, not in any formal kind of way, but just whenever one of us felt like saying something. Sometimes it was all three of us, or just me and Celia or me and Herman. I noticed that when Ashley wasn't out with her friends, she was hanging around us all the time, as if she didn't want to be left out of anything; but, unlike her usual chatty self, she was mostly silent. I couldn't help thinking how differently she was raised, as if she had a right to share in whatever was happening and not be banished from adult conversation the way I had been and the way I treated my own children. Staying in Celia's house that weekend opened my eyes to a lot of things, to what I suppose was a normal family life. Well no, not normal, for I had banished that word from my vocabulary. Ideal, perhaps? I certainly think Celia had found the ideal in Herman; I could see he allowed her to be herself, to be free; and, with a twinge of envy, I wondered what path had led her to find her soulmate.

The most important thing I learned was that Junior had had nothing to do with Shirley's death. It was pure coincidence that his own troubles started around the same time and he went underground to save his skin. But he did feel guilt that he was the one who had introduced Shirley to Pinto, Celia said.

"Though at the time he and Michael and Pinto were just good mates from school. They had no idea at the time what a madman Pinto was."

We were talking in the kitchen, because I'd insisted on cooking dinner. Celia and Herman had looked relieved at that suggestion and both had vanished to their bedroom for the afternoon. It was Ashley who showed me where to find everything and how to work the fancy stove and oven. The latter was vital, for I let her into my little secret: I had decided to make devil's food cake with caramel icing for dessert!

"Mm," Ashley said, "my favourite. Mum's too. She always makes it for my birthday, but she ends up scarfing down most of it herself. "

"Oh really," I said. "But don't say anything, I want it to be a big surprise."

Most of the dinner was prepared and the cake was in the oven when Celia appeared, looking rested, smelling fresh with shampoo and body lotion, wearing a long wrap skirt and a tight knit top that made her look like she stepped out of *Vogue*. And though I could see how toned her body was, I still couldn't help noticing her bones. She immediately started sniffing, "Mmm, am I smelling, what I am smelling?" But I pretended innocence. "Just a little something I'm whipping up for dessert," I said airily, praying to high heaven that the devil wouldn't make my chocolate cake in any way inferior to Mrs. Reverend Doctor's.

I didn't want Celia to focus on the cake, so I busied myself at the sink with washing the lettuce and spinning it.

"Gosh, G, this is so nice. I'd forgotten what a great cook you are."

"You can thank your grandmother Samphire for that," I told her. "She taught me everything."

"Makes a change, doesn't it, to have a nice mother-in-law. Herman thinks you are one, you know."

"Yes," I said, turning back to the sink and running the water to hide my confusion, for I still wasn't sure how to take compliments, how much trust I could place in what people had to say. I changed the subject by asking her to tell me about Junior. Maybe that wasn't a good idea, as it became another emotional roller coaster ride for me. This time Celia seemed quite matter-of-fact as she talked. She went to the fridge and took out a bottle of white wine and took down two glasses and held one up to me, but I shook my head; drinking alcohol is something I had never learned to do. She continued talking as she opened the bottle and poured herself a glass.

"The thing with Junior and Michael is that they were playing with the big boys and didn't know they were just small fries. They thought they were real big businessmen, suits and ties — or kareebas when that was in, Chamber of Commerce and Rotary and everything."

It took me a while to find my voice. "You mean they didn't have a factory? What was this Samjam Enterprises, then?"

Celia laughed and, glass in hand, leaned against the door. "Oh, they had a factory all right. But it was mostly turning out ackee cans stuffed full of compressed ganja. Michael and Junior were like a pair of schoolboys among the sharks. Pinto was the one that got them into it and he was the one that understood the runnings. But then Pinto got into guns and violence and was a crazy cokehead, a real user — I don't know about Michael, but Junior at least was never into taking drugs, I believe him when he says that. They got cold feet when Pinto decided to go in with the Colombians, who were all over the place by then, introducing a new spin. They were into selling the ganja abroad, but instead of U.S. dollars they were bringing in coke and guns. I think Junior and Michael came to some kind of deal with Pinto — an amicable parting, or so they thought. They stuck to their small-scale op while Pinto went off to the States to do his thing. Junior went ballistic when Shirley went with him."

I was trying not to show anything on my face as I listened, but Celia must have sensed what I was thinking.

"Oh, come on G!" She was smiling when she said it. "Don't tell me you didn't know what Junior was up to? Those thousand-dollar suits? His cars? His racehorses? His houses?"

"Houses?" I said, as if that gave me something tangible to hold on to. "Celia, you will find this hard to believe, but though Junior came to see me from time to time, I didn't know a single thing about his life."

"You mean, not even your precious Millie made you any the wiser as to what was happening right under your nose? Come on! All the young men in the district were growing ganja for Junior. Everyone. That fellow there, what's his name again — Bertie — he was in charge of transportation. Your local MP was the facilitator with the police and customs. Everybody had their role in the operation. This is Ganja Nation we're talking about!"

Celia took a sip from her glass and then continued as if I wasn't there.

"At that time, it was still the politicians running the show, you know, not like now when it's the drug posses. Junior was nothing but the politicians' lackey, their bagman, off to Miami every minute to launder the loot or pick up fresh clean dollars. I'm sure he and Michael thought they were part of the inner circle. Then the Americans stepped in and said, hey, this has got to stop. At that time they were willing to play ball with the government — loans, all kinds of aid and fancy promises. But they also said, no more funds, no more loans until you deal with the drug trade, never mind it was all American youth buying the stuff. You must remember that time, G? How they suddenly started to bomb the little airstrips all over the island so the ganja planes couldn't land and they were spraying the ganja fields from the air or sending in soldiers to burn the crops? There were always these pictures in the papers of these bags and bags of ganja going up in smoke. Everyone for miles around getting high from the fumes. Men, women, and children. Even the parson, people used to joke. Well, the whole thing was all a big poppyshow. But some of the foot soldiers had to be sacrificed to make the government look as if they were serious about rooting out the drug barons, the 'Mister Bigs.'"

She took another sip while I chopped up the rest of the salad.

"Michael was one of the first to go. Remember how he was blown away and everybody said it was a drug deal gone wrong? Remember all the strange killings of prominent individuals around the same time? Some little boy was always arrested and some spurious motive for the killing provided by the police while the rumour mills ground out that another 'Mister Big' has been taken out. So everyone was pleased that the police were finally doing something. But it was all part of the same scenario, nothing but a purge and some scapegoating by the real big men for the benefit of the Americans."

Celia came over to where I was standing and took a piece of celery from the bowl, dipped it into the dressing I was mixing, and bit it. The casual way she was acting when making these revelations was unnerving me, but she just carried on.

"You know, G, Junior is lucky to be alive today. His name was on that list. But he got a tipoff and dived deep underground. He must have had his escape route well prepared by this time, for he just vanished. He had already met Dolly by then, which is probably why he ended up in Canada."

"How much of this did you know?"

"I didn't know anything at all about it while it was happening. It's only recently that Junior's been willing to talk about it. Or even been willing to come back home. He's been running scared all these years. Can you imagine?"

"But did you know Junior was into the drug trade and all that?"

She sipped again and made a face, as if she had to consider this.

"Yes and no. I mean, there were always rumours, but if I tackled him he always denied it. But in my heart I knew that he was mixed up in something. Like you, I found Junior secretive. Herman was suspicious of him, too, although he liked him as a person. Herman himself was a bit paranoid at the time, and he thought we shouldn't have too much to do with him. I kept in touch because of Shirley, really. He was my only connection to Shirley."

"So he is the one who told you?"

"Yes, but not until long after. Junior actually skipped the country before we knew anything had happened to Shirley. I had no idea where he had gone to. Of course I went crazy when Michael got killed and I tried to contact Junior — only to find out that nobody knew where he was. After that it was like waiting for a bomb to go off. I honestly expected any day to hear they'd found Junior's body. Then I got a strange phone call one day. At my office. The person just said in this whispery voice, 'Junior's okay. Don't worry.' That was all. Then she hung up. It was a woman with what sounded like a foreign accent — and in those days of course we couldn't check to see who had called. But at least that took a load off my mind."

"Celia, this is getting to be like something out of a thriller," I couldn't help saying, rather sourly I'm afraid, for I was beginning to find the whole thing a little unreal. I found it hard to believe I knew the people Celia was talking about.

"It gets even more like a B-grade movie plot. Next thing — well, some months later, actually — I got this letter with a Canadian stamp, I couldn't make out the postmark, and the letter was just a few sentences scrawled on this sheet of paper — no address, no signature, but it was Junior's writing, and he told me to burn it as soon as I'd read it. The only letter I got from him, actually, for many years, and believe me I was so frightened I did take a match to it."

She laughed and took a sip from her glass and stood there turning the stem round and round while I stopped what I was doing to watch her, impatient for her to go on.

"So, what was the letter about?"

"Telling us what had happened to Shirley, how her body had been identified. Of course, we had no idea she was missing. Herman used some legal contacts he had to verify that the story was true, and it was after that that we came down to tell you she had died and — I'm really sorry now — I made up that stupid story for you. Junior had this one friend in New York whom he trusted, or maybe Shirley trusted, to this day I don't know who this person is. But he used this person to keep an eye on Shirley and it was he — or she — who let him know what had happened. It was this person who identified her and buried her too — Junior sent money for the funeral, but of course he dared not go. He believed that Shirley had been killed as a warning to him, or to draw him out of hiding, but I'm not sure that was really so, because why would they dump the body without ID? Another scenario floated was that Pinto had engineered it because if he was ever arrested, he was afraid she knew too much about his dealings. Who knows? Of course, Junior didn't tell me all of this in the letter, I got it out of him much later."

We broke it off then, and I was glad, for Herman appeared, followed shortly by Ashley, and we realized that it was time for dinner. All the time we were putting the food in serving dishes and getting it on the table I felt again as if a great band was compressing my chest. I felt better when we all were seated at the table and began to eat. We talked about inconsequential things, and Ashley chattered about her friends. I'm proud to say that when it came to the dessert, Celia let the first taste of my devil's food cake with the caramel topping melt in her mouth before she declared it a triumph. Take that, Mrs. Reverend Doctor, I thought, not at all ashamed of my childishness.

109

THE WEEKEND AT CELIA'S was supposed to be for relaxation, but that last evening after dinner I sat on the couch downstairs pretending to read. I was feeling restless and dissatisfied. I now had answers to some of my questions, it is true, as to what had happened to Shirley and to Junior as well — or at least it was all in the open now — but I couldn't stop asking myself why these things had happened. To my children. Why both Shirley and Junior had chosen to go down that path. I think Celia sort of dismissed Junior's days in the drug business as youthful folly, greed, laziness, just following the path laid out by his friends, the path to an easy fortune without any thought about the consequences. Though it seems he had ended up with nothing for his pains, for he had had to run and leave it all behind. Some of it anyway. Good! I thought. I hope he suffered. I was still feeling some resentment towards Junior, and I knew that he and I had a lot to work through.

Celia had vanished after dinner to catch up on some work, but now she came and sat beside me and we chatted idly about this and that until we inevitably turned to the main topic of the weekend, which was Shirley.

When she described Shirley as the adventurous one in the family I'd agreed, she'd always been the first one out there to do anything on a dare or to try something new, she always wanted to travel, to find out what was over the next hill. But then Celia said, "Shirley's adventuring wasn't so much in search of something new as to recover something she felt she had lost. Or never had in the first place. She told me so once. She wanted to find something to fill a permanent ache inside her. Like a black hole, she said. Only she didn't know what would fill it."

"Shirley?" I was taken aback, for I'd never thought of Shirley in that light. She was always the happy-go-lucky sunshine girl. "Well, something must have happened to her after she left home," I said. "That doesn't sound like the Shirley I knew."

Celia didn't answer, she started to study her nails, looking at both her hands as if the answer was hidden there. The silence got uncomfortable, and I began to remember some of the things she had said in anger to me not so long ago, how indifferent I was to my children, how I acted as if I didn't care. Was that the impression I had given to all of them? Certainly not to Shirley!

"She felt this way from when she was little, all right," Celia finally said. "We used to talk about it the times when I came home to visit, before I went away to the States, so we would have been in our early teens then. You know that's the time girls talk about feelings, that sort of thing. Papa must have been at home still, for I don't remember visiting when he wasn't there. At least not until I came back from university and came down by myself. I'm not saying that Shirley used those actual words at that time, but she always talked about feeling this great emptiness. I mean, I wasn't feeling so hot myself, but I thought I knew what I had lost. She didn't."

It was on the tip of my tongue to ask, "And what had you lost?" but I thought better of it. Instead I asked, "So she never said why?"

"No, but I think that from when she was little she felt left out. She always said nobody loved her. She had it in her head that you loved me best, Lise was Papa's girl, and Junior as the only boy was everybody's eyeball. She was special to nobody."

"Oh, nonsense," I said. Perhaps a bit sharply.

"Maybe. But there was something else. And this you will say is nonsense. But Shirley came to feel that it was because she was the darkest one in the family."

"For heaven's sake, Celia. You know she wasn't treated any differently. If anyone could lay claim to that it is Lise. She is the one who got teased for her looks. Remember all those names the kids used to call her? Quaw. Mus-mus. Redibo? Even Junior and Shirley did it."

"I know."

"I'm really distressed to hear that. Shirley was special to everyone. She certainly had the most attractive personality of all you children."

"G, you know that how we perceive things as children is more important than the reality of our lives." She gave a funny laugh then and said, "For instance, I always thought you had given me away as a child because you didn't want me. How do you think that made me feel?"

"Oh God," I said.

"It's okay. It's okay." She reached over and patted my leg.

"I think I understand now. But I'm talking about the child's perception then."

I sort of screwed up my face, trying not to get entangled in this one.

"So all I am saying is that is how Shirley felt."

"But something must have led her to feel that way."

"Well, I don't know. It's not something you should get upset about at this stage. It's too late anyway."

"I'm not upset. But how would you feel if you suddenly learned that your children were thinking such terrible things about you?"

Celia laughed out loud then. "Oh my God, you should hear that Ashley sometimes. The things she says. I'm the worst mother on earth! Gabriel was a little more subtle. When he was small and he got mad at me, he used to tell everyone that his real mother was going to come in a helicopter and take him away and it would serve me right."

I smiled then, but I knew it wasn't the same. I decided to hold my peace. I was learning that too much talking could sometimes be as bad as silence. We sat, saying nothing, but this silence was making me uncomfortable, so I asked about Lise, for we hadn't talked about her at all. I was curious to know if she had seen Lise recently.

"Oh, Lise," Celia said in a tone that made me relax. "I haven't seen her in ages, but we've been talking a lot on the phone lately. I don't know, I guess we are just at that age where family is beginning to mean more to us. I'll dig out some pictures later to show you."

I said I'd like to see them and asked what Lise was doing.

"You know Lise, always getting her own way. She ended up in Houston of all places. Went into real estate, buying and fixing up old property, now she is quite the landlord. Lise is doing okay, let me tell you." And she rubbed her thumb and forefinger together.

"And her children?"

"Amazing, when you think of it. All turned out fantastic. Doing brilliantly at school. She might end up with two doctors, and I think the third one, the girl, wants to be an architect. Don't know how she managed it. Wish mine would do as well. And she raised them all as a single mother too. Just couldn't be bothered to marry any of the men in her life — and there have been plenty, I can tell you. Still attracts them like honey, from what she tells me. Knows how to love them and leave them."

Just like her father, I thought sourly, for certain things I still couldn't swallow. Celia must have noticed my expression. I don't know how she read it, but she surprised me by saying, "Promise me you won't be hard on Junior. I think he is trying to make amends. For a lot of things. Just try and love him, Mom, and not say anything. Forgive him. For Shirley's sake. You know what she was like. Not a mean bone in her body."

I had to think about that for a long long time. So many loaded words embedded there. Making amends. Love. Forgiveness. Shirley.

Shirley and her beautiful smile. I had never really mourned her. Because I never knew the cause of her death, it had left me in a kind of suspension. As if I was waiting for her to come in slamming doors as she always did, dumping her school bag on the table. Turning somersaults. Noisy, irrepressible Shirley. And now, now that I knew the finality of it all, I still didn't know what to think.

But Celia was still on the subject of Junior.

"He's been paying back for what he did. The drugs. Shirley. Living a lie. Deceiving all of us. It hasn't been easy. Life is testing him, though. So when you go down …?"

I just nodded, for I couldn't speak even if I wanted to. I didn't feel angry, just sad, like a child who has done something she knows is wrong and is reprimanded. The wrong I did was to close my eyes to the truth about Junior staring me in the face all these years. What a hypocrite Millie and all the others must have thought me. How could I not know?

I didn't want to talk any more about it; I needed a break from all the emotional turmoil of the last few days and weeks. I told Celia I was going to bed.

She said, "Of course. Hey! I'm sorry. I know you've been through the wringer. But things have a way of working themselves out, though, don't you believe it? I'm already beginning to feel lighter from all the talking." She leaned over then and kissed me on the cheek.

The gesture only made me feel sadder. I got up and started up the stairs.

"Hey," Celia called out. "G, before you go back home, there are two things you should know about Junior, so you won't be too surprised."

"Oh," I said, mentally bracing for more unpleasant revelations. But Celia's tone was light.

"One. Junior has lost all his hair." She was laughing when she said it.

It made me chuckle, for I remembered how vain Junior had been about his full head of curly hair.

"Okay," I said. "I can deal with that. What's the other?"

"He's found Jesus."

"What?" I said, and this just burst out of me without thought. "I didn't know he was lost."

Celia roared with laughter then, and I found myself laughing too, and we looked at each other and laughed and laughed until all the tension between us dissolved.

I went back down the three steps I had already climbed and this time I kissed Celia on her cheek. "Goodnight sweetheart," I said. It seemed perfectly natural.

110

SO DESPITE ALL THE revelations, I did feel a slight lifting of my mood. That night as I lay in bed I said to the imaginary Celia, there's still a lot to talk about. Up to now I don't know all that happened to you those years we lived apart. But small steps have been taken, we are starting the dance, you and I. It's not a waltz yet, might never be, more of an improvisation. One that supposedly tells a story as people weave in and out of each other's spaces. Not that I have managed to figure it out. I don't think I'm good at that. But at least I've learnt that I need to move forward too.

III

WHEN I GOT BACK to Ellesmere Lodge, my head was still full of the past, of the children, of all the pain we had suffered. I spent much of the day wasting time, doing nothing, trying to clear my head. Then that night in my room, I had this brilliant idea, which I offered to the absent Celia. I've thought of the best way of making amends to you, to all of you, I told her. I want to give you my notebooks. Perhaps the letters too, as they are a part of this record and I don't know what else to do with them. I foresee your reaction, your wide-eyed expression, the wheels slowly turning in your head before you say anything, for this gesture of mine will truly surprise you.

You will say, "Are you sure you want to?"

And I will say, "Yes, I am sure. I want you to have them. Read them sometime. Anytime. Today, tomorrow, when I am dead. It's up to you. They say all the things I cannot."

I think you will hug me then. I am hoping you will have tears in your eyes. Then you'll smile and say, "Okay, but why don't you leave them to me in your will? You have a lot more to write, don't you?"

And I will whip out another notebook looking identically like the others, a new one, and say, "Time to start another."

Maybe I won't exactly hand over the old ones yet. Maybe I'll think about it some more. But I will at least let you know they're meant for you. I have no other gift to give you.

I will say, "Read these. I don't fear exposure anymore."

And I hope you will say, "Neither do I."

112

PACKED AND READY TO go, nothing left but to say my good-byes. The middle of the week, so my granddaughter Ashley is driving me down and wants to stay over. She is far more excited than I am. Celia and her husband to come over the weekend. That will be a first. A family reunion, with Junior there. The beds and bedding, the new furniture, the curtains we have chosen, my daughter and I, have been delivered. I didn't feel anxious or indebted about accepting such largesse anymore, it seems a natural way of doing things. This is their family home, after all, and I'm dying to see it, repaired, restored, renewed in all its bright paint.

Right after breakfast I went into the garden to say goodbye to Winston and found him looking very much at home in his plot, which has now spread to encompass not just our original beds but also quite a bit of what was once poverty-stricken lawn. He has a flourishing pumpkin vine, a chocho arbour, a bed of calalu, and rows of gungo peas, in addition to the beds of sweet peppers, tomatoes, and cabbages we had originally planted. I have no doubt that Winston's alternative crop at the back is also thriving. Winston is a different man, energetic and smiling. Now he has an assistant. A slim, shy youngster named Lenny, who turns out to be his eldest son. To Lenny, Winston has handed over the duties he once took such pride in but which he now scorns — the lawn mowing, the massacre of the hedge. Winston himself has materialized into a real gardener.

"Winston, you have just enough here to feed your present

baby-mothers. I hope you don't plan to have any more," I couldn't help teasing.

"Cho, Miss Sam," he laughed. "You always exaggervate. Is only four baby-mother I have." He leaned then on his garden fork, took off his cap and rubbed his bald pate, and looked slightly contemplative. "But you right, you know, Miss Sam. From now on, is only ground me working. A one set of seed me a scatter."

I too laughed when he said this. But it made me think that if I could leave Winston dazzled by the notion that he could produce something other than children, maybe I did have something to offer after all.

To the kitchen next, where I was shocked to see how Cookie had aged. They still hadn't released her grandson's body for burial because the police were sticking to their story of a shootout. There were arguments over the post-mortems, a human rights group wanted to bring in an outside doctor to ensure justice was done, and the case had become an international cause. But what good would that do for this small woman sitting on the kitchen stool, looking as shrivelled-up as her future? Cookie, I wanted to say, I know what it's like. I too have lost a child to violence. But it wasn't the same at all, was it? It was hard to lose Shirley, but she didn't go down with all my hopes.

I was sad to leave Cookie and Annie. All of them. Even Matron. When the car was packed and the actual time for leave-taking came, while Ruby waved from the front door, Matron came down the steps to the car, a vision in purple and green swirls. But somehow the sight didn't annoy me anymore, for now I saw it, like Ruby's, as a flag of survival, proudly waving. We hugged each other.

"Miss Sam, I'm going to miss you," she said.

"I'll miss you too, Delice, my dear." My saying that surprised me as much as the way her name just popped into my mouth.

"You mustn't forget us."

"No, but you must come down and stay with me sometime," I said. "Anytime. As soon as you get your holidays."

"You really mean that?" I was surprised by her eagerness.

"Of course."

"Miss Sam, you don't know how I would love to do that. I don't have anyone left in the country anymore, you know. But I'm always wishing I had somewhere to visit."

"Yes, Mrs. Spence, to eat sugar cane and pick mangoes from the tree," Ashley chimed in, laughing. I had to laugh too, for though she knew nothing of country life, her idea was exactly the same as Morveen and Kyisha's.

"Well, I don't know if a certain person would leave me any of the mangoes," Matron said, screwing up her face in what I suppose was meant to be a wink at Ashley.

Winston shook his head and grinned.

"Well, now we'll get to keep our pens and pencils too, I suppose," Ruby's rusty voice came as she negotiated the steps and moved towards us. The shock must have showed on my face, for she gave her famous cackle and hooked my arm with the walking stick she had taken to using, and I turned and held her frail body close to my heart. "Ha-ha, my dear G," were her parting words. "How little you know."

And that, I thought, could well be my epitaph, as I got into the car and we drove from under the porte cochere, past the sun-blasted canna lilies, everyone waving like mad till we disappeared from sight beyond the elegant gates of Ellesmere Lodge, my granddaughter and I.

113

WHILE I WAS WAITING for Ashley to arrive, I opened my new notebook and on the first page I wrote: A New Inventory of Myself.

Person — Okay. Not bad for age.

Health — Good, thank God.

Skills — Reading, writing, sewing, farming, cooking, baking, washing, ironing, cleaning, contriving — making something from nothing.

That was it. There was nothing else I could say about myself. But at least, I thought, I had skills I could share in the place I came from in a way I had not done before. I could start literacy classes. I could start a library and get my grandchildren to help me collect books, even the ones in the United States I have never met. I could teach girls how to sew and bake, learn skills that they could use. I could invite the boys to come and grow vegetables for themselves. I was getting so excited, I was lost in this vision.

My grandson Gabriel, Ashley's brother who is studying anthropology in the United States, wants to come for a semester to study village life. His mother has suggested that he should come and stay with me and work in our area. I would like that, for I'm thinking that maybe he can find answers to all the things I want to know. About my mother's people. Who they were. What happened to my father. I won't tell him or any of my grandchildren what I believe to be true, for it is something I know only with my heart. And now I know my heart's knowledge to be unreliable.

These young people, these privileged young people, Gabriel and Ashley and the rest, can't I use them to help? How can I tap into these resources that I never knew that I had available to me? My family. Something I had never thought about before as even existing as a concept. Will I be given a second chance to gather up the seeds I have unwittingly scattered?

Maybe it is children like these, people like Cookie's Trevor, now gone, the ones we are struggling to educate, who will have to come up with the answers. To find out what happened to all our fathers. Who our mothers were and where they came from. For everything has to start here. With the fulfilment of that passionate, individual desire to know who we truly are.

One thing is certain: nobody comes from the canefields anymore, for the fields have been abandoned. Abandoned like the ordinary people, the extraordinary people, of this land.

I'm tingling with a new excitement: I can't believe I am writing this, for I truly have never thought this way before. About the world, about other people. Never felt this way before. I feel my anger coming back, but now it's a new thing. I no longer feel angry at the portion life assigned to me. I am no longer angry at what I already know. I'm angry about what I don't know.

This is what I have decided, and I will sign it with my name: Gertrude Richards Samphire. And I will send for a copy of my birth certificate so I can see my mother's name. If my mother was a slug I want to uplift her by trying to help those baby-mothers, children themselves walking down the road with their constantly big bellies. If my father was a madman, I want to help those boys sitting on the bridge rid themselves of the madness of violence in their hearts.

114

THERE'S JUST ONE OTHER thing, if I'm going to be totally honest with you, Celia. It's about the time you were born. It's not true that I loved you instantly, unreservedly. That had to come later. Months later, during which time other people took care of you — Mother Gatha the midwife, Millie perhaps, Sam's mother, Ma D, and Sam too, I imagine. For I was incapable of doing anything, I had no interest in you or anyone else. I don't know where I was in all those days and weeks and months. I had fallen into this black hole, you see, just as I had the day they took my father away in the Black Maria. It was as if his turning up in such an uncanny way at just that moment, the day of your birth, plunged me back into that spinning vortex.

I don't know how I came out of this darkness, the one I fell into when you were born, for there was no Aunt Zena to bully me, and no one ever spoke to me of that hard time. But something must have happened, for I suddenly came back to myself one day and there you were beside me, this perfect little stranger, and how my heart leapt to find you there. How I revelled in your smile, the perfection of your limbs, your toes. I wasn't lying to you about that, about my feelings for you. Only there are these gaps in my life, you see, that I cannot explain, the places where I walked alone, so there was never anyone to remind me of what happened or of that self that I was then. Maybe that's not a bad thing. It's like passing through a room full of cobweb and coming out with bits and pieces of it clinging to you. Like this vision I sometimes have, parts of it as clear as if it actually happened: a room full of women chanting and my sitting in a bath pan full of warm water with the scent of sweet herbs and spices rising to surround me, mint and rosemary, pimento and orange peel, and me sitting there naked with a cloth draped over my head and covering the entire bath pan to keep the steam in. The soft singing, the scented steam, creating this safe space for me, a cocoon that I only shed when I rise out of that water and into the large white sheet they drape me in. After that I sleep, that is part of the memory, and when I open my eyes you are there, as if conjured up from that water. But it was I who was born again that day, for the pain that was afflicting me had vanished, and I felt at peace. To this day I don't know who to thank for it or even if that was how it happened.

But, there you have it, another little slice of truth. Or memory. Of all kinds of madness lost in our dreams. Waiting to be found in the light of day.

Acknowledgements

Thanks to:

- Jean Riley for the apartment in Portsmouth where G first made her appearance, and in memory of Richard, who might have been pleased to finally meet her.
- early readers of the manuscript: Mary Jo Morris, Donna Nurse, Shivaun Hearne, and Christine Raguet. A special thank you to Jacob Ross for valued insights.
- Helene Rampersaud and Velma Pollard, sisters real and appropriated, for their continued support in so many ways.
- Daphne Hart of Helen Heller Agency for believing.
- Marc Côté for making this a better book and the team at Cormorant for getting it on the road.
- the Ontario Arts Council for a Works in Progress grant.